The Austin Highway

By Alexander Wolf

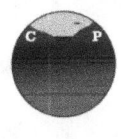

Cove Publishing

Visit the Author's web site at www.alexanderwolf.net

Published by Cove Publishing

P.O. Box 2382

500 E. Whitestone Blvd.

Cedar Park, TX 78630

ISBN 978-0-9852541-0-0

Graphic design by Lily McCabe
www.lillianmccabe.com

Author's photograph by Greg McCabe

The Austin Highway

by Alexander Wolf

To my parents, Clarice Cohn
and Samuel Stanford Wolf

Table of Contents

**"What may man within him hide,
though angel on the outward side!"**

William Shakespeare, *Measure for Measure
(Vincentio, the Duke, Act III, Scene ii*

**"Give not that which is holy unto the dogs,
neither cast ye your pearls before swine,
lest they trample them under their feet,
and turn again and rend you."**

Holy Bible, King James Version,
Book of Matthew, Chapter 7, Verse 6

**"And when he had opened the fourth seal,
I heard the voice of the fourth beast say,
'Come and see.'"**

Holy Bible, King James Version,
Book of Revelation, Chapter 6, Verse 7

Prologue – 9:30 a.m.

Samantha Barnes woke up and her eyes kept trying to roll back up into her head. Each time she tried to roll them down, the dizziness would start again. She smacked her lips and made a face at the taste in her mouth.

She thought Jack had come home last night, but that might have been her imagination.

Her radio alarm was on. She slowly freed an arm from the sheets, reached up to her sleep mask and lifted the corner. She one-eyed the clock. 9:30. She moaned and tapped the top of the clock to stop the noise.

It was Sunday, she remembered. She and Paige were going to drive up the Austin Highway to New Braunfels for brunch. Without fail, every second Sunday of the month, Samantha and her sister would skip church and make the drive to the Smokehouse. The thought of breakfast made her stomach flip. It was her turn to drive, but she was having a hard time even thinking about getting out of bed. She reached over to Jack's side; had to roll sideways off her back to reach him but she made the effort and her hand wasn't touching anything as she patted his pillow. It wasn't even warm over there, so she peeked open one of her eyes again. No Jack, but a little more nausea.

She returned to her back and the mask flapped down over her face. She groaned again. She vaguely remembered Jack had been called back to the office the previous afternoon. Something was bombing up or blowing out or whatever computers do. Hadn't he called her? That's right, he'd said he would grab a bite at Abel's, and that he'd be late getting home.

But she wondered where he was now. Maybe he was at church. Lately he seemed to go every Sunday whether she went with him or not. At least last time he'd woken her up before he left with a nice kiss, one of those full frontal, under the covers even though he was all dressed up, hand under her nightgown type kisses. Good old Jackie-pants. She'd enjoyed thanking him after he got back home. This morning, she couldn't even remember if he'd said goodbye. Her head was throbbing, really throbbing.

As her eyes slowly grew used to the light, she thought maybe she'd ask Paige to drive once she picked her up; hell, maybe she'd call Paige and tell her to drive.

She struggled to the bathroom. Jesus, she had to pee. She was glad she'd stuck that wad of toilet paper inside her panties, though she didn't really remember doing it. Damn, it sounded like the Niagara when she finally made it to the toilet and was able to let go and relax.

As the stream started to let up, she pulled her nightgown over her head where she sat, slumped forward on the seat. She flung it and her panties out the door onto the floor of the bathroom without opening her eyes. She was going to soak in a nice hot tub for at least an hour before she got dressed. She tightened her stomach flat and slapped it twice, hearing the satisfying pop pop. Her head pounded more than ever, but it was almost worth it to feel the tautness of her belly. She needed to call Paige and tell her she was going to be late. She scratched with her nails under one of her arms and decided she needed to shave, too. She yawned and winced from the sharp pain it caused. She'd take at least three or four aspirins for her head. Maybe a little drinkee would help, too, she thought.

Damn Jackie-pants. If he'd stayed home, she might have called Paige and begged off on driving to the Smokehouse. As it was, he always liked to stay after church and spend time visiting with all their friends, drinking coffee and eating doughnuts. There was no telling when he'd wander home.

Vaguely, she could hear her alarm radio blaring again.

PART ONE

I - JACK

My name is Jack Gantt. With two t's. The shirts are spelled with one... you know the kind with the button-down collars that have tabs on the back we ripped off each other when we were kids? Called them fruitloops? When we weren't using razor blades to cut the little red Levi tags off each other's jeans?

I was born in a small town in Nebraska named Burwell. My Dad was stationed at Ft. Sam Houston in San Antonio, Texas when Mom got pregnant with me and then the Army decided to send him on a Temporary Duty assignment to Nebraska for a year. After I was born we were sent back to Ft. Sam, so I never really saw much of Burwell, home of Nebraska's Big Rodeo. Dad was a lawyer in the army which meant that after he was promoted to Lieutenant Colonel, he became a judge in the Judge Advocate Generals' Corps. Probably he was involved in some trials when he was sent to Burwell, I'll never know for sure because I never asked. My sister gets to say she was born at the Nix Hospital in San Antonio; I have to admit to being born in Burwell, Nebraska. Not that there's anything *wrong* with Burwell, Nebraska....

OK. My name is really John Wayne Gantt, but everybody calls me Jack. My parents were not big time conservatives or especially crazy about the actor, I think Mom just liked the name, the way John Wayne worked with Gantt, in her mind.

I don't remember Gail or my mother and father ever calling me anything but Jack, even when Mom and Dad were mad at me. Gail was always this tall, thin, really smart older woman to me - light brown straight hair, hazel eyes, nice nose - me as a girl, I guess. Can you imagine hearing this eight-year-old sister you look up to in every way introduce you as John Wayne when your name is Jack? My confusion was mostly between hearing her call *me* John Wayne and knowing that tall guy in the movies had the same name, that I knew *him* to be the real John Wayne. Even though I was five, I had watched Fort Apache with my father and when I wasn't hiding from the Indians with my face buried in his side, I remembered John Wayne on the screen. I couldn't imagine why we shared the name and never did understand the reason. That didn't stop me later in my childhood from whistling "The High and the Mighty" constantly to annoy the family. Anyway, when Gail said "This is my brother John Wayne Gantt but everyone calls him Jack," I was shocked. When we'd walked into the room, I had developed an instant crush on the teacher, who was pretty and young and turned on the biggest smile when she looked up from the desk and saw Gail and me. As soon as she heard Gail's little speech, she shifted her smile straight to me and said "OK then, we'll call you Jack."

I guess I'm called *Jack* my whole life till someone thinks to call me *Jackie-pants*. Which is where, I suppose, the real story of my life begins.

*　　*　　*　　*　　*

We never know when the defining moment of our life is going to happen. You know what I mean? Sometimes we may sense when it's happened soon after, but mostly I don't think we do, till much later if at all. I guessed I was having mine as it was happening and I was right.

As an example, I'll never forget when I was a kid, reading *Studs Lonigan*, a book set back in the '30s during the

Depression. I'm not even sure why I read it, as depressing as it was, but I got used to taking books from my father's bookcase and I always tried reading the ones I took, though I failed with Gibbons. Anyway, and forgive me if my memories of the book aren't exactly accurate, but what impressed me about Studs, as pathetic as his life was, was fairly early on - before he smoked and drank himself to death - he had a crush on some girl in the neighborhood, and there was a time he won a fight on the streets - outfought some other bigger, young tough guy and was her hero - was the hero of all the kids in the neighborhood. Later in the book, after he was crushed by one after another misfortune related to the times he lived in, it eventually dawns on you the highlight of his life had happened early on when he fought that other kid and thought his life was really just starting. And I don't know if it ever dawned on him. He certainly didn't take the time to enjoy those early days because he thought he had so much *more* time in which to enjoy himself and his life; he had been so young. I think maybe he looked back at that experience he'd had as a kid, as he was dying, wondering how he'd let things get away from himself, I'm not sure.

The first time I see Samantha Barnes is the first day of high school. Like I said, we've just moved back to San Antonio that summer, my parents, Gail, and me. Dad has retired and bought a nice little house in Terrell Hills, part of the Alamo Heights school district, and Gail will be a senior and me a freshman. That first day all the freshmen have to go to homeroom first instead of their first real class, and mine is in Mrs. Phillips' room. No one seems to have an assigned seat so I sit halfway back. Mrs. Phillips comes in as the tardy bell rings. She is short and heavy set. She wears glasses with thick orange-red frames. Her hair is short and dark reddish brown, but she really looks like an old plodder to me. In spite of how dark her hair is, her face is covered with wrinkles and powder. Her lipstick is bright red and drawn larger than her lips. The lipstick color practically matches her rouged cheeks. I mean, she's really a sight and I can't take my eyes off her. All the kids are chattering, laughing, calling across the room to each other as they catch up on summers. Mrs. Phillips writes her name on the blackboard *Mrs. Janice Phillips* as she calls for quiet. No one pays attention.

I finally force myself to look around and count thirty-two kids in the class. As I try to size up the kids, almost every guy including me is wearing tight levi's, a button-down shirt, white socks and weejuns. Every girl has a dress or blouse and skirt with the length set just below the knees, and flat shoes or penny loafers. Some girls have scarves around their necks in spite of the heat. I notice the girl seated against the windows in the row to the left of mine but one chair closer to Mrs. Phillips has long dark blond hair trailing down her back, so I can't tell if she's wearing a scarf. I think she's really pretty, though I can't be sure, waiting for her to turn toward the center of the room so I can get a better look, but she has a great profile from what I can see. You never know how good a girl's going to look till she turns and you're monstrously disappointed when she has glasses and buck teeth or a nose out to here or something, but this girl, from the side from behind even, looks like she's going to be really pretty.

I am as... *unnerved* is the word I guess... as unnerved as a fifteen-year-old can be at the sight of her when she turns, but before she turns I know her eyes will be blue. Her hair is honey blond, dark and maybe she colors it, I don't know. She has long, slim legs, not thin, though her skirt is too long to see much except her calves have a nice shape. She wears white socks and brown loafers. There is a large red spot low on the back of her right calf, I guess from where she crosses her legs at the ankles. As she glances around, her face from the side shows high cheekbones and a perfectly ski-sloped nose, strong jaw. Maybe a splash of freckles, I'm not sure. Eyebrows are blond but dark like her hair. Her shirt is pale green. High collar. It matches the skirt color. Thin brown belt.

A girl somewhere behind me yells "Hi, Sammie!" The blond twists back to look, smiling. She has blue eyes, pale blue eyes, wears no makeup over her tan. She is holding a rubber band around the fingers and thumb of one hand. I feel my face redden as her eyes skim past mine - her eyes are wide apart on her face. They are pale blue, like I said, and make her look like she is dreaming awake. I feel my blush deepen as my face heats up. She looks through and then beyond me at the girl who'd called her. "Hiya, Fancy," she says softly, and winks. She turns back toward Mrs. Phillips, who can finally be heard as the class quiets. I watch the girl *Sammie* as Mrs. Phillips starts explaining what is going to happen this first week that will change after the week ends. Apparently there will be homeroom every morning plus right after lunch every day to give the freshman class a chance to settle in.

As Mrs. Phillips drones on, I can't take my eyes off Sammie. The most of her I can see is the side of her face, the legs from the skirt down, calves full, freckly. Her long blond hair has different shades of blond in it and I'm starting to think it's natural. She finishes drawing it up into a pony tail with the rubber band she's been holding. I've already seen five or six really nice looking girls, just walking through the school on the way to homeroom, but none of them are as pretty as Sammie.

As I watch and Mrs. Phillips talks, Sammie starts slowly undoing the rubber band again, one loop at a time, until she removes it and puts it down on her desk. She gets a brush out of her purse and brushes her hair, first back, again and again. Then she brushes some of it forward, over her eyes. Then she carefully starts brushing some of it back again. She leaves a few strands down in her face and puts the brush down, next to the rubber band. Now she must be looking crosseyed, as she seems to examine each hair in front of her eyes before she pulls it back to join the rest. She seems to be holding on to one last hair. Of course I can't really see it, but she sure looks like she's holding a hair with two fingers of her left hand, and is staring at it - still cross-eyed, I guess. She takes the hair about halfway up to the root with the fingers of her right hand and with the other hand she pulls the lower half of the hair up in front of her eyes. Then she very slowly moves the hair up and down so she can examine it. I'm guessing she's looking at the color or condition, I'm not really sure, but I'm as fascinated

15

with her as she is with the hair. I'm waiting to see if she's going to rip the hair out at the root if she wants to see the whole hair, but she doesn't. I look around, but everyone else seems to be listening to Mrs. Phillips.

And she's detailing that the early homeroom will last thirty minutes each day this first week. Then she explains she will be our homeroom teacher all four years of high school and homeroom would normally be the first period after lunch.

Sammie must be chewing gum, even from the side I'm now aware her cheek and jaw are moving. She reviews the hair a last time, much more slowly this time. I'm hypnotized.

Mrs. Phillips snaps for quiet as some boys in the back of the room laugh, and then continue to laugh after she snaps at them again. Sammie finally pulls the single hair back and then runs a hand through all her hair, pulls it together like a pony tail and then, running both hands through it, she lets it spill down over her back, and finally shakes her head quickly, leaning back. At that moment, a bell rings loudly and everyone starts to talk again and stand up.

*　　*　　*　　*　　*

For the rest of high school I never have a class with Sammie except homeroom. We never speak for more than three of those years, but then we both get leads in the Senior Play and become friends. She tells me my name seems familiar to her when she looks at the list on the bulletin board to see who got which parts, but at the time she isn't sure where she's heard my name before. Sammie is never reluctant to speak her mind and she tells me I'm cute so if she'd seen me before she would have noticed. I tell her I've changed a lot in three years, I've even grown two more inches. I say I've been on both the football and baseball teams and am varsity on both this year. She says I'm lying that I sit a chair away from her in homeroom and she laughs about it the next day in homeroom when she comes in and sees me sitting there, grinning at her.

The crush I had on her as a freshman never goes away, I guess. Like I said, I've changed a lot since the beginning of my freshman year, a lot more than she did. Maybe her face has narrowed, and she's grown another inch, and her body's filled in some, but she has really changed little over those years. She'll always be the most beautiful girl I've ever seen up close, and all I remember during that senior year is rehearsing the play, learning the songs, learning the steps to the dances, practicing a kiss with her. Me the king, she the queen, happily ever aftering....

I drive her home after rehearsal once when her car's in the shop. We are in my hand-me-down excuse for a sport's car - Mom's old black and white Karmann Ghia. Sammie asks me to pick her up the next morning and I do. Her car gets fixed but we continue the rides while the rehearsals go on. She's obviously not interested in me the way I am in her, but she enjoys the conversations and she loves teasing me the way she teases all the boys. She starts calling me Jackie-pants and tells me about the time she's out on a date with a guy in his early twenties and he's trying like hell to get in her pants. As I drive, Sammie repeats it over and over in an imitation of the guy's deep voice. "You lat mah *fahr*, Sammie, you lat mah *fahr*! Oh Sammie gal, you lat mah fahr!!" All the way to her house, she's imitating him. We pull up to her gate and I push the button. When the butler answers, instead of letting me talk she leans over me, still talking like the lathered up guy on her date. "Hah, this's Billy Bob lookin fer Sammie cuz she really lats my fahr, she *really* lats mah fahr, no whut ah mean in thar?" The butler says "yes Miss, I'll buzz you in now," and Sammie says in the same deep throated voice, "Wah, thank you Knowles, Ah preshate it, y'hear?" and she pulls back from the window.

My whole body is keening from her breasts pushing into my arm when she leaned over me to talk. Of course I know she was doing it on purpose, but it really doesn't matter to me.

"Jackie-pants," she says in her normal voice, "why don't you park on the drive and sit with me on the porch. We can study some more or talk or something." I look at her and she actually flutters her eyelashes at me and then laughs. At least, I'm thinking, she isn't trying to make me think she's meaning any of this seriously. Of course, I'm thrilled anyway.

The porch is wood, painted white. It goes all the way across the front of the building, and she tells me to sit on the swing while she goes in to change. While I sit and rock the swing with my feet, I look up. Three stories of Texas limestone, small old-fashioned windows, and columns that go all the way from the porch to the roof.

When she comes back out she's in shorts and a shirt tied in a knot under her breasts. I'm close to not being able to breathe but she's oblivious to my reaction. I don't remember much of what we talk about but we laugh and she does impressions of some of her friends and I remember we did a scene from the play with her doing all the parts but mine - she makes fun of the voices of all the other kids in the play, so I squeak my lines as if I'm five with a lisp and she roars with laughter.

A limousine comes through the gate. It takes the other fork in the driveway and goes around to the back. She stands up as it disappears behind the building and says "This has been fun, Jackie-pants, but it's gettin' late. Do ya mind takin' off now?" I'm shaking my head *no* and she adds "You'll regret it to the end of time if you get roped into meetin' anybody else in the family. I promise!" She rolls her eyes and I get up saying something like "Sure, no problem" and she gives me maybe a grateful smile, kisses my cheek and mumbles *y'all take care*. I'm in the car driving away and looking in the rear-view mirror when someone comes out the front door and walks up to Sammie, but I can't tell who it is from this distance.

Twice more I stay after bringing her home, never inside. She remembers how she used to climb these giant oaks in her yard. She made David, who I'm guessing is a brother, build her a swing in one of them. He bought a wooden slat and punched holes in it for the ropes. She insisted on climbing the tree and tying the knots to hold it up there. She broke the bone in her forearm two years later when one side came undone. David paid a company with a crane to come in and re-position the swing. I looked out where she was pointing at the trees and thought I saw the swing under the largest of them, the ropes disappearing up into the green. We talk a lot, and she even listens to some of my stories. Cars come and go, but no one ever parks out front, no one ever walks out the front door to greet us with lemonade and cookies.

On the way to school with her the day after my third visit, she tells me I'm coming to dinner.

*   *   *   *   *

I meet the Barnes family the next weekend. I'm really ambivalent about this, because on the one hand, I'm mysteriously sent packing whenever anyone from her family comes home. On the other hand, Sammie calls her parents by their first names. I can't imagine rich people acting like hippies, being on a first name basis with their kids, so I can't wait to meet them. For another, of course, it's a step up with me and Sammie. I'm telling myself not to get worked up about it, but it's cool anyway.

She tells me not to dress up, but not to be *too* casual either, so I show up in jeans and a nice shirt, my usual white socks and weejuns. Sammie had told me to be polite if I want to make a good impression. I spend some time wondering why she would care, but can't figure it out. She seems to enjoy hearing my accent because I don't sound like I'm from Texas, she definitely loves teasing me because of my inability to hide my feelings for her. I'm sure she wouldn't even be messing with me if I wasn't tall, but I don't kid myself - Sammie has men panting after her that look better and are smarter than I will ever be.

The same man's voice I always hear answers my ring, asks my name, and buzzes me through the gate. I'm in my Mom's Impala and I drive it through the gate, watching in the rear view mirror until the gate rolls back closed, then I drive down the short road to the house, though I will always think of it as the Mansion, the Barnes' Mansion. Sammie laughs whenever I call it that. I park and walk up the front stairs to the main entrance. The porch swing is empty, but swinging. Maybe she'd been sitting there when I buzzed the house.

As I approach the front door, Sammie opens it. She stands there. My heart sinks and I stop short. She's wearing something she would go to a cotillion in. Her waist is cinched into a plum colored short formal that is kind of bell-shaped from the waist down and ends just below her knees. It is strapless, with purple strips at the neckline, waist, and hem, with the kind of neckline that shows the tops of her breasts. Her high heels match the plum color. A jewel hangs from a gold chain around her neck. The jewel is a globe, encrusted with diamonds and plum colored sparkling stones. The globe sparkles and rolls around the space between her breasts whenever she moves. Her blond hair is twisted and turned into a display above her head. Her earrings, smaller replicas of the globe, dangle. She lifts her face and laughs. She takes a step and twirls to show off the dress.

My first reaction is that I'm here on the wrong night - that she has a date to the Country Club or something. Then when she shows off the dress to me, I figure it is the right night for me to show up, but that she's told me the wrong thing to wear, as a joke. The whole family is probably dressed up like she is and I'm in jeans.... *Oh damn*, I think. I turn around and start back toward the car.

"Jack!" she shouts. Then she does the singsong voice "Jackie-pants...." I look back.

She is hugging the doorframe, her face down, her eyes looking up at me sexily from beneath her lashes. "Come on in Jackie-pants," she says in her steamiest voice. "We'll get through this together." She chuckles. I pause and then turn back toward her. I realize this is going to be all I'll ever have with her, this teasing and giving a little and teasing again and on and on. But I can't really see not giving in to her.

"You'd look better if that was lime green," I blurt. I walk past her into the foyer.

Her eyes flash annoyance, but the smile never leaves her face. Before she can say anything, I try again, "or maybe the blue of your eyes."

She makes a face at me and grabs my hand to keep me from walking past her. Then she leads me into the living room.

Her parents and sister sit in high-backed stuffed chairs. Her parents seem to be having a heated but low-voiced argument, and stop when we come in. Her sister is reading a magazine. She looks about fifteen, sixteen.

"Belle, David... Paige.... Jack." I shake hands with her firm-gripped parents, neither of whom say more than *Hello*, but smile as they greet me. It flashes to me that on my other high school dates I usually get a father saying an insincere *my daughter has told us all about you....* Paige's eyes stay on the article she is reading during the whole greeting thing, she even holds out her hand without looking up, and smiles at the magazine when I take her hand. I read the title *Cosmopolitan* upside down. Belle, David and Paige are all dressed casually, like me. Sammie's high heels click on the floor tile as she walks me around the room.

"I'm going to change now. You guys entertain Jack while I'm gone?" Sammie is gone before anyone can answer, and no one answers. I'm still standing next to Paige's chair while Belle and David have resumed their argument or whatever it is halfway down the room.

Paige looks to be about her mother's height, but without the figure that her mother and sister have. She's definitely not thin, she's just not curved. She has the Barnes' cheekbones, but her Mother's brown hair and kind-of-hazel eyes. Mrs. Barnes has a beautiful face, again that perfect nose, pouty mouth. Her face is rounder than Sammie's, and she is several inches shorter, maybe twenty or thirty pounds heavier. She could long ago have been a cheerleader for Mr. Barnes - David - whose thick neck makes him a former athlete, old but still trim, dressed casually but looking like he belongs in a three piece suit. He's looking down at his wife from beneath shaggy eyebrows. She seems unhappy and looks at the arm of her chair as she strokes the fabric.

I wander to the wall that is bookshelves and examine them. Sammie's father is talking about "drillin'." *Sons and Lovers* by D. H. Lawrence. Belle asks how long he'll be gone "this time." Guy de Maupassant. Doestoevsky. Chaucer. "Till the end of the month." She sighs. *Kidnapped. The Decline and Fall of the Roman Empire.* Several volumes of that one, written by Gibbons of course, and I shudder. "Well, OK, when'll you be leavin', deah?" *The Sun Also Rises, The Complete Works of Shakespeare* in four volumes. "In the mawnin'." I take a book off the shelf because I've never heard of it before - *The Idiot* by Dostoevsky - and start reading where the book opens.

Eventually Sammie returns. She walks to me. I look her up and down. Her hair is down below her shoulders. She's in tight Levis, bare feet, a lime green t-shirt with no writing. "Nice shirt," I grin.

She ignores me. "Whatcha readn, Jackie-pants?" she asks.

"My autobiography." I put the book back in its place on the shelf.

She laughs and puts an arm through mine, pressing a breast against me. I'm so used to the teasing that I ignore it. "Have you read many of these?" I point to all the shelves with my free arm.

"Awl of em, dear heart," she says casually, "Wanna test me?"

"Well then, what do *you* think I should be doin?" Belle says rather loudly to David, then looks over at us, her hand up over her mouth.

He looks at us, too. "Sammie," he says loudly, "can y'all keep Belle busy for a few weeks, you and Paige? Ah mean in between all her charity drives, benefits, bridge tournaments and luncheons at the Club?" He looks at his wife. She shakes her head slowly as she returns his look, but her face remains calm.

"Anyway, y'all, I am gonna go check on dinnah. Paige, come with me, please?" asks Belle as she rises and walks from the room. Paige follows her, but not before several heavy sighs and a big show of marking her place in Cosmo by folding a page.

David and I exchange glances. "So you were a runnin' back on the Mules' team this year, son? And now you're an actor?" he asks.

"I just have a part in the Senior Play, sir. I'm not really an actor," my cheeks are burning and I glance over at Sammie, who's practically rolling around on the floor at my discomfort.

"Ah see, Ah see," says David absently. "Well, excuse me, son. You and Samantha go play somewheah until we're called to dinnah. Ah have some things to attend to upstaihs." And with that he rises, kisses his wicked daughter on the cheek, stares at her for a moment and leaves the room.

Sammie turns to me critically, with one hand up, first finger to her lips as if deep in thought. Finally she says, "Well, Jackie-pants, you're doin' right well so fah. If y'all don't soil yoahseff or faht too loudly at dinnah, Ah'm thinkin' y'all might pass the mustahd tanight. Y'all might ackshally be able to retuhn some tahm foah anothuh go at it!" Her accent has gotten so thick I'm having to concentrate to be sure I'm following her.

"Why are you talking like that?" I ask.

"Oh, sometimes Belle and David put it on so thick, I start doin' it, too. It's fun to do it, sometimes. It's hard to believe they don't talk like that when we're alone. I have *no* idea why *they* do it, but when I do it I think it's cause I'm enjoyin' the actin', you know?"

I am nervous, but I think the rest of the evening goes well. I'm sure I use the right forks in the right order. I've never had a shrimp cocktail as part of a meal in a home before, and never been served by a "man-servant" named Knowles. These are also my first lamb chops, after I realize they aren't just small, strange smelling pork chops. And all of us "kids" are served half a glass of red wine. I've had years of tasting it in church, but this stuff is quite a ways beyond the blood of Christ, if you know what I mean.

Sammie walks me to my car at the end of the meal, and pecks me on the cheek while I thank her for the evening. "You're welcome, Jackie-pants. You done good!" she says.

And I do go back - fairly often, actually. Sammie says her parents like me; she says they like few of her dates, boyfriends, whatever they are. We see each other less after the play finishes it's short run in the auditorium at school, but we remain friends and I feel much more popular with the other kids than I ever did before that play. Twice we go out to Edge Falls with a bunch of other kids. The jump the guys all make seems about a hundred feet. The warning signs that we ignore, prohibiting the jump, say it's only forty. Sammie is among the few girls who make the jump.

We both have other dates to Senior Prom but we dance together a few times and laugh at each other most of the time we're dancing. She is with an older guy who I think she's been dating a lot, off and on, most of senior year. Of course, he's a real nice looking guy. I'm with the girl I've been dating, going steady with actually, most of my senior year. Sammie tells me she's been accepted at Wellesley and a few other Ivy League schools and I tell her I'm going to UT.

In homeroom on the last day of school, Mrs. Phillips walks by each desk and tearfully says goodbye to each of us. She even hugs some of the girls, including Sammie.

I expect to never see Sammie again, but I know I'll have this sad little crush on her for the rest of my life.

*   *   *   *   *

My freshman year at UT is pretty interesting. I pledge a fraternity and then de-pledge. I smoke my first and probably only weed. I find out what I want to do for a career. I meet Alice and almost get over Sammie.

Oh, I go to classes most of the time and UT invites me back for my sophomore year. Many of my friends drink and party too much and play pool and poker and bridge and spades instead of studying and are either placed on scho pro - scholastic probation - or sent packing. One really cute girl from Houston is caught turning in someone else's work and gets kicked out of school the next day. It's a pretty big scandal. I guess that happened second semester.

When I smoke that dope I get absolutely neurotic.

But first, I move into the frat house with all my pledge brothers and then move into a dorm when I quit after 6 weeks. I'm sure I would have continued to enjoy pledging and the parties and even hell week, Phi Sig was a really cool fraternity and taught me all about Everclear and everything I know about not choking while catching jello cubes and olives in my mouth dropped from a second story landing. The first time I hear Bob Dylan is at the frat house. I laugh out loud when I hear him, thinking it must be a comedy album, but when I look around no one else looks amused. I guess I get used to his whining because of what he's saying, but I still prefer Bud and Travis and a few other coffee house types. Anyway, I really enjoy the fraternity, but I can see me heading toward flunking out so quickly I panic and quit. Mom and Dad locate me a dorm where two-man rooms have postings for roommates. It's on the Drag and is called the A-Bar Dormitory; I meet this guy who needs a roommate and he is OK so I move in. He introduces himself as Trevor Livingston "of the New York Livingston's" and then introduces me to his bare feet by dropping his cigarette on the linoleum floor in the room and stomping it out with his heel. When I stare at him he smiles and admits he's from San Diego, not New York, and says he's lived most of his life helping his dad the fisherman, on a boat and a rocky beach, so his feet are solid calluses. I make friends with a few other guys on the floor and when we aren't studying they are teaching me bridge and spades. The dope happens because Trevor asks me if I'd mind if he sneaks his girlfriend upstairs one night so they can smoke dope without worrying about driving afterwards. I say I don't mind, and does he want me to go on a date or the library to give him the room for the evening. I start to say I'd still want to sleep in the room later when he interrupts to ask if I'd like to share his "stuff" with them. I say OK. I don't want him to know I've never smoked before, and then I start to worry about whether he's talking about marijuana or something worse.

When we gather that night, I'm so relieved to see it's marijuana we're going to have, I confess to never having smoked before. They think it's cute. We joke about it until we start smoking. They show me how, and instead of puking or choking like they say I might, it's like I'd been sucking this stuff down for years. I may not choke but it seems like a really long time before I feel it. And when I do, whoa. I am suddenly stoned. They tell me the next day I must be really susceptible - probably to any drug including medicine - and I should always be careful about quantities of anything I take. This means I shouldn't have kept smoking the stuff after I'd taken in a lot. I mean, have you ever smoked dope or at least seen it done in movies? You know how you hold it in till you need to breathe and you blow it out and there's some smoke there but less than you took in? Well, with me that first time, I never saw *any* smoke coming out, Trevor says it was like I was taking it *all* in. So I'm sitting there using Trevor's bed to lean my back against and he and his mystery girl are on his bed so I'm not seeing them, just hearing them behind and above me. They are talking in really low voices and maybe chuckling every once in a while. I'm sitting there looking at the window across the room, seeing it get darker by the minute, but I'm thinking about Trevor and his girl and I'm certain they're talking about me and laughing about how stoned I got so fast. I mean I can't enjoy what I'm feeling, all that euphoria you hear about going on when you get stoned, I'm sitting there thinking how this is a clean drunk and man am I feeling it and why did these guys plot to get me high and why are they laughing they got me this high. I guess by the next morning that feeling has gone away, and I end up just pleasantly drunk off the stuff and we walk to a place that is opening for breakfast and we do what stoners do, we order two or three doughnuts each, and eat them and giggle.

I also take an advanced math class because that had been my best subject in high school. One of the first things they teach us is numbering systems (sorry, "they" was a kind of zoned-in guy named Mr. McDermott) - he loved math, got all excited when he talked about the concepts, actually got me excited about it too, especially first semester when we got to non-decimal numbering systems. For computers, you have to forget the decimal system except since it's the one we're familiar with; we translate the computer's numbering to decimal so we'll know where we are. Anyway I learned about binary and hexadecimal, the numbering systems for zero through one and for zero through fifteen. Unimportant concepts unless you are talking to computers and they are talking back, and that's what grabbed me, the idea I could talk to computers if I understood these other numbering systems well enough. Base two and Base sixteen became all I was really interested in from then on at UT. I transferred from the English Department to Business and started learning Assembler Language and how to add and subtract in those weird numbering systems - most of this stuff would make a normal person's eye glaze over immediately, but I felt that giving instructions to a computer *and have it perform correctly* was about as cool as it got.

Then I meet Alice, Alice from Alice. We date for about two years, until she transfers to Oklahoma State for her senior year. But while we date, we are very hot and heavy. She is pretty and smart - and good to me - I might be as grateful as I am in love.

I meet her because I always go for coffee between my English class and my Chem Lab that first semester. English is eight to nine, Monday, Wednesday, Friday and I always sit at the counter studying for the Chem Lab that starts at ten. I will *always* hate Chemistry. After a few weeks I realize I am sitting with the same people at this counter, every time - the kids studying for whichever class comes next for them, are all eating breakfast or sipping the dime coffee till a few minutes before ten. This cute girl sitting next to me looks up when I do, when it occurs to me we are all the same people sitting here every MWF.

"Hi!" she says, "Chemistry?" and points to my open and hated Chemistry laboratory work book.

I smile and nod.

"Yeah, I took that last year," she says, probably innocently enough, but I take it to at least mean she's letting me know she's a sophomore before I get any ideas. Then she confirms it when she says "You're a freshman?" She eyes me up and down and smiles.

"Yes, I am. My name's Jack."

"Hi. I'm Alice. I'm a sophomore."

We shake hands formally. I say "I'm actually majoring in Financial Management. What are you studying?"

"What am I in for?" she laughs, "I'm in the science department. I want to get a Doctorate and teach somewhere, but I haven't declared a major yet. Do you mind if I ask you a personal question? Would you like to take me to a show or something this weekend?"

"Was that the personal question, or just something you were wondering while I decided whether you can ask me the personal question?"

She laughs. "Sorry, I didn't really wait for you to answer did I? Look, I'm not dating anybody right now and you're cute and," she looked me up and down again, "quite the long drink of water. You're not a jock in addition to everything else, are you?"

"Mmmm, I assume being a jock is a bad thing, so lucky for me, I'm not a jock. Where are you from, Alice? Somewhere in Texas?"

"Actually, I'm embarrassed to admit I'm Alice *from* Alice, Jack."

After a smile, I tell her I'm from San Antonio and admit I don't know where Alice is.

She leans back like I've become a freak. "You're from San Antonio and you've never heard of Alice? Ever been to... Corpus Christi? Beeville? South Padre Island, for God's sake?"

"Corpus, yes. Now I remember seeing a sign for Alice somewhere on the way there, yes. Sorry."

"That's OK," she leans back again. "So do you play handball? It's my favorite sport, keeps you in shape, good for the heart. We could buy you gloves and sign up for a court at Gregory Gym...?"

I am just staring at her. She talks a mile a minute, unlike any Texan I've ever met. She has to be from somewhere else. I'm studying her while I think. Her chin is a little too long to be perfect and her lips are a little on the thin side and her nose... well, I'm comparing it to a perfect nose, of course. But I think my first impression was accurate enough, she *is* pretty. Shoulder-length brown hair brushed behind studded ears, flat against her head, big chocolate colored eyes. About as tall as Sammie. She is maybe a little thinner all over and from what little I know about handball, that probably explains it. I've heard you need to be in great shape to play it for more than just a few minutes, and Alice looks like she could play it for hours. "Uh," I say to slow her down and gather my thoughts, "uhm, I haven't ever played handball but I guess I could learn."

"You want to see a movie, say Saturday? Do you have time some afternoon this week to use a court at the gym? I haven't played myself in forever. Had a boyfriend who played but I dumped him a while back. You have a girlfriend, Jack? Not that that matters for playing handball cause I bet your girlfriend is more the cheerleader type than handball, you being blondish and hunkish like you are. I'd guess you're, what? Six two, six three?"

I remember thinking I need to get up and head for my lab, but Alice is making me feel pretty good, I don't think I'll be able to get up quite yet. "Yes," I say about playing handball in the afternoon, but she's asked me so many questions she can't possibly know which one I'm answering.

"Great!" she says as she stands up. "Well, I have a class to go to." She takes the pencil she is carrying behind an ear and writes on my UT book cover. "Call me and we'll figure out when we can play and what movie we're going to." Then she walks away. She really looks great walking away, all slim and athletic. She swings her arms from the shoulders, her hands swinging loosely as she takes great strides, not looking around, not looking back. She's actually at least an inch taller than Sammie, but can't weigh 110, 120 tops.

I look down at the book. On it she's written *Alice Kaplan, Kinsolving*.

*   *   *   *   *

Once, while we're making out on the bed in Alice's dorm room, instead of undressing herself, Alice surprises me by grabbing my shoulders and pushing me down toward her waist. When I kiss my way down from there, she becomes very helpful lifting her skirt and raising her hips so her panties can come off. Then, by shifting, nudging me, and whispering at me, she guides what I'm doing till she no longer needs to help, no longer *can* help. For me, it has become my instant favorite thing. I have unsuccessfully tried this twice before with girl friends in high school. The first time I tried was because she wasn't interested in anything but making out for hours, and the second was because I'd begun visualizing it and it excited me. In both cases I was pushed away.

I ask Alice afterwards whether it is unusual she enjoyed having that done to her. I tell her about my two experiences in explaining why I'm wondering. First she scoffs at my sad little high school floundering but then she thinks about it for a while. "Maybe most girls, whether they enjoy it or not don't want to *have* to reciprocate and they know that the guy's going to want it too. In this day and age, it could be that some women look on doing a guy as a male domination thing, not pleasant at all. But I enjoy doing you - really! - except I'm not thrilled about the taste, you know? Sticky and too salty? Bleh." She makes a "too-salty" face and laughs.

I admit I'm shocked at how freely she talks. I also realize I need to think about her reciprocating, even though that possibility hadn't occurred to me while we were making love because as soon as she'd been satisfied she pulled me back up and made me very happy without it. My only experience with a woman doing *that* to me was once back in high school with a prostitute down in Nuevo Laredo, and although I found it to be pretty pleasant I remember that woman made it seem like what it was: a job. Alice adds, "You didn't act like what you were doing was unpleasant." I grin at her and she smiles back and adds, "on the other hand, your breath sucks now. Go brush?"

"Yes Ma'am" I say, kissing her bare shoulder as I get up.

*   *   *   *   *

I ask her about being a Kaplan. I've never known a Jewish person before, I mean personally. She says she isn't very Jewish, her family belongs to the Reform Temple in Corpus Christi because there aren't many Jews in Alice. She is actually quite normal; normal acting and normal looking, well, better than normal but you know what I mean. I guess she is also more liberal than anyone I've ever known, if that's a Jewish indicator - like she believes in free choice on abortion rights, and the government should spend a lot more on food stamps and the job corps.

Oh, on another subject, she's gotten into computers and programming. The more English-like language named COBOL was what she wanted to learn and she started taking some computer courses to do it. She's still trying to decide what to Major in, but she loves Chemistry. Now she's also thinking about animal husbandry.

Anyway, we decide that neither of us is religious enough to let that hold our relationship back. We're much too into enjoying each other to let our religions interfere. She does tell me about the blessings over the bread and wine on Friday nights and I tell her about receiving the Body and Blood on Sunday mornings - I mean they are both about bread and wine, right? Neither of us goes to church or temple the whole time we know each other.

*   *   *   *   *

Alice says, "Jack you are like a boyfriend and a brother all rolled up in one. Do you know what a dichotomy you are, my friend?"

I think and then answer, "Which half was having sex with you on your dining room table last night? If it was your brother, he should be arrested."

Without hesitation, she replies "No, no, no - I'm serious and you are purposely missing the point - your Astrological Being, the traits of the Gemini, the masculine, positive, mutable air sign makes it so obvious that you are the two faces pointing in opposite directions - there can be no other explanation for the two of you, blissfully naive and blatantly loudmouthed."

"You realize that my eyes glazed over when you said 'astrological'? Are you even listening to yourself?"

She smiles sadly. "It's just like handball, darling. You panted like you were dying five minutes after we started, the first time I dragged you onto the court. Now you are beating me senselessly every time we play. So too will you begin to understand what I'm saying about the stars."

"'So too' Alice? Nobody says 'so too'! Seriously, have you come here from another planet? Were you sent here to teach me to become an alien? Did your people see me wander onto campus from some far off world and send you to guide me to some higher level of awareness? Who can I write to thank? I mean really, I never believed 'Alice from Alice' from the very beginning, you must know that. And why am I talking like this? You are ruining me Alice! You have me talking like *I'm* from Alice, Alice!"

By then she has turned away. We are sitting at an outdoor table at the Kerbey Lane Cafe, a twenty-four hour Austin landmark that serves the only sweet potato fries she will eat. She is either reading for a test coming up tomorrow or pretending to, in order to ignore me. I am studying for a test in a class I hate - Business Writing. OK, to be fair I hate the University of Texas Business School's Business Writing course. But as much as I hate it, when Alice turns away, all my excuses for not studying turn with her.

Alice is a junior and considering her options for transferring closer to her parents, who have moved to Enid, Oklahoma because her father's business has transferred him there. I had just told her she should go ahead and transfer and she seems to be reacting badly. I'm sure she feels if I *really* love her I wouldn't want her to go. That's what all the dichotomous stuff is all about, I'm guessing.

Two real problems exist between us, in my opinion. The first is Sammie called me last summer and we spent a lot of time together. Called me the day I arrived home, as if she was having my parents' house watched. Alice knows all about

Sammie and my crush, because we talk about everything, Alice and I. The summer had left my feelings for Sammie reinforced, because at the end of it, when we said goodbye, she'd kissed me for real; God knows why. When school started again Alice and I picked right up from where we'd left off last year, and I haven't heard from Sammie since she said she'd write. Deep down, though, I was already planning on breaking up with Alice. That's the second problem between us. Regardless of whether anything would ever actually come of me and Sammie, I want to... I don't know... be available just in case? Besides, deep down, I'm ready to break up with Alice. I know I'm acting picky, and it's truly embarrassing to admit it because it shows how shallow I am. She makes noise when she chews. She makes noise when she spits after brushing her teeth. I can hear her swallow when she drinks. I don't like her nose. What makes these reasons worse is even when I'm saying them, I *know* they're just excuses. I know no matter what she says about not wanting to move to Oklahoma, or maybe moving in with me, or whatever she comes up with, I'm going to come up with some reason to break up. Maybe I'll regret it. Maybe *she* is the defining moment in my life.

* * * * *

The summer before my senior year, after I get home from an Army ROTC Summer Camp, Sammie calls crying a few days after I've gotten settled in.

"Come over?" is all she says after we exchange hi's, but she's saying it through tears.

When I get to her house she's on the porch swing in a polka dot bikini top with an unmatched pair of brown swim trunks. Her face shows she's recently cried but she seems alright now. I mean her nose is red and there are splotches on her forehead and cheeks, but she's composed. She has her hair up in a pony tail. We cheek kiss and she's obviously distracted and says "I want to go to the pool. David's trunks would fall off you so we need to swing by your house for your suit." What I translate this to is I'm going to the San Antonio Country Club to go swimming. The Barnes' mansion doesn't have a pool although with all the room behind the house, I'm not sure why not. The family *does* spend a lot of time at the Club, eating, swimming, golfing, bridge and mahjong tournaments, and partying.

"OK, but what's up with you - you OK?"

"Let's go, Jackie-pants," she smiles and shakes her head, like she's getting her hair out of her eyes, but it's in a ponytail anyway so it just flips around back there.

We get in my Impala, the parental hand-me-down.

"I just got kinda dumped, is all," she says by way of explanation, as she settles into the car.

"You?" I blurt without thinking.

"Of course me, God damn it! Don't go stupid on me!" She is looking away, out the side window.

"Sorry" I say quickly and let the silence go on till we get to my house. She continues to stare out her window and I just say I'll be back in a minute and run in for my suit and a towel. When I get back to the car she seems pretty much composed and asks if I have some flip flops for the pool and when I say I forgot them inside she says I'll need them to go into the Club for a snack after we swim. I run back in the house to grab Dad's since I don't really have a pair. Then she guides me to the Club (I could get used to calling it "The Club," like a big shot) and when I start to pull into a spot in the parking lot she stops me by putting her hand on the steering wheel. She tells me to drive all the way up to the circle drive at the front entrance. She tells me we *never* park and walk to the front door. I flip my eyebrows and she sees it and laughs. We look at each other and she looks much better now. I roll my eyes and flip the eyebrows again, clowning. By now we're standing across the car from each other as these young guys in forest green uniforms have opened our doors. She laughs hard at the face I've made and we start to go in. Still giggling, she takes my hand as we cross the Club's threshold.

She looks up at me and smiles and says "Thanks, Jackie-pants."

"De nada," I say.

*   *   *   *   *

I'm in the pool and she's lying out on a beach towel next to the edge where I'm holding on. "I'm sure it's because I've gotten so fat. I had to put on Belle's shorts because the bikini bottom to this top would have torn in two if I'd forced it on. I just can't believe I'm so out of shape and hippy. Danny must have just lost interest. And after three years, for God's sake. I can't believe he lied to me about that slut."

Sammie looks great to me. Sure her hips are a bit wider than in high school, but this is as close to undressed as I've ever seen her so of course I'm enjoying all the skin I'm being asked to examine. Her arms are not as "tight" as they could be but they certainly aren't sagging. Her breasts look really nice to me. She's always had nice calves and her thighs are really quite muscular, considering how out of shape she's claiming to be. I even notice both her finger and toe nails are cut short and perfectly trimmed and painted the same silver color. I'm thinking that color doesn't look like it goes with her coloring, but what do I know?

I act like it isn't news to me she's been dating whoever Danny is for three years. I'm guessing they must have been pretty serious. "May I make a suggestion to get you into shape?"

"Shape? Oh, you mean I *am* fat?" She throws her arm over her face. Very theatrical.

"Have you ever played handball?"

"Handball? Yuck! That even *sounds* sweaty, Jack - for God's sake!"

"Well, I learned to play from a... young lady...at UT, and she was in really good shape, Sammie."

She drops her arm and sits up leaning on her elbows, bending one leg at the knee, looking down at me as if in shock. "You've been dating... another... woman?"

I laugh and she joins in, but I'm also blushing. She looks at me squinty-eyed and says "Jackie-pants - you've been getting sweaty with another woman, you sex fiend!" She reaches out with one hand and tries to push my head under. I let her, but when I surface, I flip my head to get the water out of my eyes and some of the spray hits her and she yelps. I laugh and tease "You've been going with a guy for three years I've never even heard of and you're surprised *I'm* going out? You silly, silly girl."

She grins and closes her eyes and sticks her tongue out at me, waggling her whole head. While her eyes are shut I pull myself up out of the water and quickly put my mouth over her tongue. She shrieks and pulls away and we both laugh hysterically. I flop back into the water, and push off to do some laps while she laughs and settles back down on the towel. I'm swimming and thinking maybe Danny just didn't *get* Sammie and her... ways. I am thinking she maybe does a lot of this goofing and sarcasm and teasing stuff to cover for herself. Mostly I seem to spark a positive response from her when I *don't* show her how I really feel about her. I mean, it makes me uncomfortable but that's pretty much how she is. I think *she* thinks she has to be that way because she's rich and blond and tall and has that nose and those breasts.

I pull up next to her after counting eight lengths and she's waiting, up on her elbows again. "You seriously can teach me hand ball and get me into your kind of shape?" she asks.

"Yeah. Do they have courts here?"

She sneers. "Who knows? Who the hell cares? I am *not* going to be seen sweaty at the Club, anyway. No way. One can come to lunch here *in* sweats but never sweaty. *You* find a place to get me in shape this summer, Jackie-pants." She looks at me like maybe this is the first sincere moment she's had in her life. "I really can't stand myself right now." She's probably still play-acting, but you never know.

"So order me a drinkie and tell me about your sweaty little girl friend," she adds, settling back down on her towel and putting an arm back over her eyes. "Why did you say she dumped you?"

*   *   *   *   *

We have sex once later that summer. It isn't very good, but it's still good. I have no idea why we're having sex. I mean she's what? Thanking me for toning her up with the handball and the swimming every day? So is it handball sex? Maybe gratitude for being there when she was upset about Danny? I want it to be more than that but we planned for this date to just be a quick dinner cause she said she wanted to get to bed early and when I picked her up the first words out of her mouth once we both were in the car was "let's get a burger at the Frontier and come back here and have sex. No one'll be home till late." Strange? Like, if this was a movie I'd be looking around the car to see who she's saying this to, right? And in the back of my mind I'm already wondering what the joke is, I mean what it's going to be when we get back here.

My first big memory is how scared I am the whole time - first of being caught. Her parents or Paige coming home and coming upstairs and catching us. We are in her bedroom. I mean think about this from my perspective, I'm in Samantha Barnes' bedroom! Me and Sammie, in her bedroom! So... that's the other, the more obvious thing I'm scared about.

She walks me up the main stairway and leads me into a large pink room, with a large pink bed at one end. She says "Wait here while I clean up" and goes in the bathroom. When I hear the shower start, I sit on the front edge of the bed. I have seen movies where the guy gets undressed and under the covers and the girl comes out and says *what are you doing I just wanted to show you my doll collection*, which is exactly what I'm expecting her to say, so I'm not taking off a stitch till she comes back. The shower stops pretty soon and I hear a shower curtain and she's humming tunelessly in there. I see that there actually is a big dollhouse at the other end of the room. It's maybe as big as those cartoon dog houses in a Bugs Bunny cartoon, the one that has the name SPIKE over the door. I get up and kneel in front of the dollhouse and see it's filled with miniature stuff. I mean it's a completely furnished layout with little people and fancy furniture and chandeliers. Three floors, just like the Barnes' Mansion. There is a Lincoln Towncar and a Lamborghini parked in front. There are little books on little shelves in one room on the second floor like a library. I'm betting I could read book titles on those little shelves if I had a magnifying glass. I see a little blond headed teenaged Sammie sitting at a table downstairs.

The real Sammie opens the bathroom door and comes into the room. She's barefoot and wearing an oversized big fluffy white robe and she's grinning.

"Nice dollhouse," I say and her grin moves from a smile to a laugh, and then to a big laugh. When she stops I say "Well it is," defensively, and she says "I know, Jackie-pants," with that big sarcastic grin. "Now go shower. We've still got oodles of time before anybody gets home." We had stopped at a Walgreens' on the way to the mansion and marched in together to buy prophylactics - me feeling pretty confident that this was going to end up as a joke on me. We even joked as we stood in front of the five rows of packages about which rubbers we should get - finally, and with plenty of poking elbows, settling on a variety pack. After we got back to the car she ceremoniously opened the three-pack as I drove, giving me that head down, eyes up sexy look she does.

After she tells me to go shower, she flashes one of the rubbers back at me as she heads to her bed and I'm closing the bathroom door.

Nice shower, biggest shower stall I've ever been in that wasn't also a tub. Then I'm clean and start toweling off and I see another robe hanging on the bathroom door, big and fluffy and white like the one she was wearing. Since I have nothing clean to put on, I leave my clothes in a pile on the tile floor and put on the robe. When I peek out after I finish she's standing right there by the door. She takes me by the hand and leads me to the bed.

My second memory of that afternoon is of a single blond hair growing out of her right nipple. Well, OK, not the nipple, it grew out of the color, the areola surrounding her right nipple. Awful that I even noticed, but there it was. It was maybe two o'clock in the afternoon so it was impossible to darken the room with just the sheers she has in the windows. Who doesn't have blinds or shades on a window? I can't imagine being able to sleep in that room after dawn. Even if we're embarrassed about the bodies we are about to show to each other, covering up or hiding is impossible in this light. She lets go of my hand and goes to the other side of the bed. When she sits facing away from me and drops her robe to slide in under the covers, it is a modest move except then she throws the covers open to let me in on the side I'm on - so I can see all of her except her toes, anyway. She *is* blond. Even her nipples are pale, a shade of pink I'd never imagined, almost as pale as her lightly tanned skin. I drop my robe and lie down next to her, instantly excited. I touch her breasts and she smiles, watching me. As I feel and squeeze them and lower my head to taste them, that's when I notice that one long pale hair on her nipple. I pause and stare at it for a few seconds and she brings me back to what's going on when her hand, which had begun moving with a lazy spiraling descent from my chest to my abs, has finally settled between my legs. She begins caressing me there so I put my mouth over the nipple I've been playing with and squeeze the other one, gently. As my breath quickens, it flashes into my mind that I should be trying some of the stuff I've learned before it's too late. I guess it sounds clinical, but I'm really dreading and anticipating I'm going to be bad at this with her, so I really am being clinical, trying like hell to do well. I interrupt us both and leave her breasts to bend lower. She stops what she's doing, too, because I've gotten in her way. I think she was starting to breathe harder, too, when I began playing with her breasts, but when my head starts moving down toward her hips she stops and lays back. I put my free hand under her buttocks and begin by kissing her stomach. Then I move lower. I part her legs. This is really different - although I hadn't been thinking about Alice at all, hers was where all my experience with this kind of foreplay has been and she'd been dark and curly and kind of mysterious down in there. Sammie is all blond and light and smooth and exposed and perfumed. I'm kissing those lips. The smells and scents and taste of her have me completely dazzled as I open my mouth and kiss her deeply where I feel the bud in her and she says *whoop* in a high pitched voice and gasps. I don't want to stop, but before too long I do. I go back up to her face and kiss her and take a breast in my hand. I gently squeeze the nipple with two fingers while I caress between her legs till I find the bud I'd made wet moments before, and she eventually stops me and when I look at her to find out why, her pale blue eyes are only half open when she reaches to the side table with one hand and grabs the package. With the other hand she's playing with me again, without really needing to. She hands the package to me, so I open it and lie on my back and pull it on and then she grabs my shoulders and pulls me on top of her. Of course everything from that point on happens too quickly and can't be any more satisfying for her than it is for me. There is a moment in there when I stop what she's trying to pump out of me and say "wait" and try to move my hips sideways just by pressing into her hips sideways, then not, in the same rhythm to which she'd been moving me, but I'm trying to move without moving in and out of her. It feels good and I know she's enjoying it, but I find it impossible not to start moving the other way again, and that means losing control.

When we dress and go downstairs later, she leads me straight to the front door. "We smell like sex. I don't want anyone to get home before I'm showered again," she explains. She kisses my mouth and makes a face at the odor. Then she smiles again and says, "On the other hand, that was nice. Very interesting stuff while we were playing around there, Jackie-pants. You read about that or did 'handball' teach it to you?" She pushes me out the door without waiting for an answer. "I'm glad you like my dollhouse," she laughs as the door closes.

I don't hear from her again, that summer or the next year. I graduate and break up with the girl I've been dating after Alice moves away. This one is from Dallas, a girl my Mom has been trying to get me to date since high school - good family connections, Mom says. She's cute, dark hair, olive complexion, and we get along, but I can never get past second base with her, maybe she can sense my heart isn't in it, maybe *she* just isn't really interested or she has better sense than I. Anyway, we break up easily at the end of the year, Donna and I.

I'm in the Army. ROTC has kept me in school till graduation, but I can't avoid Vietnam forever, I know. We have only two-year commitments to the Army after ROTC, so we all expect to go to war either the first or second year. The first year I'm assigned to a programming unit at Ft. Benjamin Harrison in Indianapolis and Sammie sends me a birthday card two months after my birthday that Mom forwards to me from home. It's a "friend" birthday card and Sammie has scratched out the word ~~Friend~~ and written *Jackie-pants* above it, but no note, just signed with her full name *Samantha Franklin Barnes* at the bottom, to tease me. I tease her back by not answering, pretty certain she won't notice anyway.

For my second year I'm handed what I've been expecting, orders to Nam. The Army is in a rush to get us over there and to have mid-level officers as cannon-fodder to fill the ranks of those who've come home after their duty tour dead, badly wounded, or with no intention of volunteering to go back. As a result, I'm promoted twice the first year. I'm now a Captain with absolutely no combat experience, just a year in the active reserve, writing COBOL programs for an Army personnel system. My war zone "experience" as an Army officer is a few overnight bivouacs where I play at calling in and receiving calls for fire. What I really remember are the charley horses from standing up for twenty-four hours at a time.

I am praying I'll get to serve my year in the war zone next to some computer, underground at headquarters in Saigon. Of course, the Army sees me as an artillery officer first, so I don't get what I want. Mom calls two days before I'm to leave for Vietnam and tells me Donna called and asked about me and left me a number to call. I think about it for a few hours, and just don't see the point of calling her back. Letting her or Alice know I'm leaving seems irrelevent, really. I also consider calling Belle to let Sammie know where I'm going, but I'm pretty sure just how sad that would sound. With Vietnam looming, I'm thinking Sammie probably got all she wanted out of me anyway and I got all I'm going to.... I'm also thinking there must be a Danny replacement back east by now. I'm honestly not sure how that makes me feel. Certainly no better.

*   *   *   *   *

I've been on this plane for about twelve hours. One brief stopover in Manila and now we are taxiing to a stop in Saigon. Through my little window is like I'm seeing a newsreel I've seen hundreds of times on the TV news. Little Vietnamese laborers with those funny hats and bare feet working all over the airport, men, women and children. Planes landing and taking off. Trucks, jeeps and artillery being unloaded from transports. Huge crates filled with God knows what being shuffled back and forth. Warehouses, doors open to reveal ceiling-high box piles. Every sight is surreal, marked and washed out by the uncompromising brightness out there. The plane jerks to a stop and everyone rises to get in line. We wait for the steps to be rolled up to the plane. Once the door is open we slowly shuffle forward. The stewardesses smile and welcome us to Saigon International as we pass by. Eventually, I take my first step through the door into the harsh and blinding white light. I pause involuntarily at the door, the heat is so... scorching... so amazingly humid, torrid, nearly suffocating... after the coolness of the past few days in Seattle it instantly bakes me and sweat literally springs out of my body. I feel the drops form in the small of my back and begin their trek buttward. I wipe my forehead with the sleeve of my fatigues not realizing that I'll be wiping off sweat for a year and eventually my skin will permanently ache and stay red from rubbing it. After I wipe, the sweat returns immediately and drips down into my squinting eyes as I look out at the airport, finally able to move again. No one behind me complains about the delay I cause - everyone in front of me paused the same way and even the men returning from R&R or for a second or third tour have psyched themselves out of remembering the wet heat and the brightness and how flat the world is here, how much sky.

A lieutenant in the airport looks at my orders and sends me to a gate with a much smaller group of soldiers and officers. Half an hour later, we are escorted back out on the tarmac to a small transport that flies us to Can Tho, which everyone pronounces "can toe". Before we take off, the guy next to me says it's the largest city south of Saigon; after we take off, it's too loud to talk. We sit like we're paratroopers, in two long rows facing each other, swaying in unison as the plane dips and swerves. When we land, we all shuffle in to the airport and line up at a desk that has a cardboard box sitting on it with the words LINE UP HERE written in red ink on all four sides. One at a time, we show our orders to the sergeant manning the desk. Everyone in front of me is either sent on their way out the front entrance of the building or told to sit down in the waiting area. I on the other hand, am immediately escorted back out to the field to a small nasty looking helicopter that is a gunship of some kind. Seems to me I've seen this kind of helicopter whenever they show air battles on TV news. As far as I can see, it has a pilot and co-pilot up front, and a soldier in the second row, sitting across from me behind a mounted 50 caliber. There is a seat between us, but it's empty. I strap myself in, once I figure out how, next to the open doorway. On the flight, whenever the chopper turns I'm either looking straight up at the blinding brightness of the sky or straight down at rice paddies and dirt roads. I'm guessing they're rice paddies we are flying over because the sky reflects off the ground - otherwise you can't really tell from above; they look like normal, planted fields.

An hour into the flight I see helicopters off in the distance, maybe four or five of them. They are in a line diving in turn at something on the ground. As each one ends its run and starts back up, the flames and smoke on the ground get denser. It's happening far enough away, and the chopper I'm in is so noisy I can't hear any explosions - it isn't different from watching a newsreel on TV, except for the noise and hot wind trying to blow me out of the chopper while I watch.

When we land, wherever we are, the airfield is one strip of asphalt and a hut. A jeep is there with a sergeant and a captain standing alongside. There's a canal with huts next to the strip. If you don't look at the huts or that woman and the kids squatting on the side of the canal, Vietnam doesn't feel much different from a hot summer afternoon in San Antonio with a lot more humidity. The captain introduces himself and the sergeant. All I hear because the chopper's taking off, is his name is Mike, until he says "Welcome to Vi Thanh, Chuong Thien." I'm only sure he's saying those words because the orders I'd been given said that's where I was being assigned, to the town of Vi Thanh, in Chuong Thien Province, Republic of Vietnam. The sergeant's nametag says Pedersen. My gear is next to him in the front of the jeep and I'm in the back with Mike.

I have come to Vietnam to die. It is a crazy feeling to be *in* the war movie you've watched. I'm resigned to a fate I feel is inevitable. Dad may have survived World War II and Korea, but I am convinced I will die now that I'm here; there's no returning alive. I'm an artillery officer. I've been shown the statistics for officers, especially lieutenants and captains, surviving a firefight for more than five minutes. Not good. I am literally scared shitless for the first three months of my tour, and after that I still only need to sit on a bowl every week or two, as if the stuff is somehow leaking out of my pores. When I'm finally able to fall asleep every night, it's only because I have finally trained myself not to think about the fact I'll probably never wake up. I develop a technique where I pretend Sammie and I are on the swing on the porch at her house and we're just talking. I try to talk seriously about something, some boring subject about school or a movie or something that's come up during the day, and she smiles and says *that's nice Jackie-pants* a few times and I drift off to sleep.

The images that stay with me from my time over there are few. I am running out of the ready room toward the fox holes dug at the perimeter of the camp. Machine gun and rifle fire are all around us, but I am only concerned about me. I glance back at the table in the middle of the room. Playing cards are drifting to the floor and poker chips are rolling around where they were dropped when the shooting began. I remember watching a card floating like a leaf toward the floor as I run. Slow motion. Then I'm through the door snapping the chin strap on my steel pot and scrambling for my foxhole. I hadn't learned to tighten it correctly so when I land in the foxhole the whole helmet comes crashing forward on my nose and I see stars.

I remember Major Anderson's body brought back to camp after a firefight when the ARVN infantry unit he's advising is overwhelmed by a large Charley force.

I remember the Huey I am in when the smoke that popped in the landing area isn't the color we are told our men are popping and our pilot turns sideways getting away.

I remember the Regular Army officer who we called Captain America behind his back raging at the staff personnel officer, the Team Adjutant, for losing the bronze star paperwork he had written for himself toward the end of his tour. After Captain America ships out, the Adjutant tells me he lost the paperwork on purpose, just as he did the paperwork one of the Majors none of us liked wrote for himself.

I remember calling the transport helicopters *Shithooks* like everyone else, even after I find out they are actually Chinooks.

I remember getting letters once or twice a month from Sammie. She always asks me where I am and how the pot supply is "over there." She always tells me about her new boyfriends and all the fun stuff they are doing. It depresses me but the letters smell like Sammie. She always ends with "I'll never forgive you for not telling me you were leaving, Jackie-pants. Luv ya!!" When I see her later she tells me she was full of shit about the boyfriends, just teasing me the way she always has. "Ah didn't want you to think Ah was pinin' away for you, Jackie-pants," she will drawl, wrinkling her perfect little nose at me.

Mom forwards a sad little letter from Alice. She's missing me in Oklahoma.

Four times during my tour Sergeant Pedersen drives me and a few other officers to Can Tho and I call home at the phones set up at the Post Exchange. The one time I try Sammie's house in San Antonio, I have to leave a message for Belle to pass on to her. I get a letter three weeks later from Sammie, with her dorm room phone number. I call it the next time I'm in Can Tho, but end up having to leave a message there. My Mom always seems to be home when I call. I never tell her I am going to die and not make it home. When I get home I'm glad I kept that to myself; I also never tell anyone I passed up R&R in Australia because I didn't want to die ironically, in a plane crash on vacation.

I am on an advisory team in one of the least secure provinces in the delta. My work in Nam is as an advisor to my counterpart, Major Nguyen, the provincial artillery officer. We never discuss politics, especially the obvious failure of the so-called "Vietnamization" of South Vietnam.

The time we aren't practicing or actually fighting, Major Nguyen and I only see each other about once a week when I join him for dinner at his home. When we go there, I am Jack and he is Vuong. Boiled chicken. Blood oysters. Flash fried baby bird. Sticky rice. The baby birds are small, not really babies, but the bones seem to melt away when you chew. Everything but the beak goes down. When we eat the boiled chicken, it looks as if it's been chopped up with an axe. We throw the bones on the floor with a flourish, following the lead of our host, as if we're all playing in a King Henry VIII movie. I don't remember women and children being there; they may have been scrambling for the bones. I'm thinking his wife may have served the food but I honestly don't remember. We toast each other for hours with warm gin. I throw up in Vuong's shithouse and then return for more toasts.

My own sergeant, a hillbilly from West Virginia named Robert Edward Lee Singleterry, I call Bobby. About six months into these feasts, the Major presents me with a war trophy, a Browning semi-automatic 9mm hand gun, stamped with its origin, *Belgique*. It's a nice, dangerous looking pistol and it fits in my .45 holster, so I wear it the rest of the time I'm in Nam.

My CO Colonel McArdle, his Adjutant, a fellow Captain named Fescola, and I are in a chopper with the pilot and his gunner looking for two 105mm howitzers that have gone missing during a firefight Major Nguyen and his ARVN were involved in yesterday with Charley. The Major and most of his people get out of there alive, but abandon the guns. We're supposed to find them and a Shithook is already on the way to lug them home, anticipating we'll find them. The Adjutant is worthless, but my Sergeant, Bobby, couldn't make the flight for some reason.

We are flying low, looking in some kind of grid search maneuver I don't pretend to understand. Colonel McArdle, who seems to know everything, is a little guy, fearless and all RA, Regular Army, through and through. He's directing the pilot, with a map spread out on his lap. The pilot, the gunner and I are watching for the howitzers - which we should see any second unless the VC have already taken them. Of course, there is also the possibility Charley has left them where they are so they can kill all the stupid Americans who come flying in to rescue them.

I spot the 105's at an angle, because they can't be seen from directly overhead being under a canopy of netting. The pilot makes two scary fly-by's going sideways first with him on bottom, then with me. We don't see anyone so we set down.

As soon as I unhook my seat harness and hop out I hear shots that sound like little pops and see the dirt around me jumping. I dive and land on my elbows with my M16 at port arms. I've only done this a few times so both my elbows are bleeding from landing hard on the rocky terrain. *You are supposed to land on your knees first*, I tell myself too late. I'm struggling to remember where the safety is on my M16 and if I remembered to put a loaded magazine into it before we left. I've also got the 9mm on my hip and I know I have 2 extra clips with me for that, worse comes to worst. I'm also seriously numb. I know the helicopter I was in is still there behind me, because I can see its shadow and the blades are going, but I'm not hearing them. I'm looking at the flat land in front of me and I'm thinking I can see smoke puffs pretty close. I aim at one and fire, and fire again.

I'm trying to sweep my rifle around, guessing at targets when I see those puffs. I glance over to my right and McArdle is down in a good prone position five yards over. I'm thinking he looks good lying there, firing. I think I'm day dreaming, *where did he learn to shoot like that - he's old!* I lazily look back in front of me and there's a guy, I guess a VC, running laterally across the field in front of us. McArdle is shooting and I'm the idiot watching and I try to snap out of it. I sight a yard in front of the VC and fire twice and he drops. Our pilot yells he's called in for support, but when the Colonel and I stop

49

shooting at the same time, we realize no one's shooting at us any more.

I'm too scared to get up, but when the Colonel does I shake my head, hating him for being so gung ho he's going to get me killed. I get up anyway. As we run back to the chopper I see the Shithook coming in low to start hooking up the guns.

Fescola's sitting in the Huey, slumped, looking bored. I take a second look at him and now he looks asleep which I think can't be possible in all this noise. There's blood all over him, chest down. McArdle glances at him. "Oh, shit!" he yells over the engine noise. We clamber on board and I see a hole up high in the Captain's side. We pull him around and there's a gaping exit wound on the other side. *Sweet Jesus*, I'm thinking. *Fescola.*

We leave him in the seat and the Colonel and I scramble to put our harnesses on, each of us to one side of his body. The chopper takes off, straight up, then straight out, parallel to the tree tops. The Captain's eyes aren't quite closed and he is swaying hard with the chopper's turns. McArdle and I each have hold of the shoulder closest to us. The pilot calls MedEvac and sets up to have them meet us back at Vi Thanh. A couple of our noncoms meet us with a stretcher when we land. There's a seldom used supply tent close to one end of camp that is used as a morgue whenever it's needed. That's where they head with Fescola.

When I think back, I don't remember many more names than the ones I've mentioned here. Mike, the Captain who greeted me at the airfield was in the Artillery, but he was already short when I met him. Great moustache he played with all the time, fingering it, chewing on it when it got too long. The best officer there besides McArdle, was an infantry captain who really knew his stuff, was really brave, already had been wounded and was on his second tour, I have no memory of his name.

I remember we watched movies on Saturday nights when we weren't out in the field.

And Vietnamese girls would come to our camp at night, whispering to each other behind hands, giggling. They were the girlfriends of some of the officers. When one of those officers left or died, his girl would continue to visit and become the girlfriend of someone new. Not too many of the officers were single. I was one of the ones who didn't want, didn't have a girl friend over there. It's funny, they were so normal, those women. Just like all the Vietnamese girls, they hid their mouths with a hand when they chewed, wore those long, tight dresses called *ao dai*, smiled all the time.

Sergeant Pedersen drives me back to Can Tho for the last time. He also helps me pack up the ceramic elephants I bought in the Can Tho market to be shipped back to Mom, and fills out the paperwork to have my 9mm carried back with me as a war trophy. Pedersen is in Vietnam for the duration; he's married a Vietnamese woman and has a few kids, even lives in Vi Thanh with her, rather than in our camp. I don't remember his first name. But I do remember telling him I'll write and tell him how things are back in the States. He tells me I won't. He tells me everybody tells him they'll write when he drives them out and no one writes him. He says he doesn't mind, everyone wants to forget this place as fast as they can.

When the airliner takes off from Saigon and lands in Honolulu and then takes off again, I am sure it will crash all along the way. Every air pocket causes my hands to resume their death grip on the armrests. When the noise comes from the wheels locking into place as we descend, I jump and look around wildly till I realize what happened. I only start to relax after the plane lands back at the Seattle/Tacoma Airport. Even that landing bothers me, the wheels bouncing and the shuddering and the noise of the engines reversing to slow us down. For the rest of my life I am pretty sure I'll be uncomfortable on planes. Before I leave Nam, I've already vowed never to ride in a helicopter again. But planes bobbing up and down in air pockets and landing gear clicking into place will bother me more than anything else.

*   *   *   *   *

As soon as I get back I'm given my discharge papers at Ft. Lewis and fly halfway across the country to San Antonio to see Mom and decide what to do next. I change out of my fatigues in the men's room at the airport in Seattle; a lot of people look at you like you are scum, dressed in any kind of military uniform. It is going to take a long while for people to start acting like we were OK to have gone over there and not some kind of villains - it will probably take another war, but it will have to be a *popular* one, for some of the respect the soldiers in the new war are getting to leak over to some respect back to us.

A year later, I'm engaged to Sammie and driving us to a dance at the Country Club. It's hotter than hell in San Antonio, even with the air conditioning. Not as muggy as Nam had been, but hotter. Sammie's hand is in my lap and she's teasing me about how uncomfortable I'm acting because she's got me excited. She's threatening to keep her hand in my pocket the whole time we're at the party. I can finally laugh and remind her we're meeting her sister's new boyfriend tonight.

"Fred," I say I think his name is.

"Fred *Klein*," she responds, wrinkling her nose.

I say it'll be a thrill, him meeting me with a circus tent poking out the front of my pants. We both laugh hard and she finally pulls her hand away. For some reason the sweat really jumps out on my face, I guess from the excitement, but it reminds me of all that sweating I did in Vietnam. I'm back in the jeep on my last drive out to Can Tho with Sergeant Pedersen and we're both sweating hard.

I'd never written him, it dawns on me.

I pull up to the entrance at the Club. Two uniformed kids spring out to open our car doors; they are still wearing those hunter green uniforms. The guy who opens my side is about my age. He's sweating about as much as I was in Nam, but for a different reason.

II - CHOLO

My name is Cholo. OK, that's not my real name, but its what I made the guys call me, all the way back to when I was eight, maybe ten. Cholo.

I like the name. Its Mexican for halfbreed. Mom told me she has about an eighth Indian blood, Choctaw maybe. It was a relief to me cause I thought maybe I was Mexican the way my nose gets wide at the bottom and this broad flat forehead.

I've always been strong. I always worked harder on my muscles than the rest of my friends. I was twelve, thirteen when I started liftin with some other guys. And it was like my body'd been waitin for me to start. Lifted weights more and heavier. Pushed myself more. It made me... wider, you know? Like a tree trunk, Black Leon used to say. I don't remember back to what it was like, bein able to let my arms just hang down straight. I wasn't ever the tallest but always the boss. Not stupid enough to take orders, I guess. I stayed in school, at Alamo Heights, long enough to learn some stuff, but when I had to repeat the eleventh grade I dropped out. My father didn't give a shit and I really couldn't afford clothes like the other kids so I quit. No friends there anyway, I was a hood, collar up, hair greased back on the sides, cigarette behind my ear when I could get away with it. Didn't take shit from nobody.

Got a job at a gas station. The Texaco on the Austin Highway? Between New Braunfels and Montclair?

That was when gas stations were more than filling stations. That was when I had a grease rag stuck in my back overall pocket cause I used it. I checked oil and the water in the radiator, filled the tank. I could replace belts and hoses, do a brake job, check the timing - we were pretty much full service, you know?

It got me plenty of action too, not braggin. Women and some jobs for my little troop. The women were just for me, dont misunderstand. But the jobs were like if I got called to deliver a car after a tune up or to take the tow truck to pick one up that wouldn't start, then I could case a house and see what's what. I mean I wasn't exactly an arch criminal and me and Leon and a couple other guys maybe just hit a few of these places, but we were very very careful, you know? We never did more than one, maybe two jobs a year. No guns, no knives, always an escape route so no one got caught, no one got hurt.

Anyways. Back then, single, workin at the Texaco station, I didn't need much - cheapo apartment, didn't eat a lot, all the ladies drivin around, needin, you know, gas.

So one day I've been at the station a couple years, this old powder blue '67 Deville convertible pulls in. Four young ones givin me the eye while I fill the tank, clean the windshield. Tell the short-haired blond drivin to start the engine so I can check the radiator. One of the chicks in the back says "Yeah Angie, if you can't get the engine started for this guy, maybe I can get mine goin!" and then leers at me. All the girls twitter, and Angie starts the car. I can't think of nothin to say, but I look hard at the backseat girl. She looks older, long brown hair, big dark eyes, nice tits, pretty. When they leave, all four of em are wavin, laughin. Don't remember ever seein any of em before, think maybe they'll start usin the big bright Texaco star now.

Couple days later I am doin an oil change under a car and Beau the owner hollers down into the pit "Hey Cholo, company!" I haven't heard no ding so it is probably a buddy parked and walked up to talk. I tell Beau I am fixin to finish and I climb out of the pit a few minutes later. It is the hot chick from the back seat of that Caddy. She is big too, you couldn't see that from her sittin in the car. When I walk up to her, wipin my hands on my rag, we are practically eyeball to eyeball. I'm not tall, but I'm not short either, maybe five ten, five ten and a half. She is also not skinny, big tits like I already said but also the rest of her fits the tits, you know?

"Hiya," she says, smilin that same smartass smile she had on when she made that crack a couple days before. "I was in the neighborhood."

"Oh yeah?" I grin back. "In the neighborhood? *This* neighborhood?" I'm not much for smartass conversations. I feel stupid tryin to be smart, you know? "Anyways, if you wanna talk or somethin" I look over at the wired-in clock on the wall over the bays and then look back at her. She has a great mouth on her too, I am thinkin. "I can take a break any time you want."

"Yeah, let's go to lunch," she says, and I'm not knowin if she means it or somethin else. I'm hopin she means somethin else. "I'm Peggy," she smiles. She looks me up and down. "Maybe we could clean you up first?"

*   *   *   *   *

We're together for two, two and a half months when Peggy tells me she's knocked up. Doesn't bother me at all telling her it is OK with me. Hell, I asked her if she wanted to get married right away, when she moved in. She said no, she wanted to see how things went with us. That's Peggy, no bullshit.

So a couple months later she's knocked up. After I say I dont mind she asks me will I pay for her to get rid of it if she decides to go that way. I lose it and say "shit, Peggy. Why the fuck would you do that?"

Don't get me wrong. Peggy was my girl from the first time she took me from the gas station that lunch. We went over to my place, showered together, other stuff. I never got back to work till the next morning. I'm uncomfortable talking about this so lets leave it at that. I mean, I may screw around on Peggy a few times, but Peggy is my woman and I have feelins for her I have for no one else.

Anyways, she says "cool down, Cholo. I'm not saying I'm going to get rid of the kid, but I'm considering my options. This isn't something I've ever had happen before." She smiles.

Long pause. "After this, I'm going on the pill. No more rubbers, you hear? We're never careful enough." I take that to mean at least she wouldn't leave cause of the situation we're in. "You get out of here for awhile," she says, pushing me toward the door, "I need to do some thinking." So I'm out the door and she closes it behind me. The plan I come up with is to buy a six-pack of Star at the 7-11 and settle in at the Frontier with a couple burgers. Anyway, the only reason I'm tellin this part of the story is to get to what happens when I get home. That burger and beer doesn't take me long to finish.

I'm a little high but not bad. I knock anyways instead of usin my key, so Peggy'll decide if she wants me to come in yet. She opens the door and we smile at each other.

"You still pregnant?" I ask.

She smiles. "Yeah. Think I want to stay that way, too. But I want you to do a couple of things - make me some promises first."

We're standin pretty close at the door - eyeball to eyeball, really. She's doin this thing where she looks from one

57

of my eyes to the other and then back. Back and forth, you know? Its a real turn on to me, she's concentratin that hard, lettin me know this is important cause she doesn't do it every time we look at each other. So I'm lookin back and forth at her eyes too and I say we should sit down and talk after I piss out some of that beer and she laughs and says OK.

After I get back from the bathroom I join her on the couch.

I say what I'm thinkin. "You wanna get married now, Peggy?"

"Not so fast," she says. "What I want is for you to decide how serious you want this to be." She says "If I don't have the kid, I'm gonna move out. If I keep it you're gonna have to get serious - about me and about... look Cholo, I... I don't think you're really a grease monkey, do you? What I saw that first day, and then when I came over later was some serious stuff in you - I mean sure I saw that face and that big body, and I was right about us having some good things goin together, right? - but I don't think you're gonna be happy doin what you're doin for long either, right? I know you've been happy so far, me and your buddies, you workin and screwin me, us havin plenty of laughs, and you and the guys out doin whatever, but I have your kid and... you don't know shit about me... we don't ask each other *anything*, do we? And all I know is your parents don't give two shits about you and you quit high school."

"Whoa," I say, holding up my hands cause I'm confused. I mean this is like she's pukin all this... stuff... she's been savin up to throw at me. I'm wonderin where in the hell we're goin with this. I'm thinkin maybe I dont *wanna* know where she's goin with it. "Peggy. Whatta you want? Just tell me."

She takes another deep breath. "We have to start telling each other stuff. Talking. And you gotta meet my parents - at least once - and I gotta meet yours." She holds a hand up to stop me cuz my mouth is opening. "Even if it's just once,

58

dammit." She takes a breath, pauses some more like *here comes the big one*.

"What?" I ask.

"You gotta get your GED, that's what," she answers.

I'm just starin at her. I'm not saying *holy shit*, I'm not sayin *fuck you*, I'm not talkin, I'm just thinkin *what in the hell is she talkin about? What does she think I am?*

"Look," she says, "if we have a kid don't you want to live better?" She looks around the apartment and I know what she means but I'm thinking *damn* anyway, and maybe I'm thinkin *oh fuck* too. Then I'm seriously thinkin and I'm not seein whats around me, I'm just thinkin and then I think some more and I end up admitting to myself *I'll probably be tryin to do this, just like she wants me to for Christ's sake.* Then I surprise myself cuz I'm thinkin *maybe a couple years of college, too, after I get my GED.*

I blink and holy shit I'm gettin a stiffy. I'm just sittin here talkin to her, makin this decision and I'm not thinkin about sex, but man am I feelin it down there. This must be how a man feels when he agrees to makin a baby with a woman. You just want to get right down in there deep as you can, and you want to make it special, make it a big one to show the decision is important.

Peggy's lookin at me funny. And her eyes widen. And she grins.

*   *   *   *   *

Crickets when they are all singin together in the heat around this part of the country its almost like hearin the ocean the way the noise will go louder and then softer in a kinda rhythm. Its all part of the heat in Texas. Leon, Charlie, and me are standin on a corner about 2 blocks from the house waitin for it to get dark. They are both still in high school, Alamo Heights, my old school. Leon's a skinny kid I call Black Leon or sometimes Four-Eyes, dependin on my mood. Charlie I call Charlie the Chunk so you know how he's built but he only lasted his freshman year in football cause he hated the work. Me, I also quit football my freshman year cause I smoked too much back then, and cause I didn't like bein bossed around the way that coach did.

Anyways, this guy who owns the house we're gonna visit is outa town I know, cause he tells me so when I'm droppin off a car at his house earlier in the week. "I wanted to make sure the car'd be safe to drive to Florida this weekend - brakes and oil and all" he says. I ask him is he drivin all that way just for a weekend and he says he meant they're drivin this weekend to *get* there, then they're stayin a week at one of them rental suite places, then drivin back the next weekend. I'm thinkin it seems like a lot of drivin if you can afford the plane tickets, but I don't argue with him.

These crickets. I heard there's a way to tell how hot it is by the crickets, but I don't know how. Anyway, I'd guess its still close to 85 and its comin on to midnight I reckon. Hell, I remember one August night it was 91 after midnight.

We're all smokin, lit cigarettes hangin from our mouths, heads back, squintin, and I say "hey Leon, you know about tellin the temperature from crickets?" Leon pushes his glasses up closer to his eyes, thinks a while and says, lookin at a car rollin by, "Don't know, don't really care, Cholo."

We wait a few more minutes and I think I'll give Leon a hard time, I love pushin his buttons. "You reckon you'll care about the crickets if I pound on you for a while, Four-Eyes, you simple shit?"

Leon squints over at me and quick says "Whoa hoss, I

didn know this was a test. What's so fuckin important about crickets - they can't tell *time* unless its knowin the difrence is it light or dark, so how'd they know how *hot* it is?"

Charlie's watchin us both.

I let some time pass. "You bring your watch?" I ask Leon.

"Yeah," he says, and looks at it. "Its about 11:20."

"You sure?" I say right away. "Why don't you double check with those crickets over there" and I point to the house on the corner where we're standin. Leon isn't sure if I'm kiddin or not so he stands there. His cigarette glows at the tip as he takes a drag with the cig still hangin from his mouth. The smoke pours out of his nose and mouth as he lets out his breath. I let myself get angry for a show. I say "Well what are you standin there for," and I take a step, then a second one at him, raisin a fist.

He backs away, hands up and open, scrawny little four-eyed shit. "OK, OK, for Christ's sake, I'm goin."

He's halfway into the yard and he turns to me and asks "now what'm I supposed to do with these fuckin crickets?" Charlie laughs, then stops quick, lookin at me.

I take a last drag and flip the butt at Leon. I can really power a cigerette when I squeeze it between my thumb and second finger, and it hits him in the chest. Sparks explode all over him like New Year fireworks. "God dammit!" he yells, rubbin his shirt real quick to make sure no sparks are stickin. "Brand new god damn shirt, Cholo! You fuckin crazy, man?"

I act disgusted with him. "Ahhh, fuck you, faggot! Anyway, forget askin the crickets what time it is. I think it must be about time to go visit my old friends over on Auburn."

We move out.

Auburn's a nice little street, full of well kept hedges and trees and neat homes, it dead ends in a circle but the houses on one side butt up against the Austin Highway so they may not be the most popular houses in Terrell Hills. The other side of Auburn I guess are nicer houses, there are even some swimming pools on that side. Most houses anywhere on the north side of San Antonio are fenced in the back, but we can jump or climb over most of them. This is a week day so its already pretty quiet except for the car and truck noises comin from the highway. That hum is good for coverin most noises we might make.

So we hop the fences between Auburn and Morningside to this guy's house. I try the back door and its locked of course. Charlie has his hammer stuck down the back of his jeans, its good we all wear em so tight. I can take one good shot at the door knob and that's usually all I need so I take one practice swing like I'm at a carnival, and then I pop it. Twang!! We wait maybe ten minutes and nobody comes by, no sirens, no yellin, so I let us in. We got three rules, no lights, no noise, and a guard. Leon covers the back door. There's stairs up from the back of the kitchen, so we can get out if someone shows up at the front. Its light enough inside we don't need our flashlights.

I go up the front stairs, Charlie goes up the back. I find a jewel case, a jar of change I don't take and a stash in one of the kids rooms. Why they didn't take it to Florida with them I don't know. I hear Charlie usin a toilet in the back to take a leak so I go back downstairs. Leon has a brown bag from under the sink he's loadin up with cleaners.

"You're robbin this place for window cleaner and Brasso, you dumb shit?" I say in a low voice to Leon.

"I'm out a this stuff at home, Cholo. Come on, man."

I just shake my head and look disgusted. I don't really care what Leon does, but I'm lookin for what they have hidden someplace, somethin I'll say *bingo* when I find it. If I have time, I'm goin to go back up to the big bedroom Charlie's already gone through before we leave, but for now, I start searchin the downstairs. "Stay in here, Leon," I say before I leave the kitchen.

I look under every wall hanging and any loose rug I can move the furniture off of. I'm thinkin most people probly take their stuff with them on trips if they can carry it with them. Probly knocking off cars and vans in nice hotel and motel parking lots is where you'd be sayin *bingo* all night. I return to the kitchen. Charlie's back from upstairs with nothin, so I tell him to watch the street out front while I make one last trip upstairs. There's a big painting over the king bed in the master. Nothin behind it, nothin under the carpet. There's a... there's something, I don't know what, right under the bed in the middle, maybe an old sock. Bed's a heavy bastard but I move it. It *is* a dirty sock but its half in and half out of a floorboard sticking up.

"*Cops, Cholo!!!*" comes a loud whisper from Charlie up the stairs.

Holy shit, I'm thinkin, just when I *bingo*. I'm thinkin fast. I stage whisper back. "You guys get out the back NOW. If I make it out I'll see you back at my place. GO!!!"

I peek out the window down onto Auburn. The cop's car isn't in front of the house, its just makin the turn half a block away in the circle at the dead end. But its movin real slow and the cop behind the wheel's workin the spotlight in yards, checkin out trees and bushes, flashin on doors and windows. I guess this is either a normal check up or my guy called in his vacation plans and asked the cops to have his house checked while he's gone. I run back to the loose floorboard and lift it up. There's long white envelopes and large manilla folders folded up. We all wear gloves on these trips, so I'm rippin open the white envelopes. There's cash in every one I check so I'm stuffin em down in my jeans, in the back. The first large folder I look in has paper, official lookin maybe birth certificates or stocks I can't see well enough to be sure but I don't care. I fold that shit back up and dump it into the hole under the floorboard. I'm just gettin too antsy to stay still so I go back to the window. I don't see the cop car on the street, but I'm not stayin anyway. I stick the sock halfway into the hole and put the floorboard back about where it was and slowly push the bed back in place. Even slow, the bed makes a moan sound moving over the hardwood. When I get downstairs those assholes Black Leon and Charlie the Chunk are still there, hidin under the kitchen table.

"What the fuck?" I whisper.

"What? We're gonna leave you with the cops, Cholo?" says Leon, as softly as he can without whispering, "Why the hell else do we go on these missions, man? *This* is the cool part."

"Well, OK." I say, "but we leave and split up and meet back at my place - and you're just out for a stroll and lost track of how long you been walkin. Don't look guilty," and I stare both of them down, in turn. "You first Charlie."

Leon scoops up his brown bags and looks over at me as Charlie walks to the back door. I glance through the kitchen door to the front hall and I see the light of a flashlight bobbing around out at the front door, so I quick grab Charlie before he can make it out the back door, which is half open because the knob's gone now.

I whisper "They're here in front. We're gonna have to run." So we all three take off out the back, but I'm careful to keep the door from bangin. Leon's throwing his brown bag over the fence and we all leap over. The bag makes the noise a couple glass bottles and a Brasso would make landin on a guy's lawn, so while Leon's reachin down to pick the bag up, I fist him on the back of the head and say "leave it" low but with force. He pauses but leaves it and we run for the next fence. No flashlights behind us yet. They'll check the back though, so we continue dashing through the yards. Charlie's the out of shape one, so he's puffin. I'm thinkin *this'll be a story to use on these two assholes for years to come*. I'm really thinkin that, while we're tearin through the yards. Can you imagine? One thing occurs to me then, I'm absolutely sure of. If Peggy ever hears this story it'd better be when she nice and old.

* * * * *

I spend nine months takin night classes at SACC for this GED - math, english, social whatever but I passed all the tests. I know I still can't write worth a damn, can't spell for shit, but now I know I *know* I can't - just used to not care. So now Peggy's tryin to get me into St. Mary's but they're sayin I have to take some starter english stuff and pass it before they'll let me in. Of course to Peggy that just means they're *gonna* let me in. So here I sit, lookin like, feelin like, Frankenfuckinstein with this broad forehead and short hair and blocky jaw. They're probably most of these kids scared shitless of me, so nobody talks to me. Teach calls on me and half the time I have an answer. I'm learnin this stuff, I guess. I'm diagramming sentences for fuck sakes! I have to stop thinkin like this cause it means I'll talk like it. If my neck wasn't wider than my head... some of them probably think I'm a dumb jock. I'm thinkin what the hell... I'm thinking what am I gonna do with it, anyway. Peggy says findin something will be easy after this, but who knows. I'm glad I'm doin it anyway - I'll tell you what, it's worth it with that little baby girl at home, Lucy girl, man she's something, layin there smilin, rolling over now, googlin around. Yeah, she's something special, worth every miserable minute I'm spending, listening to this dick preachin about spelling and conjugations, all this shit... all this stuff, I mean. I never once before remember seeing *forin* was spelled *foreign*. "Apply what you're learning," Peggy keeps saying. How was I supposed to know, she rolls into my station in the backseat of that fancy old ragtop, where I was gonna, where I was going to end up? And her already with a two-year degree and older than me. She also made me quit smokin! Pretty cool, huh? I feel healthier for God's sake!

I'm makin the effort, really. I'm also pulling a few more house jobs with the gang, but bein as careful as I can. No way will I mess with this life I got now with Lucy and Peggy. Black Leon's moved on, but my buddy Charlie the Chunk is still hangin with me since he's out of high school ... best man friend I have now, even with or without the jobs we do. And he's good with Lucy, loves her like us, like an uncle, you know?

*   *   *   *   *

I was never short on brains, I left school because they were goin to leave me back my junior year. I didn't show up enough they said. What I've learned for the GED and this remedial English class hasn't been as tough as I thought. Anyway, I pull into the carport at our apartment and go inside. I'm tired from pulling a double shift at the garage to make up some time I missed studying. Note from Peggy says she and curlylocks are at some park. Next to the note is an open Express News classified section. She has drawn a couple circles in pencil all the way around a big official looking help wanted ad. There's a San Antonio PD badge and they're lookin for recruits. I laugh, put the paper in the trash and get out a beer, turn on the TV. What's she doin at a park at ten at night, anyway? I doze off and I wake up when Peggy straddles me in the chair and starts kissin all over my face. I look around and Lucy's already in her little bed asleep.

"Where ya been," I say, tryin to stop her kissin me with my sleep breath.

She sits back. "You remember Beth, my friend from school, the one with a son about Lucy's age? We were at the

66

park and then went to her apartment till her husband got home. He's a cop and doesn't get home till after midnight."

I say "then I bet he's as tired as I am, but I gotta get up for my shift at the station and I bet he sleeps in when he works late. A cop is your what, best friend's husband?"

"You know you're my *best* friend, Cholo," she says in a teasy voice, dry humping me a little and biting my ear. She knows I hate that and laughs while she does it.

I jerk my head away and say "Seriously, Peggy, I'm tired and I've got bad breath. You want I should brush my teeth?" I know she's just doing a late night tease and she's as tired as I am so I know the way I can get her off me, so I say real soft and low. "I could brush my teeth and then I could help you get sleepy."

She slides off me right away and says "Never you mind, Mr. Hornyman, I'm tired too. We'll talk about Beth's husband tomorrow, don't you worry. I really want you to think about applying for that job."

I'm thinkin about it, but I'm smilin when I fall asleep.

*   *   *   *   *

I put my feet up on the couch and watched a late movie after school tonight. It's called *Streetcar Named Desire* but I didn't see much desire in it, mostly tension between this "brute" named Stanley Kowalski and his wife's sister - though I guess he rapes her at the end, they fade out of that scene without spelling it out. His wife's name is Stella and when I hear her name and watch this Kowalski guy for a while, it suddenly hits me between the eyes.

Once in one of my first college classes, I mention my

wife in answering a question. A guy a couple rows back says "What's her name, Stella?"

Some people laugh quietly and I say "Nah, she's Margaret. I call her Peggy." I twist around in my desk and look at the guy and he stops smilin but I never knew what he meant, what he was *really* saying until I see that movie. Now I'm pissed by the time Kowalski's screamin *Stella!* at the end. I ever again have another class with that little pipsqueek motherfucker, I'll Stanley Kowalski all over his ass.

*   *   *   *   *

To prepare for this interview at the Police Department, Beth's cop husband has told me when I walk into the room I should wait till someone tells me I can sit down, so after the secretary in the waiting room tells me I can go in, I stand in front of these guys, who are all sitting down. The man in the center, who looks older than the rest, tells me to sit down.

"Relax for a minute while we look over this paperwork..." he glances at the papers in front of him, "...Hartmann."

"Yes, sir."

I'm in a small conference room on the second floor of Police Headquarters, sitting on one side of a rectangular table. Around the other side of the table are five men in police uniforms and one in a suit. The older guy, who says he's a Lieutenant, introduces himself and everyone else at the table. There's the Lieutenant, a Sergeant, three patrolmen, and the guy in the suit. He has a weird little goatee and the Lieutenant says he is a psychologist named Bryan something.

First we talk about how hot it is outside and if I played football in high school. I tell them just the one year but I've been lifting weights all my life, and no one looks surprised when I say that. One of the patrolmen asks me what I normally bench, and I say after a warmup set, 140 plus the bar till I max out, three sets.

We talk about the facilities available for cops to use to keep in shape, firing range, all that stuff. I'd guess that goes on for thirty minutes. Mostly the patrolmen talk to me about how important the Academy and the first years after are to a member of the department, and then the Sergeant and Lieutenant talk about the Academy basically being a place to learn the use of common sense and good judgment.

Then the Lieutenant asks me about crimes, like Beth's husband warned me they might. I had answered the same question at least twice on the forms Peggy and I'd filled out when I first applied, *have you ever been convicted, have you ever been tried, have you ever been arrested*, stuff like that.

"Have you ever committed a crime, Hartmann?" asks the Lieutenant. I notice the suit, Bryan, picking up his pen and looking at me expectantly.

Interesting. He's asking me I ever didn't get caught, like I'm gonna confess to something in an interview for a job as a cop. First I'm thinking I better hedge. "Speeding? Rolling through a stop sign? I suppose."

I pause. Here goes. "In my youth I have done some things, committed some indiscretions I may have gotten away with, but things I regret doing, now I look back." As I answer I'm looking around at these guys, trying to concentrate on their eyes the way Peggy's told me to.

One of the patrolmen smiles at what I'm saying, the Lieutenant is looking upset. He kind of glares at me and repeats, "Indiscretions? What was the nature of these... *indiscretions*?"

"Sir, I drove, several times, while under the influence of

alcohol." I make a face like I'm sorry I'm having to relive these moments. I mean, I *am* sorry as I'm saying these things to these policemen, you know? "Also, when younger I took a few items from a drug store and didn't ever pay for them, didn't get caught." I wanted to say my Dad caught me and made me return the items with an apology, but these guys might have interviewed the old man and there's no way he could have told them a lie like that. "Also, I and my friends have been rowdy a time or two on a Saturday night. We may have accidently broken a street lamp or something similar."

The patrolman who smiled before has a coughing fit and pulls out a handkerchief to blow his nose. Bryan the suit is staring at me, fingering his goatee. The Lieutenant shakes his head and asks "how long ago would you guess these 'youthful indiscretions' took place, Hartmann?" A couple of these guys have their arms folded as they watch me. Peggy told me folded arms might mean they weren't liking what I was saying and I should talk to them, mostly.

So I do.

"Well, I dropped out of school at seventeen and have worked at the gas station like I put in the paperwork I filled out - I guess you've talked to my boss there? Anyway, I've gotten married since then and had a kid. I've gone back and gotten my GED and have taken some college classes too. I've been pretty serious since all this has happened and I'd have to say I have tried very hard not to do anything wrong in the meantime." I can feel the sweat has popped out on my forehead while I talk.

The Sergeant, whose nameplate says *Pike*, leans forward. "Does your wife have any idea what it would be like to have a policeman for a husband? To not know every day when you leave the house what kinds of potentially dangerous situations you'll be dealing with? Have you two seriously discussed this aspect of the job?"

Peggy and me also talked about this stuff with Beth and

her husband, can't remember his name as I'm sitting here. "Yes sir, we have and she does understand. Her best friend is married to a policeman and the two of them have also talked about it."

They look at me. I'm expecting them to ask me who the friend is but no one says anything so I say "Beth. Beth Anderson's husband is on the SAPD." Several of the officers leaf through the folders in front of them and pull out a sheet I'm guessing is either Beth or her husband's interview. I spent a Saturday afternoon with him talking about what he had gone through so far, he's only been out of the Academy for a year, plus we went over to their house one time to drink beer and watch TV. He told us about the interviews that would go on, gave me permission to use their names.

I can't remember his first name so far, kind of in a panic, so I'm trying like hell to remember it while these two read the sheets and some others leaf through the folders.

"Would you mind telling me the officer's first name, Mr. Hartmann?" asks Sergeant Pike, looking up from his folder.

"Um. I think his name is Ron. Ronald."

More sweat. I feel like my shirt must be soaked under the sport coat Peggy bought me for this. I pull down on the collar, just above the tie, and jerk it back and forth to try to get more comfortable.

"Yes," the friendly patrolman says, "here it is, Officer Ronald Anderson." He holds up a sheet of paper and looks at the Sergeant.

There's another long pause as the men continue to read or shuffle papers.

Bryan the suit is writing something in his notebook, still playing with his facial hair.

Then the Lieutenant fires off another question: "Why a

cop, Mr. Hartmann?"

I look at him blankly, which is exactly how my brain is reacting to the question.

"I mean," he says, "why are you applying for this job? Why do you want to become a policeman?"

"Oh!" I'm actually surprised at the question, but at least I feel like him rewording it for me like that, at least now I know what he's asking. The first time, I didn't even know what he meant.

"Well Sir... first, the pay's good... better than what I'm makin now anyway, and I feel like I need to be bringing in more with the wife and kid. I mean, I made some promises to her and I've been doin all this schooling to make good on it, you know?" My mind's really clickin now and I go on. "Also, it's the way I am, I think... this is hard to put into words, but look at me.... I've been bustin my... tail... almost all my life to toughen up, to be bigger and stronger and quicker than everyone around me. And to be the boss of them, too. I don't know, I mean I don't think I knew it when I was doin all this, but maybe I've been gettin ready for this job my whole life, sir.... I... I guess that's about it...." I look around the table and they mostly look back for a while.

Finally the Sergeant says "There is a very real possibility, if you become a police officer, you may during your career come face to face with decisions which may involve the use of force. Have you considered that?"

"Yes, sir. Officer Anderson and I talked a lot, and he told me many officers go a full career without ever having to face life or death situations. Still, we all have to understand the possibility will always be there, and that's why we are trained to handle it. I'm sure if I get to go to the Academy I'll be able to absorb everything I need to start handling whatever comes up after I graduate, until I get to the point where I can be on my own."

So for what seems like an hour these guys pepper me with questions, sometimes they give me choices and sometimes they just ask what I'd do in a situation. They also want me to explain why I say what my answer is. As I listen and weigh and answer I begin to see some patterns in their questions and in my answers. I see policemen are never supposed to show any doubt in any situation. Right or wrong, they have to be in what they keep calling "absolute control." It's dawning on me I'm really going to like this being a cop, you know? I mean I've been my own version of the boss, even working for Beau at the station, especially when he's not at the shop but even when he is. Telling people what to do and all.

Oh, I do remember a few of the questions. I'm sure they're tryin to catch me in a lie when Bryan the suit asks me how I would handle stopping a guy for excessive speed, 60 in a 45, and as I'm checking him out on the computer it turns out he's the city attorney. I say I'd still give him the ticket and go on for a while about how important it probably is to treat everyone within the law - you know, I'm spouting off a little, figuring cops have to be that way. So, about - I swear it seems an hour later in the questions - a different guy, one of the patrolmen, asks me what I do if I stop somebody for rolling through a stop sign and when I pull her over it's Peggy - only he just says "your wife." I think a second and flip a coin. I'm thinkin I gave a ticket to the city attorney cause the law's the law, I better give Peggy one, too. So I shake my head cause I'm sorry to say it, but I say I'd give her the ticket cause I gotta be consistent. I see nods all around, so I'm thinkin the coin landed heads up.

The other thing they quiz me on a lot is deciding when it's OK to shoot somebody, when I need to kick some ass, and when I have to soft pedal. Of course, they don't say it at all like that, I'm just translating to what they *meant*. I'm not really sure whether my answers are right, but from their reactions to what I say, common sense answers don't bother them at all. I'm thinking I'll probably be taught the rules at the Academy for when it's OK or not, by rule, but I'm thinking in the middle of some dangerous situation the most important thing is not losing your head and doing what makes sense.

Anyway, after a while of this the Lieutenant looks around the table and asks if anybody has any more questions for me. Everybody shakes their heads *no*.

So then the Lieutenant turns to me and says "Hartmann, if you become an officer in the San Antonio Police Department, your first few years on the force will be the most important, in terms of learning the things you'll need to know, not only in order to survive, but also in order to become an instrument of the law, "to protect and serve," as the saying goes. As such, during this intensive training period, you will be working long hours, probably during off shifts and weekends. You'll miss big holidays. Your family won't see much of you during this time period which could last as long as two or three years, depending on how you do. Do you think you, your wife and your child can handle a long period of time like the one I'm describing?"

"Yes sir, I do. We were told about this by our friends and we talked about it between ourselves, too. We're ready to make it through whatever it takes for me to be a success with this."

He nods and says "OK. Thanks for coming today. Please wait outside the door and someone will come out in a few minutes and discuss the results with you."

I say "Thank you, sir" to him. I stick my hand out and he shakes it as he and the rest of them stand up. All of them except Bryan the suit appear ready to shake with me so I keep shaking hands till I've looked them all in the eye, thanking them.

I'm pretty tired as I stand in the hallway. I start to lean against the wall and think better of it. So I'm standing there close to the wall, but feeling better for *not* leaning, like a weakass. I'm hoping the air conditioning is going to work in Peggy's car. It's only reliable when it's dark out and right now it's mid-afternoon and hot enough the car will be an oven. I'm sorry I didn't drive mine, but we traded cars this morning after deciding my rebuilt '67 Chevy Super Sport 383 with dual Holleys and glasspacks might make the wrong impression....

Finally Bryan the suit comes out with his hand cupping his chin and smiles at me and says I've passed the interview, only the way he says it is "Congratulations Mr. Hartmann, you've passed the oral board" and I guess that means the same thing. He says I'll be getting an official letter in the mail that'll tell me where to report for the Academy and all the other details, you know, when, what to bring, what to wear, all that. We shake hands and he wishes me good luck and I say thank you to him again and I'm walking out of the place feelin pretty damned good.

So I find Peggy's little Pinto in the lot and unlock it. I roll down the windows all around and feel the heat pouring out, so I stand there and wait. I'm thinking about the interview and what I learned. I'm also thinking I got the job - at least the going to the Academy part of the job. I'm kinda shaking my head, you know? Me, a cop? Whoda thought that, man! I take off the coat I'm wearing and put it on the hook above the little window behind the driver's seat. I loosen the tie. Then I think, maybe I'll stop by the gym on the way home, call Peggy from there and tell her. I feel like a workout, work my muscles out through how tired I am. You hurt your muscles when you don't feel like you can even do much lifting, they still come back even stronger than if they were rested - that's my feeling.

Then I'm thinking I'm gonna miss the gang. I think I'm surprised I'm thinkin that. Is being a cop going to replace the feeling you get when you're doing something can completely screw your life if you're caught? I'm guessing yes, but who knows? I can't explain the feeling, can't describe it very well, but it's like feeling cool, feeling adrenaline pump you up, but instead of being nervous and shaking and maybe out of control, you're all cool and your mind and your body are just pumping, pumping away, all under control, all waiting for you to, I don't know, do something. Do something crazy, maybe. Like I jumped off a roof once. I mean it was a one story, but still. I landed practically on all fours but took the shock by landing straight up and kind of absorbing it by coming down quick to that squat. I'd have never thought you could do that without hurting something in your body. Anyway, I landed all down and didn't feel anything hurt so I did the next crazy thing. I realized I was down in a four-point stance so I whispered *hut hut hut* and took off like I was back on the field. Black Leon was watchin from the other side of the fence and loved telling everybody that story, sayin I took the fence like it was a hurdle on a track, but of course that was bull shit, I had to do a side straddle to clear it. Even so, I remember how cool I felt when I did it, ice cold, and like I was watching myself, my muscles working and me not breathing hard, a machine.

"So, Hartmann, how you feelin now?" asks a guy behind me. It's one of the patrolmen from the interview standing there in the lot, still in uniform. It's not the one gave me that encouraging smile, one of the other two. He's a bulky guy, dark with a pear shaped face and a mustache slashed across the middle, built like an ex-linebacker. He's sweating through his shirt, big time.

"I'm OK, I guess," I say, "I'm a little tired from talkin so much, but I'm OK." He reaches out a hand and we shake again.

"Say, you go by George? That's a little formal around here."

"No, most people call me Cholo - it's just a nickname."

"Well, I think you're going to be a pretty good cop, Cholo, so I reckon a nickname might be better to use than George, you know? Congratulations, man." He puts his hand on my shoulder. "My name's Frank, by the way." His name tag says Rodriguez. Frank Rodriguez, huh? I'm gonna remember that name, that face.

I'm not sure what to say, but I'm guessing he's been

around long enough to be able to say something like he did and be comfortable saying it. I can't help grinning and thanking him. "Man, it's a relief to know I made it, that interview was tough."

He nods and says "It was a little touch and go for a second there, after you were excused. The Lieutenant thought maybe you weren't respectful enough. He called it 'flippant' but several of us said maybe you were a little raw but we thought we could see a lot of good potential. He always asks us at the end of the review if we'd serve with the candidate, and we all said 'yes' about you, including Sergeant D'Angelo."

I tell him how much I appreciate everything he's told me. He looks at his watch and says he has to go. We say *goodbye* and *see ya*. I call him Officer Rodriguez and he smiles and waves and walks off, back toward the building.

I get in the car and still have to be careful touching the steering wheel and gearshift not to burn my hands. I leave the A/C off and sweat it out all the way up Broadway to Alamo Heights and the gym.

While I'm driving I'm also thinking about the lies I told to get the job. *Lies of omission* is what they are called. I'm not worryin about lying, but Charlie the Chunk has said he maybe will apply too, and I need to tell him how careful he needs to be. I'm thinking also maybe he should apply to the Alamo Heights PD so we don't need to worry about stories, cause I'm not sure I can trust him like I could myself.

Anyway, I walk into the gym and head straight for the pay phone and call Peg. She's on phones at the office she's working at, and answers first ring. We're pretty happy on the phone. I'm telling her about the interview and all the stuff she guessed right about, and then what the guy said after, in the parking lot. She says she'll call Beth and thank her and I say yeah, maybe you should. She says she'll also tell Beth what the patrolman, Frank Rodriguez, told me after.

I tell her I'm gonna work out to celebrate, she says she can come home early today, maybe help me get cleaned up when we see each other, and celebrate some more.

I'm in for that, I say.

* * * * *

So Jerry and I are sitting in our unit, getting calls to be on the lookout. We're idling, parked on Houston Street in what we call the Jungle, east of downtown. Sometimes Jerry likes to park here, just to be a deterrent for the folks driving on Houston. You see an empty DPS unit parked up on a berm on a highway? Same thing.

Black woman left the scene of an accident, a 10-57, near where Eastwood's was out on St. Hedwig. She's in a '72 black Plymouth Fury says the dispatcher. Plates are unknown. Then another call. Rapist thought to be in the area, but although the rape was reported at the Nix five minutes ago it took place about an hour ago. Full description pending, but the guy's black. Jerry looks over and we shrug at each other - like the guy was gonna be Asian, this part of town.

About five minutes later a black Fury comes by. It's a '70, '71. It's maybe an old police unit re-sold and painted over all black. The big police spotlights are still hangin out on both sides. There's two women in the front seat, a guy in the back. They're makin time, but maybe less than ten miles an hour over the speed limit on East Houston. I see no body damage on the car and normally that kind of speed wouldn't put us in pursuit, but Jerry says something like "let's check 'em out, Cholo," and I don't answer because he's not expecting me to. We light 'em up and they pull over a block, block and a half later in front of a five and dime. I call in the plates while he gets out of our unit, people are already starting to assemble on the sidewalk next to us. By the time I get out and stand between our car and the Fury, Jerry's walked up to the driver and asked for ID and proof of insurance. I notice he unhooks the strap over his .38 but I figure it's SOP for this neighborhood, with that crowd building on the sidewalk.

"Whatcha bothering these ladies about... Officer?" This from a bigass buck in overalls with no shirt and a comic afro I'm not laughin at. He's got a nasty tone in his voice and that long pause before he says *Officer*. I know from my training I can't let things get out of hand, so I say "None of your business," loudly to the whole crowd, "Checking a license and insurance here, doesn't concern you people."

They are talking louder from what I've said, muttering is what I'd call it really, and I'm starting to tense up. I'd like to tell Jerry the car already checked out with the DMV, but I walk back to the patrol car, driver's side, and reach in for the unit radio to call for backup. I say 10-78 twice after I identify the unit and then I see Jerry jumping a couple feet back from where he was talkin with the ladies and the guy in the car. It's not the occupants have him twisting around. He's turning and bending at the knees and pulling his weapon and I see four or five punks in the crowd already have guns in their hands pointing them at both of us.

As I start toward them all, things start moving slow. I remember a time made a big impression on me back when I was maybe five or six, in the car with my folks. The car wouldn't start and my old man put the car in neutral and had the old lady slide over behind the wheel. He told me to get out and we both went to the back of the car. He said "push" and we both leaned into the car. It was a big old heap of a car. I was useless as tits on a boar hog pushing, but my dad grunts once and then things slowed down. Like I'm watching a football replay. He's down low and this car is unmoveable and he grunts and his arms grow. I see veins standing out on his temple, but his arms seem to enlarge as I watch, from hand to bicep. His feet gain traction like a bull moving to charge and slowly, slowly as the tires roll they make a distinctive popping noise against the road's surface, slow motion

Shots are fired and there's smoke and I'm not doing a very good job of drawing my own revolver, fumbling at it and trying to keep an eye on this street scene in front of me instead of lookin down at the strap over my piece I'm fumble-fucking with. Jerry starts firing as some of the men on the sidewalk break ranks and shoot and dive and run. The rest of the crowd is screaming and running, some down the sidewalk and some into the street between the guns. Smells like the firing range only it's smokier. My gun is out and I point it at a guy standing so close I could as easily try slapping my bare hand at the piece he's pointing right at me. I fire and see the revolver tip up and fire shoot out but I'm hearing nothing or maybe it's like the noise a breeze through a tree makes the leaves rustling hard I feel like I get punched in the chest and then slapped across the face. I've slowly dropped to my knees like the thirty pounds around my waist is weighing me down. I look down and there's a big red splotch on my shirt. There's a hole, too. I'm thinkin *that wasn't there. Did one of those motherfuckers*

I see Jerry's walkin funny as he limps past me to our unit. I think I see blood on both legs of his uniform pants. I can't turn but a few seconds later he's limpin back around me with the twelve gauge. He fires twice and my ears absorb the concussion of the blasts made by the shotgun, and through that I'm hearin sirens and three of the civilians are down, one is next to me face down, one is on the sidewalk on his back and the other's on his stomach and his head is down in the gutter and he's the one with all the hair. Otherwise the sidewalk's empty except for a couple handguns now.

I'm pretty tired. The Fury has squealed out, tires shrieking, smoking, the whole car fishtailing before it turns right at the next corner. *Rambling Drive,* I'm thinking. I'm startin to fade in and out. I must have missed Jerry falling because next thing I'm seeing him pulling himself toward me using his arms, elbows. I'm not on my knees any more; I'm on my stomach straining my head up to be able to see him crawlin toward me. I'm still hearin sirens, but I can no longer tell if they're getting louder or not. Jerry rolls me over. He wipes the water out of my eyes and holds his hand out and we're both lookin at the red on it. Must not be water. Like my shirt.

You ever faint? The noise starts in your ears till it takes over everything? It's like ocean without waves - like a big shell up to your ear. You start by hearing it, and end up getting confused about what's real, the noise or the asphalt of the road you're lying on. Then you're not feeling the road, you're floatin in the noise. You're up and you're down. Siren seems to be everywhere, pain floats in and out, it's silent, then it's not, the noise filling your ears, screams in the air but they're not screams *sirens* really something else and then it's all sirens and buzz buzz in your head, your ears. Your head feels like it might bust open but that wouldn't stop it from bein so suddenly quiet again.

Someone's ripping at my shirt and putting something heavy on my face. I feel hands trying to rip the skin off my chest. I swear to God. The thing on my face is so heavy. Who's screaming? The siren.

I'm being rocked side to side it's making me hurt I'm strapped in and there's an engine roaring around me with the double scream of a siren warbling traffic out of my way now I can hear the monitors beeping in time to my heart beat and there's a guy with a stethoscope hanging from his neck leanin over me maybe I'm in an ambulance he's got brown eyes and sweat on his forehead and one of those white strappy masks over his nose and his mouth - I'm suddenly not foggy for a second. I say "Peggy" but my mouth ain't workin. Then I try "Lucy." Same thing. My face is half covered with somethin but the pain's in my chest. My whole chest hurts deep but low like a gigantic dull cramp. You ever cramp a thigh workin out? I try to stretch to stop the cramping and that makes the pain turn into somethin I can't really describe and I fog back up and the noise in my ears is back, louder and louder, taking over again

*   *   *   *   *

The pain of physical therapy heightens the soreness in my chest. Not sleeping except in fits while slumped in front of the TV. I'm finally doing the PT three times a week, but Peggy or cops have to drive me there, as well as to the office where they let me sit at a desk in the detective branch answering phones. I'm told when the soreness goes away is when I'm well enough to be able to leave the desk bullshit; I'll go back on duty but I'll be driving my own new unit, I'll be on my own and a "made" cop, so to speak. Peggy's driving me to school full time during the therapy and I'll have credit for two full years I hope, by the time I'm back at work full time. I'm majoring in business, pre-law, but there's no way I'm really thinking about following through on the lawyer bit - I'm just enjoying the mix of statistics and business writing and civics and U.S. law, you know?

Besides, things are really going well for me, I've survived two operations repairing stuff in my chest; didn't lose any significant parts inside except some muscle and a chunk out of one rib. Lucy's heading for three, Peggy's keeping herself nice and they dropped my probation as soon as I got out of the hospital; plus I have the battle stripe, the scar I got on my face on East Houston Street. It causes me to squint that eye, my left eye, cause I lost enough skin close to my eye they had to pull the good skin together - at least that's what they told me after I woke up and was thinking enough to actually hear what they were saying. It's a stripe starts an inch from the eye, above my cheek bone, and ends right where the eye starts. The bullet went in my chest is, of course what's causing me to take so long to get back on the streets, but that's OK. Thank God they are giving me a choice of assignment after this.

The Sergeant from my initial interview, Pike, who has become what they call my rabbi on the force, helped me with that. The street commander was clear I could stay at a desk and retire in 20 years, if that's what I want. I even discussed it with

Peggy and she agreed I'd have a chance of making more of a career if I went back to the field for awhile. There'd be plenty of chances to get back into a staff position after I spend more time getting experience on the line, so to speak.

Frank Rodriguez from my interview came to see me in the hospital a couple times. Let me know Jerry and I are famous now, from the shootout. Guys shake their heads about the rookie with the eye and the bullet in his chest.

My old partner Jerry picked the other route. He was shot in both legs below the knees and one bullet broke the tibia in his left leg. He was hobbled for awhile and the bone had shattered so he was still getting around with a cane. He and I skated through the internal investigation and though there was some initial noise from the NAACP and ACLU, the papers were full of accounts made us sound like public heroes. Maybe in Houston or L.A. Jerry'd have faced more scrutiny for firing the shotgun the second time, maybe not. He told me he'd have kept firing if there'd been any more of them still on the sidewalk standing up, but the two he shot were the only two there, and he said they were both still pointing their guns and shooting at both of us, they were just bad shots in the heat of battle, I guess. I don't remember aiming when I pulled my trigger; we're taught to go slow, to line up the sights first, to squeeze not jerk - you're better off not firing the first shot if you're good at being careful because they'll miss and you won't. Of course fast and careful beats slow and careful, and trained is better than untrained, either way. Anyway, Jerry decided to stick with a desk, he said he figured he'd never have his legs working a hundred percent again, and he admitted he wasn't really sure he wanted to shoot it out with a mob again - I guess once in a lifetime was enough for him. Me, I plan on doing better next time I'm in that situation. I walk with a cane I don't need but the PT lady says it is useful to remind me to walk careful. That is bullshit. I walk as hard as I can. I walk to *make* it hurt, to get my body to work through the pain. You don't move your arm around after a tetanus shot, it hurts longer, you know?

*　　*　　*　　*　　*

I'm in south San Antonio now, dealing with punks and gangs and unpaved streets. It's funny, you're standing in the dust with a chicken pecking in the grass growing in the gutter, a kid sucking his thumb at you from behind a sagging wire fence. He's wearing a dirty shirt and nothing else in what could just as easily be Nuevo Laredo, but you look up above the little shack houses on this street and see the Hemisfair Tower looming north a few miles away, downtown, shimmering in the heat. I remember driving through this neighborhood with Black Leon, seems like just a few years ago, looking for trouble. I still am of course, only now I'm looking to stop it; back then I was looking to join in.

Everything looks cooked, wavy like in a desert, unnaturally white like a bad photograph. You know your retinas are getting too much light even when you squint, and you'll have to close them for a minute when you go inside someplace.

I get a call, domestic disturbance. Usually that means a woman has called after she gets beaten up by the man of the house; she'll call once he leaves or once she manages to lock herself in a room where she can get to a phone. Once one even coldcocked the guy with a bat when he turned his back, and trussed him up like a chicken while she waited for us to show up. If she didn't have two black eyes we wouldn't of known who was beating up who. I 17 back I'm meeting the complainant as I pull up to a small house on Sadie. I walk up the path and hold open the screen door, knock and identify myself.

I don't hear anything unusual inside or outside. There are tall live oaks all around the place, shading it. Through the weight of the heat I'm hearing the monotonous noise made by the crickets, rising and falling. I think back to me and Black Leon discussing crickets and temperature one night long ago. Then I think that also means probably no screaming has been going on or there'd be less chirping. It's really damn hot here, even in the shade - humidity bad, too. Probably less shade would make it drier heat. I see the mostly white smoke stacks of the Alamo Iron Works off in the distance while I'm waiting for an answer. I knock harder, identify myself again, and I unhook the flap covering my new pistol. We've been promised new holsters won't be covered at all and I'll be happy when we get them in. I'm thinking which way should I go around the house to see if I can see inside.

The door whips open and there's a gangbanger standing there pointing a revolver at me. I can see the tips of the bullets in the cylinders of the fucking thing, pointing at me like they're waiting their turns. I've been back on patrol maybe four goddam months and this guy's motioning me into the house with his gun as he backs in. He's shaved bald, has a little Mexican moustache, bare-footed, wearing a wife-beater so I can see both arms are tattoo friendly all the way up and over his shoulders and there's tattoos on every knuckle. He's shorter than me but in good shape.

I don't move. I know I'm probably dead anyway, if he's a good shot or a lucky one, but if I go in there or, worse, hand him my gun, it's just making it too easy for him. I'm feeling pretty cool, partly because of the Houston Street shootout, partly because you train for this shit to happen and we're like airplane pilots: we're supposed to be ready for the bad stuff. I'm saying to myself *here goes*.

I bend at the knees thinking I'll try springing to my left out of the doorway. As I push off, the little shit fires. He's still in the process of backing up and the screen is closing on him and I don't even hear the bullet zinging by, I'm so close to him. The noise of the explosion out of his gun is pretty loud but my springing to the side maybe saves me and I'm pulling my gun out as I land on the porch. Thank God my chest feels ok. He's shooting into the wall between us and the bullets are coming through, but high. I'm thinking this lousy house must have no fucking insulation, what did they make it from, plywood? He runs out of bullets after he pumps seven or eight shots over my head. I hear him running away deeper into the house and I'm up, running in after him.

This is what we call a shotgun house, standing at the front door you can fire a shotgun straight through to the back door. I grab the radio from my belt and start calling in man with a gun and shots fired and 10-13.

After I hustle through the front of the house, I'm faced with a narrow opening into a hallway where the bedrooms and bathrooms are going to be. He's back there maybe reloading; the back door is closed and I haven't heard any slamming doors. It's quiet but my ears are a little stopped up. I've got my pistol up in front of my face, both hands on it to keep it steady but I'm not sticking it way out like I was at a firing range, I don't want him jumping out from someplace to knock it out of my hands.

Which is what he does. As I slide myself down the hall he comes out of nowhere swinging his arms and hits my wrists and the gun goes flying. His hands are heavy with the knife he's holding when he hits me, and I see it's a big motherfucker knife. We push into the wall and both my hands are on his wrist trying to hold the knife against the wall so he can't use it. He starts punching me in the side with his free hand and he curses me "*Fucking puto cop.*"

I free up a hand and reach back for the knife I keep in the scabbard under my belt in the back. He keeps hitting me with his left fist while he's trying to free his right so he can use the knife. The fist is hitting me mostly in the arm so I'm OK so far and when I free my knife I stomp one of his bare feet just as I swing my knife around and stab him as fast and hard as I can in the rib cage. I mean James Jones was right in *From Here to Eternity*, when he says knife fights don't last long; if they do you're watching a movie. The kid screams and frees his knife hand as he starts to drop. I have to kneel to follow him down and he takes one chopping swing with his knife and hits me in the face. I'm thinking it's just the butt of the knife and his fist, which hurts plenty anyway, but I'm still grinding my knife into him.

He lets go his knife and it clatters around on the floor next to him. I realize I've got blood on my face and I'm blinking it out of my left eye. I rub at the spot where he hit me. No wonder I'm having trouble seeing out of that eye. I can feel I'm sliced through the eyebrow! I can't believe it! He's cut me just above the same eye that's already fucked up from being shot! I curse and roll him over hard and cuff him. I'm hearing sirens approach. I've got his knife and I pull out a twenty from my wallet to measure the blade. Fucker's longer than 6 inches!

I'm gonna write him up for that, too. He's screamin where he lays, so I think he'll live.

*   *   *   *   *

Couple months later, I'm home early, got to take the rest of the day off after the Captain tells me the news, so I'm home playing with curlylocks. I went by the pre-K and picked her up early, called Peggy and told her to come straight home after work but I wouldn't tell her why. I'm just so fuckin full of myself right now I could put my fist through a wall - but in a good way, you know?

Lucy and I are sitting on the floor facing each other. She's looking at the jacks with a strain on her face. There's no way she's gonna do fours and she knows it, but she's seein *how* she can do it. I mean she's done about a perfect throw because there's two obvious groups of four and the other two are off by themselves. She's got her mother's hair and big brown eyes, but right now her face is working, narrowed down to the floor, the jacks.

"Take your time, Petunia, do you see how you can get the job done?" I mean, her little hands, you know? She does have quickness in them for her age, but not quite the size, I don't think, at five. But she does look up at me and smiles with a nod. Then she points right at each of the groupings I saw, too. Damn she's good, gonna be great.

She's taken right to gymnastics, loves the trampoline and flips, all that stuff, can almost do a walking handstand, for shit's sake - you know, the Chunk taught her a lot of that stuff, I'm glad he's straightened himself out and is on the AHPD. He's gotten back in shape now and he and curlylocks are tight. *Both athletes*, he says, *me and Lucy*. I hope he marries that broad he's going with, that Elizabeth, he should settle down by now.

Anyway, Lucy's hand is down by the first set of four, rubber ball nestled between the bases of her middle fingers like I've shown her. She takes her two soft practice lifts and then flips the ball up. She scoops at the jacks and they are all in her hand in plenty of time to catch the ball after it bounces. She uses her thumb to center the ball on her hand and quickly starts her practice lifts again. She flips up the ball and goes for the second set of four. My God! She's got em and her little hand is under the ball before it lands a second time! I keep quiet, but my mouth is open ready to shout if she can... oh, shit. A couple jacks come out when she tries pulling the ball to the middle of her hand and my reaction is to pick them up and return them to her hand so she can try the last two jacks, but when I try to give them to her, she'll have none of it, dropping all the jacks and the ball between us calmly. She has always refused to cheat, dammit. She has Peggy's ability to handle setbacks, dust herself off like the song says. She definitely doesn't have my temperament. Thank God she *looks* like Peggy, too. Anyway, I get up and scoop her up in my arms - I'm excited she did so well.

As I throw her up, I scream "Close, curlylocks, you

were as close to fours as you are to the sky!" and I throw her up again. She's shouting too, laughing and screaming *Daddeeeee* and maybe a little burp of excitement thrown in.

"What in the world...?" Peggy's coming into the apartment, big handbag over her shoulder, an excited smile on her face. "What are you doing to this little girl, Daddy, you're going to give her the hiccoughs, poor thing. Come here honey. Come here to Mommy, my little Lucy Goosy," so she has her and is kissing all over her face while the little girl giggles and hugs her and lifts her head so Mommy can get down there under her chin and blow air bubbles into her neck.

Peggy's in a dark suit, stockings and heels; what I think of as her work clothes. She's got her hair up, pulled tight to keep it out of the way. I can smell the great perfume she uses, probably just put on before coming inside. She had made that a habit, primping when she first pulls up to the house. While they nuzzle each other and Lucy is giggling, I'm looking Peggy over, her great body. I guess she's a little plumped up since I've known her, but not to put me off at all.

I walk up to them and embrace them both, lifting them off the ground, but *my* air bubbles are for Mommy's neck and she does her own giggling and asks me what's going on, what's the occasion has me taking off from my shift practically middle of the day.

"Donnelly called me into his office today to tell me I passed the test first try. They want me to head up a task force eastside to organize a civilian support group, with my new stripes on. I'm a Sergeant."

She looks up at me and so does Lucy, but Lucy's first finger is in her mouth and she's still flushed from excitement and breathin hard and wondering why it's suddenly so quiet in here.

"Oh Cholo," Peggy says and her eyes fill with tears, "I'm too too proud of you! Damn, I just don't know what else to say, honey. I'm so happy for you I could just bust." By this time Lucy is squirming to get out of our arms. She's locked up in our hugging and is suddenly determined to get some stretching room away from the hugs, so we both lower the arms we are cradling her with and she wriggles down. She looks up at me and says "Make me some poppy corn, Daddy?" and I say "When Uncle Charlie gets here honey," and she grins and dashes for her room.

Peggy and I face each other. Peggy's blotted the tears with a handkerchief she got from God knows where and I pull her to me. I'm doing the eye to eye to eye thing with her face, making sure she sees how important I also think this is for us. "I made reservations at *Naples* on the way home and called Charlie to babysit."

"*Naples*, Cholo?" she looks at me with a grin, "You know the way to my heart is through Ralph's shrimp *congelia*, you sneak!" She's laughing and she snuggles in closer. "Kiss me for a while before Charlie gets here, would you mind?"

*   *   *   *   *

The eastside townhall meeting is going full blast when I'm introduced and stand up to speak. I'm dressed in what I like to think of as my police civvies, a blue muscle shirt I bought with a small SAPD Peggy sewed where the penguin or polo player would normally be, and brown corduroys. Chief Torres has welcomed everyone, and Mrs. Eunice Washington has thanked them for coming and asked for their willingness to listen to "these fine policemen who have come to speak to us today" - has asked it in fact, on behalf of her late husband the Right Reverand Thomas Ezekial Washington late of the First East Baptist Church of San Antonio - and she has offered these words in the form of a welcoming prayer, so everyone says "Amen" and she nods in my direction and says simply, "And now a few words from Sergeant Hartmann." I get up to speak. I'm not very nervous, but I'd have to say I'm anxious, you know? I have a script I've been rehearsing for days, but I don't know if this mostly black group of people who feel they've been mistreated by the police all their lives, how they'll react to a "new" group of policemen telling them things are going to be different now - especially when the one speaking looks like Frankenstein's monster.

Anyway, I've been introduced by Chief Torres as a guy who has been through the wars in San Antonio, which I have, and as a guy who understands the problems of the east side, which I just kind of do, not having lived through anything in this part of town, but as someone who's definitely *seen* a lot of it. So there's a little bit of applause when I first stand there. I wait, first I watch Mrs. Washington get settled back in her chair, we nod and smile at each other, and then I face the crowd. I pause; mostly I'm getting used to being up here in front of them all, and am also letting the crowd take a good look at me. Peggy says I look like I'm "of the people," which I'm sure she's right about, with this mug. I've just got the one tattoo, mostly not noticeable if you're not looking for it, but I've got the Indian forehead, the scars and the squinty eye, and the muscles could put me on either side of the law.

So I start my speech. I know the words we wrote by heart and I am saying them, but saying them in a way that sounds more natural than the way they were written. I welcome everybody again. I tell them I know why they're here, and I tell them why I was selected to try to make this relationship between them and us work. I say I've been a "have not" and whether I lived in these neighborhoods or the ones up north, I still know what their lives have been like. Being available to them is real, I say. All the guys working for me and me are available to them twenty-four hours a day, every day of the year. We will make sure the kinds of things that have been allowed in the past will never happen again. Then I go through six cases we've decided are the ones everyone knows about; I say these are the ones have been the six nails driven into the east side's hate coffin in terms of the animosity and distrust in them toward the police. By the time I finish detailing the sixth incident, we're *all* upset with how *we've* been mistreated - if you get my drift. Then I tell them that's the past, and I tell them what's the future. I tell them I'm *of* the police, but not from the *six nails police*. I like that as I say it, it isn't anything I've said in any of my rehearsals, but it just seems to flow out of me when I say it - and everybody listening in this crowd has been nodding at my words before, is agreeing out loud now, like we're having a revival meeting. I saw *Elmer Gantry*, so I know kind of instinctively it would be good if this turns into one of those crowd-moving scenes. I say louder the time of the *6-Nail Police* is over! And someone shouts *Yes!* I'm even louder when I say to them my team is going to stand up *for* them not *at* them, and many of them stand and shout *Please!* I beg them to give us a chance and trust us - I invoke the names of the six men and women, name them slowly one at a time, and say they were questionably jailed or beaten or shot, and praise each one as a hero who caused my team to come here and work for justice *in their name*, and I'm hearing *Hallelujahs!*

I have no idea what I'm talking about, really, or if I can back up what I'm saying, or... if the Chief's going to fire me as soon as we get in the van to head back downtown. I glance over at him. He's a Latino, third generation in the U.S. and maybe the second non-anglo Police Chief San Antonio has ever had. When I turn, he's looking at me hard, but when our eyes lock, he makes an almost imperceptible nod at me. He mouths *finish* at me. So I look back at the crowd and pause a long time. The shouting out slowly winds down in the crowd. I end the meeting by thanking the people, the Chief, my men. I tell them we'll be advertising the phone numbers to call, starting tomorrow morning. I thank them for their kind attention. I bow slightly and go sit down.

The applause isn't bad, I'm thinking. A lot of nodding heads and smiles, too. I also notice quite a few white heads in the crowd, especially toward the back. I'm guessing some retail owners who have a stake in this too, have been listening.

92

Maybe they are saying *Praise the Lord!* too, but only inside and also thinking *only if this works.*

The meeting is over and a lot of hand shaking is going on. I'm being introduced to a lot of people and I'm not going to remember any of their names, but I'm thinking sometime in the future I'm going to hear a lot of people remind me I met them at this meeting - maybe even more people than could fit in this hall. One guy makes me tell the stories about my two scars, but I downplay that stuff as much as I can. That's the past, I remind him and everyone else who's gathered around. Finally Chief Torres works his way through the crowd to me and tells everyone I need to get downtown with him. We start toward the door and everyone makes a path.

Just outside, a group of white guys are gathered in the parking lot. I recognize most of them from the audience. One of them, a little guy with a big nose and dark wavy hair, steps forward from the group and asks Torres if he can talk to me for a minute, to introduce himself. The Chief says sure and says it like he knows the guy. He introduces me to him. "Cholo," he says, surprising me by using my nickname, "meet Fred Klein, head of the San Antonio Chamber of Commerce."

"Well," says Fred, kind of looking down like he might be blushing, which he isn't, "I'm not sure what the Chief means by 'head' - I certainly don't run the organization, Sergeant; but I do have a few fingers in a few pies, haw haw. Tasty pies, some of them, if you get my meaning."

Already I'm not sure I'm going to like this guy, not really seeing in the first place what the Chamber of Commerce's interest could be in this little eastside police watch group, and in the second, frankly, what this little shit's got to do with anything except he's wearing some very, very expensive looking duds, Italian loafers, a cream colored suit is maybe an Armani, one of those five thousand dollar watches he can swim in but probably never gets wet, dressed like that on the eastside, in the Jungle, if you can imagine. So I'm already put off by this guy and then he says "Nice speech, Sergeant... you mind if I call you Cholo?"

"I guess not... Fred." I figure he wants me on a first name basis, but I don't work for him so he'd better let me call him by his first, too, or it won't work out for me. He looks at me like he's not thrilled, but I can see him working it out and I think he finally comes to understand what I'm saying and says, "OK, Cholo. Anyway, I liked the way you handled things in there... *we* liked it," he changes the subject of his sentence to include the men hanging around him, with a little wave at all of them, "and just wanted to let you know you've got our support, however you can use it."

There's no way I can use the help of the Chamber of Commerce to limit the repercussions or liabilities involved in police brutality in the Jungle in San Antonio, but I guess politically we need all the support we can get, so I thank Fred very much for his kind words and support, etc., etc., and the Chief and I are walking away, toward the van we came in.

"Perhaps we can have a lunch some time, Cholo?" comes Fred's voice from behind us.

"Perhaps," I say, looking back with a wave. *I'll have my people call your people*, I'm thinking to myself.

But what I'm already back to worrying over is how I'm going to convince a police force the necessary show of force we are used to using on breakers of the law, that we are *trained* to use to keep these people in line, is something we need to keep more in check, within ourselves. Most of these law men know, either through class or on the job, that a kick to the ribs after the cuffs go on is at worst a tension release, and at best a useful reminder of their future to the person we've just chased down, or exchanged gunfire with, or pulled off the man they've just been beating. It may be, I'm thinking, a few examples may have to be made of some of the cops, in order to cause a hesitation that leads to a *safe* threat, rather than an unjustified beating. I don't want to stop the things we do in the heat of battle, those instant decisions can't be questioned, but I've seen too many cops, hell, I've *been* the cop who kicks a guy in the chest after he's tried to kill me. I kill him with the knife while we're fighting is saving myself and part of a good arrest, I kick his nose up into his brain after I've cuffed him and I'm a murderer, you know?

III - FRED

My first Rolls was a used one a customer signed over to me in payment for a big shipment of PC's. I mean, he was buying a new car anyway. What I got was white, spotless, another great deal I just wandered into. I'm telling you, there is nothing in the world including sex that matches the feeling of pulling into the San Antonio Country Club circle drive for a dinner and dance in that Rolls, flipping the keys to a boy dressed in his dark green uniform and heading into the building with Paige on my arm. I suppose if it was Samantha that would be better, but... haw haw haw.

I digress. My father died when I was nine and he had already gotten me interested in cars. Interested, hell. I was fascinated. I collected models of racers and expensive sedans and convertibles until I was old enough to drive them instead of just owning them in Matchboxes My Mom was worthless in most ways but I talked her out of a chunk of what she'd saved from Dad's insurance to buy my first Corvette. I raced that baby weekends while I worked my way through a little college in Houston. At the same time I'd gotten interested in PC's when I was looking around to make myself some money. I decided to move to San Antonio about the time the Corvette crashed and I broke three ribs and my desire to race (but not my desire to own nice cars). San Antonio was perfect - growing but about as naive a big town as you'd ever need to meet to be able to perfect your "business" skills. I was born, was gifted, with the Jewish equivalent of blarney - I think my grandmother would have said something that sounded like *plyoot* - and this town must be the easiest place this side of the Atlantic Ocean to get yourself raised up to the top. You know anything more exciting than money, power, bullshitting your neighbors, the city, the state and national government into unloading their pockets into yours? Well I do. It's getting them to let you get away with stuff normal people can't get away with. Tax relief and fraud, zoning restriction relief, parking ticket's getting torn up, I could go on and on. It's getting into the German Club when you had a grandmother who spoke Yiddish, for God's sake.

I have to admit, there isn't anything I've ever done didn't have dollar signs for me at the end of the plan. I've done some really good things, too. Some really giving things, about as altruistic as you can imagine, but believe me nothing I didn't get big things out of in the end. I'm rich. I live in a mansion. I'm an Oh-Niner elite. San Antonio politicians ask my opinion before they ask the Council's. I'm the second Jew asked to join the Club - and not because my wife's people were already in and old family, either. Of course, that didn't hurt, but I wanted in on my own and wouldn't go there with Paige after the first time we went in since we got married till they asked me to join separate from the Barnes's. My understanding was that aside from the token they already had, and any loose Jews who were members by marrying into the right family, was about all the kikes they were interested in having in there except for those coming in as guests to peddle diamonds or decorate for a wedding. Of course, that was long ago and it's different now. Now there are rich Jews and even Orientals and Blacks in the Club. So that makes it not so important any more. Maybe that's why I keep buying nicer and more expensive cars in which to drive there. Hmmmm. Never thought of that before.

I'm as Jewish, of course, as most Reform Jews are - which ain't much. It is really a burden in this town being a Jew, even as relaxed as things have gotten, at least as far as what you can see. But there are still literally cigar smoke-filled back room decisions being made I've managed to get involved in wouldn't even include your local bigwig fish eaters, much less someone with a nose my size.

But money, at least *enough* money, is a great equalizer. I'm pretty sure it had something to do with my winning over the Barnes clan when I started dating Paige - that and her being comfortably convinced she is lucky to get me, of course. That girl is fucked up, I must say. Of course, my philosophy has always been there isn't a woman in existence isn't screwed up one way or another - and you seldom have to dig very deep to find the fucked up part. Samantha may be the exception, but may not be, I'm not sure. I may have to kill Jack to find out, haw haw haw.

I hope it's OK I'm wandering like this, I was talking about being Jewish - not much - and meant to talk about how much of a bastard the Jewish God is in the Old Testament to show why. But I'm thinking I don't need to; it's probably just the excuse I use to not practice my religion except when it suits me. It's much, much easier to just go to Alamo Heights Baptist with Paige and shake everyone's hands and then go eat a nice supper at the Club. But you've got to admit there *are* some pretty fucked up things in that Old Testament - like King David sending Uriah off on a suicide mission so he can *shtup* Bathsheba.

I'm on maybe my second date with Paige when I go to the Club with her and meet her sister Samantha and her fiancé Jack. He's just gotten out of the Army and they're engaged. Of course, I have an instant lust for Samantha and hate Jack from the minute I meet them. They're tall and leggy, she's wearing her hair long and spicy blond and his is darker but maybe blond from the sun and it's still military short. and they're pretty, both of them. You'd puke on their shoes there's so much sugar coming out of them, lovebirds both. Jesus Hallelujah Christ. And the noses on those two. And his fuckin hand on her ass as they stand there chatting with us. Now I can see although Paige is kind of nice looking, she's just got some hints of what Samantha's got all of. Paige's nose is a bit too pug to be as cute, nice figure but much more on the pudge side, and as they talk you know Samantha's actually got brains and Paige has lived off what she can manage as *cute* so far for her whole life. Jack's not showing much brain power either, keeping mostly silent and nodding and smiling a lot, which just pisses me off to no end. I'm thinking how good we'd be together, Samantha and I, what a great team - but while I'm thinking it, I know it'll never happen. I can face it: I'm just a kike. Maybe I'm going to be a *rich* kike, but everybody in this fucking Club is probably looking at us right now and saying to each other behind a hand "Look at the Jew-boy poor Paige's brought to the Club." My ears are burning just imagining it. Damn, damn, damn. It's really frustrating because even without the Barnes' money, I'm already pretty successful in this town. After all, I met Paige in the first place going to some fucking charity event in the St. Anthony Ballroom to raise money for the Children's Hospital.

Samantha's telling me the plan. "Jack's going to relax for a while up in Massachusettes while I finish my Master's, and then we'll move back here."

"Where are you going to school," I ask, "somewhere in Boston?"

"Close - a little bit west of there in Wellesley."

"Ah yes, Wellesley." As if I know anything about Wellesley except I think it's a woman's college and I know I'm going to study up on it tonight when I get home. I'm also thinking it must be an Ivy League school, fancy shmansy. I don't even know where Paige went to college, yet. Did she even graduate, I'm wondering.

"And you, Jack." I turn to him, thinking how can I put this guy down, "What are *you* going to be when you grow up?"

Jack smiles at me, all friendly, shy and sweet, God damn it. "I have a business degree from UT but I learned a bit about computers there and in the Army so I may do something with that. I really don't know what, though." He glances at Samantha. "I'm really looking forward to just relaxing with Sammie for awhile first." His arm is still around her, slung low. His hand,

I'm sure, is still resting on the top of the left cheek of her ass. *My* cheeks are burning.

Paige says something about us needing to say hi to her parents and pulls me away. I look back at Samantha *Sammie* as we pull away and shrug like I wanted to talk to her some more and then I begin girding myself to meet the Barnes's - Belle and David.

Which turns out to be quite easy actually.

Paige's parents seem very eager to make my acquaintance. David says he's been hearing all about me from Paige. I'm suspicious immediately perhaps their younger daughter has not attracted many agreeable suitors. Agreeable can come in many flavors, I'm thinking: old money, old name, successful possible future, new money. I would fail in any examination that required my resume to contain the words *old* anything, but I'm thinking the young men with that qualification in San Antonio maybe weren't acceptable or weren't interested in the bubble-headed daughter of another old-name family. Maybe I can turn things around for Paige's parents if they are worried about what she might end up attracting into the family, if they have to pick between a short balding *successful* Jew and some tall good looking *unsuccessful goyishe kop*.

*   *   *   *   *

I research the Barnes family as soon as I realize maybe Paige and her parents are interested in me. I might be the first Jew they've seen up close or something, who knows. The Barnes' are rich, not of the filthy variety but close, and only just close because so much of their wealth is just sitting around. Paige is a direct descendent of Matthew Barnes, who is credited with being among the younger men sent from the Mission San Antonio de Valero, the Alamo, as messengers to attempt to induce reinforcements to come to the aid of the trapped Texians against the Mexican Army of General Antonio Lopez de Santa

Anna. The family, based on nothing factual that I can find, believes he is the first man to be snuck out, and his ride is to Gonzales, just down the road. My research places him third out, and he rides southeast to settlements around Victoria. Whichever, he returns to the Mission too late, survives the battles at Refugio and San Jacinto and receives a grant from the Republic. He becomes an early Texas Republic Senator and then a State Senator and in his old age is rewarded by being sent to Washington, D.C. as a United States Senator. He tires of that duty after one term and returns to San Antonio to continue building his estate.

He ends up leaving acreage, cattle, several successful businesses including a bank, and a lot of land in and around San Antonio. He has nine children but only six of them survive their first five years, all boys. Matthew's will leaves almost everything to his oldest son, who is told to see everyone in the family is kept with work and to want for nothing. Several generations later and the current Barnes' clan is about a hundred strong, all involved in oil and gas, mercantile, banking, and real estate. They have gigantic blocks of developed and undeveloped land all over San Antonio and the suburbs, including downtown, Alamo Heights, Terrell Hills, Castle Hills, and virtually all the undeveloped land north beyond the airport, from Interstate 35 west to Bandera Road. Paige's father David holds title to most of the land and is the senior partner in the bank, but he spends most of his time dealing with the family's oil reserves - he majored in petroleum engineering at UT. My eyes light up every time I think about it.

Haw, haw, haw!

*   *   *   *   *

Eventually (like our fourth date) I get Paige in the sack. I think she was ready sooner, but I was taking my time, playing it cool. I really want to marry this broad, so I'm playing hard to get at first. Understand she's got plenty of money, or will have, but that's not the only point of this union. I'm talking name, family, what's that Fiddler song? Oh yeah, *tradition!*

She's about as exciting as a rock - absolutely no idea what she's doing. Hasn't she ever talked to a guy she's sleeping with? I mean she thinks going down on me is the foreplay and then she just rolls over and spreads her legs. So that's fine with me of course, but don't you think it's a screwy way to have a sexual relationship? How can enjoying sex like that last more than a week or two - in this case she's got a lot more than a cunt that interests me, so say that helps it last a year, year and a half tops? After even just a few weeks of this, and hurting her every time I try to get in her, I'm already not enjoying myself - something I never thought I'd say.

So tonight I finally stop her when she's heading south and I ask her straight out, "Hey hon, I really enjoy what you're doing, but... uh... have you ever... you know... had an orgasm yourself?" She looks at me with no expression, probably doesn't even understand the question, stupid broad. So I say, "I mean, what gets *you* excited?"

So she's still staring at me, honest to God. I'm getting annoyed. I decide I'm not going to say anything till she says something, the little bitch. She's playing with me? What's up with her anyway, can she actually *be* this dumb? So we stare at each other. And then we stare at each other some more. *Finally* she says "You mean what makes me have a... you know...? Cause if you must know I've never had that happen having sex." Meanwhile, since she paused to answer me, half crouched over my dick, now she's acting like she's not sure if she should continue her mission or stop and lie back down so we can talk.

"Come back up here so we can talk," I say.

"OK, Fred."

After she settles down next to me and kisses my cheek, she says "Yeah, I'm not sure I can even have one of those when we're doing it."

"You're fucking A you're not sure. Doesn't something excite you? I mean have you ever *had* an orgasm?"

"Yesssssss," she reluctantly replies, "But this is embarrassing, Fred. I mean it's something I take care of myself. Don't... I mean, isn't that what most girls do?"

"You play with yourself, you mean? I mean that's good if you do, it shows you can have one, anyway - I wasn't sure."

"Well, yes, of course I can have one. But I've never met a guy who... who cared enough to ask," she said, lowering her head with what I took for embarrassment. "No, I don't exactly play with myself. Let's not talk about this, OK?" She's pleading with me but I'm not having any of it.

I try to explain. "Look, I want you to enjoy this. I actually want to have a serious relationship with you and if you enjoy sex with me then maybe you'll want to have a serious relationship with me, too." *And let me play with your money*, I'm thinking.

She looks almost bewildered. "Are you serious Fred? I'm already enjoying this! You seriously want to have a relationship with me? Just tell me what you want! I don't care about me, I just want to make you happy!"

There are tears in her for-Christ's-sake eyes! I really hate this part of it, you know? Can I separate what she brings to the table from *this*?

"Look, tell me how you do it when you're alone."

"Ummm, a friend bought me a little thing that massages me." She looks scared for a minute and says real fast "I mean a girl friend, Fred, not a guy. A friend who said it would help. Anyway, it makes me feel good... down there. After a while I... have one."

"You mean a vibrator?"

"Yes, a vibrator." She refuses to look at me this whole exchange. I put my hand under her chin and pull, but she won't lift her head.

"Look," I say, pointing toward the next room with my jaw, "I have a vibrator somewhere in the bathroom. I'll find it and we'll try it out, use it while we have sex. Want to try?"

"I guess," she's still looking down at the bed. How she can go down on me but not want to talk about orgasms, I can't imagine.

So the rest is easy. We start her playing with herself when we have sex. Of course we don't have "normal" sex any more, but now she gets excited before we start so it's a lot easier and a lot more enjoyable. I'm doing my thing and she's doing hers whether I'm behind her or she's on top or whatever. Good stuff, finally. I'm also relieved she didn't bring up *me* going down on *her*, because that's where I draw the line. I can't imagine putting my face anywhere near that thing, much less my mouth, for God sake.

She comes now, most times. Plus, from a "relationship" point of view, I don't really have to talk to her much any more - certainly not about anything important. She's happy just telling me the stupid things that are going on in her life, the leather mules she just bought, where she ate, Sammie being mean - and she looks panicked when I ask her anything other than "what's up?"

And we're everywhere together, and she's hanging all over me all the time and I'm thinking it's just about the right time for me to propose, when she saves me the trouble, telling me she's missed her period, crying like I'm going to stop going out with her or something. God, she's pathetic.

*   *   *   *   *

So we end up getting married, beating Samantha and her big dud to the finish line. It's half hurry up because of the baby cooking along in her, and half gigantic production because little Paige actually hooked herself a man!

After dinner one night, I tell David about a little deal I have going, over cigars in the library. I know this sounds like Clue, but that's how I'm living now.

Some acreage is up for sale I paid first rights to, I have insider knowledge it's going to be in and around where the new freeway is going through Brackenridge Park. I have three months to purchase, but I'm cash short about half the asking price and banks want collateral and interest - even *his* bank. So I ask him if he wants in and he studies my plans and likes it and even brings Samantha and dumbass into the limited partnership we create. Somewhere down the line this'll bring in big time millions for us, but right away we get involved in all the emminent domain stuff on just a small percentage of the land we've bought and that alone pays us back the original investment. David is very pleased with himself. And with me. Life continues getting good.

David invites me and Jack on a little vacation down to Corpus Christi to celebrate - just us men - and introduces me to his old boat. I fall in love. Seriously. The boat's big and has sails, which I've never been anywhere near before. It's not for speed, except when you're pointing leeward, or whatever the expression is for letting the wind push you till you're going faster than hell. Of course Jack gets seasick and is hanging on the whole time, staring out at the horizon, puking when there's nothing left in him to puke. Haw haw haw. I just fuckin love it, man.

This boat of his, this *White Lightning*, is an old beauty. I want to fix it up, you know, put in new wood everywhere, polish it up, buy whatever I need to, to return it to the luxury it must have been, new. It is just so much *fun*. As soon as the kid's born I can turn Paige loose taking care of it while I drive down here every chance I get. Shit, I can even work from here as long as I have a phone, the accounting staff at my office, a *Wall Street Journal*, Chinese contacts, and a cartel in my pocket. Hmmm. Maybe getting away from the "family" is why I fell in love with this beast, but the reason doesn't matter. I mean it is really fuckin' fun, learning how to drive this thing, salt air, sea spray, slammin down on your butt when you drop off the crest of a wave. all that shit. And sleep? You get in the bunk after you tie this mother down and you can sleep for *hours*.

*   *   *   *   *

I'm sitting in my office downtown, stereo on, listening to Clapton sing. I've got the song set to repeat. I'm feeling really good, just leaning back, listening, planning my day. I've got some meetings, one with the Planning Board, one with some of the guys from the City Council. Lunch with that guy Cholo, that Sergeant from the SAPD who I have maybe got some plans he can help me with, maybe not. I'm gearing up, feeling good. Rubbing leftovers across the gums above my teeth.

Somebody wrote that this isn't a drug anthem, the guy who originally sang and wrote it meant it to be anti-drug. Can you imagine? I fly to L.A. and watch him perform this shit and you're trying to tell me this isn't an anthem? I jumped up with everyone else there, shouting *cocaine* with everybody. I got so interested in the song, matter of fact, I researched it. J.J. Cale wrote it but Eric Clapton made it famous. I went to see Cale once. *They Call Me the Breeze* made me want to learn the guitar, I've got to admit. As if I have the time to learn the *guitar*.

The other thing I have to worry about, though I'd never let on to friends and family anything ever bothers me, is the effect of this stuff on my nose. I'm fucking committed to not doing anything worse than snorting this stuff, so I need to be very careful I don't ruin my nose. I actually *dread* the possibility that I might end up with a bleeding problem or a fucked up lining in there between my nostril holes. You know this nasal septum I've also been reading up on. My nose isn't a small one and I have a lot of septum to worry about! Haw, haw, haw.

Well, something else. Paige's getting closer and closer to term with this kid. Now they are saying it's going to be a boy, so I can relax on that score. A girl would have been a problem, this first baby in the Barnes' collection. Jesus fuck, would I be hearing about that - especially if Samantha gets knocked up and has a boy. Talk about a shift in the balance of power! But thank God it's almost too late for that to happen. Anyway, what's got me a little worried is Paige has taken to this shit like candy to a baby. If she could buy rocks of it she'd use it like fucking snuff. Holes all over her mouth, she wouldn't care. As a matter of fact, she likes it better than sex. In that way it's cool for me too, her wandering off at night smoking and snorting, it's really a kind of relief. I need to balance her though while she's pregnant, says her doctor. "Just like she's eating for herself and the baby, *everything* she's ingesting goes to the baby as well."

So I'm restricting her to a few toots a day, and letting her smoke dope the rest of the time. It balances her out, I tell her, and frankly all she really knows is what I tell her, you know? Stupid bitch.

There must be something to my little theory the *weaker* you are the more prone you are to things that can make you dependent, like drugs. That applies to more than just Paige, but it definitely applies to her. Keeps her off me, anyway.

Sober she's even come up with a name for Junior, and I'm cool with it - Jesse Marshall Klien. The Jesse's unusual enough and the Marshall is a grandmother's maiden name, so it adds up to fancy shmansy and better than anything Samantha and ass wipe will come up with if he ever knocks her up.

I am sure now I can get Samantha on my team. I know she's as smart as a whip from the times I've been able to sit down with her and talk about the business. She really understands trade, real estate, banking and accounting - every fucking thing I tell her I'm into, that's for damned sure. She did her thesis on *Modern Accounting under the Restrictions Imposed by the United States Government,* or some such shit. Let me read it and it made plenty of sense to me, just on the boring side with all the fucking citations. She could be a high-priced lawyer or even the CEO of a corporation, whatever she wants, *if* she wants, which is her problem of course. Talk about opposites attract - that's Jack in a nutshell, everything she's not. Dragging her the fuck down, the way I see it.

But I can suck him in too. He loves these fucking computers and I can give him pleanty of misery there. These shitty boxes belong up the asses of the people who came up with them. I've never seen such undependability in anything not human. First they need climate control, then they need programs, and finally they need twenty-four by seven care so they don't screw up every time you turn them on. Yeah, I can keep him busy.

So Samantha. Yeah, that's gonna happen. David and Belle can be happy, we'll all be happy together, and busy guiding the family fortunes. Haw, haw, haw.

Most of this elation I feel is really inside me, not just the effects of some drug or other. This is really exciting, what I've fallen into. This family. These people. The money, the fucking Club.

Clapton's starting up again. Love it, man!

Think I should call Paige for lunch. Maybe get the sisters to meet me at the Club. That would be very cool, eating there, talking to those two. Well, Samantha. Maybe Jack might be off somewhere living his dream.

Oh shit, wait. I'm meeting that cop Cholo downtown today. What's his last name? Cholo, Cholo, Cholo... Hartmann I think. Double-n to make him German. Got a pie I want to stick his finger in. Been thinking about needing a big old cop-type like him on my team. Right? Am I right? Yeah, you're fucking A I'm right. Haw haw haw, I'm always right! Yes sir.

I mean, Cholo may not be the right person for the kinds of things I have in mind, but he might be. Really impressive that one. Big. Scares the shit out of everyone - including me. Smart, too. Has a feel for the politics of being a cop.

Mmmmm.... Could be I might hire him someday, say as head of security for... *The Barnes' Conglomerate...* that sounds good. You never fucking know how these things work out. Interesting thought, though....

Say, I probably should check my schedule. See when my meetings start. Pencil in lunch with Paige and Samantha... say, tomorrow... probably fucking Jack, too, need to get him in the bandwagon... on the bandwagon... too. Better work on drying Paige out by morning. Gonna take a big old train ride with these guys, I sure am! Alla board!!

This is weird, making all these plans, sounding good, feeling like I should be getting more excited about it than I am. I'm actually feeling just a little bit depressed. Don't understand that at all....

...maybe I could use another line or two.

*   *   *   *   *

The Greater San Antonio Chamber of Commerce started around 1894, but until I joined it, I think more commerce was throttled by it than anything else. Houston and Dallas, hell, even Austin passed us by until we stopped sticking with the military and tourists for all our income, and I take most of the credit for that. You have to be needy and greedy I like to say.

Don't get me wrong, I love making money the old fashioned way, cheating, but putting those gains into land and enticing people like Omni to come in and buy my land pays off just as well and I sleep better than when I'm wondering if the government is going to ask questions about where I've hidden my withholding tax accounts.

It's easy to notice new activity at the Chamber, when Lou Tonzerelli and Frank Bonello buy their company into a seat on the Board of Directors right out of the starting gate. It doesn't require a gigantic amount of money, but it isn't a donation you can write off, either. And any company that lists "Investments" as their line of work gets my attention. These guys seem to be connected out of state. I wouldn't have been surprised if they'd said their business was importing olive oil. Much as I'd prefer doing business strictly with locals, these guys are more financial than anybody around. Lou, especially.

We do an investigation. I have it done offline not wanting to insult anyone, but I do it to make sure me and the Chamber stay out of trouble and don't generate a surprise embarrassment to the city - like a Paul Thompson exposé for example. Or something that involves a grand jury. Of course I'm mostly concerned that it could make *me* look bad. Shhhhhhhh.

The report comes back that the complications are impossible to follow. Well, not impossible, but no newspaper will devote the time and money I could to trace this corporation back to actual people behind Tonzerelli the CEO and Bonello, the President. Now the police might be willing to spend the time and energy running this mess down, and I'm thinking I should want to, also. These guys have the potential to raise me up to another level, so I'm letting my people know I need everything they can dig up on these guys.

I even ask Cholo if he can find out anything, him not quite being *my* cop yet, but close.

In the meantime, I'm welcoming Lou and Frank to the Chamber at the Board of Director's meeting tonight.

*   *   *   *   *

So how was I supposed to know he'd get so high? I've never seen a guy get this sick with just a little pot. He said he was susceptible, but this is ridiculous. I bring home this really good shit, this stuff they're calling second cousin to the original Maui Wowie, just a little tobacco cut in, and he passes it around like the rest of us, looking like he knows what he's doing. I've sampled this stuff so I know to take it easy, and I tell them that, like a good boy. Paige could give a shit "take it easy" but Samantha listens, begs off on about every other toke. Little Jackie paper tries matching me drag for drag and he's incoherent in a half hour. Sicker'n a dog.

While we were starting up, Samantha teased him about Nam. She reminded him he always denied seeing any drugs over there, but all we heard on the news was how rampant it was. "That was probably non-coms, and probably in the infantry units that did the real fighting, not in my advisory team," he choked out trying to hold his breath and talk at the same time. She snorted like she didn't believe him and they laughed at each other after she snorted, so that just pissed me off some more. I said "So you weren't actually in the real fighting?" And he slowly turned toward me. He thought about it for a minute and then slowly nodded yes but didn't say anything.

He's a heavy mother, this one. I get him up with his arm over my shoulder, Samantha on the other side. I maybe have pulled a muscle manhandling him up from the couch but if he's gonna puke I'd just as soon it be in his wife's old room on that waterbed we put in there, then down here in the living room. Belle has already complained about us smoking - how *disappointed* she is, and it *smells* funny.

We get him up the stairs don't ask me how, but Samantha's talking to him and she's telling him every step to take and he must be listening. We turn him to face away from the bed and he just drops backward, bouncing up and down on that bed and moaning. I mean he's making me seasick just watching him; even after he stops the bouncing he's kind of sloshing around on the bed. He curls up and she pulls the blanket up and over him from where it's folded at the foot of the bed. Of course as soon as the blanket's on him he starts shivering, so she gets all concerned and tells me to go back down and she'll be there in a few minutes.

So I leave them and go downstairs, being quiet so I don't wake up Jesse. That's easy, him sleeping hard ever since we got him home.

Paige has pulled out several bags of chips and is chowing down. I take the bag with the ones that have little ripples and turn on the TV. The news is on, but I'm really just watching the newscasters, seeing their lips move and watching the voices coming out of them. They smile most of the time and glance at each other as they read the news, these two guys, good looking guys too, all that strong jaw, perfect teeth stuff. My fucking mother never looked into braces so my fucking teeth look completely fucked.

Paige comes over, sits on my lap. She hasn't been smoking while I was upstairs; there's powder on the bottoms of her nostrils. She nuzzles into my neck and I have to keep shifting around so I can see these guys doing the news. They go to commercial and Paige's sucking on my neck to make me a hickie. I don't mind, I can use that at the office, but if she thinks this is somehow exciting, I cannot for the life of me remember a time when it worked on me.

So she's kind of hanging onto me by my neck, like she's a leech or something. I've got my hand on her fat stomach, and she takes and puts the hand under her skirt and I'm just absolutely turned off by that and pull my hand back out; rubbing her stomach some more, the news boys back from commercial.

This big blond guy kind of reminds me of....

Samantha's walking back into the room. She's worried, of course, Jack hasn't puked but he's *so* dizzy, she says. Of course the first thing that occurs to me to help him is a little blow. "I can give him something to balance him out, if you think he might be willing," I say. "A little of my white powder always helps me when I smoke too much, you think he'd try some?"

"I don't know. Can't hurt to try. Bring some upstairs, and I'll see if I can get him up."

So she goes back up the stairs. Fat ass is still eating chips, playing with my lap, so I have to disengage her and head up to my office to get my stash.

I bring my little mirror into Samantha's old room. I've got three lines already built on it, one per. Samantha comes over and I tell her he should just do half a line each nostril, only I say *each nose* and she and I can't help but giggle. Anyway, she gets him up and tells him what to do. After, she leads him back to the bed and lays him out, covering him up once he's back on the bed. I hear her say "If you get dizzy again, stare at the wall, Jackie-pants." He mutters something and I can see him try closing his eyes. *Jackie-pants.* Sweet Jesus!

Samantha comes over and does a line like a pro. She pinches her nose twice and walks out the door. Damn!

So I'm in the room with her and the lamebrain, and she just walks out the door like she fucking owns the place and doesn't give a shit who knows it! It's like she is so cool, she naturally knows what to do all the time. I cannot get over it. I'm standing over Jack now, looking down at him. He's really her match, looks-wise. Has that big old strong chin, smooth fucking skin, I know when he opens his mouth the white teeth are perfect, the son of a bitch. Nice nose, I notice, straight, no hook. I head out to come back downstairs; it's scary how much he looks like those news guys... something about his mouth.

I get downstairs and Samantha's walking what's left of the chips back to the kitchen. Paige's pouting, crumbs all over her blouse, pants. I could lick her face and O.D. on the salty crumbs stuck around her lips and chin.

I do just that, I kneel on the couch next to her and lick across her mouth. She misunderstands of course and opens her mouth wide, trying to catch my tongue. I give in and kiss her, hoping that maybe Samantha will come back in the room and see us. Later when we go to the kitchen, she is sitting yoga-style on a chair at the breakfast table, drinking bourbon rocks - the bottle's next to the glass - and reading one of those cookbooks Paige has never opened.

*　　*　　*　　*　　*

Paige and I are having dinner at La Louisianne with Samantha and the *schmuck*. I'm using colored sugar in my coffee, waiting for the Italian wine I ordered, *Lacryma Christi*. Fancy French restaurant, fancy Italian wine.

We've just come from Belle's funeral and a visit to David in the hospital. While I waited for Paige and Samantha to visit the old man I was on a pay phone and let Jack hang around the ICU. I like the hospital phones because they are usually set up like those isolation booths on TV quiz shows. Someone would have to be prepared in advance to hear what you say in one of those things. I'm on the phone with some people I know south of Nuevo Laredo. The one I'm talking to calls himself Silvio and his English is pretty good. The way he has described himself and "his people" is like they are all related like a *familia*, but I'm not sure if that's to be taken literally. We've slowly grown to trust each other over the years to the point now we're doing seven figure deals. I'm talking about a shit-pot load of money here, sports fans. Big action, fairly quick turnaround, three degrees of separation between me and the grunt level activity; this phone call is about the only point where I can be traced directly to the bad guys.

Paige and Samantha are sitting here going on and on about the shock of their mother dropping dead like that in the middle of a conversation with David, and David having the stroke when he squats down next to her to see what's wrong. I got home from a trip to California a few hours later and found them, still lying where they fell. Murder suicide was my first thought but that was a crazy reaction just because what I saw was so crazy, those two lying there like that in the library.

Very little hope for David, the specialists say, and Samantha is trying like hell to prepare Paige who doesn't want to hear it. We, meaning me, didn't find him soon enough, she says. He'll probably never come out of the coma the doctor said to her. Just be prepared for the worst, she says.

114

Tears are streaming down my wife's face. Snot'll be next so I ask her to go use the bathroom and clean up before our dinner comes out for God's sake. Both of them get up and head out, so you can imagine my relief.

I sample the wine for the *sommelier* and we share a smile.

Jack's been quiet the whole fucking day, hardly saying three words since he and Samantha arrived at the house this morning. Samantha did a great job arranging for everything related to the funeral, including taking care of Jesse till the nurse/babysitter arrived (Jesse's just about through his withdrawals from Paige's hand-me-downs), hotel rooms for out of towners and so forth, and I used the contacts I have at the SAPD who owe me big time, to arrange for the extra motorcycles for the police escort from the church to the family's mausoleum and then back home for the extended family and guests. I'm thinking we should have waited for David to cork off too, so we could do two for one and really have something to celebrate.

Jack's playing with his salad.

"Are you alright?" I ask him politely.

His glance bounces from the salad to me and back to his salad.

"Yes" is all he says. What a *schmuck*.

"Have you given any more thought to my offer?"

"Sure I have Fred. I'm interested, of course, but I'm not in the mood to talk about it now. Let's just have dinner and get the girls home so they can rest up. This is a tough day for them, you know?"

I pause, taking a slug of my wine and smacking my lips, feeling enough anger at his talking down at me the way he is I make sure I'm cooled off before I respond.

"Well just don't fucking take too long - this is big money I'm offering you, more money than you'll make for years slaving at these mainframe shops you put so much stock in. The offer's on the table and I can take it off just as fast. You want to work for the family, you need to make up your mind soon."

"Hi girls," he says as Paige and Samantha return to the table.

"Here honey," I say, jumping up to pull out Paige's chair while Samantha pulls her own out and Jack sits there with his thumb up his ass.

Paige's face is dry now, but she still looks like shit, puffed up and red-nosed.

I turn to Samantha. "I was just telling your boy here he needs to hurry and make up his mind about working for me. My offer is *very* generous, Samantha."

She glances from me to her husband. He looks at her and shrugs, shaking his head *no.*

What the fuck's *that* supposed to mean?

She shrugs back at him, and smiles but he must miss it, because he's already looking down, shoveling salad into his mouth. Instead of answering me, she's taking a sip of her wine and picking up her fork to work on her salad, too.

Oh well, I'm thinking, he'll end up on the team. It's too much money for him to pass up; he's not stupid - especially with the family torch about to be passed to us. I can outwait him, make him look selfish.

Fucking waiters finally show up with our dinners and much fanfare, but I'm not having any of it.

I'll get Samantha on the team, too. Jack doesn't know it, but she's really the main reason I want him to say yes.

Interlude: 9:56 a.m.

Sammie laid the phone down on the side of the tub, satisfied her sister was agreeable to picking her up for their Sunday brunch in New Braunfels. She'd been in the tub for maybe twenty minutes and it wasn't scalding any more, but at least she'd gotten her underarms taken care of. She needed it hotter, so she sat up and slowly slid down to the faucet end of the tub, making a face because of the grit she felt under her. She turned the knob to let water out of the tub and turned on the hot water. She waited while she felt the tub heating back up and then when she could almost not stand it, she turned off the water and used the other knob to stop it back up. She slid backwards so she could lie down again.

The aspirin had kicked in and she was feeling fine, completely recovered from last night. Next to the phone was a tall glass of orange juice and vodka, half emptied. She had a tub pillow behind her neck and she got comfy, stretching the muscles in her thighs, working her calves by stretching her Achilles' tendons and wiggling her toes. She arched her back and settled down into the heat.

She reached the glass and took another long sip. Then another and the glass was empty. Perfect, she smiled.

She closed her eyes. She thought about Jack and how surprising, how satisfying that this had all worked out, marriage with Jackie-pants. He was so sweet, shy... and yet smart, really sharp in that quiet confident way. Big and good looking, but... though she'd cared for him since high school, she'd been hesitant about him for so long.... because for the longest time she hadn't understood - had misunderstood - the love he'd shown her all those years, for a weak kind of neediness that put her off. Yes, he'd seemed so quietly needy. Until... until she finally knew for sure he must be the one for her. She remembered why and her smile deepened. She squirmed in the water, sending tiny ripples through the tub.

The water was cooling off again. Her head was still feeling ok, though she could feel the throb lurking.

If she could ease up on the drinking, she knew it had really started bothering Jack and, face it, it was starting to interfere with just about everything. She'd always loved the taste of alcohol but she had to admit that lately she was drinking to get drunk. She didn't have to think about the job then and where it seemed to be taking her.

Finally, she grabbed a towel and carefully stood up, wrapping it around her, tying it tightly under her arms and over her breasts. She dried her hair with a second towel, and then made a hair bun with it. She dried her legs and arms with a third and spread that one out on the carpet in front of her basin and mirror so she wouldn't drip while drying her hair. She decided to go without makeup so her timing would work out with Paige arriving in half an hour. Her hair was really too long for a quick dry so while she worked the dryer, she idly considered getting more than just a few inches taken off on her next visit to the salon. Nah, she decided.

Her throat. She had a table mirror set up next to the basin. It was a large square mirror set up on a pedestal. She could angle it so that she could turn her head sideways and use the reflection in the table mirror to see her profile in the big mirror behind her. The nose is really perfect *she told herself every time she did this.* But that throat. *There was the slightest puffiness that started maybe an inch below the tip of her chin and disappeared just before reaching her neck.* Not yet, *she thought,* but soon. *She idly wondered if she was doomed to plump up like Belle had in her last few years.*

Her nails. The color was really not a good one for her, made her hands disappear. She wore it so she didn't have to visit her manicurist so often because of work. If she could take the time now, she should remove it and try that new one she just bought, that really dark blood red. She'd still not be able to use lipstick or she'd need makeup to keep herself from looking like something out of Dawn of the Dead, *and besides she wanted to be relaxed and dress relaxed all day today. She decided to live with the nails. Her hair was finally dry enough and as she turned the blower off she thought she heard the doorbell being rung. That would be Paige.*

"Just a minute!" she shouted. She grabbed her drink glass, put on her after-shower heels and headed for the front door.

She looked through the peephole to make sure it was her sister, then opened the door and turned and walked away. "Make yourself at home, Sis," she called back, "I'm about 15 minutes from being ready!" She headed to the kitchen for a refill. She also wanted to leave Jackie-pants a note.

IV - JACK

Here's how I get engaged to Sammie Barnes.

She knocks on my parent's door about three hours after Mom gets me home from the airport on the Tuesday afternoon that I fly in from Fort Lewis. I'm already asleep on top of the covers on my bed when Mom kisses my forehead to wake me up, just like when I was a kid before I started using an alarm. I can't get my eyes open and I'm foggy and I ask her if it's morning already and she sits beside me and says, "No, Jack, Samantha's in the living room. She came over to say hi. Would you like me to tell her something and send her on her way?"

"No Mom, I'll be out in a minute. I just need to try to wake up. I'd like to see her."

"Then you might want to take a shot of your mouthwash before you come out," she says with a smile in her voice.

When I do join Sammie in the living room, she's winding the music machine Dad brought home to Mom after an assignment in Germany. It's a small, realistic looking bird cage, with a mechanical looking bird sitting on a perch. The key is on the bottom of the cage and you wind it till it stops. When you turn it on, this little red bird sings. Its head turns and tail bobs as it sings. I think it's supposed to be a tune a nightingale

120

would sing. You can set it to sing constantly, or to sing patches of the song every few seconds. Sammie's got it set to sing straight through. We stand there next to each other after barely a glance, listening to the bird. She actually takes my hand while we listen. As the singing eventually starts to slow, I let go of Sammie's hand and turn off the machine. "Pretty," she says.

She sits at the end of the couch. It's Danish modern. I think this is the first time she's ever been in my house. She says "Wow, what an uncomfortable couch!" And she's right, of course. The construction is not only stark, it's hard, with shiny wooden arms that have no material to soften their feel. The material on the couch itself is made from woven wool, in alternating dark and light gray stripes.

"Thanks," I say, "I'll be sure to tell Mom. You want me to let her know how you like the color?"

"That sucks, too," she smiles. "Sit," she adds, patting the gray stripes next to her.

"On that couch?" I joke. "It's too hard for me." I walk over to my Dad's old leather armchair and sit.

She mutters something about her big mouth, and gets up. She walks over to me and sits in my lap with her arm around me. She looks down into my face. Her eyes work their way around till they land on my eyes.

"I really worried about you, Jack. I was scared for you the whole time you were gone. You've got no reason to believe me," she adds, seeing the look on my face, "but God dammit, I did." She kisses my cheek. Her eyes look almost green in this light, but pale, pale. I've forgotten how pretty. Mesmerizing.

"Well, let me ask you something then," I say. "You know I like you, and I wouldn't mind being friends with you and seeing you like we've always done, whenever you let me know, but what about these other guys you've been telling me

121

about, Buddy and Ryan and Richard to name a few? I mean what are you doing, really? Sitting on my lap is tough enough without knowing all these boyfriends you've got."

She shrugs and smiles. No, her eyes are really blue, pale blue. "Oh, Jackie-pants! Quit playing so hard to get! You believe all the crap you read? I was just trying to entertain the troops with those stories. You *know* you're the only one for me... I mean I can *feel* how much you believe me, Jackie-pants." and she squirms her hips to make sure I know what she means. I aim a kiss for her lips and she returns it, but cuts it short. She looks down at me and says "Whoa, Nellie! Save that, young man, there'll be plenty of time for that later, I know I owe you! Right now," she says, standing up, "I've got an appointment at my salon. You are taking me out for a late dinner at the Club so I can show my hero off."

I guess my mouth's open looking up at her. She grins again and says "You walking me to the door, or do I have to go searching for it all by myself?"

Of course we both know I could just point at the door it's so close, but I smile and get up. At the door, she holds out her hand, and I shake it as we are back to clowning. "I'll drive tonight, soldier," she says. "Pick you up nine-ish. Byeeeee!" She air kisses with a loud *smack* and is gone.

*　*　*　*　*

We are dating pretty steadily now. We play handball twice a week. We hold hands in movies and she puts her arm around me in the Club. She introduces me to her parents' friends and the friends she has that I don't know. She tells them all I'm her boy friend. She's been to my house for dinner a few times and is surprisingly charming with Mom.

We've had sex a few more times; we've even talked about how to make it better and the last few times she's had orgasms... or faked them so well that I didn't care if she was acting - if that was kegel control, more power to her.

Her Dad is hardly ever home, with what he calls *bidness trips* all over the state. Paige is dating some guy that Sammie calls "Paige's Jewish friend," when she's feeling charitable, and "Freddie the Jew," when she's not. Belle is at the Club most nights, so Sammie and I watch TV and drink beer at the Mansion a lot.

I'm starting to feel more relaxed about Nam though I'm having two dreams fairly often. Fescola's in his harness in the chopper behind me, while the VC soldier is running in slow motion in front of me. My bullets don't hit him. I feel Fescola behind me trying to reach out to me but he's harnessed in. The other dream is I'm watching that card floating down by the table, as I run for the door, but the door never gets closer and I'm staring at that card as I run, mortar shells exploding outside the room.

Sammie is talking about me maybe going with her when she goes back to school to complete her work on her Master's.

"We could get a nice apartment - I've got one on hold now but they have really nice bigger ones walking distance from the building I have my classes in. You could be my sex slave and maybe start thinking about what you want to do with me for the rest of your life." She blinks those eyes at me and they crinkle up when she grins. I don't remember her ever talking about a future with me before, but it could be teasing so I don't respond.

"I'm really into computers, Sammie," I try to explain again, patiently. "I don't know what I'll end up doing with them, but something. I could be a programmer at a few places in San Antonio, but there really aren't many companies around here big enough to use mainframe computers."

"USAA? What others?"

"Actually, USAA and Datapoint are the only ones I'm sure of," I reply. "Otherwise, I think I'd have to go to Dallas or Houston to stay in Texas and still do computer stuff. Ross Perot has a company in Dallas that sounds cool."

"Well," she says, thinking about it, "don't you think you have plenty of time to decide that kind of thing? I mean don't you *want* to spend some time with me at Wellesley while I get the Master's?"

I don't answer. I'm looking at her and thinking about it, but I really have no idea what to say, since I don't have any idea if she's serious about a word she's saying.

Maybe to find out if she could possibly be serious, I pull her closer and kiss her. Her mouth opens and she gets aggressive fast. I mean her tongue's right in there, right away, like she's been thinking about this for a while like I have. She's fumbling at my shirt already and I'm holding her face with my hands trying to keep up that great, tongue swirling kiss.

She pulls away. I'm starting to really enjoy the eyes half closed look she gets on her face when she's getting excited. She takes my hand as she stands, and leads me upstairs. She has one-handed her t-shirt off by the time we get to her room, and I'm shutting the door while she's getting the rest of her things off and pulling down the covers. I can only get my shirt and socks off before she pulls me down on the bed, pushing me by the shoulders down to her hips. Her legs are spread and she's already moaning when she arches her hips up toward me. I kiss her, my hands under her buttocks, holding them up off the bed. In what seems seconds, her hips are rolling in time with my tongue, and I've managed to get myself naked, and then she's stopping me, pulling me off her, breathing hard. Without thinking, I don't get on top of her. I want to be able to touch her while we make love so I try a new position I've seen pictures of somewhere. I think it's really for pregnant women but I've thought about doing it this way with Sammie just so no one's on top for a change. I lie on my left side right where I was and swing her closest leg over me at my waist. I put her other leg between mine and we are scissored together, perpendicular and touching where we meet in the middle. I'm able to enter her easily, and I can rub her legs, belly, breasts, while we move. Moving seems to be what she's most interested in, using her hands to pull my hips closer where we are joined. I rock slightly to the side each time we are at our closest. We rock back and forth, and now she's pulling and pushing my hip to keep the rhythm. I'm rolling a thumb around the nipple I can reach and her face slowly shuts tight, mouth making a small o, and her breathing is starting to make a noise down in her throat. I force myself to not speed up, to not break that rhythm. I know that's the way to mess things up for her, speeding up. Over time, with the movement and the control, I feel myself get into a state where I'm excited but it's not increasing, as if I can do this forever. She's getting closer; she is holding my hip tighter as she rocks me back and forth. Now she pulls her free leg up and back, wanting more contact between us. I roll up onto her, allowing her other leg to go up and back; she bends her knees, practically up into her armpits, smiling and moaning. We continue our slow rocking but so much deeper now and she is gasping. Her lips have pulled back in concentration. I'm pinching the nipple lightly now as she gets close, following a suggestion she made a while ago. We aren't rocking now, we're pressed against each other and I'm still rolling my hips to the side in the same rhythm. In effect, I'm massaging her where we're joined. Her knees are lightly brushing the bedsheet in rhythm. Her moans increase in volume. She tightens inside and I have to strain to keep my hips rotating. I have to move slightly in and out just to be able to keep the rhythm within her tightness. It's enough to suddenly bring me over the top too. I begin pulsing. She can feel this throbbing going on inside of her, and it seems to intensify her waves. She arches her back, crying out with *Oh!!* over and over to the rhythm of the waves, my noise lost under hers. Her hands finally unclench their grip on my hip, and though she continues to say *Oh!* with each wave, her cries are slowly ebbing, losing cadence. She moves her hands to her knees to help keep them in place till she finally stops. Our breathing continues to rasp as we lay there. My hand has moved to her stomach, and she finally lets her knees go and places her feet over me and against my butt, to keep us together.

"God, Jackie-pants, I *must* love you!" she blurts between breaths. "That was the most unbelievable feeling I've ever had! I didn't even know if it was ever going to stop! Jesus!"

I'm aware that her leg muscles are quivering. Eventually that stops and our breathing starts to sound normal. She lifts her feet and pushes me out of her and onto my back with a shove. She crawls around and pulls herself on top of me, not minding the smells or the wet.

"Marry me, Jackie-pants." She looks down at me, into my eyes. She looks at the rest of my face, then back at my eyes. Her hands are on the caps of my shoulders, and then she moves them, placing them under my arms and forcing me to arch my back so she can hug me.

I whisper into her ear, "Sounds good to me, Sammie. I'm actually starting to think you might be serious."

"I am," she whispers back. She kisses me softly, opening my mouth with hers and swirling her tongue around mine like earlier. She pulls away and looks down at me and my face again. Her eyes crinkle with a grin. I really love those eyes.

*   *   *   *   *

Sammie and Belle and Mom are planning the wedding, thank God I'm clear of that.

The announcements have already gone out, and the Barnes clan is popping out from under every rock in the great State of Texas. Not too many Gantts *anywhere*, really, besides Mom and my sister Gail and her new husband and baby boy.

I'm also seeing much too much of Paige's Fred Klein, since they hustled the two of them through their wedding. It's recently dawned on me that I've never really had a lasting friendship with any of the men I've known - there were plenty of guys in high school that I goofed off with but none of those were lasting high school friendships. The poker buddies, the teammates from football and baseball, the guys I double dated with, were all friends but I just never felt the kind of kinship with any of them that we continued to talk or write after we all left for college. The only young men I knew in college, I never saw or even thought about after I went straight into the Army. And I still don't remember much about the soldiers and officers I knew in the Army.

He did reintroduce me to a guy he was talking to that I knew in high school. A jock I was on the football team with for a year before he quit. He's an up and coming cop now; I've seen him in the paper a few times and now he's a Sergeant.

But this Fred guy. Strange character, with his stupid laugh. When he says the things he says that are supposed to be funny and he laughs, it's like he's looking out from behind those little brown beady eyes to see if you're going to laugh with him. I mean the eyes aren't laughing; he is behind them, *inside* them, peering *through* them at you. I imagine I'm not doing a very good job of describing this, because it is very hard to put in words. It's eerie, the feeling that there's something weird going on inside that guy. *Almost* makes you feel sorry for him, unless you dislike him enough.

Frankly, he's a sarcastic son of a bitch. From practically the night I met him I haven't liked him. I mean he's obviously got a brilliant mind and has explained to us some business deals he has going, the concepts of which just literally whizzed right by me - I had no idea what he was talking about and felt that it was obvious to him and Sammie that I was the dumb one in the discussion, right next to Paige. Sammie seemed to understand what he was describing because she asked a few questions about the timing of the two sales he was talking about that he got completely into when he answered. She suggested that he "structure" something or other and he smiled and said he'd talk to his accountant about her suggestion. He'd take her suggestion to his accountant! I was impressed. Sammie doesn't let too many people see her like that very often. She prefers being a smartass most of the time.

Fred has talked to me about computers, not just the kinds he sells, the PCs in one of his side businesses, but also the one he needs to set up to keep track of all the stuff he's into. He's interested in my knowledge of languages and has asked me to get involved in computer security so I can help him set things up, and, as he put it, "to keep all my secrets a secret." I'm not really sure he's interested in what I know as much as that he is trying to ingratiate himself to me as a potential fellow member of the Barnes' "clan". There's no way I'm ever going to be sucked into his business. To me it's like something oily: slick, greasy stuff.

*   *   *   *   *

"Jesus, Jackie-pants, we just got back from our honeymoon and you have an appointment for a job interview *today*?" I'm sitting on the bed showered and dressed, and she's in it.

The honeymoon was a three week cruise around the western Caribbean, so I thought it wouldn't be pushing things to start thinking about what I'm going to *work* at for a living. I'm thinking if kissing Manta Rays off Grand Cayman is one of my life's highlights, then I'd better get busy. Although... many nights on that cruise ship with Sammie *could* serve as highlights for most peoples' lives. God am I lucky.

And, we have been home almost a week, so it isn't like I ran off the boat when it docked in Galveston and started making calls at the first pay phone I could find.

"Yes dear, I do." I smile, hoping she won't drag this out. "I actually have two if you count meeting Fred K for lunch as one. He *says* I might be interested in some of the computer work he's doing with the new System/38 he bought."

"Oh yes, that wonderful fucking System/38," she says sarcastically, as she snuggles back down into the bed, pulling the night mask back down over her eyes. I put my face down just above hers and lift one corner of the mask and she opens one pale blue eye, squinting up at me. Her breath isn't the best thing I've ever smelled coming out of her (or the worst), but she *is* pretty, so I kiss her quickly and say "Love ya, mean it," let the mask pop back down over her eye, and stand up. She groans and rolls over onto her favorite side, flopping around to find a comfortable position in which to fall back asleep.

I've been sitting beside her on the bed. When the alarm had gone off earlier, she hadn't moved. I remembered when she'd joined me in bed because she woke me when she snuggled, and it had been pretty late. I'm not an early to bed person, but she's always preferred getting to bed later and sleeping in even later than I. I don't think her position changed from the time I got up to the time I came back, showered and cerealed. I am getting used to seeing an empty drink next to her on her nightstand - I mean, one is on my side too often enough, especially when we stay up together. But it helps explain why she sometimes sleeps in so late. At least she isn't doing drugs, like her pregnant sister and Fred.

I'm still driving my old Impala, but it is definitely on its' last legs. We never drive it when Sammie's coming someplace with me, Sammie's really weird about that, being seen in the old car. But today I hop in it and drive off for my interview with EDS. They usually do their initial interviews in the home of the interviewee, but an exception is being made in my case, since we're about to move to our new home and are temporarily in my in-laws' mansion. I'll never get Sammie to move to Dallas, but I know I'll learn from the interview anyway because I've heard it's a tough one.

*   *   *   *   *

We've been in the house we just bought for about a month. It's a nice little place and Sammie's turned our bedroom pink, so I know she's getting used to it. She even has the dollhouse set up in it, across from the bed like her old room, except now there isn't much space between it and the bed.

Sammie says she wants to show me something. We are in our underwear, getting undressed for bed when she stops me. She gets me to kneel next to her facing the side of the dollhouse.

"See the fireplace in there?" she asks, giggling like a little kid.

Of course I can see the chimney on top of it, on the side where we are kneeling, so I look through the open back of the miniature mansion and there, on the first floor, is a fancy fireplace with a little metal fire guard screen and a set of andirons or whatever they're called, with fakey little logs glued onto them. "Yes, dear," I say, "I see the fireplace. It looks really nice, but I don't underst -"

"Jackie-pants! Look at it on the second floor!" She's practically hopping up and down on her knees, she's enjoying this so much.

130

So, I look up a floor and there in the "library" is another opening under the chimney. This fireplace is not formal at all and not even very realistic looking, for being in a mansion. It's just a flat faux-cement space with no andirons or fake logs or screen in front of it.

"OK, now I see that one. It's kind of unfinished, though. What, are you going to ask me to use all the interior decorator knowledge I have to finish it for you? Hey, *that* sounds really exciting, Sammie! What a great idea!"

She says "Ha, ha, ha Jackie-pants. Nope, this is our secret place, this upstairs fireplace. Stick your finger up in there - probably your middle one would be a perfect fit," she grins.

So I'm clowning, I mean Sammie may be serious or she may be clowning too, but there's only one thought that comes to my mind after what she's just said and I reach my hand across my body and down to her crotch and shove it down the front of her panties. I'm working at getting a finger, any finger, into her while she's laughing and grabbing at my wrist and half trying to stop me and half opening up to let me rub at her, in there.

So we're wrestling around and laughing and now I'm half on top of her and, giggling, she sticks her tongue on the side of my jaw and licks up the side of my face. I make an "Eeeew, gross" noise and we laugh and tickle each other for a few minutes before she finally stops me and says, "Right finger, wrong hole, Jackie pants. Just let me show you the *other* secret place, first? The one in the dollhouse? It'll only take a second, I promise. Then we can get back to acting like sex-starved teenagers."

We get back to kneeling and straighten up what little clothing we have on, which is only underwear after all, and she tells me to go ahead and stick that finger into and up the fireplace. So I do and actually it's a bigger space than I thought and I can get two fingers up in there. She says "now pull your finger away from the wall," and I do and the wall above the fireplace snaps out in my hand, revealing a long vertical rectangular opening. It's deep enough to hide plenty of stuff, maybe intended to hide jewelry or something, but at the moment there's only a piece of paper in there. It's pink, probably from Sammie's private stock of correspondence stationary. It's one of the cards she writes thank-you's on, folded in half.

I look at her and say "can I leave you notes there, sometime, too?" and she grins wide and nods and says "Sure. So go ahead, Jackie-pants, open it."

I take the card out of the hide-space and open it and read slowly.

Hi, Jackie-pants!!! Whenever I need to tell you a secret

this is where I'll hide it for you!!! Always check this place

when you need to know what I'm thinking, OK? Right now

you should look around, cause when you find me you'll see

that I have a present for you!!!

So I look up and Sammie's not kneeling next to me anymore. I haven't even noticed that she's gotten up.

She's on the bed, she's naked, and she's not lying down with her head on the pillows. Her feet are on the pillows and her head is halfway down toward the foot of the bed. She's up on an elbow smiling at me.

"I've been thinking about doing this all day, Jackie-pants. Now drop those drawers and get over here!"

*   *   *   *   *

When we talk about it, she says "I don't know, Jackie-pants, I'm not sure I ever thought I'd get serious enough to get married, but here I am. Now I'm thinking we'd have a seriously good lookin kid, wouldn't we? I'm thinking going shopping together would be an unbelievable kick too, me dressed up like Belle? Her dressed like me when I was a kid? Cruisin Nieman-Marcus in Dallas or Saks in New York?"

So, from the time we talk about it, we stop using precautions for getting pregnant. We agree that it won't matter to either of us if we get pregnant any time. But as time goes on, Sammie's periods keep coming and we keep trying. For several years, we keep trying pretty hard.

We find a cool book that tells how to have sex if you want a boy, or the different ways, if you want a girl. We go for two or three months at a time, religiously following the instructions for one, then we go about the same amount of time for the other, and alternate back and forth. I think in general it's more work for Sammie and more fun for me because of the positions this book says work best depending on the sex of the kid we want.

You know, like for instance wait till you're horny, and the woman starts to ovulate, and have "deeper penetration" to make a boy, or have sex as many straight days as you can starting some number of days before ovulation to have a girl. Things like that. Oh, and for a girl Sammie couldn't have orgasms! Orgasms were bad for the sperms that would get us a girl! After four or five days of that, she wouldn't let me touch her or shower with her because she claimed she'd come if I even *walked* too close to her! So when we had sex, we had to get me "ready" before I could get anywhere near her and then try to just make a "deposit" - like a boy fish just drops his sperm in with the sack of eggs - so I wouldn't excite her! How strange is that?

Yeah, I enjoy much more trying to make a boy - many great ways and positions to be in to make sure we meet all the "requirements". If I was Fred K, I'd be laughing "haw haw haw," now.

But... nothing works.

After a few years we just go back to being married. I eventually quit my job at USAA because I let Fred talk me into going to work for him in his Data Processing department downtown, running his security group and helping code some upgrades to the applications he runs.

Sammie has already joined his Payroll group but is soon shifted to Payables and then Receivables and ends up running his whole Financial Accounting Department. Sammie talks salary with him and he winds up paying each of us twice what we're worth, which is OK with me.

Once Sammie rolls a copy of the Ten Commandments in our hiding place. We read them to each other and she says "where's rape?" and we laugh; once she writes me a four page note on paper from a legal pad about how pissed she is, having to get up "early" most every day and having to go to work.

Once we get so busy at work that a note I put in the hiding place goes unread for a week before Sammie thinks to check. All it says is

I love you, Sammie

So when she finally reads it she's really upset that she didn't think of checking for a week.

She insists on make-up sex for missing that note. I feel really good afterwards of course, so when we get in bed after cleaning up, I take her hand and squeeze it. I have swished a lot of mouthwash as I washed up, but I know she won't kiss me after, no matter what I do with my teeth. So we're both staring up at the ceiling, holding hands when she says "Let's go on another cruise, Jackie-pants. I need a vacation."

I think about it for a few minutes and she says "Maybe to the east this time? Like Jamaica, Key West, that sort of thing?"

"I don't mind," I say.

"You don't *mind*? What's *that* supposed to mean?" She has turned her head toward me. I can tell she's looking at me by the way her voice's volume increased as she asked the second question.

I can feel her eyes on me, but I'm still staring straight up. I'm thinking *Wait. This isn't fair. I should be drifting off to sleep now, not catching heat for saying something before I thought it through.*

"I didn't mean that, honey sweetie beautiful wonderful woman of mine, I meant 'Let's do it, it sounds like fun.'"

Now I'm looking back at her, smiling. She crinkles her eyes as she rolls them up in her head, letting me know she isn't buying the names I'm calling her or my story about what I meant. "OK, then! I'll call the travel people tomorrow and have them set it up." She reaches over and pecks me on the cheek. "G'nite, Jackie-pants!" she exclaims and turns to her nightstand to grab her sleep mask.

She's pretty damned proud of herself.

*   *   *   *   *

"I love that word, don't you Jackie-pants?"

I look over at her. We are sitting next to each other on the couch with the TV on. My hands are behind my neck and I am looking up at the ceiling. I'm thinking about a line of code I'd written that wasn't working. We've been home from the cruise for about two weeks.

"Shlub, Jack," she said impatiently, leaning forward to put her drink on the coffee table, "I said you are being a shlub, And I think you do it on purpose to piss me off."

"Hmm" I say. *I'm wondering if I put a period at the end of the sentence I inserted into the middle of that massive if statement I was messing with. If I did then the whole piece of the statement* after *the line is screwed up. I need to check that when I get in Monday. Maybe I should go in now and*

"*Shlu-ub*," she says in the God-damn-it voice.

"Yes, dear?" I ask, absently. I glance over at her and stop. Her honey blond hair is in a pony tail. She is wearing the dark pink sweats she's been in all day, but the zipper is now down between her breasts. Now I'm remembering this is Saturday and I've been sitting here thinking for several hours, and she's just returned from her workout. Her cheeks are flushed and her pale eyes are narrowed. She is glaring at me. Just looking at her knocks all thoughts of code out of my head. I lean toward her to kiss her. She smiles by the time I'm halfway to her and she puts a hand behind my neck as we kiss. She clamps her hand back there, and I know it's to keep me from making it a quick kiss, but I'm not minding at all. Her mouth tastes part Sammie, part vodka and orange juice. I hear the zipper going the rest of the way down.

*   *   *   *   *

We don't drive together very often, because she likes to leave the office at a normal time, no matter what's going on in her department. She has made a few exceptions over the years, but she mostly sticks with it - 6 o'clock and she out of there. I'm not as disciplined, I admit it. When I feel like something I'm working on needs to get fixed, I hardly ever leave till it is. It's like solving a murder mystery mixed with being involved in a spy ring to me, when I'm snooping around in the systems, checking code for errors, running the programs through different input scenarios to see how the results change, watching something I've tried suddenly get the correct results after I figure out the problem....

I guess church is about the only thing I refuse to push away when I'm hot on a project. Sunday mornings are becoming more and more important to me; it's gotten so that *God Blessing* everyone I can think of makes me feel good for the week between. Wish I could get Sammie to come with me more often and she should, as sour as she has become on her own work. I should mention to her how much better I'm able to handle Fred's bullshit now that I'm trying to get to church every week.

We are driving home together tonight. It's about eight and she's talking.

"...so, I'm going to start looking for something else. Have you heard anything? I think I'd rather bag groceries or park cars at the Club."

This signals that it's pretty serious, her naming maybe the two most demeaning jobs she can think of like that.

She changes the subject. "God, I could use about four drinks. Let's stop at the Club on the way home."

"Yes,dear," I say.

We glance over at each other and smile. Now we're looking back at the road and we just drive for a while. I've taken Broadway north out of town. I really don't like driving the freeways, too many crazy people driving. I take a right onto Hildebrand, so I can loop back to the entrance to the Club on New Braunfels.

I'm thinking this might not be the most pleasant meal I've ever eaten at the Club, Sammie's upset and flushed and not too forthcoming with why; she's going to drink to "unwind" while we're there and so she'll start calling them *drinkies,* and eventually I'll be trying to get her to talk softer when she begins telling me about all the people sitting around us. "Maybe we can call Belle and David to join us when we get there?" I ask.

She snorts. "You know David's in Corpus talking to that lawyer about selling *White Lightning* to Freddie the Jew, and Belle's probably already heading home from the Club after mahjong." *White Lightning* is an old Pearson 365 sloop that David bought and rebuilt a while ago, but, if not for Fred, would be sitting in dry dock in Corpus Christi.

"Why doesn't Fred just use it instead of buying the boat?"

"Freddie needs to own it, Jackie-pants, like he needs to own the mansion free and clear someday. You know that. That motherfucker...." I glance back over at her and she's looking out the window, shaking her head.

After a few minutes, she turns to me and says, "he also loves to just sit in her at the Marina, sit in the cabin and mess with the controls, maybe take some mechanical part on it apart and clean it and put it back together, cook, sleep, he loves the life, Paige says. She says it's the only time she sees him relaxed. When she goes with him, they pay Knowles extra to stay with Jesse, and Fred spends his vacation snorting coke and banging her in that boat. He keeps in touch with the office, but mostly that's where he relaxes, so he wants to buy it, he just needs to work a deal instead of paying for it. He's trying to work a deal that'll help David with his taxes, too, at least that's what he's telling David."

"What, do you think he's trying to get away with something, with *David*?"

As we pull into the driveway at the Club, she says "I don't know, Jackie-pants, but I told David to have a lawyer go over the papers for him. Now let's go get me drunk, y'hear?"

So we go in to the dining room. Belle is still in there and she waves. She's sitting with a woman I've seen her with many times before, Mrs. R. J. Belton. All the times Belle introduces this woman to me, I've never heard her first name, she's always RJ's wife. We walk over and say hi. The maitre d' is setting us up a table halfway across the floor at Sammie's request ("not too close please, Armand"), but we're spending some time standing at Belle's table, finding out what's good tonight.

Finally we head for our table and, as soon as we sit, I ask the question I've been waiting to ask: "So how much would a boat like that run - what is it, thirty feet long?"

"More like about forty, honey bunch. I'd bet with all the shit David and Freddie the Jew have added or replaced it's probably worth a couple mill by now.... Why, you want to buy it out from under Freddie, Jackie-pants? You don't really need to, he'll let us use it whenever he isn't."

"Nope," I smile, "I was just wondering. I don't even like sailing. It's much choppier than a boat with a big motor on it - that's my preference, that's why I love it when we take a cruise. I mean except for the medicine we both have to take to keep from getting seasick, of course."

"Yeah, I prefer smooth sailing too." She looks up at the waiter, who has been hovering. "Bring me two double vodka's with splashes of OJ. He'll have an iced tea." She points to me with her jaw as she says *he*. After the waiter leaves the table, she looks at me with a smile, takes my closest hand in one of hers, and says "so how are *you* doin', darlin'?" She bats her sexy blues at me from under the lashes.

* * * * *

I have two interviews tomorrow so I'm taking the day off.

Wake me when you get home tonight if you want a piece

of ass!!!!!

Normally a note like this would do more than cause me to chuckle as I read it, kneeling next to the dollhouse. I'm holding the note up so I can read it in the light from the hall. Sammie may wear a night mask, but she's a light sleeper so I try to be careful with noise and light.

I'm weighing my options. First, Sammie disappears tonight at the office - left me a note on her desk that she didn't want to wait for me. So she cabs home and leaves me the keys to her car. I figure she might be mad at me and I don't go to the show we were going to see, just head straight home. Even so it's almost midnight. Sammie's asleep on her back so her snoring is approaching chainsaw level. The empty glass by her side of the bed is now sitting next to what is, over time, becoming a standard: ice bucket and bottle of bourbon. I can't see much of her face because of the size of her sleep mask, but I'm sure she must be wasted and the last time we made love while she was drunk, she didn't remember it the next morning and, when she came out of the bathroom she asked me if we'd been fooling around the night before.

So I'm smiling but I'm going to pass, I guess. I fold up the note and snap the fireplace wall back in place. The snapping noise echoes in the room and Sammie makes a little mewing noise. "Uh?" she asks.

"Hi, love," I reply in a whisper, "you go on back to sleep."

She turns toward me and snuggles deeper into the bed. All I can see is a wild splash of blond hair and the mask and a smile poking out of the covers. Her whisper is louder than mine. "No sir, Mm awake now, you cain't get out of it."

"You sure? You think you'll remember tomorrow if we fool around tonight?"

"You bet, Jackie-pants. Mm aready naked n everthing. Rarin ta go." She's saying all this in a whisper and it sounds like she's maybe only half aware of what she's saying. Or maybe she thinks she's dreaming, I don't know.

"OK," I say and go to the bathroom. I get undressed and take care of my teeth. I would do all my teeth stuff anyway, but I use extra mouthwash tonight figuring it will overpower the breath coming out of her when I get in bed. I wash my hands and after they're dry I carefully open the door, in case she's fallen back asleep. The light is still on in the hall, so I go turn it off and close our bedroom door. I feel my way back to the bed. She is breathing heavily and from the noise I can tell she's facing back away from me and asleep. I spoon up behind her and she *is* naked, so I put my arm around her. When my hand rubs against her hand, I feel something wrapped around it. It could be a bandage from the feel of it. She mutters and pulls her hand away. I'll have to remember to ask her about that tomorrow, but right now her naked flesh feels *so* good to rub up against. I feel for the breast closest to the bed and slowly work it away from where it's half under her so I can cup it with my hand. She shifts slightly back and into me, and that frees it up for me. I bury my face in her hair and breathe whatever she's using to condition it. Nice.

The sun in the room hits my closed eyelids and wakes me up. I realize it's already early morning. I'm on my back, so I do a crunch and put my elbows under me. When I open my eyes and glance over, Sammie's not in the bed. Now *that* is unusual. This is way too early for her to be up unless we've been up all night or we're catching an early flight somewhere.

I slip out from my side of the bed and grab my clean underwear and head for the shower. When I open the bathroom door, Sammie's in there. She's still nude, but she's on the floor in front of the toilet, one arm up on the bowl, her forehead resting on that arm. When I open the door her head pops up and she smiles but her eyes stay closed. "I'm OK," she says, keeping the smile going. I can smell the vomit, though she must have flushed and cleaned up the area around her. "Good," I reply, "Can I turn on the light?"

"Could you wait on that please? I'm still a little nauseous and the aspirin hasn't really kicked in yet."

"Well... did you throw up before or after you took the aspirin?"

She doesn't answer me though I wait for a pretty long time, so I'm guessing she doesn't remember or most of the aspirin ended up flushed down the toilet when she was throwing up. I get two more out of the medicine cabinet, and grab the water bottle from the sink. "Think you can keep this down?" as I present her with the pills and bottle. She squints one eye open and sees what I'm handing her.

"Yeah, I think. Thanks, Jackie-pants," and she takes first the pills, then the bottle. "You go on and shower, I know you want to go to work. I'll be OK now, I think."

I turn on the bathroom lights and the vent right before I step into the shower, she's still slumped on the rug in front of the toilet, forehead down in the crook of her arm, that lush body slumped with one leg curled under her, her skin pale in the glare of the makeup lights over the sink.

When I'm halfway downtown I remember that bandage on her hand from last night. I need to remember to ask her about that today, except if she's interviewing, I probably should wait till tonight. I don't remember seeing it in the bathroom this morning, anyway.

*   *   *   *   *

Her right hand had to have been a red and purple mess, but she's taken care to clean the knuckles and restore a lot of order to what must have been pretty ugly right after she lost her temper. The knuckles look exactly like my hand looked after I popped a guy on our practice field the day before a football game back in high school. I know Sammie can be hot tempered, but the thought of her slamming her fist into her office wall is one step past where I ever thought she could go. I can't imagine anything Fred could say in a memo that would piss her off that much, but she's got no reason to lie. I'm telling her I'll look for an Anger Management class she can take, and she's looking at me with a strangely wry look on her face. "I'll take a class if it's not too expensive, OK Jackie-pants? Would you take it with me?"

I'm not sure why she'd want me to join her and my face must show it. She smiles and adds, "I really think it's silly, but if I can drag you along then I'll at least know one other poor slob who's stuck in the class with me!"

We are in the car, having another of those unusual days where she's gotten up early to drive into work with me. It's the day after she's recovered from her latest late night, so she tells me that's why she wants to work a full day today, because of the sick day she took yesterday.

I finally notice her hand, in the car this morning. In order to give the wound some air she has removed the gauze bandage roll she'd wrapped around her knuckles. She says she thinks she should just wrap it at night till it heals some more, because when she's sleeping it wakes her up whenever she brushes it against anything without the dressing.

We're on Broadway. We've just left the Jim's that I forced her to let me stop at; it's where I like to have some breakfast when I don't feel like cooking myself. I enjoy sitting at the counter, I read yesterday's *Express* while I eat, I have conversations with complete strangers like all Texans do, and the waitress who always seems to tend that particular Jim's counter calls me "sunshine" as I expect she does every regular who sits there on her shift.

I'm still holding Sammie's right wrist, and whenever traffic allows, I'm still looking at her hand. "Lucky you weren't wearing a ring on that hand when you hit the wall. Bet you'd have broken at least the finger and maybe had bone bruises."

"I think I have bone bruises, anyway. It really hurts like hell." She tries to flex her fingers and winces.

"So how about we get a doctor to look at it, love? For all you know there's a hairline fracture in there someplace."

"Oh please!" she sneers. "I'm alright, for God's sake! Let's at least wait till after the weekend. Then if it starts to show that it's healing, we'll know I'm going to survive. It already looks and feels better, don't you think?"

I can't argue with that because I can picture what it must have looked like originally, smashing a closed fist into a solid wall. What must she have been thinking? I mean she must have gone berserk if reading a stupid memo could have made her lose it like that.

"What was in the memo, exactly? Was it company wide and still in my in-basket?"

144

"Jackie-pants," she laughs, "it was just to Accounting, and if I explain it to you, you'll get your deer in the headlights 'huh?' look and I'd be wasting my time. I've already yelled at Freddie the Jew about it, so please, let's drop this now. If anything's going to get me back to being upset, it could be *you*, if you keep harping on this. I'm really OK. I promise."

I've glanced over at her while she's talking and she really does seem to be mildly amused at my concern, so I'm thinking I can probably quit worrying.

"OK, Sammie, I'll drop it, but let me know if it keeps hurting."

"Yes dear.

"Oh - My - God!! Did I just say 'yes dear'?" She has that wicked look on her face. "That's just more proof that I must *really* love you! I *never* thought I'd *ever* hear myself saying 'yes dear' to *anyone*! This is just like that Beatles' song, that *Amazed* one. Look out!" She puts her hand on my bicep and squeezes. "I feel a song comin on! Uh oh, uh oh, HERE IT COMES! HERE IT COMES!

"BABY I'M AMAZED AT THE WAY I LOVE YOU ALLA TIME, KISS YOU FOR A DIME, SOMETHIN SOMETHIN SOMETHIN SOMETHIN!!!" she sings at the top of her lungs, head back, eyes closed, *"Oooooh oooooh ooooooh oooooooh ooooooh oh...."*

She's in a strange mood today. The kind of mood that she seems to be in more often than not these days. As I drive, I reflect on my lot: lover, friend, brother, cook, father, nurse, maid, nursemaid.

*   *   *   *   *

I head home late from the office Saturday night, just thankful it isn't already tomorrow. I'm hoping Sammie's waited up for me even though she has to get up and drive to New Braunfels in the morning. If she isn't up, I'm dog tired anyway, and can use some sleep.

Driving north on Broadway, before I hit my left at Normandy, the whole northern horizon is darker than anywhere else in the night sky. Something must be going on with the weather for it to be that dark. Then I start seeing little flashes. Very distracting but some electrical storm must be passing to our north. I've seen a light show like this in Dallas; this is my first in San Antonio. There is no noise coming from it but eventually as I enter Alamo Heights, the whole northern sky is pitch black and sparking, silent the way you can't hear after an explosion. brilliant balls of lightning all over the horizon that should be followed by roaring thunderclaps, foreshadowing a storm that will never come. I turn onto our street.

I park my car and walk through the garage into the kitchen. The lights are on all over the house and I hear music coming from the bedroom. There's a half eaten sandwich on a plate by the sink. I look it over. Sliced ham, lettuce, tomato, relish spread on both bread slices where I'd have spread mustard. Typical for a lonely-Sammie dinner. There's also an empty bottle of Booker's next to the plate, so now I'm thinking maybe she's no longer awake. I clean up the plate, toss the bottle and head for the bedroom, hoping I at least don't have to stay up too late putting her to bed and turning off lights.

Everything's neat in the bedroom. First I check the dollhouse. No message behind the fireplace. I walk over to Sammie. She is passed out sitting up in the recliner. The TV's on. The table next to her has another bottle of Booker's, lying on its side. It appears maybe half full. Her glass has about an inch left in it. It looks watered down from melted ice. There's a pitcher of water and an ice bucket full of nothing but cold water next to the reclining bottle. When I pick up the bottle and place it on the table it makes a little *clink*, and she stirs. "Whuzzit?" she slurs.

"Jesus, Sammie, you're absolutely wasted aren't you?" I say as I turn off the TV.

She tries to peer around with squinted eyes. "Jackie-pan's? Izzat you ol' fren? Where the fuck ya bin all night?"

"Let's get you to sleep. Want any help getting up?"

Her eyes are already closed again and she appears asleep, so I get a nightgown out of her bottom drawer. I pull her t-shirt over her head and unsnap the bra. As it comes off she mutters something with the word *fuck* in it. She grabs my arm as I slip the nightgown over her head and tries to squeeze one of her breasts with my hand. She mutters something but I think she's mostly asleep again. I pull her arms through the nightgown and do a kind of fireman's carry to the bed. Wish I understood the sudden increase in her drinking volume the last few weeks; need to ask her about it the next time I catch her sober. After I swing her legs onto the bed I pull her shorts off. I put her dirty clothes away, and then take all her drinking stuff to the kitchen. When I get back she's still on her back, snoring quietly. Her hair's in her face. I lift her head gently, cupping the back of her neck, and pull her hair back with my other hand. When I lower her head back onto the pillow, she moans. I remember that the last time she did this she wet the bed sometime during the night, so I go get a long strip of toilet paper. I fold it up at the perforations and cup it on the fingers of one hand and raise the front of her panties with the other, pushing the toilet paper down inside. I'm forcing the paper down between her legs when she says "Mmmmm" and tries to grab my hand. I let go of the paper and push her hands away. She rolls over and is silent. I open the top drawer of her night stand and grab the black silk night mask and slip it down, first the band behind her head, and then the mask down over her eyes.

I check the clock and see she has set the alarm. I check the volume and I'm sure it's loud enough so I go get ready for bed.

I'm thinking I'll go to church in the morning. Pray for Sammie, Paige and Jesse like I've been doing. Light candles for our parents, Sammie's and mine. The sun will wake me up so I don't have to worry about a second alarm.

After I'm cleaned up I crawl quietly into the bed. She's facing the other way so I snuggle behind her and she makes a nice sound and pushes back into me.

I must fall asleep instantly because I don't remember anything until the light in my eyes wakes me up. I'm facing away from Sammie and her arm is across my chest. She's still dead to the world as I get up and head for the kitchen. I boil the water and set up the filter for my coffee and when it's ready I take it to the bathroom with me. When I'm ready to leave I walk over to the bed and check Sammie out. Her face is buried under her hair and her arm is over her head. She's facing my side of the bed, so I get under the covers with her and pull her leg over me as I kiss all over her cheeks and lips and nose to see if she'll wake up. She smells of bourbon and sleep and doesn't react.

I back my face away, but keep our bodies connected. She's still beautiful, her face lightly tanned, flushed from the sleeping and, maybe, from the drinking. On the other hand, her mouth is open as she breathes heavily and there is a wet spot on the pillow by her mouth. She's got a slightly sour body odor from the drinking. For some reason, I'm humming an old George Jones song. I mean, I don't think there's anything remotely similar between the song and my situation, but I've been singing it to myself since I woke up, About the guy with a wasted crush that doesn't end till he dies.

I lift her leg and push myself backward, out from under the covers. She doesn't stir. I walk to the bedroom door and pause, looking back.

*   *   *   *   *

"Both girls died immediately, Mr. Gantt. Neither was wearing a seat belt, and their automobile struck the concrete barrier underneath the overpass. In the case of your wife - sir, are you sure you want to hear these details? As I said, there's no need for you to identify your wife's body, or anything...."

I ask him to continue what he's saying. Although I'm shaking, I think I need to hear what he has to say. Pastor Franklin and some other people are in the room with us, the Pastor's hand on my shoulder. There are also some other policemen in the room, local from San Antonio and one from the highway patrol.

Sergeant Hartmann, Cholo, is talking to me. Fred reintroduced us years ago, but I also knew him from high school. I think Fred and Cholo have done business over the years, Chamber of Commerce stuff, I'm not sure. I am guessing Fred's in the building here too, maybe with his son Jesse. We weren't driven down here together.

Anyway, this is worse than anything I ever felt in Nam, this mind numbing feeling that I can't really hear very well, like a 155 howitzer has just been fired next to me. I've already been questioned by two officers from the highway patrol, describing for them several times, and in detail, my memories of my last twenty four hours with Sammie, then an old guy from the Medical Examiner's office talked to me for a while, then they led me and the pastor to this room where some of our friends from church were standing around. I'm getting a lot of sympathy from all these people and then Sergeant Hartmann comes in and starts talking about Sammie and Paige after everyone but the Pastor and me are led out of the room.

"Well... your wife struck the windshield hard enough to sustain a massive head injury, but because of the size of the automobile and in spite of the speed of the impact, neither woman was thrown clear. Both of them sustained massive internal injuries and the preliminary indications are that both deaths were instantaneous. She didn't go through the glass so that, should you want to see her I don't believe it would be as traumatic as it might be otherwise. There *is* some bruising, though...." *I'm having a hard time hearing this and keeping it together but I'm trying. This is the third time since I opened the front door to those policemen this afternoon that someone has told me Sammie's dead. But she can't be. Last night I came home and she was there and this morning she was warm in bed when I left for church. She can't be. Dead. What will I do? What* can *I do?* "I understand that the family normally uses a particular Mortuary in Alamo Heights, and they've been contacted, though no final decision has been made by the ME - by the Medical Examiner - as to whether an autopsy of your wife will be necessary.

"Pastor Franklin, here," and the Sergeant glances at the Pastor with a sympathetic smile, "will coordinate all that for you and your brother-in-law, I'm told.... Also," he looks back at me with an apologetic half smile, "we'd like to pick you up around ten o'clock tomorrow morning and drive you to our headquarters downtown for a formal interview and statement. Just a formality, I promise, but a necessary one. Would that be OK with you?"

"Yes, I suppose it would." I look around for someone from the Medical Examiner's Office, but all I can see now are the Pastor and men in uniforms "Can I speak to someone about seeing her -" As I say that, I feel tears surfacing, but I stop talking and choke them back. I'm about to say I want to see her now, but I probably can't say it without choking up again.

Pastor Franklin squeezes my shoulder and I look over at him. He's an old guy, his hair is bright it's so white, and the hair in his eyebrows are bushy, with errant hairs pointing all over the place. He has kindly brown eyes that are smiling at me sadly now. "We should probably go back to the front office where we came in, once Sergeant Hartmann says we can go, Jack. We can ask them there, about seeing Samantha. If you don't mind I'd like to be there too, with you....?

"Of course, Pastor."

* * * * *

It isn't one of those TV scenes with a freezing room and a wall of drawer doors, where a technician looks up a name on a rolling index, finds the right drawer and pulls it open, throwing the sheet off a face.

Pastor Franklin and I follow the Medical Examiner himself into a room that maybe looks like an operating room in a hospital except that there are several desks along with the table, which is not in the center of the room, but off to one side. There is a soft hissing sound coming from the ceiling and it is *cold* in here.

She is lying on the table, with a sheet over her. I can already tell it's her, just from the profile her face makes under the sheet.

In answer to the question that I asked as we approached the room, the ME is saying, "Yes, we will probably perform an autopsy on your wife's sister, simply because of the suspicious nature of the accident: possible hit and run, no witnesses, etcetera. If we autopsy Mrs. Klien, we will probably also do a cursory one on your wife."

The cold seems to be starting to get to me, as I nod. I'm thinking about an autopsy; I'm a little shaken thinking about it, these people who don't know her....

Now my teeth start chattering a bit so I try to clamp down on my jaw, thinking the ME and Pastor Franklin will hear the noise.

I guess the ME's waiting for me to come closer or nod at him or something, but I don't know what to do. I don't know if I want to get closer, or nod, or walk quickly out of the room. I've forgotten about my teeth and relax my jaw. My teeth start chattering but I'm nodding at the man and he's pulling back the sheet. He pulls it gently down from her face to just below her throat, and folds it carefully down. A second sheet partially covers her hair so that I can only see the first inch or two.

She looks asleep, but she's so white. I can't see any damage to her face, maybe a small scratch on her forehead. There is an odd cast to her forehead as I look more carefully, almost purple, disappearing into her hairline. Her hair looks wet; it's combed back and must be pillowed under her head and neck. Her face... is so... beautiful. Her eyes are closed of course and her cheek bones are still... actually they do have a bit of color. She has no make-up on and her face looks very clean. The cool slope of her nose is there and she looks so relaxed. I don't remember the last time I saw her so relaxed. No smirk playing across her lips. Those perfect, beautiful lips. I can almost hear her talking, even now. Saying *I love you* to me, that smile flirting over her lips.

Oh my God. Oh sweet Jesus.

I really cannot stand up. I realize before I even think that I can't stand up, I'm already on my knees, my hands on the edge of the table next to the sheet covering her arm. I'm rocking, my face is down, looking at the floor, I may be about to vomit, I'm not sure. Slowly I start to get control back and the rocking slows. I look up, toward her face again. I blink the tears standing in my eyes and feel them trickling their way down to my chin. From here her nose and chin stand out in relief from the pale green wall behind her. Pastor Franklin's hand remains on my shoulder. My shoulders shake as I try unsuccessfully to hold it in. I clear my throat which starts me coughing, and I stand up quickly and bend over, trying again and again to clear my throat and stop the choking.

Eventually I can breathe clearly and I'm not crying any more. The Pastor holds me in his arms and I'm staring at the wall, dry eyed. Eventually I push him away. I lean over her and look at her again. She's always been so pretty.

I remember we fought recently about me wanting us to move. She had asked *where the fuck to* and I said I didn't care, L.A., Seattle, Dallas, somewhere mainframe computers are, and she said *Why? You can do anything you've ever wanted to do, you don't need to work with computers, God damn it.* I think I just shook my head, giving up. Later, she'd come over and sat on my lap on the couch. *Kiss me, Jackie-pants* she had vamped, teasing me with that low voice and those eyes fluttering.

Come here, Jackie-pants

I realize I will never hear her call me that again, ever again. *Jackie-pants. I love you, Jackie-pants.* When we were first engaged, I'd thought how lucky this was, the way it had turned out. *And they lived happily ever after.* I never really felt comfortable that it had ended up with *her* wanting *me,* with *her* marrying *me,* that guilt some people feel when things work out absolutely perfectly. But, as our time together lasted longer and longer, she slowly changed, and I felt helpless in the face of it. God knew I'd wanted to help her, but I didn't know how and just being there for her was obviously not enough. Maybe it was the work we were doing; maybe it was her not being able to get pregnant, maybe it was the drinking. She was becoming more... edgy... more... dangerous... the more time we were together, to herself and to the people who loved her.

153

Pastor Franklin is walking me out of the room.

*　　*　　*　　*　　*

Pastor Franklin tells me it will be cathartic for me to give Sammie's eulogy. He thinks sitting in the front row with Fred and the Barnes clan all over me will be worse if I don't have something to keep my mind off all the eyes poking me. I absolutely do not want to speak, everyone waiting for me to break down, but he's probably right.

So I have two things that I'm spending all my time on. The eulogy and deciding what I'm going to do now. It doesn't occur to me that I've got to figure out what I'm going to do the rest of my life until I go in for a second interview with Sergeant Hartmann. When we finish and I walk out of Police Headquarters downtown, Fred is walking in. He is with a guy in a suit and introduces him to me as his lawyer, but I'm not paying attention so I miss his name. I don't have anything to say to these guys, but I don't want to cut them off, so we talk for a while about the interviews and the funeral. I feel a guilty relief that at least the deaths mean I won't need to see Fred anymore or have to put up with his bullshit, now that we aren't really related. Then the lawyer asks "Have you thought about the will and how you'll handle your part of the inheritance, Mr. Gantt?"

That really shocks me. I know it's hard to believe but it hasn't occurred to me that there will be an inheritance. Fred looks at me, at the expression that must have been on my face, and he laughs, *haw haw haw*. "You'll be seeing a lot more of me, Jack," he says with a grin, "we'll have things to go over all the time, now. I mean, we can get all the holdings settled during probate."

He turns to his lawyer. "Wilson, can you represent us both for this?" His lawyer shakes his head and says something about a conflict of interest, then turns to me and hands me his card. "If you'd like, call my office and we'll give you some recommendations for one."

You'll be seeing a lot more of me, Jack.

Oh my God, he is right. This could go on forever. I've got to get out of this. I'll do anything except give him everything. The thought that everything David Barnes loved would wind up in the hands of Fred K turns my stomach. I have already started thinking about assigning whatever I end up with to some kind of trust that could just give me an allowance or something, I don't know but I decide I can get a lawyer and an accountant to figure it out. Getting away from this place and Fred has become almost a panic to me as I think about it.

Blue paint on the bashed-in passenger side of that yellow car, the papers all say. No proof, but *murder* is whispered on every page. And how can I think of anyone but him, if it's true?

I'm also pretty sure that I'm packing up and leaving town as soon as I can after all this is over. The only things keeping me here are the will, deciding where to go, and the funeral.

And that damn eulogy. I don't want to write it, but half of it is already written in my head.

* * * * *

I concentrate on looking down at the pages I've written. Then I lick my lips, clear my throat and begin.

"My wife was born into a family that epitomizes what is Texas. From Matthew Barnes to Samantha Franklin Barnes runs a straight line of outstanding, successful, and courageous people, Texans. Americans. Matthew, Jesse, Barlow, David, Samantha. Proud people, people who have helped shape San Antonio, and through this city, Texas.

"Sammie was as smart as she was beautiful. She was Most Likely to Succeed, and Most Popular in high school. She was selected a National Merit Finalist, but she really downplayed how gifted she was intellectually. She had a wonderful sense of humor and if she'd wanted to she could have been a successful athlete - I know because I had a hard time keeping up with her on a handball court.

"I've been in love with Sammie since we were freshmen in high school. I can't imagine why she married me, but I've felt myself to be the luckiest man in the world to have shared part of her life, these last years of hers. And through her, her late parents, Belle and David, and also Paige, my sister-in-law. Sammie and her sister drove the Austin Highway up to the Smokehouse once a month to share their lives with each other, and they did that to the end. Sammie loved her... and she loved that potato soup, she really did.

"Before Sammie agreed to marry me, she'd gotten her Bachelor's Degree at Wellesley College and then received her Master's in Accounting from there. I found out later that while I was overseas she was offered a scholarship to a school in England but turned it down to be with me when I came home.

"She had a true gift for balance sheets and P&L, and ran the family's affairs most of the last few years. Paige's husband wanted me to say how much he came to depend on her input, not only for running the Accounting Department, but also for running the day to day operation of the business.

"One of her few disappointments was not having children. She so wanted a baby girl. She once told me she

156

dreamed of shopping with a little girl, and I would like to think that we would eventually have brought some kids into our home. She would have made them very happy to be there. Sammie practiced for that day with her nephew, Paige's son Jesse.

"When this accident… when this accident happened, the shock to the Barnes clan was felt across the state. Texas itself grieves for her, for her and her sister. The condolences and charitable contributions have poured in from across the state, and literally from across the nation. *We* all thank *you* all so very much for having us in your prayers these last few days. It is such a tragedy that women so young have been taken from all of us; and for Sammie to have been taken from me and the rest of the family.

"Sammie was a special woman, but she was also just like the rest of us. She had many many strengths, and a few weaknesses too. She lived.... She lived her life each day. Her gift to me, to us, was being with us, sharing what she was with us. Her talents, her humor. Her looks.

"I would like to think that Sammie and Paige and Paige's little girl... ...are together now, and that they walk along together. Sammie is carrying the baby for Paige. She has the baby giggling, making funny faces at her, and she and Paige are holding hands as they walk along a sunny road together, talking and laughing...."

I return to my seat on the front row. I hear sobs behind me. I'm barely holding it in myself. I'm on the aisle and young Jesse is between me and Fred. Jesse puts his hand on my arm and squeezes but when I look over he is looking straight ahead and tears are on his cheeks. When it comes time for me to follow the casket up the aisle, all I can think is when Sammie and David walked arm in arm down the same one, Sammie beaming up at me through her veil. Now I'm following her out for the last time.

I'm missing her terribly, the thought of never seeing her again like a gigantic weight on me. I also can't stop wondering what really happened on the highway that day. As I walk, I feel the physical presence of Fred behind me. I remember how Sammie changed slowly over time after we started working for him. I changed too: as Sammie chose drink, I took solace in the church. I should have said something. I should have done something.

V - CHOLO

I'm driving back to the office after my two and a half hour lunch with Fred K, wondering what it is about men that make them so different from each other. This asshole, me, and his brother-in-law Jack Gantt for instance. I can't imagine an upbringing much more potentially damaging to a kid than mine, but Fred's an amazing example of twisted, so I wonder about how he was brought up. And what's happened along *his* way.

We run into Jack as we're walking into the restaurant and Fred introduces us. I remind Jack about knowing him in high school, but I don't bring up the football stuff. He nods like his mind is somewhere else. He and I could have a contest, trying to out-quiet each other. He seems like a nice guy, which brings me back to his opposite, Fred.

How much of his personality is inherited, how much is drummed into him by Mummy and Daddy. I mean he says he came from poor people like I did, but were his poor people unhappy like mine, give-a-shits like mine, off in their own little world like mine? I give a lot of credit to Peggy for how I seem to be turning out, but dammit, there had to be something in me, some, I don't know what to call it - "wellspring"? - of something burbling way down in there that maybe would never have been tapped if she didn't tap it, but there had to be something down in there, right? So is that in everybody and Mr. K's is waiting for someone to come along and point at it, or is what he is not equipped with the same... potentials... that I came with? Of course I don't have any answers, and I'm not even sure Fred is worth asking the questions, tell you the God's truth. But there is something about him gets you to listen anyway, if you can pick your way through the bullshit, the real live bullshit that's coming out of this guy.

I mean, he's a very important guy, right? It isn't easy to separate the crapt from the truth, listening to him, but I did some homework so I recognize at least some of the bullshit, some of the truth. OK, so he's married to a Barnes and they have a son, born "early" in the marriage. He hardly knows me and he's joking about deciding to buy the cow and stop getting all that milk for free; but that's OK he says, because now he can just leave her in a stall whenever he feels like going out, a stall in the back of the mansion, haw haw haw. What an asshole, right?

He says he wants us to just get to know each other. He tells me about all my "daring exploits" in the Department, I guess so I'll know he knows, and then asks me to tell him about my family which I do. I talk for quite some time, as a matter of fact. Him asking good questions along with pitching in some sarcastic comments, some funny, some would piss me off if I let them. The subject never comes up about much detail of the life I led between high school and the law, but I did get in that I worked at the gas station for a few years. Then he tells me about himself, a little about him being raised in Houston and about his parents, he brags about racing some cars and getting fucked up in his last race. Coming to San Antonio, getting into the real estate market here, and selling the little computers you can put together and have in your house. He throws in that he could give me one for the kid (he calls Lucy "the kid" because there's no way he's remembering her name or even Peggy's) so she can play games on it. I tell him I'll let him know and he nods and goes on talking about how rich he's getting to be. I'm thinking *is this idiot going to ask me to be his bodyguard or some such bullshit?* but he doesn't go anywhere near that kind of thing. He just keeps on describing his "empire" and throws in, of all things, some weird remark about how big his dick is, for God's sake. Like it's a cross to bear, along with all the money. Then he laughs that disgusting laugh of his. How can you not be attracted and repulsed at the same time by a guy like this?

And he's "interested" in me, he says. The last half hour of our meal, while I let him pay for it and watch him upside down throw in a gigantic tip on the credit card slip he fills out, he spends telling me he's gonna watch me on my assignment on the east side, which he calls the Jungle to let me know he knows the jargon. He says after the speech I gave, he admired how comfortable I looked up there, and how inspired he thought I got the crowd. But when he says that, he lets his eyes roll up in his head so I'll know *he* wasn't taken in by it, and I guess he also meant he didn't think I was either, even though I was, I believed what I was saying one hundred and ten percent, but I'd never tell *him* that. He says he's been following my career and will continue to, and I'm silently wondering *why's my career worth following?* He wants to know people, he says. He arches a brow at me. I'm almost expecting one of those fucked up hardee har har laughs out of him but he just looks at me in a meaningful way with one eyebrow up. *Jesus* I'm thinking, *what's he expecting me to say, thank you for wanting to know me?* I mean what kind of homo thing would that be to say?

Two days later Peggy answers my checking-in call and asks me who Fred K is. I want to know why is she asking and she says that's the name on the return address on the big box was just delivered, addressed to Miss Lucy and Mrs. Peggy Hartmann. It has one of those new Personal Computers in it, with a card taped to the top of it says call this number for free installation and unlimited lessons on how to use it.

*   *   *   *   *

I get another call from Fred K. He says he wants me to speak to the Chamber and he wants to talk to me about some ideas he has. That's exactly how he says it, "some ideas I have."

I never thanked him properly for the computer, but Peggy and I talked about it and decided what the hell, it wasn't like taking a bribe. Besides, there were so many pluses to keeping it. The really good thing about it was how much it benefited Lucy, especially with the training she got. We called the people the note said would teach how to use the damned thing, who came over when we called. Peggy even puts our household finances on it. Now she can print spread sheets off whenever she needs to lecture me on my spending. I never felt like I needed to be careful about how it would look to I.A. or whoever if questions ever came up, and as far as Mr. K was concerned, I planned on being consistent with my enforcement of the law, just like I'd promised those old boys back at my initial interview.

It's strange with Fred, I'm thinking. I'm interested and repelled by him at the same time. He's a very influential guy, he screams big bucks and power, but he's also got this way about him of not being straight, kind of a sleaze. It is odd.

Anyway, I tell him I can see him today if he has time and he says sure, how about lunch? So we meet at the restaurant in the Menger Hotel right next to the Alamo downtown.

"Hi, Cholo," he says, like we're old buddies. Hugging me, I always forget how short he is until he's standing next to me, he acts so big when we're on the phone. Or when he's interviewed by the papers for some project or other he's working on, making big bucks. "Hello, Mr. K."

He haw haw haws and says "when are you going to relax and start calling me Fred again, Cholo?" Big smile. *Never*, I'm thinking, *Just when I first met you that day.*

This dining room is special and fancy. Everything's white except the flowers and plates. Eight fancy columns inside the room. The staff is all over the place keeping glasses full, pulling out chairs, taking away used plates.

We order. I'm in the middle of trimming my weight so I order a cup of tortilla soup and the house salad with oil and vinegar. The menu says they do the soup with beef instead of chicken, but I guess that's OK as long as it's spicy. The menu also says I better let Fred K pay the bill if he offers.

"So I saw your latest escapade in the *News* a few days ago. It's like you attract excitement and danger. Like those scars you carry," he nods in the direction of my eye. "I like that. Of course, I'd shit my pants if it ever happened to me." This he says kind of loud and I have to admit I'm embarrassed for him; I'm looking around at the well heeled business people sitting around us. They've got to be hearing this, aren't they? No one is staring so maybe not.

"It was just a lucky thing, Mr. K. I stumbled into the right place, lucky I said the right things and the bad guys did what I asked. That photo...." I shook my head, like I thought it wasn't a good thing it made the paper. If someone could make me tell the truth, I am starting to get a swelled head about it, and about my rep, too. "It's also lucky my bosses think I'm good publicity for the department, or I'd be out on my ear."

He smiles and leans forward, kind of like a snake or something with those puffy eyes, and says "Oh I wouldn't worry about that too much. You have the attention of a lot of people, like even in the Chamber. Matter of fact that's one of the things I wanted to talk to you about, Cholo. Later we can brainstorm a topic for a speech I'd like you to give at next month's meeting, but for now I just want to explain I want you to get experience speaking to these kinds of people. I honestly see a future for you that I got the idea for when you spoke on the eastside. But this is a different set of folks, the Chamber of Commerce, and I think it could really round you out, making a speech there."

I start to say something about not being too excited about speech-making, but he waves me off and says "you don't have to decide right now about that, we're talking next month anyway.

"What I really wanted to mention to you is an opportunity that has come my way and I want you to get in on it too. Want to hear about it?"

"Well, what does 'get in on it' mean exactly? I'm a cop, Mr. K."

"Of course you are, Cholo. You mean is it *legal* for shit's sakes? You got to be fucking *kidding*, man; I'd try to rope *you* into something illegal? I'd have to be fucking nuts! You'd have my balls off and up my ass before I could turn around!" I'm looking around again; his voice is raised and there is a woman dressed in a business outfit at the next table staring at him. I lean forward. "OK, Mr. K so tell me what you *are* talking about."

He leans back and changes his look to serious. "OK, so every once in a while I come across... what I'd call a business opportunity. I can always just invest my money, the family money, into this kind of thing but I don't. Usually I create a little company of investors to get into them. On the plus side for me, this allows me to spread the risk. You know what I mean?"

"Yeah, more people lose but *you* don't get hurt as much."

"Well, we don't *each* get hurt as much, Cholo," he smiles. "But man, I never lose. Never. I mean this isn't my first rodeo. My father-in-law is making money hand over fist on these investments and I'm almost as scared of him as I am you! Haw, haw, haw."

I just look at him till he starts to show he's getting uncomfortable, so now I say "OK, so what are you talking about exactly and what makes you think I can afford *any* kind of investment?"

He practically bounces in his chair and starts rubbing his hands together he's so eager to tell me. Oily little shitface.

"OK, see, this investment is so safe it's crying. I already own the property, that is, my *family* already owns it." He says 'family' like that means the same thing as 'Fred K'. "All I'm doing in this deal is rezoning this city block because I'm pretty sure there's a strip mall waiting to be built there. Big nationwide investors who like to build these drive-up, outdoor malls have been sniffing around in the area and this block is right in the middle of where they're interested. I want to sell you and a few friends part ownership in the land. When it sells you get paid back in the same percentage you buy in. In this case," he leans back again, this time spreading his arms like he's Buddha or somebody, "you really can't lose because if I'm wrong and they don't bite, I'll just buy back your investment dollar for dollar. Understand? No harm, no foul?"

I'm thinking. Rezoning bothers me. Part ownership makes no sense at all. He already owns the land? Or is he making payments that I'm going to be helping with?

"Well look, I have to get back to work and I would have a bunch of questions to ask before I'd ever be able to get involved. Why don't I just pass on this one and maybe sometime later something might come up, we might do some business?"

"Cholo, I figured you might not be able to just jump into something like this, you're not that kind of person, right? That's why I picked this particular deal to offer you, see? We'll meet again after I get the whole thing set up, the City Council Committee does the rezoning bullshit, the Council votes, *then* we maybe talk again, you and Peggy could join Paige and me for a nice dinner at the Club or something like that? The beauty of this is there isn't a big rush. OK? Will you think about it? Please?"

He's smiling like a used car salesman. I can't think of a reason to say no, so I say "We'll see, Mr. K, all I can promise you is that if you bring this up again, and you can show me how I can actually afford to do anything with you, then Peggy and I will need to hear and understand everything about it. OK?"

He looks as if he's already won the deal as he stands up. The food's great, by the way. Beef in the tortilla soup makes it "interesting," and he has picked up the check.

"Cholo," he says, sticking out his hand for a shake. I make it firm enough to hurt, though I'm not sure why. "Thanks for lunch, Mr. K."

He winces from the hand shake and maybe from me not calling him Fred. "We'll hash this out with our wives some day soon. So long."

I smile and he heads toward the hotel lobby and I walk off toward the parking lot outside. I drive off, wondering what that was really all about, and figuring I probably know.

Dammit, I forgot to thank him for that PC.

*   *   *   *   *

"Well, we can sure as hell afford it now."

Peggy's speaking. The salesman has excused himself and walked off with one of the other couples wandering around. It's open house Sunday in Alamo Heights. We are in the third house we've looked at and it's not even noon yet. Lucy's off in Nebraska at some national volleyball all-star exhibition.

"Right?" she asks.

We're seriously looking at houses. Even with Lucy in her last few years at home. Peggy said it to me like this. "Even if she never comes home again, which you know she will, I want to live in a nice place once in my life, Cholo. And what if she starts a family sooner or later? How will we get her to visit if we don't have a nice place?"

"They have really nice hotels in San Antonio, that's how."

"OK, OK," I have to put my hands up to stop the yelling when I say that. "I suppose you're right, Peggy, OK? You set it up and I'll go this weekend."

So here we are and this house is affordable with the net from what we got out of Mr. K's venture, so she's right, why the hell not? Not gigantic, but a nice house in a great neighborhood - big bedrooms upstairs, bathrooms all over the place, just across Olmos Dam from a lot of nice shopping, and a roomy den area downstairs.

The realtor, not knowing we already live in Alamo Heights, explains that because the zip code is 78209, San Antonians refer to people living here as Oh-Niners as if this house would put us in the upper crust. I remember my mother calling us Oh-Niners sarcastically. I can imagine snobs in New York and L.A., even Atlanta and Dallas - but San Antonio? Oh-Niners?

I know Peggy's in love with the formal living room because she's already put some cash down on that upright piano she's been wanting since the age of 6, when she first learned how to play. Plus her books are stacked in five foot piles in a closet in our old place, so these built in bookcases have her saliva running, too.

"So let's put in an offer, huh Cholo?" she's looking at me, measuring the look on my face.

"I'd like to, Lambchop, I really would. You sure we can afford it?"

"Damn it, you know we can! Especially when you let Mr. K forgive the loan he made to us. Hell, we made enough to pay back my parents and sink a battleship. Can you just imagine? Lucy can work out here, in that room over the garage. I know you want to stay at the gym but she and I can work out together here. Plus this formal living room and all the closet space and"

"For God's sake, Peggy, *all right*! Get the man over here before you have a damned stroke."

*   *   *   *   *

Peggy has seared some thick pork chops and put them in the oven to bake. She has Lucy making a salad and I'm adding syrup and bacon to a couple cans of baked beans. The rich smells of the chops are all around the kitchen, and I'm sure the rest of our new house will be smelling like the old one soon. This double oven and the exhaust system over the stove take no getting used to, that's for damn sure. Really nice, you know? Glad I asked for this vacation, too, moving in and all. The piano came from the store yesterday, Peggy played for us. Last night was our first night in beds, before that we were a few nights in sleeping bags.

I grab plates and silverware and we put out all the food and dig in after a prayer.

We're all pretty busy, but Lucy and Peggy are talking softly about some school project. I listen a bit but I'm mostly just taking all this in.

The house has become friendly through the last few days. The more of our stuff came in, even the things we had to buy to kind of fill up the place's empty spots, the more friendly it got. It isn't curtains so much as it is pictures taking up space on the walls and mantel that makes this place seem like it's our home now, already. The wall colors are on the dark side which makes it seem peaceful to me. The lighting isn't too bright and I like that, too.

I guess for an active guy this is like the caveman's cave you come home to, to rest up in before you go kill your next meal, you know? And Peggy and Lucy seem real, real happy here too. They both glow while we're eating and they talk; softness is in the voices they use.

And Peggy came to me last night, just a few minutes after we kissed and turned out the lights. I was just lying there, quiet and relaxed after two full days not thinking about the job, not getting any calls, my beepers and radios and work phones all left at the office, Lieutenant's orders. I was happy, letting myself relax after all the moving in, all the unpacking we'd done, maybe even dozing already, lying on my back, my hands under my head. She rolled over and against me in our new bed, in our new home. She was calm and silent but I could feel heat rising from her. She came to me and kissed me and I turned to her and she helped me open her up, took me with her hands while I took her with mine, letting desire quickly build between us till she rolled me back over on my back, got on top, started moving us, almost quick, almost like she'd been getting ready for this while we worked together all day. She buried her face in my neck, growling and moaning and holding me really tight until she slowed, and I completely forgot about me while all of that was going on, you know?

So we're eating and they're talking and I'm remembering the night before and so I reach over and squeeze Peggy's hand. She continues with what she's saying but she glances over at me and smiles at what she sees on my face and squeezes my hand back, before she looks at Lucy and listens to what she is starting to say.

I fold my hands in my lap and lean back into the straight backed chair I'm sitting in. The room we're in looks nice I'm thinking, as I glance around. Then I picture the other rooms around us, and then the house itself around the rooms. The yard, the grass and trees and hedges and flowers. What we own now, this is the *where* and the *what* that we've come to. I'm not a man to feel peaceful without there's some uneasiness under it somewhere, but this is as close as I can get to comfortable. Hard to describe it, but the girls are finally getting up and starting to take things into the kitchen, still talking to each other.

I kiss Lucy's cheek, the back of Peggy's neck. They are talking about algebra, sounds like.

I go back and sit in my chair in the dining room, still feeling pretty damned full of myself, the smells from dinner, the clicking of silverware and chatter from my women coming from the kitchen. I think how far I've come. I have tears in my eyes, I swear.

But it's ironic, you know? It's like a Greek tragedy, the chorus telling the story, the feeling of doom, too much good foretelling something bad could be coming. I can't help but think of Fred K, like some festering *thing* out there. Ahh, I'm just thinking like a goddam cop or something.

*   *   *   *   *

Chief Torres calls me at home one Saturday. He wants me to consider joining his inner "team" by *allowing* him to promote me to Lieutenant. *Christ sakes*, I almost remind him, *seems like I'm a Sergeant for just a few years*! Of course I don't say it, him being Chief. He reminds me about the success of my work with what the papers are calling *Cholo's Gang* on the eastside, so it isn't much of a stretch him thinking of me as being promotable, at least that's what he says. I'm not uncomfortable thinking there may also be some outside influences at work here. He also says he's already gotten the approval of his Commanders, which means the Captains, and also from the Mayor. *Christ sakes*, I'm still thinking.

Inside, I'm getting used to this pretty fast, but I wonder out loud to him that since I'm so comfortable - and good - at being a line officer, *then why would I want to do it?* He mentions a few things like my probably not having to stick my neck out much any more, and my salary would be about double what it is now. I try not to pause too long, hearing that, when I say maybe I *like* sticking my neck out, maybe I don't. *How about the politics?* I ask, and he says he gets appointed, and no Lieutenants have ever been thrown out with an old Chief that he's ever heard of. He laughs when he says that. I ask him can I think about it and he says he's got the other two Lieutenants in the north splitting the shift I'd be responsible for. *They are going to crash and burn if I don't make a decision by the end of the month*, he says. *They know you're being asked to join them so you're welcome to talk to them about it, too.*

I tell him *OK, I'll talk to them, if I decide I'm interested.* And he says again he can give me till the end of the month which I say sounds reasonable to me. He says there are people high up who are very interested in me, in getting me "up the ladder." I thank him and tell him to thank them, whoever they are, city councilmen or whoever, but I'm not sure yet the job is something I want to take on.

First thing I think when I hang up is that I might be boss to some people I've worked with over the years, probably even some men I interviewed with back in the day. Funny. Then after I think about it some more maybe I should be calling Fred, thanking him for what he's been doing behind the scenes.

I may not like him being the man who can have the kind of power needed to pull this off, but I am more and more liking the thought of becoming a leader in the SAPD. He's still a slime ball, but....

I'm also thinking about Torres' admin, the one with the legs, the one he's had read to the press a few times. I will need an admin if I take this promotion, and she'd be good. We've gotten along, the few times we've worked on something together. I don't even remember her name for sure - Doreen, maybe.

Captain Hodges is the Commander who oversees the operation these other two Lieutenants and I would be splitting into thirds. Now *his* job would be even more of a challenge.

*   *   *   *   *

Chief Torres, Captains Hodges, Arriaga and Bowman and their wives, Sergeant "Charlie the Chunk" Briscoe and his wife Elizabeth, a couple other old friends of Peggy's including Beth and Ron the cop, Peggy of course, the mayor of San Antonio and his wife, for God's sake, other people I've never seen, dressed up like nobody's business, the San Antonio Country Club, oh and Paige and Fred K, with Mr K acting like the party's for him which, what the hell, maybe it is.

I'm pretty sure the promotion was pushed by him and of course I'm grateful, I mean who wouldn't be? But I'm also keeping my feet on the ground. I owe Peggy a debt more than anyone.

"You've had an unbelievable career, Lieutenant Hartmann," the Chief is saying. Peggy's arm is squeezing my bicep through the coat while he talks to me. "And I'm comfortable thinking you have a long way to go before you're finished." He looks around and smiles at everyone listening. "You know, even I will have to retire someday!" Everyone else laughs, I smile and look at Peggy and she's blushing and looking around at them all, all these people. I'm really soaking this in and I'm sure Peggy is too.

These people are all drinking pretty hard, too. We are holding waters, water with lemon squeezed in. I'm trying to keep an eye on Charlie the Chunk because he's a two-fisted drinker, but I can see Elizabeth's doing a good job slowing him down. As a matter of fact I'd be more comfortable if I'd ordered a Lone Star myself, but I passed on that. I figure I can loosen up when we get home.

The speeches are over and people are breaking into smaller groups. Peggy squeezes my arm one more time and walks over to Paige K. They head for the ladies room, laughing at something Peggy has whispered in Paige's ear.

Captain Hodges and his wife are standing with me and Hodges is telling me he's looking forward to having me on his team. I'm nodding and thanking him for the opportunity. He and Chief Torres cooked up the new structure for the Detective Bureau that has opened up things for my promotion.

"It really started," he's saying, "With a visit from your friend over there, Fred K."

I'm surprised and say "Really?"

"Yeah. He and a few of his cronies from the Chamber suggested we centralize Major Crime. Can you imagine a citizen's group getting involved that way? If it hadn't made sense, of course, it would have been easy to dismiss, but I liked it and so did the Chief."

"I guess it was good for me, too," I say, feeling like I have to say something.

They laugh like I'm delivering the punch line to a good joke and thank God some other people join us and the conversation moves away from being about me.

I can see Peggy and Paige head back into the room and pick up Fred as they come. They join the group I'm in and Fred says something to me, but I don't hear it over the laugh coming after one of the Captain's wives says something. So I just smile and nod at Fred K, and he seems comfortable with that.

He must have said something about the food being ready because everyone starts drifting toward the dining room.

Good. I'm starved.

* * * * *

When I get in bed tonight, the lights have probably been off for three, four hours. Peggy sleeps through me pulling myself down, under the covers.

I lie here, listening to her breathe for awhile. I'm thinking about I'd like to wake her up, man. I'm thinking... well, you know what I'm thinking, but she's asleep. I close my eyes and relax, but I can't sleep. I'm just lying here, hot. Tired from the day. I can't stop my mind from wandering. Fred K is pushing me for a favor, I hear Peggy breathing softly, and something strange happened on the job today. I had to go downtown, got called in by the Chief for an Eastside planning session. Had to wait for awhile and there was that Admin again got me coffee.... There is something about her. I mean she wasn't dressed sexy at all, don't get me wrong. Really pretty though, and really sharp. She didn't give me a look or anything, strictly business. But there was just something strange there, I felt some weird kind of something between us. Hell, I didn't even catch her name when the Chief's other Admin introduced us, but I'm sure there was something. Also I noticed, when the Chief buzzed her and said they were ready for me and she led me to the conference room they were in, I noticed the part of her calf showing under the dress as she walked. Nice muscle in that calf, I mean *nice*. You couldn't tell the way she was dressed that she might be in that good of a shape; it was a dancer's calf, a tennis player's calf. I'm thinking maybe she's got shape like that all over, who knows? Also, trying to stop myself but I'm thinking about what else might be under that dress. You can't really tell with the way women dress, you know?

Now I'm thinking maybe I'll get up and take a shower.

*   *   *   *   *

I'm on my way to the Medical Examiner, called in because of some high profile deaths that have occurred out on the Austin Highway, a one-vehicle traffic accident way out of our jurisdiction but the victims, sisters, are from San Antonio and, like I said, high profile. They are being brought to our ME for an autopsy on the driver, I'm told. The Bexar County Medical Examiner's Office is where I'm driving now, over on Leona, practically under Interstate 10.

I've been called into this because, according to the Chief, I'm "just what this case needs," whatever the hell that means. He knows everyone will always remember me as being a minor celebrity in town, and he knows that the work my people have been doing in the Jungle the last few years has been damned good.

I'm told the two husbands should be at the County Morgue by the time I get there. Many jurisdictions are involved, the accident taking place on the Interstate out in Comal County, the women initially transported to the New Braunfels hospital, the women residing in two suburban San Antonio municipalities. I have already spoken to the Highway Patrol people, the first troopers at the scene and the investigators called in by them from their office in Austin, plus some detectives who showed up at the scene from the New Braunfels PD. I took very careful notes so I can frame what to say to these two husbands about the accident, and then I wrote down some questions I need to ask them both.

Of course, the obvious reason the Chief has put me in charge of this case is that I know both of them, can probably ask them questions at perhaps the worst moment in their lives, and I can judge from their answers if there's anything can help me figure how to work all this out.

The husbands are Fred K and Jack Gantt.

And there was fresh blue paint ground into the scrape marks on the side of Mrs. Klein's faded old yellow sports car. Jesus.

*　　*　　*　　*　　*

Between Captain Jeff Davis of the Texas Department of Public Safety and me, I think we've covered all the bases, but not much has turned up so far. We have a statewide alert out to every business resembling a body repair and/or paint shop with details included on the blue paint and what it probably was painted *on*. We have also sent the details to all our border states and a general description to all law enforcement agencies nationwide.

The crash scene was discovered maybe half an hour or more after it occurred when smoke was seen by a couple, a man and his wife, who were taking the overpass to u-turn back toward San Antonio. They'd gotten mixed up from directions they had to a friend's house. I interviewed the friends, too. When the couple saw the crumpled car and the smoke down in the ravine made by the culvert under the bridge, they drove straight to a Gulf Station one exit south, and the manager helped them call the highway patrol. The wife was hysterical the whole time I interviewed them.

Less than an hour before the accident a dog walker, Frank Carswell and "Tinkerbell" - a blue Weimaraner - saw a yellow sports car matching the description of Mrs. Klein's pulled over in a bank parking lot right at the base of the Austin Highway, didn't see two women but does remember a woman was standing outside the car, leaning into the back seat and he was more interested in her ass than remembering anything else about her or the car. No idea height, weight, color hair, "maybe she was a little overweight, maybe brown hair," Mr. Carswell said.

A truck driver and young guy in a Corvette remember dueling to get around a pale yellow sports car that wouldn't get out of lane one. The driver of the eighteen wheeler had originally called the DPS from his home just outside Fayetteville, Arkansas when he heard about it on the news, but when I interviewed him on the phone he was stopped overnight in Knoxville, Tennessee.

The kid with the Corvette remembered a blond in the passenger seat. Neither could remember the kind of car, whether it had Texas plates, nothing about the driver except the car was sticking to the speed limit and not moving over for them.

No one has reported eye witnessing the crash, and two people who don't know each other report they saw a yellow Sunbeam at two different car washes in New Braunfels two hours *after* the crash occurred.

No one has called in about seeing a blue car anywhere in the vicinity of what we are terming an "accident" and thinking privately as being of the hit and run variety until and unless we are given information that sends us in another direction. I've had samples of the blue paint scraped and sent to the crime lab for analysis. The tech who did the scraping says it looks like GM paint, but we'll wait for the report.

Autopsy results are pending on both women. Both of the husbands are behaving the way grieving husbands should, though I'd say that Mr. Gantt is taking this worse, of the two. What I'd expect, all things considered.

Both of them are coming to see me again, once I hear back from the M.E., in the next few days. They've been warned that they'll be making recorded statements in response to "a few questions."

*   *   *   *   *

The police stenographer has packed up and the door clicks behind her. Jack is looking attentive, but his eyes are obviously tired from the ordeal he's going through.

"Off the record, Mr. Gantt, I appreciate your coming in again like this."

He nods. I don't think he's going to be smiling for a while, but under the circumstances at least he's trying to be civil.

"You and I have lost track several times over the years, Lieutenant."

I'm wondering how much to tell this guy. He seems nice enough, but I have a lot to consider, like how friendly can I afford to get with him. Even if he had something to do with the "accident" it might strike someone as odd that I'd trade biographies with him, but I could do it to get some insight into his character. And even though I *know* this is not a man who could have anything to do with what came down, it can't hurt, can only help to get to know him. It could be important to be on good terms with him in the future, him being related to Fred K. You never know. So I make up my mind.

"You want to get out of here? Go get dinner someplace and relax?" I smile easily, "We can stay off the record as long as you want, Mr. Gantt."

He thinks about it and shrugs. As he stands up he says "Call me Jack."

*   *   *   *   *

"Burger? Pizza? Feel like something fancier like Italian?"

Jack is settling into his seat, looking around the insides of my car. Of course he's surprised a cop is driving something souped up like this, so his mind isn't on eating yet. I turn the ignition and the car starts its rumbling. It's an old Impala I've been working on lately, a 63. I mean it drives like a tank and all, but it's a 409, so it's a *fast* tank. My old 383 Nova is back in my garage.

"How bout we go to the Jim's on Broadway?" I ask.

"That's fine, Lieutenant."

"If you want, you can call me George."

He doesn't say anything, just nods, and we drive in silence. It doesn't feel like a strained silence, I'm just thinking Jack Gantt has enough on his mind not to have to deal with a policeman asking him questions on the ride. Besides, I have my police scanner on, and he may be listening to what's going on, like I am.

We pull into the restaurant parking lot, and I back into a space close to the door.

When we get settled inside, we're both drinking coffee and waiting for our burgers. I'm getting a regular, no cheese, and he's ordered the one with hickory sauce, no pickles.

My memory from when we met in high school is crystal clear. I finish my cup and am looking around for the waitress when I say "You mentioned earlier I look a little familiar. Do you remember me from high school?"

He looks at me puzzled. "*You* went to Heights?" I can see on his face he realizes as soon as he blurts that out, that he knows how it sounds, but I laugh, "Yeah, I know I don't look the part. I'm an Oh-Niner from the other end of the scale. I was a hood and I dropped out before I graduated. But I thought everyone there knew me cause I was such a thug. I guess I thought too much of myself, if you don't even remember."

He looks at me for a long while, but shakes his head. "I'm sorry, man. I'm really drawing a blank."

I think of something else in addition to the football thing I want to tell him about, that might remind him.

"Back then most people knew me as Cholo...?"

He thinks again, but shakes his head a second time. "Sorry."

"Well, anyway, you've got to remember this: I played football and so did you. You were varsity third year and I was a freshman scrimmaging against the JV. I remember helping pull you off a guy one day. You were beating the living shit out of him, you've gotta remember that."

Our orders arrive and between mouthfuls, Jack says "Of course I remember that fight. My knuckles were ruined for weeks. I had to tape them for three or four games after that. But *you* pulled me off him? You'd think I'd remember, but I swear I don't."

180

"I think I even said something about how hard you were hitting him, telling you not to kill the poor bastard."

His eyes widen. "You've *got* to be kidding! I remember somebody saying that!"

I nod my head. "I picked you up in the air to get you off him. You were already taller than me back then, but I was big time into weights. Football was my excuse to work out hard for free."

"I guess I was so into the fight that I just didn't see anything else. The guy tried to break my leg when I came through the line and I saw red. It was practically a walkthrough of a new play we were learning when he did that. I remember ripping his helmet off and trying to rip his head off, too."

He stares at me again, and laughs. "I remember the guy - it was Chris Cooley - but I don't remember who pulled me off him."

If nothing else, at least I have him smiling.

VI - FRED

Today I see the stupidest bumper sticker ever produced. It says "I Believe in DIVERSITY". And to prove it, the artist has each letter in *diversity* made out of a different symbol. Like the *T* is a cross, of course. The D is a quarter moon and star - how they came up with that for a 'D' I can't imagine. What is that, from the flag of Turkey or somewhere? The V is the bottom of a Jewish Star of David. The E has a man arrow coming out of the side and a woman plus sign coming out of the bottom. So this bitch believes in diversity? Well, I'm driving right behind her and I'm a Jew in a Rolls Royce, does that count?

I mean does she believe in giving jobs to idiots because they wear sombreros? Giving some sand nigger a job he really can't handle because EEO government agency *schmucks* say to? The President appointing a black guy to the Supreme Court even though some Italian or Jew has more experience, but the president wants to get reelected....?

I think she does.

See, what you need to do is force equal education down everyone's throats. Then when everyone's educated to the same level, you check them all out and start giving the jobs to the people who deserve them. Maybe a few minority people will get some of those jobs as a result. *That*'s diversity, not forcing it on us. I've worked hard to get where I am, damn it. Nobody gave me a fucking thing, I missed out on taking advantage of this diversity bullshit. EEO my ass.

Stupid bitch....

OK, I just passed the car and it's a guy who's driving. Must be his wife's car.

Still, that cross and the Star of David remind me about something that happened when I was a kid back in Houston. I think about it nearly every time I see a cross, actually. Which is just about every day, I mean think about it: Paige, Samantha, even Jack wears one. Every woman at work, it seems like. Tattoo crosses are everywhere here. What? San Antonio is probably 70% Latino - all Catholic, right?

I'm something like four or five years old when this happened, so this is the best I remember it. I find this dead bird, probably just died and dropped off a tree or something. My idea is to bury it. Full honors and all. So I dig a hole with my hands. I'm young, so I just plop the bird down in there, I don't know any better. Now I'm finding sticks to make a cross. I find a couple and I'm trying to figure out how to get the sticks to stay together so I try a strip of grass and it won't hold the sticks. I get a bunch of grass and wind the strips together by twisting them. Then I start looping this grass rope I invented around the sticks and tuck in the ends when I run out. When I let go, it holds! Maybe I was six, I don't see how I could have been anything but a fumble fingers when I was four or five.

So I'm carefully sticking my cross into the soft earth where I've buried the dead bird. And this redheaded dickwad with a big nose, my cousin Davey, has been watching me. He's three years older than me. He walks up and kneels next to where I'm crouching. Fat fucker has to kneel because he's too fat to crouch. He's practically puffing just from getting down there to talk to me.

"Hey Freddie. Whatcha doin?"

183

"I'm buryin a bird I found. He was already dead, Davey."

"Yeah I saw. But Freddie, we're Jewish."

I hear him but I don't know what he means. "OK," I say.

"Jewish means you can't use that cross, Freddie. We don't believe in Jesus. See?"

I don't see, of course. I say, "I can't put a cross for the birdie?"

Davey nods and says "Right. You have to put a Star of David there. Star of David means Jewish, Cross means Christian, Freddie."

I'm Jewish? I'm thinking. *I can't use a cross? But I like the cross.*

Davey pulls my homemade cross out of the ground. He looks at it, turns it over and says "You sure made a nice cross, Freddie. I really like the way you twisted the grass into a rope."

For a second I get suspicious and think maybe he is lying about that Jewish stuff just so he can steal my cross. But then he carefully undoes the grass rope and hands it to me, throwing the two sticks back on the ground. "Here," he smiles, "keep the cool rope."

I think about this Jewish Christian thing for a few minutes, squatting there over the birdie's grave and then I say "Davey, can you draw a star? I don't know how to make a star for the birdie."

"Sure. Here." He picks up one of the sticks and draws a star on top of the bird's grave. I remember how he drew it. I didn't know till much later what it really was all about, but as he drew I remember thinking that all he is doing is drawing two triangles over each other. But when he finishes, it does kind of look like a star.

I look at it and feel sad. I think to myself that I really liked the way the cross looked better than the star he's drawn, but I don't tell Davey. Also, I had really been proud of the way I tied the grass together into a rope.

I remember looking down at my hands and seeing they are grimy with dirt. My nails are almost black from digging. I wonder if my give a shit mother is going to make me wash my hands ten times like usual. Davey and I walk slowly back to the house together.

*   *   *   *   *

My secretary buzzes me that Jack is on the line. Normally I'd tell her to have somebody who's calling in screw off when I'm getting ready to leave the office for a meeting, but this is *Jack*. He never calls me.

I say hello all warm and nice and he just says "I'd be interested in talking about that job at your place, if there's still an opening."

"Why sure, Jack. You know I'd always have a place for you here, that talk about not bringing you on was just bullshit. You're family! Haw, haw, haw."

I'm thinking *excellent*. "Why don't you come by..." my calendar is booked solid for a week and I'm already late to meet a guy about some property up north. "Well, when would be convenient for you? I'm on my way to a meeting, but I'll be back in the office later or you could bring Samantha and come by the house tonight."

185

"No thanks, Fred. We have plans for tonight, but I could come over anytime you say this afternoon, after lunch. If you want it later in the week let me know and I'll take some more time off."

"You're taking the day off today?"

"Yeah. I'm spending some time with Samantha and Paige right now, and they've talked me into hearing you out about this job."

Well, I'm not sure how to take this news. He's called me because Samantha and *Paige* have talked him into it, for Christ's sake? It's not about the work or the money I've been dangling, it's what, *family*?

"Oh Kay," I say, talking slow and thinking fast while I look at who I have appointments with this afternoon, "I can squeeze you in at four thirty...."

There's a long pause, and I'm thinking the son of a bitch is worrying about his *date* tonight, and how long it might take with me in the afternoon.

So I say, "Look Jack, I don't think we'll be more than an hour, talking about this...."

"Yeah, you're probably right," he says back, not sounding like he believes it. "OK Fred, I'll see you downtown at 4:30." And he hangs up before I can say anything.

Man, everything this *schmuck* does pisses me off.

*　*　*　*　*

I win. Samantha's already running the Accounting Department and dumbass is happy as a clam with his desk in the middle of the programmers downstairs. I actually think the only reason she took the job was to keep an eye on her husband, but it doesn't make sense to me. There's no way he could get interested in any of the tail around here when he has her to go home to, as opposed to the rest of us swinging dicks. Personally I'd rather be running down to South Padre on the *White Lightning* than balling Paige, anytime. But that's just me, haw haw haw.

But back to the Gantts. Samantha's getting high marks on her work. Now I have confidence in knowing where I stand every morning when I come in. All the investments, all the expenses, all the bottom lines. Like I always say, I like all the loose strings tied up, you know?

What I'm thinking... she seems like she might be interested in being brought into my confidence about the other stuff that's making the family the big bucks. She's already noticed that not everything I'm doing is getting rolled into the P&L, and I've had to put her off with some shuffle and dance that I'm thinking she won't settle for, forever. Smart cookie.

Anyway, when Jack can free himself up, they disappear for lunch every day. I followed them once but lost them by the St. Anthony. Jake Foster, one of my real estate guys, saw them coming out of a Mexican restaurant over near the Buckhorn Museum, once. One other time that I've heard about, and she's only been here a few months so habits may not exactly be formed yet, but one other time she locked them both up in her little office for lunch. I'm not thinking they were in there for an hour and a half just for lunch, but no one around there heard any noises. And I can imagine that after an hour, the people at the desks in the vicinity weren't doing anything *but* trying to hear what was going on in there! Makes me question my decision to install blinds over the glass in my manager's offices so they can have some privacy when they need it. I thought it would be so they could do reviews and chew somebody out without everyone in the place watching. I'd like to chew *her* out.

Sorry, my mind is wandering. I was thinking about bringing her into the big time. That's why I've promoted her quickly to running the Accounting Department. She's wasting her time in Payroll or any of the other groups. I want to see how she'll handle the pressure of the big time.

I've got plans for that one.

*   *   *   *   *

So Hartmann's a Lieutenant now, for fuck sakes! Man, he's living the dream and I'm handing it to him, you know? I'm just home from the promotion party that I hosted at the Country Club, and believe me it wasn't cheap. I'm relaxing in my upstairs office, Paige's already said goodnight and wandered off, drunk.

Cholo's wife and Paige still seem to get along, which is good, and she's damned easy on the eyes, that one, that Peggy. Built like a brick shit house. I bet Hartmann needs every muscle he's got to take care of *her*. Haw haw haw.

Now the main thing this party was for, was to make sure he knows who's watching his back, you know? I really appreciated all the nice things his Chief, that Mexican, Torres, said about me - with Hartmann standing there to hear it. Pretty hard to argue with all the bullshit coming out of the guy, even dressed up like he was in that silly uniform, looking like a minor South American dictator with all that shit on his hat. And *gloves* for Christ's sake. What a *shmoozer*.

I can see Hartmann and his wife both enjoy being at the Club whenever I take them. Shit, anyone would. Even when you dress down here and eat in the lounge, it's nice. Especially when someone else is signing for everything!

Plus we drew a good crowd, a couple mayors, another Police Chief, three Captains from the SAPD, and friends of the Hartmann's - really a bunch of people. I'm a little pissed about the Gantts, but they're off in the Grand Caymans or somewhere. I wouldn't have minded being dragged off to the Caribbean with *them,* even if I had to take Paige too, but of course Paige and I were left off the guest list. I picture me at the pool on the boat signing for Paige's booze, watching Samantha sunbathe; Jack probably in their suite, seasick, puking his guts out.

Those two didn't even mention it to me at the office till a few days before they left, she telling me it was a last minute vacation, and she said she didn't really give a shit if I liked it or not. *Last minute my ass*, I said, *no one goes off on a* cruise *last minute*. She just fucking laughed and walked out of my office.

Don't get me wrong, I couldn't care less. I'm busy enough, got my wife and kid, got my *White Lightning*. Got all my plans... yes, I'm plenty busy enough.

Still... when she flounced out of my office like that, I got a flash of thigh from when she turned. She wears short fucking sun dresses to work most of the time, because it's "hottern hell," she says. If I'm not catching thigh shots, her tits are hanging out. I can't help picturing her....

Anyway, I'm still glad I arranged this celebration for Hartmann as soon as Torres told me he agreed that the reorganization would be perfect for moving Hartmann up.

Now if I can just get to bed without stirring up Paige, that sloppy whiney drunk.

* * * * *

A few years ago I went to North Star Mall in a hurry. I needed to pick up a present for Jesse because I forgot his birthday. I mean I was in a *real* hurry. So I drive up to the front of the mall and stop my car there, turn it off and lock it, and run in. When I come running back out with the whatever I bought the kid, there's a mall cop standing by my Rolls.

He's got his fucking foot up on my running board, I get a little annoyed and I say to him "Hey, get your fucking foot off my car."

And he says "Excuse me?" kind of like he thinks he's hot shit, so I stop walking right next to him and put my hands on my hips and say "I said get your fucking foot off my fucking Rolls Royce before you lose your fucking job!"

He looks down at his foot, moves it off my running board and says "Sir, you can't park in front of the mall like this. The parking's right over there." He's pointing to the parking lot, what, twenty feet away, like I'm blind or something.

While he's talking, the guy puts his hands on *his* hips, too, one of them is resting right on the holster his fucking flashlight is in.

I wave the bag I'm holding, from Kay-Bee, and say "Look. Take down my license plate number and report me to mall management or the SAPD or whoever the fuck you want, but my kid's birthday party is going on right now and I'll be fucked if you're going to waste any more of my time."

I get in the car and as I'm driving away I look in my rear view mirror and see that the guy's writing down my license plate number.

I only mention this because since then I've never stopped parking my Rolls Royce next to that curb, smack in front of the main entrance to North Star Mall. I don't go there often but when I do, I get some fucking respect. I got a call from the guy who manages the mall a few days after that first time when the mall cop had his foot on my running board. The manager called and was kissing my ass from the second I got on the line. *Mr. K this* and *Mr. K that.*

Now that mall cop and the rest of the hired hands always tip their hats when they see me, always say *hello Mr. K*, and always tell me *have a nice day* when I leave. I love it. It's not only what I consider a verification of my standing, like when I got the invitation to join the Club, but it also just makes me feel really fucking *good.*

One of these days, if I see that same mall cop when I pull up, think I'll toss him my keys and ask him to go get my car washed, see what he does. Haw, haw, haw.

*   *   *   *   *

I'm meeting some of the boys who've just flown in to see me, for lunch at *el Mercado*, which is Spanish for what we call the market square downtown. It's San Antonio hot, so I drive over from the office. You get off the interstate around Commerce and there's parking under the freeway. You walk a block or so and there's this area about two or three city blocks long that they call a marketplace but it's really a great touristy area for buying stuff from Mexico and eating Tex Mex. The Barnes' family owns one of the big buildings in the Square. I go for the food and to listen to the music, soak up the atmosphere.

So I head for one of the restaurants and poke around inside till I see some familiar faces soaking up the suds at a big table. It's next to a window so we can watch the crowds listening to Mariachis, buying hand-painted shirts, looking for one of those imported onyx chess sets to buy. There's a cart right outside our window selling the Lord's Prayer on a pin, and a group dressed like Aztecs or whatever are playing those funny bongo-looking Jamaican things and singing in *español.*

I sit down at the head of the table facing the window. These guys are all dressed like Italian gangsters, I'll never understand why since that's mostly what they are. I keep expecting Stallone to walk by in a leather jacket and that funny hat, shadow boxing.

"You got everything set up, Mr. K?" asks Lou Tonzerelli. He's the only one of these guys I've ever heard speak.

Before I answer I give my order to the waiter who has appeared at my elbow. He heads off and I turn back to the table.

"I always like to tie up the loose ends. My part of this action is absolutely ready. How about you boys?" and I look around the table at four nodding heads. "We've been smooth with this for almost three years now, right?" Again the nods. "So, except I'm moving in some new security this time, I see no reason this shouldn't be as smooth as any other time; just a bigger payout."

"I like the way this business is taking off, Mr K," says Tonzerelli.

"We're just giving the customer what he wants, right Lou?" I grin.

A waiter comes over with two more baskets of chips, and I grab one of the baskets. The salsa's excellent here. Another waiter brings a large platter with food and sets it down next to us on one of those folding things you put your suitcase on in a hotel room. My order's there with all the others; these Mexican restaurants can really bring on the food in a hurry. And lordy is it good. Picture beans and rice and a couple of pork enchiladas getting mixed up together in your mouth, the music outside, the bright sunshine and everyone laughing and singing.

"So let me ask you, Mr. K: some of the boys back home are wondering if you might be interested in expanding our association to the transportation business."

I smile and swallow a mouthful. "Explain." I'm pretty sure I already know where he's going, but I like to play and see how they've thought out what they're going to propose.

"Sure. We can provide trucks and drivers and have what we could call "distribution centers" in a couple cities up east, and you have contacts south could be hooked up with - so we're thinking maybe we can combine forces and cash in."

I consider. I'm spreading butter on a flour tortilla before I salt it and roll it up like a cigar. "You think there's enough business and enough demand?" I ask. "I'm not sure about the supply, but I'd be glad to do some research on my end."

"We'd appreciate that, Mr. K. I can vouch for the demand, *maestranza, puttana, lavoratore a giornata,* whatever you can bring up."

Sometimes Lou starts talking Italian and I'm not sure I follow of course, but I've lived in Texas all my life and spent a bit of time in Nuevo Laredo in my youth, so I know what a *puta* is - *puttana* can't be much different. Maybe I can ask one of my *Latino* employees to confirm, but I'm pretty sure he's talking immigrant labor and prostitution.

I nod and smile again. The Empire grows another tentacle....

*   *   *   *   *

Look, take my advice. I'm as serious as I can be when I say this: there isn't a woman in the world who isn't fucked up, *fakakta.* Your job is to figure out how... maybe even why...

because that might help. But basically, every woman under the sun is absolutely, irrevocably and forever, fucked up in the head. You might have to go searching around for a while, or what's fucked up might come right out and bite you in the ass, but either way, believe me, it's there. They are nuts, hung up, stupid or crazy, somehow someway every one of them is fucked up in the head.

Somebody told me that truth when I was a kid, just starting to date, and ever since then, I'm always on the lookout to see, even with the most normal, or nicest, or sweetest of them, I'm always on the lookout for where the fucked up part is.

And it's always there, I always find it, whether right away or after close examination, sometime, somewhere, there it is. She'll be cool or she'll be smart or maybe nice looking, but she'll wind up fucked up, like all the rest of them.

I bring this up because I'm thinking right this minute that I might need to make an exception of Samantha Franklin Barnes. She's got all three of those qualities – gorgeous, brilliant, and absolutely comfortable in her own skin - and one more quality that I'm just discovering. She's the only one I've seen it in besides me; of course she's relaxed in every situation I've ever seen her in, has genuine smarts, is drop-dead beautiful - money or not, and she has plenty of that too – *and* she's got the fourth ingredient for the perfect woman, namely *she has larceny in her heart,* she's an *unmensch.* That's right, like me, she thinks she's entitled to anything that's out there, anything that's being dangled in front of her that she wants, whether it's on a silver platter or there may be a few strings attached, as long as she can figure out a way she can avoid a jail cell or bad dreams at the end of the struggle, she's willing to do what it takes to figure out which scissors to use to cut those strings and get that thing, whatever it is. And maybe she's even more special, come to think of it, because *she doesn't need to be that way.* She already has whatever she wants *and* whatever she needs! A rich bitch, through and through. Jesus Christ, what a woman!

It's really been a joy working with her. I mean it hasn't been a one way street here, me just training her in the ways of politics, government, and bullshit. She's figured out plenty on her own and taught me a trick or two taking care of business. We once played around with the calculations for tax withholdings, and then with the money we 'withheld', made some money, covered it up - impossible to detect - and it was all her idea! She even figured out a way, through the accounting for it, to write herself out of what we'd done so if we got caught *I'd* be the only one they could trace the scam to. I mean, is that a work of art, or what?

This woman is a charmer, and as sarcastic a son of a bitch as I've ever met. I don't admit to understanding the relationship she has with her asshole husband, but they do seem... I don't know... content? Jack is OK, good at what he does, but the man certainly has blinders on. He can be shown any problem and the inputs and outputs and boom! he's gone. You won't see him for days and then he shows up and the problem's fixed, no matter how complicated or buried. Sammie bats her eyes at him and they go off to make the "trophy presentation" and then they come back and they're both laid back and calm until she sees something else in the books or the IRS codes or wherever and he gets another problem handed to him, and they're both gone again.

She's really jealous of her free time, I could put the Earl Abel sign that's next to the clock in his restaurant up on the wall in my Accounting Department. Only I could reword it to say *This clock will never be stolen. Samantha Barnes is always watching it*. Six o'clock and I see her heading out the door. No matter what! We could be closing a deal that has to have paperwork postmarked today and when it hits six; I'm on my own. Honest to fucking Christ, she's gone. She doesn't give a shit what's going on when that clock strikes six.

So tonight I'm walking past her office after 7, and she's in there. I do a double take and look in through her window and she's sitting in front of what looks like one of the Master Tax

195

Guides we buy to help us sniff out the holes in this year's tax laws. So, I knock a couple of times and walk in.

She looks up and grimaces at me and says "Jack is in his office working on a problem."

"And you're *waiting* for him? He could be here all night."

She shrugs and says "We have tickets to a late show that he wants to see, and I promised I'd bring him back down here after. We're leaving in about an hour."

I already don't care, but while she's talking I'm looking down the top of her blouse at those titties thinking that Paige can't even wear a push-up that would make hers look like these jugs. Well, maybe when she was pregnant with Jesse and wouldn't let me touch them, anyway. Now, I'm starting to think Samantha and I have known each other a pretty long time. We've also gotten along pretty well and she's probably been wondering what a meal of good old Freddie K might taste like. She can't help but have wondered, right? Us being together at work as much as we have? It's not like I haven't acted on the same impulse and done the same thing with a few of the good looking secretaries we've had in this office over the years. No complaints from any of them!

I'm thinking fast. "So what are you looking at in that Tax Guide? Anything interesting?"

She looks down at what she was reading and while she launches into an analysis of some new business tax code change, I'm moving around beside her. I'm thinking maybe I should try closing the blinds of the window into her office before I make my move, but then I think so what if Jack does walk by and sees me? What's he going to do, the pussy? I mean the chances of him coming by are nil anyway because when he's working, like I said, the blinders go on.

But what if he does catch us? I'm looking at her mouth thinking about those lips and what it would be like to have my tongue down in there and I'm getting hot thinking about doing her, bending her over the desk with my arms around her squeezing those tits, banging away, and Jack catching us and seeing her crying out with pleasure with me coming into her from behind.

I'm breathing hard just thinking about it, and I've got a bit of a boner even though now I'm just looking blindly down at the book, thinking about her. She's pointing to a paragraph that has a sentence in bold type, but I have no idea what she's talking about or what it says. She asks a question, I think it's something like "Do you think we should give it a try?"

I know what I want to try and I'm really not thinking about anything else. This is what is meant by lust, now I know. I can feel my fucking heart hammering in my chest and my groin, and my ears are even starting to make a low waterfall noise and I know I'm taking a small chance doing this but I'm only thinking about the rewards, so I stick my hand down the front of her shirt and move my face down in front of hers and start to kiss her.

Well, I'm halfway there anyway. I've got all tit with my hand - the slut must not even have a bra on! She's trying to avoid my mouth and pull back and already her hand has pulled mine away from her chest, but I'm fighting back - this is like hand wrestling with her chest the prize.

And I'm losing. This bitch must work out like hell because I'm breathing ragged and she has just gotten my fucking hand in one of those grips where she's jamming my thumb back. It hurts like hell! She must have gathered herself while we were hand wrestling because suddenly she springs up and pushes with all her might and I'm staggering backward. I get my balance back before I crash into the wall. Now *I'm* gathering *myself,* God damn it. I make a charge at her, my arms open for a bear hug. If I can pick her up and somehow throw her down on the floor, dammit, I'm gonna make her pay for this.

And she hits me! This God damned teasing *kurveh* hits me! Closed fucking fist! I was centered on getting my arms around her and she must have been winding up and I didn't see it coming. She smashes her fist into my God damned face! I can't even see straight, the little cunt!

And then she's screaming at me! And she's yelling "You dirty Jew motherfucker!! You come at me again and so help me Christ I'll cut your dick off and stuff it down your throat!! You slimy bald headed pathetic mother fucker!! How dare you come at me!! Get the fuck out of *my* office!! *NOW*, you pig!!"

And she's pushing me from behind and I'm holding my aching cheek and being run through the doorway. If I don't grab the doorknob and turn, the cunt would have put me through the glass, I swear to God.

It's all I need is for Paige to get the story from this crazy person, is what I'm thinking, this slutty cock teasing bitch. I'm having trouble breathing, and a little trouble getting downstairs to the parking garage. I have to hammer on the elevator down-button a few times, and I'm looking over at her office while I'm waiting to make sure she doesn't come out with a gun or some fucking thing, but the elevator finally shows up and I'm gone.

I'm shaking while the elevator slowly goes down the floors to the basement. My cheek hurts like hell and I'm pressing against it with my hand. I'm also sweating like a bitch and my breathing continues to rasp and hurt. Man, I could use some more blow when I get in the Rolls, sure could. I'm finally able to start thinking again. I really need to get high to relax before I get home. Don't want anyone to see me upset. Maybe cool myself off with some weed, too.

I was right. Samantha's as fucked up in the head as the rest of them. She'll pay for this.

*   *   *   *   *

When I get to my office today, there's a note on it from my secretary. *Samantha has the flu, will probably be out a few days* it says.

Oh shit, I'm thinking, *wonder if dumb ass is out today too.*

Jack refuses to have a secretary or an admin, so when I call his desk, one of the other programmers answers. "Yes sir, this is Hal. He is in, but his phone's set to DND while he debugs a code fix he's testing for Payroll."

I thank Hal and buzz my secretary for a cup of ice. My fucking head is throbbing where that cunt - I mean, *Samantha* - blindsided me. I need to keep my mouth talking nice, can't afford to piss the family off, damn it.

I make sure I'm not forgetting anything on my calendar and I'm not. If I can concentrate long enough, and here I'm cursing *her* again, I have all day to investigate in depth whether a scam I've cooked up to work on those idiots at the Railroad Commission will hold.

Now *that* is a board ripe for the pickings, and me with a close personal friend elected a Commissioner and just starting his first six year term! The TRC was created in the late 1800's, mostly to prevent railroads from unfair pricing practices. The weird thing, the *Texas* thing they did in the 1910's was when the state Senate passed a law that *defined oil lines as common carriers.* So first they say that people, cattle, and goods riding on a train need to be protected and then they decide *oil and gas* is the same as *people* for regulating prices! *And,* topping it off a few years later, they put this board in charge of regulating *who can drill, and how much!* I mean come on, how sweet is that?

The Railroad Commission, for Christ's sake! Not exactly an invitation for payoffs and scandal there, huh? And they think they are mostly there for energy conservation, is that a riot?

I'm knee deep in open regulatory books and binders and my fucking head throbbing when my secretary comes in with a lunch that I ignore. She comes back midafternoon to take it away. Paige calls around five and I tell her to leave me alone, but in my nicest way.

Actually I'm regretting this mess with the cu... I mean with Samantha... because I could use her input. But never again. I'll treat her with kid gloves but she's never getting off my shit list, and I'll never be able to trust her again.

Once I get resolved in my mind how I'm going to move on this TRC thing, I have a few other calls to make. Things need to be taken care of, and it's time to call in a couple favors.

*   *   *   *   *

Knowles knocks at the door of my home office on a Sunday afternoon. It's two cops at the door, he tells me. So far I've been careful all day to stay sober, while I'm reviewing the reports I'm getting, almost every two or three hours, on progress at the "secret" TRC meetings taking place in Austin, discussing my proposals.

My guy on the board seems pretty confident things will go our way, and he's keeping me updated whenever they break. I chuckle when the *mamzer* includes himself and says "our way." If I take more than my share of the allocation what's he going to do, announce he conspired to do TRC business for personal gain? He might as well slit his own throat. Haw, haw, haw.

So I tighten up my robe and follow Knowles down the main stairs. He's moved the cops to the drawing room - living room to the uninformed. I hardly ever smoke cigars but I have an unlit one sticking out of my face, I think it impresses people if they know what a real Cuban looks like.

Two cops I've never seen before, they have Terrell Hills patches on their uniform. First I'm thinking maybe my trash cans aren't being put in the right place, but then I remember they are always behind a wired fence in the alley behind the grounds, and Knowles and Paige have to take trash bags out there every so often.

One of these guys is way too dressed up. The bill of his hat has fancy gold stuff looks like scrambled eggs so I imagine he's a big shot in the little local police department. Torres wears the same bullshit on his hat, but at least he's the Police Chief of the metropolis, not this little burg I'm living in.

I've been daydreaming while he talked. I know I was smiling when we shook hands but I'm not listening, I'm thinking about the Railroad Commissioners. I finally start paying attention just as he is saying "...regret to have to tell you this, sir, but your wife and her sister have been involved in a terrible accident out on the Austin Highway, just short of New Braunfels."

I can't stop myself from saying "Oh, shit."

Now I ask, repeating him "A *terrible* accident?"

And he says, "Well, sir, they've been transported to the hospital in New Braunfels: McKenna. We were notified to come alert you and offer our services to assist you in any way." The guy with him gets beeped and excuses himself back out toward the front door. This is not going well. "What happened, do you know?" I ask.

"I really don't. The DPS was on the scene of course, and I understand some officers from the New Braunfels PD had also been dispatched out there, but being your wife and sister, we were called to come notify you."

The other guy comes back and says he needs to speak to the one talking to me, the big shot he calls *Chief.* They whisper and I'm thinking the guy who's been doing all the talking at me, the Chief, must have introduced himself before I started paying attention. I sit down and hand the cigar to Knowles. The cops come back in and the Chief is looking grim.

He puts his arm on my shoulder and I flinch without thinking and he says "I'm sorry Mr. Klein, but your wife and her sister didn't survive the accident. I believe that it will be too late for a trip out there. The women are in the process of being moved here, to the County Medical Examiner's. Would you like to have a family member accompany you there?"

I curse inside, thinking about the Railroad Commission. My mind is racing. "What about Jack, Jack Gantt? My sister's husband."

"Yes sir, I know. Because of his home address, some officers from the AHPD were dispatched to notify him, sir. They'll probably drive him to the ME's office when he's ready."

I say "Knowles should stay here with my son." When I glance at him, Knowles nods at me, eyes wide. "You guys wait down here and I'll go upstairs, attend to a few things and get dressed."

"You want me to call anyone for you, sir? Someone we could pick up on the way? A close friend or a pastor?"

I stand up, shaking my head. I need to get upstairs.

A close friend... shit... is dumb ass the only person I can think of? Or a pastor? Is he kidding?

A pastor? Me? I'm remembering me, a little Jewish kid who didn't understand what I was, my hands dirty from digging that stupid bird's grave and my cousin Davey drawing that Star of David over it.

All I really want to do is call my TRC Commissioner from upstairs before we go.

*　　*　　*　　*　　*

I'm glad Chief Torres buys in to putting Cholo on the investigation team; I'm surprised he puts him in charge. It's a great relief. Among other things, he's a good investigator and he'll have everyone's attention because of his reputation. And it gives me a confidence I have maybe lost a bit of since the accident. Torres is showing me respect.

I'm driving in for a statement, second one I've had to make since the accident. Wilson's meeting me down there; he says we won't need my criminal lawyer unless something goes wrong at this interview, or maybe if it turns out to be a criminal deposition, for some reason. *What could go wrong?* I asked him. *I have nothing to hide, do I?* Privately, I'm thinking maybe I didn't act sad enough when they came to the house or when I went to the morgue, unlike Jack who was all over his Pastor with grief, I heard. He's such a pussy. I wanted to be sad, to show it, but my God. Face facts, you know? I'm sorry Paige bought it, but Samantha? Under the circumstances....

Parking's tough around this place, I'm glad they have a lot I can park in that takes care of my car. These lot attendants understand that special automobiles need to be treated with special care. Plus they know I tip well. I walk up and into the lobby and there's Wilson. What *is* his first name? Anyway, he leads me up an elevator to where we're meeting Cholo and whoever.

I'm trying to stay somber but I'm chuckling inside about when I saw Jack last, how horrified he looked when I reminded him we are now the new Barnes' partners. He and I are going to get to know each other really well. Really well. Comical.

This meeting room looks like what you think of when you think of an executive briefing room, or something. I've got to get heavier furniture, like these chairs. Man! Feel the weight of this table....

"Good morning, Mr. Klein." I look up and it's the Chief, all dressed up like he's a General in the fucking army. "I hope your trip in was fairly easy. Once more, I'd like to extend the Department's deepest sympathy for the loss of your wife and her sister." Cholo is watching me from behind the Chief. He doesn't look so good, himself. Uncomfortable.

"Thank you, Chief Torres, I appreciate that." I reply. "Say, is something wrong? You people look worse than I feel." Nice touch I'm thinking, saying that I feel bad.

"Have a seat," says the Chief, pointing at the head of the table. Then he looks at Wilson and points to the chair next to that. Cholo is pulling out the chair next to the one Torres had pointed to for me. A pretty woman is standing close to the door, and she says "Would anyone like a drink? Coffee? Juice? Water?"

She leaves with our orders, closing the door. She looks young but has prematurely graying hair cut really nice to her shoulders. Excellent body.

"While we're waiting, Mr. Klein, has anything come up since we spoke last that you've thought of, that might mitigate the things we've already discussed?" This from Cholo! *Mitigate!*

"No, Sergeant - sorry, no, *Lieutenant*," I correct myself and smile. As I'm answering the secretary is coming back in with a tray full of the drinks we asked for. Someone must have been out there helping her, that was so fast.

I don't think to thank her, but I sure could use the coffee, so I take a sip before I go on. Good coffee.

"Nothing's come up in my mind." I glance at Wilson and he nods his agreement.

"Well," starts Cholo, and he's looking really uncomfortable now, pale too. "I'm afraid there have been a few new developments from our end, Mr. K. Some things you need to hear. Naturally you will be provided copies of everything, you and Mr. Wilson."

Holy fuck is honest to God what I'm thinking, *what is this son of a bitch about to tell me?*

"Yes." Cholo shuffles some papers in front of him and finds one, pulling it to the top of the pile. "The Medical Examiner has filed his report - we just yesterday received our copies and I called you to come in shortly after we reviewed them ourselves. The report is based on the results of the physical examination - the autopsy - and the toxicological lab results that the ME received from their lab.

"Chief Torres and I," he glances over at the Chief, "thought this meeting might be more appropriate than just sending the paperwork to you. A few things that you would be better off hearing from us. These reports will become a matter of public record over time, so in our judgment, you'll want some time before they're heard, even if it's only at the inquest."

Well, I'm sure I'm pale too, by this time. I'm starting to feel a little shaky. I mean I have *no* idea where this is going.

"What the hell's going on, Lieutenant?"

"First, briefly, the toxicology report indicates that your wife had cocaine, or rather the chemical resulting from its use, in her system. Now, Mr. K, the Department feels that unless some link can be established between the accident and her use of this drug, the information won't be used as part of our investigation simply because of the low amount found."

Well, needless to say, my mind is spinning overtime. I mean, I'm not stunned by the news, but it never occurred to me that her using might come back at me - even though these cops are trying to play softball with the knowledge, somebody who isn't on my team could try to make this a wedge into all the shit I've got going. Politics, all of it. Great. God damn it.

"How much of the stuff does it say she had in her?"

Cholo answers "Less than an amount that would indicate she was driving under the influence, which is about 150 nanograms per milliliter. The report put her level at 63.

"But, there's something else, sir. The autopsy also showed that your wife was pregnant. Since you haven't mentioned this fact to us in our conversations, we're assuming you weren't aware of it, even though your wife must have been. We've checked with her ob/gyn's office and they recorded test results a few days before the accident. Mrs. Klein was in her sixteenth week at that time. I'm sorry to drop this on you like I have, but there's really no good way...."

I'm so genuinely shocked at this news, I'm not hearing him anymore. I'm sitting here choking to death or something, as if I can't breathe. It isn't possible that she was going to have a kid. I would have known that, wouldn't I? I think my eyes are closed because I can't see a fucking thing -

"Mr. K!!"

"Sir!!"

"Fred, for God's sake!!"

I'm trying to say something. Oh yeah, I'm wondering if Samantha had anything in her blood stream. It seems important, somehow. "What about Samantha?" I manage to croak.

There's a long pause before I hear Cholo say hesitantly, "well, we've met with her husband about her toxicology report and autopsy, but she wasn't driving and at this point in time the results are confidential, just as the results of your wife's report are confidential to you, sir. Or... did you mean was his wife also pregnant?"

I realize my eyes are clamped shut, so I open them and blink till what seems like a haze goes away from them. "No, no. I meant did she have cocaine in her system."

"Well, Mr. Gantt would have to be the one to share that with you, sir. I'm sorry, sir."

After a pause I start thinking about another baby being in Paige. "Holy Shit." I actually get choked up. Somebody's patting me on the back. Jesse could have had a sister, brother, something.

"Was... was... it... a boy... or a girl?" my voice is embarrassing, still croaking.

"It's in the report I think. I believe it was going to be a little girl. I'm really sorry, Mr. Klein."

Sweet Mother of God, I'm thinking. *A little girl.*

* * * * *

It doesn't look to me like anyone's ever going to be arrested for having anything to do with the accident. Not that I thought anyone would, but it just proves to the reporters crawling like roaches over everything that it was an accident, there being no witnesses and the police not able to find anybody who might have been involved.

Paige pregnant and messed up with coke and Samantha maybe drunk or something, or at least a better driver than Paige ever was, but not driving. It just goes to show you that you never know how things will end up.

And Jack's gone.

It's a little frustrating him taking off almost as soon as the funerals. I'm just starting to think I'm going to have some fun with him over the years and he's gone, off for some new life somewhere. I'll track him of course, can't let him disappear on me, but the way he's having Wilson move him off the various boards he inherited, selling me his interest in other stuff, why it's almost like he doesn't want to have anything to do with me, now! Me, his only real link to the family! Haw, haw, haw.

It's maybe why I asked him about his house. First you have to understand that I got rid of everything in the mansion that reminds me of Paige, I got all that stuff moved up to the attic or out of the house. Not a lot of stuff, really. Most everything here is real ancient antiques, or stuff from Belle and David - furniture, fancy throw rugs, paintings, books, and on and on - all worth a great deal. Paige's clothes went fast, out the door. All the frilly stuff from our old bedroom, and Paige's collections of crap, went to the attic. I moved into the Barnes' old master bedroom and gave Jesse our old room. He's outgrown his room and all the old toys and baby stuff, anyway.

Just call me a sweet old sentimental guy, but I also went through Samantha's stuff at Jack's house after he left. I had almost all of it moved upstairs here, too. Can't really explain it, hell, I don't really understand it myself and am not interested in finding out some - what? hidden meaning for it? - but I spent some time going through all her things, putting her shoes in one bag, folding and stacking her dresses and skirts and blouses, on and on. That all went in bags too. I remember all those sundresses she wore to drive me crazy at work. Funny, looking back.

And the smells in her old chest of drawers.

Shorts, tops, night things, bras, underwear. Got them all into bags for the attic. Eventually.

Interlude: 10:43 a.m.

They were in Paige's old Sunbeam, and Sammie's head was starting to throb again just as they turned onto Broadway. Paige took the turn too sharply and was forced to swerve back toward the island to get into the high speed lane. Sammie cursed as she was helplessly swung around in her seat. Paige was working the steering wheel like a truck driver, blinking her eyes rapidly, squinting hard.

Sammie moaned and brought her hands up to cover her face. "Do you have any aspirin? The stuff I took when I woke up is wearing off."

Paige told her her purse was in the storage area behind them. Sammie struggled to twist around and get on her knees in her seat to be able to find it. Paige said it may have dropped under the driver's side back there. "Do you want me to pull over?"

"Yes, I really need it, Paige."

They were fast approaching the Austin Highway so Paige waited for the left turn lane and turned her blinker on. The blinker wasn't working correctly; it lit up but didn't blink. There was the Pegasus sign at the corner.

After they turned, Paige pulled into a bank's empty parking lot and got out to retrieve her purse.

Paige handed Sammie the aspirin bottle and a bottle of water from the glove compartment.

Swallowing, Sammie groused "This Sunbeam is really getting to be quite the piece of shit, Paige. Can't Freddie the Jew afford to buy you a new car?"

The two girls stared at each other. Sammie knew Paige really loved her car. It was the nicest thing Belle had ever given her sister besides the requisite Master Card and Diner's Club. It was a 1960 Sunbeam Alpine Series II hard top that Belle bought new a million years ago and had painted her favorite color, creamy yellow. When she'd tired of it, she'd kept it around for the girls. Sammie had sneered at it all through high school so it was taken for granted Paige would get it. Paige told Sammie it was a sporty little thing, and she was going to learn standard transmission on it for her first driving test.

Sammie couldn't hold the stare any more; she giggled through her headache. Paige started laughing as soon as Sammie did, and though Sammie had to put her hand up to the side of her head, they reached for each other and laughed through a hug. Sammie's eyes were wide open. As they held each other, she couldn't remember ever holding her sister before.

They finally sat back in their seats. Sammie closed her eyes again and asked through a smile "Does your gas gauge work as well as your turn signals? I don't wanna run out on this trip. That's all I need."

Paige glanced at the gauge and said "We have a quarter tank. I guess we could get some gas before we get on the road. There's a 7-11 just past the light up here."

"No, hon. A quarter tank is plenty for this drive - please let's not stop unless we have to till we get there, OK? I'll feel better if we just drive till the aspirin kicks in."

Sammie tried to relax. She thought about Jack's reaction to her hand. It had been awhile since she'd thought about what Fred had done, had tried to do, to her. She'd dismissed out of hand telling Jack. He was, at best, a slow burn; so introverted at times that he seemed only to react to things hours or days later. She'd only known of him losing his temper once; the time in high school. She hadn't seen it, but the whole school buzzed about it, when he nearly killed that other boy at football practice, that Chris Cooley. Chris was not much in the looks department, but good family. Club people. Oil, she thought. He was stocky, built, wore his hair too short but dressed nice.

Anyway, he must have done something to Jack and Jack went at him. The story was that Chris was a bloody pulp and Jack wouldn't stop beating him till that hoodlum, Fred's new friend, the one with the hooded eyes and swollen lips who'd become a cop, lifted Jack in the air and walked off with him. It must have taken a week for the story to die down.

Originally, Sammie had told herself she'd handled Fred and wasn't about to tell Jack. She was changing her mind about that, but she hoped he'd drop the talk about the anger management class. And she was going to find another job; no way she would work for that bastard any longer than she had to.

VII - JACK

I am on the road, somewhere between Ft. Stockton and Balmorhea, Texas. The Interstate won't really go into a town till Van Horne, or into a city till El Paso, so I have all the time in the world to think, look at flatlands and twirl the radio dial. I've found stations in Oklahoma City, Las Cruces, and I swear for a few minutes a country station in Chicago.

I am headed west, but I haven't decided where exactly. I can settle anywhere from San Diego to Seattle, or try one place and move on if it doesn't feel right. There are mainframe computers up and down the west coast and I'm looking forward to just working for awhile, no personal life.

God, no personal life, *please*.

I packed, took care of the last minute details to keep me in cash for awhile, picked up a few maps and travel guides from Triple A, and that's about all I needed. The feeling of doom or whatever that was, has slowly ebbed since I left San Antonio, taking the Loop west to Interstate 10 and heading out.

I've been working on it and working on it and all I can come up with is how could that have been a chance accident? I mean the blue paint on the passenger side. No blue car showing up anywhere resembling an auto repair shop - Cholo let me leaf through the reports. The truck driver, a few others on the road around then, some of the calls that came in on the hot line, nothing.

At first I couldn't imagine anyone doing something like that on purpose. What would anyone gain from those two women. Well, Fred. He gets his boat, he gets everything Paige had, and I don't think he liked her much anyway. He also enjoyed talking to me about the accident too much. He was having fun knowing I wasn't.

I pass a rest stop. There are two school buses and an eighteen-wheeler parked in the lot, empty BBQ pits and a bathroom. Live oaks and mesquite.

Hills on the far eastern horizon, otherwise the land here is flat and uninviting. Where are the families sending their children to school on those buses? Back off this interstate, for sure. Must be quite a round trip.

I'm fiddling with the radio dial. 'Seek' goes through the radio without stopping, but cranking on the dial with the volume up, I can pick up an accasional newscast, a few local Spanish stations and some country and rock and roll music.

Wherever I end up, I need to keep calling Cholo, bug him, remind him to keep this case open. Sooner or later someone will say something or make a mistake. Cholo's a good cop. I need to call him maybe once a month after I get settled. That couldn't have been an accident, not with the damage to the side of the car. Fred, that bastard.

Never saw Balmorhea. I've picked up a Los Angeles rock and roll station. Faint but I heard them say so. Missed the call letters but the DJ has the weirdest bass voice, almost sounds like he's making his voice do that, scratchy like a frog or like he's smoking five cigarettes at a time.

Maybe it's a sign. Maybe I'll try L.A.

PART TWO

VIII - FRED

Already ten years since the girls died, ten years since I've seen Jack, ten years since I've been on my own raising Jesse, my church mouse. Even so, I have a hard time believing that Tonzerelli is retiring. I've known him what - fifteen, twenty years? I thought these Eye-talian guys stayed in "the business" till they dropped over to the side of the road.

We've seen or talked to each other just about every month at least once or twice, all these years. We make plans together, check our notes on how we're doing, discuss new ventures and problems that have come up. Sometimes he has to go back and straighten something or somebody out, sometimes I do. He might visit me down here, I might go up there to New York, or we might meet in Corpus or the Jersey shore depending on the weather. We've been close, but you never want to be too close with these guys. I mean, they may let a Jew be their accountant, but they stay pretty close knit about the business-end of their dealings. That makes me a Texas connection I don't want to get too pushy about. Ever.

I didn't notice till he's talking to me how fucking old and skinny he looks. Thinned down in the face. Deep lines down his cheeks. Lost his jowls, looks like. Probably cancer is what I'm guessing.

Me, I'm as fat and bald and healthy as ever but this *putz* looks a hundred and five. He tells me he's got to retire for his health. I have to laugh, haw haw haw.

I ask him if he means his health, or is somebody getting ready to kill him. Now he's laughing and saying *no, no, no. I'm retiring to be with my family, I've got grandkids now. I'm turning everything over to Frank, been with me since I started this little business.*

I've known Frank Bonello as long as I've known Lou, but I've never heard him open his mouth. After the retirement announcement, Frank sits in on the rest of our discussions, seems to be listening, I even see him taking some notes for Christ's sake. Anyway, Tonzerelli and I said goodbye after last weekend, we were in New Jersey and I just got home, flew in last night. I'm going to have an even harder time trusting Frank than I did Lou - and that wasn't much. These guys never lose that cold-eyed look, no matter how long we've been working together.

Jesse's already gone to class, a freshman in college, yet! Knowles is getting me a lunch ready. I'm enjoying being home. I call the office and ask my admin to tell me about my calls. She's already screened them and gives me the highlights. I need to deal with a few things, but mostly if I don't get something started, my businesses just float along. The bank too. The land just sits, the malls, the investments. If I wasn't in the middle of a drug move, or capitalizing one thing or another, or shipping illegals north or east, this life would be as boring for me as I guess it got for Lou.

Matter of fact, I should start planning a trip to the left coast. Maybe I can talk Jesse into going with me. It's fucking hot as hell around here now anyway, so maybe he'd like to see a few Dodger games and a show or two. I'll have Knowles check what's playing at the Hollywood Bowl, maybe the Greek. Or I could pretend I like one of these bullshit bands he listens to, the ones with the singers who whine or scream or both, instead of sing.

Jesse and college don't seem to be agreeing with each other now, anyway. I bet he'd welcome an excuse to blow it off for a while.

Knowles walks in with a tray, puts it down on the desk, and starts to walk out without saying anything.

"Hey Knowles?" I say, wanting to start a conversation.

"Yes, Mr. K?" he says, turning back toward me and looking like he doesn't.

I really don't have anything to talk about with this guy. He's been my servant since before the accident and I still don't know shit about him, not a thing.

Also, it's strange how, no matter how long it's been since, I still just call it "the accident" and everyone around here knows exactly what I mean - it's ten, but it could be fifty years later and people will still call it that, at least around here.

Sometimes I'm actually sorry I let that dumbass leave town....

"Uh, Mr. K, you alright?

Knowles standing there waiting and I'm acting like a stump. "Sorry Knowles, never mind," I mumble, hoping he won't notice I drifted off like that.

He shrugs and turns away to leave. "You buzz me when you want me to pick up the tray, Mr. K."

"You bet, Knowles," I say.

It's a toasted BLT on sourdough, plenty of mayo, with low salt chips and ketchup on the side, glass of lemonade. At least Knowles knows what I like.

*   *   *   *   *

I'm getting tired of this run around. I'm in my office downtown and I just got back from L.A. this morning. Because of this fuck up south, I had Knowles pick me up and drive me straight here instead of home to get cleaned up first. As a result, I'm not only getting pissed off about these Mexicans, but I'm feeling... I don't know, gritty... from the trip. I have tried the two numbers for these guys, the primary one and the backup one, and neither of them are being answered. Of course the calls don't go to some recording when no one answers, but I mean that makes sense. I just thought these guys *always* had someone answering the phones. I imagine the connections have to be changing all the time to prevent any conversations getting bugged by somebody. Never occurred to me before to be worried about that, the numbers themselves haven't changed in a couple of years.... Jesus, maybe I *should* be getting worried. I'll ask Sylvan the next time we talk.

Anyway, I'm sitting here drumming my fingers on the fucking desk, wasting my time. I'm thinking I'll call Knowles to come back and pick me up. Maybe I'll ask Joseph, the new accounting guy to come up here and go over some things while I wait. He's pretty good; he's keeping up better than most of the people I've tried running the department.

"Francine," I say when she answers the intercom, "Send for Joe Reilly, I want to go over some things."

"Will do, Mr. K" she says and clicks off.

I'll talk to Joseph about the write-offs at the bank and then call Knowles.

And I'm still pissed off about Jesse not going on the trip with me. He isn't really interested in school but he insists on going, wasting his time, switching from Financial Management to English for God's sake. My God, he got an A in Latin, can you imagine? What's he going to do with that, *teach?* Jesus!

Francine buzzes through. "Sylvan's on line one, Mr. K."

About fucking time. I can't be too hard with these guys but I also have to keep them in line. It's a tightrope. Sylvan's got the second coldest eyes I've ever seen.

*　　*　　*　　*　　*

My theory is that if I come back as a tree, it'll be a live oak. Live oak is the state tree of someplace, I think Georgia, somewhere around there in the deep south. I don't know about any of the other states' versions of the live oak, but in Texas, I think live oaks are distinctive from other trees, in how different they are, except maybe mesquites, but mesquite trees that I've seen always seem so small and shrubby and too close to the ground, hardly a tree at all, so they don't count in my theory.

Live oaks are called live oaks because they are one of the oaks that don't drop all their leaves in the winter, that aren't *deciduous* if you can handle the scientific parlance. Now, I don't actually know how many oaks lose their leaves and how many don't. Hell, I don't even know how many types of oaks there are, probably 500 for all I know. But live oaks keep their leaves in the winter *ergo* they seem alive; *ergo* someone named them live oaks, God or somebody.... Actually, to me live oaks are a nuisance-shedder. They drop these sharp little leaves all year but seem to grow them twice as fast as they lose them.

The trunk of most live oaks looks as sturdy and straight as any other oak. I suppose everyone knows that oaks are one of the thick woods, one of the heavy woods that are better for furniture than chopping up for firewood. Anyway, at that first branching is where things go wrong for live oaks. Seems like they all change right there where branches start forking out. Seems like nothing stays straight after that. Every inch of every branch looks to me like the trees are screaming, they twist and shudder and reach for the ground one inch and the sky the next. They look like supplicants and that famous painting of the screamer - you know that one? By that Scandinavian? Expressionist crap, except that the woman in the painting (OK, maybe it's a guy) and the ground behind him and the red sky above him, are all tortured and wavery and are just like the twists and double-backs and triple forks in a live oak. There are other trees, that when they get really large you have to put supports under the branches that have reached too far out and down instead of straight and up; the supports are to keep them from breaking under their own weight. Well, I bet you can't even *find* a really large live oak that hasn't either broken itself apart or doesn't have those large supports stopping those big branches from cracking off.

You know, large trees in other parts of the country seldom spread their branches sideways, most are like ornamental pears, reaching pretty much straight up. I think it's because south Texas soil is so rocky - limestone and all. Roots are spending so much time finding their way through and around the rocks in the soil that trees don't, or *can't*, climb straight up. So they spread and bend and twist.

Inside, that's me, is my theory.

I'm thinking about how gnarled I've become, this old tree has become, all the gigantic, twisted branches, the thick chunks of wood carefully cut and placed between the branches and the ground to prevent collapse. I guess I'm a lot like that fictional guy, who was it? Silas Marner? Dorian Gray? I don't know, the guy with the painting in his attic; it was one of those old books they made us all read back in school.

Anyway, back to live oaks, the branches toward the top are just as "gnarled" as my painting, but reaching eventually up to the sky, constantly shedding and growing thousands of tiny leaves.   Like, I own a District judge.   Mayors and City Councils. Cops, State and Federal Congressmen. Guys high up in the IRS infrastructure and the TRC.   You don't always need the head guy; mostly you need the people who don't get thrown out less than a decade in, with exceptions.   You provide and then you ask back.   You always remember to tie up the loose ends, I'm always preaching that.   You get private help to find out things you need, things you can use.   And drugs, of course. Don't get me started on drugs - drugs helping, drugs getting in the way, drugs making you *another* fortune.

But you always have to stay careful.

Like family.   I never cheated on Paige.   I tried, but I never did. I don't consider screwing a few secretaries cheating. They ask for it, anyway. It's funny, you see a movie where the boss is sitting behind his desk, and his secretary is under the desk chewing on his salami?   Not nearly the fun they make it look like - believe me.   First she's going to get sweaty down there, not enough ventilation.   Then, how are you supposed to get excited enough when you're lucky she can reach anything with her hands, cramped like she is down there?   Also you have to be built gigantic, or slump way down in the chair for her to even get at you, and how's that look if someone comes in your office and your head is barely peeking up over the desk?

Nope, cheating on Paige never entered my mind, having a woman full time on the side.   That slut Samantha would have been the only... but that's water under the bridge and kind of sick to even think about, at this late date.

So right now I'm sitting in my home office, ruminating. I put what I like to call the 'cookbooks' away in my safe place. I do some lines. I lean back in my Big Boss chair. I put my feet up.   I like looking at the Magnanni loafers I'm wearing even though I'm in my morning robe.   Wearing good shoes without socks is something I picked up a few years ago.   You have to get cleaned up first, of course.   Nothing worse than seeing your feet turn brown from sweating in an expensive pair of Italian loafers.

To me it's like something I expect Jack, that *schmuck*, did back in college in his fucking fraternity house, whichever one he was in. None of the Jewish ones invited me to pledge, not that I spent any time with any of them pledge week. Even Jews grow snobs, you know? I remember one of the frat houses stuck me in a room with some Bobby Fischer type chess player who stomped me a few games and wandered off shaking his head, leaving me in that room till I finally got up and left, no one making a fucking peep at me when I left. But fuck 'em, boys and girls, none of them have a net worth anywhere close to the -

Doorbell. Sunday morning, for God's sake. Who the hell could even be on the grounds without ringing at the gate? I haven't seen Knowles all morning; don't know if he's here or not. Probably out doing his Sunday morning grocery run. Whoever's at the door must have gotten around the gate and the alarms.

I'm guessing I have one of my special visitors, now that I think about it. I have a plethora of silent and invisible people who I pay to take care of me and my businesses behind the scenes. My Live Oak caretakers, so to speak. God I love thinking like this. Plethora - straight out of *The Three Amigos*! Haw, haw, haw.

Maybe reporting in. Maybe it's the guy I have overseeing that rezoning I'm forcing the council to approve for the land I need, to develop the Olmos Basin Mall - that "pipe dream" the editorial called it in the *Express-News* - I should rename it *The Pipe Dream Mall* when I build it and cram it down that writer's throat, that Jacob O'Neal piece of Irish fuck. I've already gotten the dossier I ordered on him. Plans are being made to screw up his life, you can believe me when I say that.

I trot on downstairs to the main door and whoever it is hasn't rung the doorbell again. Very patient. I look through the keyhole and I'm surprised. You never know who the hell's going to show up at my mansion on a lazy Sunday morning. Some of these "big shot" assholes I own think they can drop in any time they fucking feel like, no matter who they are - no matter who they *think* they are....

So I open the door. He smiles and says "Hi, Fred."

He swings the hand around he had down by his pants leg and I see he's holding a pretty scary looking gun, capped by the kind of metal cylinder you see in a movie that I'm guessing means it's a silencer. I'm suddenly feeling just a little nervous, but he hasn't killed me yet, so maybe he's just going to try to strong arm me. This one *is* a cold son of a bitch under the nice; I've certainly seen some of his work up close. Now I'm feeling half chilled, half scared shitless by the look in his eyes, you can never tell about some people. I'm trying desperately to think of the perfect thing to say but I'm not able to. "We going to discuss this?"

I'm lifting my shoulders and holding my hands open and out to show I've got nothing to hide, no hard feelings.

"No, Fred," he says, "Like you always say, it never hurts to tie up loose ends," and I hear a pop that snaps my head back.

IX – HAROLD KNOWLES

The last time the police buzzed around this place was at least, what, ten years ago? The girls got themselves killed. I've been here, well I was hired by Mister Barnes way before the Missus died and he took ill. My memory is not as sharp as once, but I would guess the girls died after I'd been with the Barnes's somewhere over ten year.

So I'm here maybe over twenty year now, I think a lot over.

I always do my Sunday shopping at the HEB on Broadway.

I come home this Sunday just like ever Sunday, and drive up the driveway to take the fork to the back of the house. Only the front door stands open and I'm absolutely positive it was shut tight when I left, absolutely positive.

So I park in front, grab the bags and come up the stairs. Of course I see Mister K right as soon as I get to the door, his fancy Italian shoes and all, layin there lookin deader than a doornail.

He is flat on his back, a pool of blood under his head that has slowly seeped over a ways to the left where there's a little dip in the Mexican tile has caused it to form a second pool. His eyes are open and lookin at absolutely nothin, like what war's for in that old song.

His bifocals are also open and are lyin next to his head as if they'd been thrown off when he fell. His mouth is also open. He has an expression on his face that could be happy or sad, I can't tell except he can't be too happy.

He is wearin the Italian loafers without socks, and he has on his silk robe which has opened enough to show his bare chest and boxer shorts. The ones with the little stars. He must not of tied the robe's belt well enough to keep it from openin when he fell backward.

And he has a bullet hole in his forehead and I might get sick right here, I can smell the smoke and the blood and he must of gone to the bathroom, too; I can't help but think this is the part they leave out of movies.

Instead of passin out I walk as fast as I can to the pantry, about 20 feet from the body, and I'm breathin hard.

I spend a long time in here starin at the Log Cabin Syrup thinking things through about the chances that someone might try to pin this on me. I finally work that out in my mind, and so I call the police, 911.

I'm forwarded to a detective who tells me to do nothin, touch nothin, and call no one else. We are on the way, the man says. Now I'm thinkin about two other things - what to steal before the police arrive and whether any of Mister K's family or houseguests would catch me, whether anyone else is even home.

Mister K is a great one for havin stashes in a couple places in the house. Maybe I can hide some of the cocaine in my pants' cuffs or underwear or - wait, there are two, maybe three other things I would love to take from this place, given the chance. It has been several minutes and I'm still not hearin sirens from outside, or footsteps inside, so I think I will need to get upstairs as fast as I can. I can get the coke that I know where Mister K has in one of his nightstands, and also the stash in his office if I have enough time.

But then I think I'm hearin the soft paddle of bare feet on the wood of the main staircase. It sounds like someone comin down the steps. I rush out of my hidin place and see it's Jesse walkin quickstep toward me. He nods when he sees me.

"Knowles?" He seems calm. I put a hand on his shoulder and try to lead him away from the vestibule.

"I've called the police, Jesse. Your Dad looks like he's hurt bad, over by the front door. An ambulance is on the way. They'll do everythin they can, son, but you should stay away from the door."

Jesse stops our march toward the kitchen. He knocks my arm from his shoulder. "I called the police just before I came down the stairs," he sneers, "Dad was dead when I went back upstairs. His brains are all over the floor and the wall. Relax... I wish I knew what's taking them so long to get here."

"You mean *you* found him first? God, Jesse, I'm sorry." I don't know whether I'm sorrier about my boss's spoiled-brat kid findin the body, or that I'm probably not goin to have any alone time to snatch anythin.

Then we both hear one or two sirens wailin in the distance. Jesse looks at me. "If you want any of the old man's shit, get into his bedroom fast. I'll talk to the cops first. But do it quick, cause they'll be here any second. Forget the stuff in his office, I already moved that."

Although I'm not fond of the kid and don't want to respond, the cool of the hazel eyes staring at me help me realize that what is being offered is worth more than pride. So I scamper up the stairway, and hear the sirens gettin louder, probably gettin close to Wilshire by now.

My own car is parked in the back; I can toss the new TomTom in the trunk, along with that set of gold coins. I wonder if I have time to run back down to the kitchen for a sandwich baggy.

X – JACK

I am reading the *Times,* sitting at a table outside the cafe, mostly hidden from view by the flower boxes. I prefer the table on the far end, which is where I sit this morning. I am having an early breakfast here at Rex's, just as I do almost every day. I enjoy watching and listening to the people who either eat here, or come by walking, running or on bikes. Occasionally the place will get so full someone will ask to share my table. I'm not much for conversation, discourage it really, but I love the looks of the people, the snatches of story, the clothes, the smiles and arguments, laughter and frowns.

Of course I realize it is mostly because I'm a pretty lonely guy. But that is OK because that's the way I've set my life up. I am awfully busy once I start into my day's work and I often forget to get up from my desk to stretch, much less to spend time eating or going out. This morning ritual at Rex's and my work are really about all I *have* of a life, all things considered. I work from my house as a consultant and when I get a call from any of the corporations that need my help from time to time, the requirements of the job force me to devote everything I have, everything I am, to resolving the challenges I'm handed. I mostly get calls to resolve security issues on mainframe sites at the largest of bank and insurance holding companies. But I also receive many calls to do the same kind of work for massive networks of servers being used to run retail outlets and support centers all over the world. I've also advertised myself for hacker and programming services, but that ended up making me *too* busy. I tried working mainframe security all day and hacking all night till even I couldn't keep up.

Ethel, my waitress all these years, approaches. "You're thinkin too hard, Mr. Gantt! Why don't you relax and let me bring you a big ol breakfast! Know whatcha want this mornin?" She pours my coffee and sets down a small cup of fresh fruit, the way I always like to start my mornings. This is San Pedro, California, a few blocks away from the marina and about a ten minute drive from my condo, up the hill a ways.

"Yes, dear, I do. I'm missing my old stomping grounds this morning - think I'll have the fajita omelet, no sour cream, chicken."

"Texas, right. I hear it's pretty hot over there right now, though - you're better off missin it 'sted of bein there! Fajita omelet chicken no sour cream, comin right up, Mr. Gantt! Enjoy the fruit while you're waitin!" And off she goes, large and happy, sticking the pencil back behind her ear.

Three extremely thin men, dressed in the full regalia of the Tour de France, are standing in the street in front of me. Two are watching the third working at removing the tire from the front of his bike.

I pick up the front page of my Monday morning *L.A. Times*. My interest in current events has flagged over the years, but I do like to try to keep up. By the time I get to The Nation pages, my omelet is in front of me and the strawberries and melon slices are no longer in the cup. At the bottom of the page, I do a double take. The slightly bug-eyed, unlikely face smiling back at me is Frederick Klein, "Noted Texas Entrepreneur and Philanthropist." The article above and to the right of the photograph, is headlined *Foul Play Suspected In Death of Noted Texas Multi-Millionaire.*

As I read the article, I snort at the *Times* reporter's use of the word 'Suspected'. *The man has finally been murdered,* I think to myself. I glance up. The three men have locked their bikes to the side of the bike rack and are heading toward Rex's front door.

I continue to enjoy the omelet, and Ethel comes by to refill my coffee and remove the fruit cup. I fold the paper to the article on Klein and re-read it. When I finish my second reading and put the paper down, I continue to stare at Klein's picture. Fred has aged considerably since I last saw him. When I knew him, his baldness had just looked inevitable; now it is complete. The horn rimmed glasses he had worn were only for reading when I knew him, but now they look permanent. The bags over and especially under his eyes have puffed out considerably. I can picture him sitting at his desk, face aimed down and raising just his eyes - those bags have gotten to the point where you might not see his eyes when he looks up. Poor guy, I think wryly. He also looks like he has gained and lost weight several times since I last saw him. The blotchy face is unhealthy looking and his skin sags. He is probably still doing the white candy too, I think. I'd like to believe he had constant sniffles and nosebleeds by the time he died if he never stopped feeding that habit.

I am definitely having a hard time feeling sorry for the guy, all things considered. *All things considered.*

So, no more brother-in-law. The article covers the whole background story about the accident; I skipped over it the first time through. Wife and sister-in-law dead about ten years. Their accident the impetus for the Texas Department of Transportation to require filled 55 gallon drum containers be placed in front of concrete abutments and road forks on all state and federal highways in Texas, anywhere that an automobile was likely to crash into concrete on a highway. In that strange and ironic way, the sisters saved some lives after theirs were taken away.

After a thorough investigation, no one had been able to prove the accident was anything more than an accident. The possibility that another car may have been involved had been strongly suspected from the first, but also had never been proven.

It doesn't really matter to me, of course. My wife is dead. I sigh, leave money for the bill and tip, put the Nation section under my arm pit, and leave the rest of the paper next to my half finished meal.

Instead of heading directly home, I go straight down 22nd Street to the Marina. Pulling up to the water's edge, I think about Fred for a while. I've hated the man for a long time, and am pretty sure he had something to do with the girls' deaths. But if Cholo and the rest of the police department haven't found proof... idly, I wonder if his death and the accident could be related too.

Finally, I head home.

My beeper goes off on my way up Crenshaw. My answering service is requesting a callback.

I park in the garage under my condo, and trudge up the stairs to my first floor. I have lived relatively simply for many years; the condo suits my needs, basically a kitchen and small living area on the first floor and a combination bedroom / office on the second. I grab a bottle of water out of the fridge and walk up to the next level. I turn my phone to speaker and call the service I use. I prefer someone else screen my calls, so I have no dialable home phone number. The woman's voice mechanically instructs me to dial my 8 digit code and once I get through that security drill, the woman who comes on the line tells me I've been called by someone claiming to be a policeman from San Antonio, Texas. If I am willing to return the call immediately she will place it for me and, whether she dials for me or not, she will be glad to tell me the phone number I can use at my discretion.

I ask for the name of the policeman - it is Hartmann - so I give her my permission to dial. After a Sergeant and two secretaries pass me along, I hear a lower-pitched version of Cholo's voice saying "Hartmann." "Hello, Lieutenant." I say, "this is Jack Gantt returning your call."

"Thanks for calling, Jack. I'm sorry to take your time like this. You remember me after all these years?"

"My memories of that time in my life have remained clearer than anything that's happened since, Lieutenant."

"I completely understand. Of course. However, time hasn't stood still. Actually, I'm no longer a Lieutenant."

"So what is your title now? Whatever it is, congratulations. I remember you were always in the middle of whatever excitement was going on."

"I'm a Captain now, Jack." He sighs. "Big fish, but they've practically thrown me out of the water now, making me *plan...* and *speak...* and, worst of all, *organize.*"

Captain Hartmann! I'm shocked, really. I remember George Hartmann as being a bulky, serious guy, a weightlifter in a uniform that looked as if he would split the sleeves the way Bruce Banner does when he turns green. Hartmann isn't stupid by any means, but I'm surprised that he has been ambitious enough to rise this high. I figure he must be next to Police Chief as a Captain. What's his nickname? Oh yeah, Cholo.

We talk for a while about the old days, even laugh again about Cholo's memory from our days playing football in high school. It's still our little joke that I can't remember Cholo being the guy who saved me from beating that other football player to death. We could joke about it even back then, back when Hartmann worked on the girls' accident. I remember

233

making the statement downtown, and then Hartmann taking me out to dinner. Where had we gone?

Cholo was getting to the point.

"Have you heard about the death of your brother-in-law?" he asks.

"Former. Yes, I read about it in this morning's *L.A. Times*."

Hartmann chuckles. "I'm not surprised it made your paper. Fred K was in L.A. at least a couple or three times a year for some premier or other, or for receiving an award for giving away some money."

"But why exactly have you called me, Captain - should I call you Captain?"

Hartmann chuckles again. "Captain, George, Cholo, I'm fine with whatever makes you comfortable. May I still call you Jack?"

"Sure... Cholo. So, tell me why you've called me."

XI – CHOLO

I punch the button on the phone to end the call and pick up his folder. *John Wayne (Jack) Gantt* is typed on a sticker on the folder's label. I smile and think over the conversation we'd just had. I shake my head. I could really like this guy. Still, I need to call my contact with the LAPD, that Sidowski guy, and get a name from him in the Palos Verdes / Rolling Hills area so I can confirm Gantt's alibi and get some background information on the life Gantt has been leading since he left San Antonio. Personally I don't like doing it, but I have to. It's what I do.

Then I write notes of as accurate a replay of the conversation we'd just had as possible, so I can review it later if I need to. I'll have Doreen type it up and let Charlie and Lieutenant Buckhalter read it.

I'll think about, and note, the change in Gantt's attitude after I'd mentioned the will. I was notified by Klein's personal lawyer, that Wilson guy, that Gantt figures prominently in the will. It is one reason I called him - to see if he'd come back for the reading. And the second I was notified of Klein's death, I figured it must be obvious to everyone that this death and the deaths of the girls could very well be related, even with as much time as has taken place between them. So having Gantt back to interview might be interesting; a lot of time has passed, and people remember things differently with time passing - maybe I should depose the guy again and talk him back through the whole thing. I feel myself slowly turn grim as I think about Klein, those poor girls on the highway (I can still see Mrs. Klein's body in the morgue), setting up security for the funeral coming up, appointing a lead for the murder investigation, and working out a partnership with the AHPD and the THPD on this thing, which means I have to iron out my problems with the new Chief in Terrell Hills. It is amazing, I think, how much of a cluster fuck Mr. K's death has caused with three jurisdictions trying to peacefully investigate the murder, when Terrell Hills obviously should be handling the whole case.

I also miss being out in the field. My rise to head the units that investigate homicides, sex crimes, overnight felonies, and youth crimes seems like it has taken a few days in comparison to those years of being a young cop in a city when every minute has been etched into my mind in slow motion. Once I left the Academy, the adventure had begun almost immediately and didn't really end until my promotion to Lieutenant, when I left the squad in the Jungle. Man, that was such a hot area; the men and I were involved in so many wild-assed situations back then!

Anyway, I sigh, that part of my life is over for the most part, except for whenever I can force my old thirty pound loaded belt to buckle over my gut and get out there with some of my current line officers: Charlie the Chunk and Black Leon when I can.

In spite of having that intercom button set up on my phone, I raise my voice a little and say "Doreen!"

"Be there in a sec, boss," comes a voice just outside my office.

Soon she comes in, steno pad in hand. I hand her the notes I'd made on my phone call with Gantt.

Doreen glances at the title on the top sheet. "Shall I type these and make copies for Lieutenant Buckhalter and the file?"

"And one for Charlie. I think I'm going to spend most of the day in the field today, but when I get back I want to work on setting up a special team to work on the Klein murder."

"Good. I've been trying to free myself up some time to set up the new filing system I've worked out for your personnel files, so I'll do that while you're gone...." she hesitated, then added, "You mean Charlie *Briscoe,* Captain?"

Irritated, I just nod so she won't comment further. "OK, I'll have these notes typed in a few minutes, if you want to review and initial them before you go. Oh, and Paul Thompson called again. I swore to him that you'd call him back before Christmas, and he actually laughed!" She walked out, her heels clacking on the linoleum.

I groan because Paul Thompson is the front page political editorial writer for the *Express News.* To me Thompson is a sensationalist who will turn this murder into a gigantic conspiracy against something or other. I'm also groaning because of Doreen. I think, first a new filing system, and second she questions my judgment on giving the notes to Charlie. I'm not sure which pisses me off more... probably the filing. Seems like once a year she has to screw around with systems that are working like a charm. It's like I hear about in companies, nine to five type companies like where Peggy works, where they reorganize shit every once in a while regardless of what's going on, or if it's necessary or not. Busy work, I grump to myself.

I stand up and stretch. Think I'll stop at the gym first. I am going to lose this weight, starting today. Peggy and Lucy have been after me to get my weight under control for months. So has Doreen.

Then after a good workout, I'll get cleaned up and see where everyone is. Maybe I'll join that surveillance team out on Roberts or just respond to calls like the old days. First I'll see what the Chunk and Leon are up to, maybe they'll work out with me this morning.

I grab an extra shirt. I have workout gear in the locker at my gym, so I'm ready to roll. I walk out to Doreen's desk and as I approach her she holds out her hand and a sheaf of paper.

"What's this?" I ask, taking them from her.

"Three typed copies of your notes ready for your initials, a letter for your signature that you dictated late yesterday - you wanted to mail it to the new Chief in Terrell Hills - and some mail you received from the Catholic Men's Club about making an appearance at a week-end retreat coming up, to speak on 'religion in law enforcement, or a topic of your choosing' as they put it. I think that's a week from Saturday... yes, a week from Saturday," she confirms, pointing at the large calendar that substitutes for a blotter on her desk.

"Good God," I say, sitting on the edge of her desk. I quickly read my notes and initial all three copies. "Call whoever wrote you and say I'll be glad to speak to them. Will you come up with an outline I can speak from? Or maybe just the one I used when I spoke at the Jefferson High career day last year?"

"Uhm, boss, they want your talk to relate religion to law enforcement. I don't think the high school talk is appropriate. How about the Mt. Zion Youth Ministry speech from last year?"

"Whatever," I say impatiently. I *really* need to get going, get to the damned gym. Get out *cruisin.* "And just hold on to the letter to Chief Newton. I need to talk to him in person anyway about the Klein investigation. See if I can have lunch with him... or not lunch, dammit, just an hour of his time sometime tomorrow morning." *That beady-eyed son of a bitch.* "I'm fixin to go work out now."

"Yes, sir," she smiles. "I'll take care of it while you're gone. Are you still planning on returning before the end of the day?"

"Yes of course, Doreen."

"Excellent, Captain, I'm looking forward to your review of the new files when you get back."

I stand back up as she bends over the paperwork on her desk. I stare down at her, knowing she won't look back up unless I say something else. Maybe I can tell her I'll call Thompson back; I don't really want to, but I'd like her to look up at me again. She makes me feel like an idiot when we're in the office.

*   *   *   *   *

"Doreen!" I yell, exasperated. I can't find anything in my office since she moved every damned thing around. Even the filing cabinet is in a different corner, and the files! She's filed everything in a sequence I can't figure out!

"Doreen, God damn it, where are you!" I'm wasting my breath now, imagining her taking a break or maybe even already gone home, since I've been concentrating on my work and have no idea how late it has gotten. I check my watch and it is just a little before 7:00, but I still have heard nothing out in the outer office. And here I am, cursing at her knowing how she hates me using foul language. If she *is* still around, she might walk out the front door just *because* I'm cursing.

I open the file again. I'm looking for Charlie's personnel file. The roster files, as near as I can make out, are not in alphabetical order. *Maybe it's by rank*, I think. *No, Aarons is my highest ranking Lieutenant and he isn't first in line, Why not just have everybody in alphabetical order? Why did she have to fuck with -*

Suddenly, Doreen flies into my office, heels clicking furiously. "Sorry Boss, sorry, I could hear you yelling all the way into the Ladies' Room, but there was no way I could make it back here till now!"

I'm nodding OK the whole time she talks. I've already realized I'm not upset about the filing system, I'm upset she didn't come running as soon as I called. Doreen is such a sight to behold, I can't imagine anyone staying anything but respectful around her. In spite of the fact that she is as smart as a whip, I'd keep her around just because she brightens up the place. I stole her from Chief Torres back when I received my last promotion, back when she was one of the Chief's two Administrative Assistants. Back when she was the Chief's favorite "Police Spokesperson."

"Just please find me Charlie Briscoe's file so I can look it over."

"Of course Boss, but may I show you how to find it so you won't have a need to get upset when I'm not around? When you work really early or late, I may not always be here."

I look at her cool, smiling face. I wouldn't mind just staring for a while, but I've done that too many times, so I just agree with her and she explains the new system, and I don't want to argue about it so I just nod. After the explanation she breezily announces that she is going to go on home, unless I have something else for her to do. She reminds me that it is after seven, and I say she can go. She nods politely with a smile, and I watch her leave the room.

She's wearing a dress, a work dress she's worn many times, a simple green collared thing, buttoned to her throat, the length halfway down her calves, the dress cut to successfully hide her figure. I reflect that, in fact, she never wears anything the slightest bit revealing. She is very serious about how she appears at work and that she maintain that look. I must take our intimacy to my grave, but I often thrive in the knowledge of it.

I've been staring at the door she closed when she left. What I need to do is study the personnel file of Charlie the Chunk. Will it help me justify handing Charlie the lead on a murder investigation of this importance? I blink thoughtfully, and finally walk back to my desk, tossing Charlie on the blotter. Can I assign Charlie the Klein case, in spite of its importance, in spite of the journalists covering it and the THPD having jurisdiction? Can I give enough of my own time to Charlie to help get him through this if he can't handle it? I'm thinking I have to play this very carefully, but weighing everything I'm thinking yes. Even so, I know I need to gnaw on this one for a while longer.

I call Peggy and tell her I'm in the middle of the Klein thing and ask her to put my dinner in the microwave for later. I ask her how Lucy is doing; she's out on a date, and while Peggy launches into a description of the kid she's out with, I see my other private line start blinking and I think to myself that maybe it's Doreen and I feel a weird sense of relief. I tell Peggy I love her and hang up. I tap the blinking line. I answer the call by just saying "Hello."

She says "Hi. I've missed you."

I pause, imagining her. Yes, I'm more than smitten. I pause long enough she says "Hello? George?"

"Yes," I say. She only calls me Boss or Captain in the office, she calls me George in private conversation. It's like she imagines we are being watched in the office. "Yes, Doreen, I'm here."

"I'll be at my friend's house, whether you want to see me or not. They've decided to extend their trip for another six weeks. The garage door will be open till late." And she hangs up.

*   *   *   *   *

"From a political perspective, it could be a disaster if he doesn't do a good job. Or worse yet, I suppose, if he botches it or embarrasses himself. I'm thinking... I don't know... it's a mistake. I know he's your old friend, George, but this is *such* a big deal, too big to let friendship get in the way of common sense... good police work... that any number of other detectives on the staff can provide."

I've got too many reasons for using Charlie to head this case, but Doreen just needs to be reassured and I'm hoping she'll drop the argument. She's feeling my tension through her hands. When they get to the middle of my back, it's like there's a rock in the muscle - the deltoid sheath back there - and she can't work it out. I think the muscle has seized up, cramped, and won't let go. One of my Sergeants had something similar happen and he got a cortisone injection right in the muscle and the cramp went away for good.

She says it's tension from not cracking the Klien case. It's actually become a political hot potato, my first. Hard to believe, but as many reporters are assigned to this story from all over the place as I have detectives assigned!

Doreen has her robe on. The sheet is up over my hips, and my arms are supporting my forehead while she works on me.

She continues. "And it's also important for another reason not to select him. Your men will question it, whether they say anything or not - and I doubt they will because of how they feel about you. Look, if this is an instinct thing, then follow your instincts, but... is it?" She straddles me and rolls the heels of her palms over and over the cramp. She must have removed or at least loosened her robe to mount me the way she has, so I roll over. She adjusts to stay on top of me while I complete the maneuver.

I put my hands on her arms at her elbows. "I don't know," I say, "I've been looking for something good to give him, and think this might be it. I understand the down side, of course. There are a couple other open cases I could give him.... Give this one to either Buckhalter or take it on myself. One thing's sure, I need to go in tomorrow morning and announce my decision at morning roll call. You need to set me up a small press conference mid-morning. I'm still leaning toward Charlie, but I'll let you know for sure tomorrow."

"Maybe you could also announce Gantt coming back to town to participate in the investigation?"

"God no, Doreen, I don't think that would be wise at all. I don't think the guy's going to be that much help, and I think drawing attention to him will do nothing but dredge up all the past shit he's been through. Besides, he's still a suspect until I hear back from a few people out there."

She nods. "OK," she says, "I'll have the press come in at... 9?"

"Yeah. 9 or 9:30's fine, and clear it with the Chief's office too, so he doesn't feel left out."

She is nude above me, the robe spread wide open. I've been idly rubbing her stomach with the back of my hand while we talk. Now I slide it down into her hair. She is hot down there.

She looks down at me, amused. "Slow down, cowboy," but she is bending down to meet my lips with hers.

*　　*　　*　　*　　*

"Sorry, no questions people.　That was my statement - coördinated investigation with Terrell Hills' Chief Newton; Detective Charles Briscoe leading the SAPD team; full support from the entire San Antonio Police Department; you all heard me the first time."

I ignore the shouted questions and follow the Chief, Charlie and Lieutenant Buckhalter from the room.　The "press conference" has taken all of seven minutes.

"Norm," I say to Buckhalter, "You and Charlie come see me in half an hour.　I'd like to go over what we have and see if we can make some plans.　I'll touch bases again with Chief Newton and see if he wants to meet with us and actually *have* a coördinated investigation.　With as few detectives as they have, he told me yesterday he could only afford to assign one to this mess, so maybe we can just attach whoever it is to Charlie."

"I'm taking off, Cholo," Chief Torres breaks in, shaking hands all around.　"I've got a luncheon to make an appearance at."

I choose not to mention that it is only about 9:10 a.m., letting him escape.

"OK," Buckhalter says to Charlie as they walk away, "let's talk at your desk and get something down on paper for the Captain."

"The Captain" watches them walk away.　I am relieved the announcement has seemed to go smoothly, Buckhalter isn't bothered at all by the Chunk being named to head the investigation and Torres hasn't made a peep.　I am convinced Charlie will be perfect for the job and whether he solves anything or not, it will reflect well in his record that he's been put in charge of an important, high visibility case.

I ride the elevator up to my floor. My office is in a corner at the end of the hall. Doreen's name plate is below mine next to the door that I open and walk through.

Doreen looks up from her desk. "How'd it go?" she asks.

"OK. Briscoe and Burkhalter will be here in about half an hour, if you could keep everyone else at bay while we review everything? Say, two hours?"

"Sure boss."

I head for the door to my office. "Quick press conference," she says as I walk by.

"Yup," I say, not wanting to stop and chat. "I need to make some calls."

I closed my door behind me and head for the desk after removing my sidearm. I want to check back in with my west coast contacts before the meeting. *Maybe Gantt has been a bad boy in L.A. That'd be nice.*

Interlude – 10:57 a.m.

Sammie's head was finally starting to feel better now that they were building up some speed. The wind, the sound of the road, and the loud whining of the engine was relaxing her and making her feel better.

Sammie began thinking about her meal. With the aspirin working, the Smokehouse potato soup was sounding yummier and yummier. She ordered it every time they went. She could just taste it right now, the thick creamy potatoes, the bacon and chives stirred in, mmmmmm. She also got a side salad with it to eat while she watched her sister devour whichever heavy German meal she would order. And Paige wondered why she took after Belle rather than David! Jesus Christ....

She peeked open an eye and glanced out the window. They were really just starting the drive, merging onto the Interstate. It wouldn't take long to get to New Braunfels but it was just too bright to open her eyes and sit up.

Paige had noticed her looking out the window. "Awake?" she asked.

"Nope" came Sammie's dull reply.

246

Paige sounded a little upset when she said "Sammie! I thought the idea of doin' this trip is so we can relax and talk!"

Sammie thought it over and smiled and said "In that order, Sis, and I'm relaxin' first." She rocked and squirmed in her seat, as if she were in bed softening up the mattress and pillow. She smiled and said "Mmmmmm."

She felt Paige push a bit harder on the gas pedal. "That's not true, Sammie. Come on, let's talk. Please?"

Sammie shook her head but kept her eyes closed. "Paige, you are the world's whiniest person, you know that? My God woman, you're married - you have a child, for God's sake, you're a mother - you're rich and you can afford anything you can get Freddie the Jew to spring for, so quit complaining," she finished weakly. And she thought dammit, I didn't bring my flask.

A truck roared by in the slow lane.

Paige let out a scream as a current of air blasted the little sports car. Sammie opened her eyes and sat up quickly at the noise as the steering wheel whipped back and forth under Paige's hands. She could see INTERSTATE TRUCKING painted on the back of the speeding eighteen wheeler.

She tried to grab the wheel to help, but Paige screamed again and pushed her away.

Then, as Paige finally seemed to regain control and the wheel steadied, a Corvette, all tricked out in candy apple blue, roared by after the truck. As soon as it cleared the Sunbeam, it screamed around the truck. The bright blue car had Texas plates that read NU GEE.

Sammie was glad they hadn't been killed and angry that Paige wouldn't leave the high speed lane no matter how slow she was going. She wouldn't move over for God or the

Governor. Sammie closed her eyes again and breathed a deep sigh of relief.

Paige was breathing hard at the near miss, but Sammie, slumped back down in her seat, eyes closed.

"Damn it, Sammie" her sister said. Tears were in her voice. "I had a nice surprise to tell you and all you can do is... be mean. You are just such a shit sometimes." And she was crying, sniffling as she drove. Sammie sighed and waited till the noises stopped.

She opened her eyes and looked over at Paige. "I'm sorry, Sis," she made herself smile, "you know how I get when I'm hung over."

Paige had her handkerchief out. "It's just I wanted to tell you my surprise before we get to the Smokehouse, Sammie, and all you can do...." Paige held the handkerchief under her eyes, catching the tears that were starting to flow.

This isn't making sense, anyway, *Sammie thought.* Wasn't I telling her the things she should be happy about? I thought I was telling her why she shouldn't be complaining. She's just acting so fucking hormonal, I don't get it.

Hormonal. Jesus H. Christ. That's it.

She was also vaguely aware, out of the corner of her eye, of another car coming slowly alongside them in the slow lane.

XII – JACK

I'm getting ready to travel. Still not keen on flying, so I'm packing my car. I only have to pack one suitcase because I plan on using a hanging rod across the back seat of my car for my shirts, coats and pants. I've never made the drive from L.A. to San Antonio before, but I came the other way once.

I am playing a song on my stereo, set to repeat. It's a song I often play on repeat and I never tire of it.

A guy wishing he could be different things mostly so he won't have to be himself. Fits.

After a while of playing the song, I stop hearing it with my ears but hear it somewhere, on some level. I can't explain the hypnotic effect if you ask me, but it is there. And yet it isn't like white noise, doesn't have the effect of soothing me to drowsiness because there are words, a tune. I feel when I work long hours it helps keep me sharp for some reason.

I am going to head on out first thing in the morning. I remember stopping once the last time I made this drive in reverse. Was it in New Mexico or Arizona? Damned if I can remember, but I do remember the total drive was a long one, something like... was it thirteen hundred miles? Something like that, I think. It had just been so long ago. Ten years or more.

Why haven't I kept in touch with anyone there? At first, I called Cholo a few times a year, just to check in, but after a few years I stopped. Hartmann had just been promoted to Lieutenant back then and is now a Captain. Captain George "Cholo" Hartmann. A local hero - a celebrity after some shootouts. He and I had even been at the same high school for awhile.

Maybe something someday might have broken on the case if I'd kept pestering him about it. After all, I was certain they'd been murdered, and I was pretty sure who made it happen. Eventually, people make a mistake, don't they? You can't get away with something like this forever, can you?

I've beaten myself up about this many times over the years. It doesn't help me to think it through, over and over, through the years. Nothing stops me from waking up sweating, or missing a beat while I am hammering away at the keyboard doing a job that is basically rote work for some bank or other; I end up staring at nothing, gazing just above my monitor.

It is *different* now, I tell myself. Fred is dead. Fred hasn't just died, he's been murdered. I think, and guess Cholo thinks so too from the tone of his voice coming through the phone line, that maybe this is what he's been waiting for, some kind of break in figuring out what had happened. And to me the more important *why*.

I am looking at the map. Halfway from L.A. to San Antonio looks like it is somewhere between Tucson and Las Cruces, maybe Lordsburg or Deming, in New Mexico. Lordsburg sounds familiar, probably where I'd stopped for the night, going the other way. Maybe I should check with my motor club, see what nice motels around there have vacancies tomorrow night. People probably don't make a lot of reservations at those places, but regardless, after dinner in the summer they probably fill up quickly.

The guy in the song is wishing he could be anywhere but where he is.

I change the subject in my head. I have a theory, certainly not one I think I came up with independently, that every relationship involves someone who loves the other more. I know I had cared more deeply in my relationship with Sammie, and Alice had in ours, so the theory seems a natural conclusion for me. I think my Mom had probably cared the more in my parents' marriage. Belle probably loved more in hers, yet David's reaction to her death seemed to belie that. Painfully obvious was the Paige / Fred relationship.

Yes, I will make myself drive on to Deming and use Lordsburg as my "tired stop" if I can't make it all the way.

I wonder about the possibility that my love theory can handle some kind of seesaw effect, where the strength of one partner's feelings can diminish, or the other's love can become stronger, causing the *dependence*, if that is the right word, to switch from one to the other. Can one's feelings become stronger, even become dominant over the other's over time? Surely needs change, and consistent demonstrations of the qualities that go into love could have a deepening effect, one on the other, that could enrich, widen the emotional dependence? Somebody can grow up or grow past. Of course, that might happen as often as not in any long relationship. Who knows?

I guess I should take every pair of socks I own, just in case, plus my t-shirts which I roll into cylinders as I'd learned to do in the Army. I figure I'll be in my Lucchese's or sneakers most of the time, but I'll still pack some nice shoes, too. I also bury my 9mm in the middle of my underwear, along with the holster. War trophy or not, I always kept it clean and available.

I have notified every company I work for in emails earlier in the day. Although I'd said personal issues were calling me back to Texas for several weeks, I privately think I might be away as long as a month or two. I left it open ended in the memo, promising to let them know within a few weeks if I'll be "out of pocket" longer than I'm guessing.

I wonder if I'm shortchanging many people with my "love" theory. How many couples are on a fairly even footing with their feelings toward each other? Just because I can't think of anyone having that kind of relationship proves nothing. It would be interesting to read a study, if anyone has ever conducted one.

On the other hand, thinking about it is making me tired. But I want to load up the car, eat, and settle the questions about where I am spending tomorrow night on the road before I will allow myself to go to sleep.

Although, I think, how many people will tell an interviewer they don't love their spouse much? Or are pretty sure they get more than they give back? Not many, I'm sure.

While packing the car, I start thinking about Alice, Donna, the few other girls I've dated over the years. Jane Foster is the only one I've almost dated since I moved here. She is an HR rep at one of the banks I work for. We became good friends in the office and she flashed me once as I sat in a meeting and she stood in the hallway outside, unseen by the rest of the people in the conference room. By the time I got up the nerve to ask her out, she was involved with someone else.

I'm folding t-shirts and laying them over my underwear and socks, the music thrumming around me, remembering Jane's laughing reaction.

"Your timing sucks, Jack! I finally gave up on you, buddy boy! Donald and I are going steady now," she raised her voice so Donald, who was sitting three people down the bar, could hear - "aren't we Donnie - going steady, I mean?" Donald got up and walked over to us, leaning down, putting one arm around each of us.

"Now what are you people talking about down here? Who's going steady?"

Jane leaned in. "Donnie's so shy, Jack," she said in a stage whisper. "He's a little embarrassed to admit that he finally nailed me after months of working me up to it." She reached up and put her hand to Don's cheek. "Isn't he just too cute?"

Donald looked a little pained, but smiled gamely. I couldn't help laughing at them both, Jane's big mouth and Donald's awkwardness. They'd make a great pair. I looked at Donald looking down at Jane. Jane was still holding her hand up against his cheek and gazing at him with a smile.

I smile to myself as I remember the three of us, the fun we'd had on our bar nights after work, Jane flashing me at the office, that freckle-breasted chest. I am finally ready to go to sleep so I can get up early and start my long drive home.

I turn off the music, the song full of unfulfilled wishes.

*   *   *   *   *

The first place I go after I check into the hotel downtown is Earl Abel's.

Although the fried chicken and pies are what bring people in, my comfort food is Abel's open faced sandwich, hot turkey with mashed potatoes smothered in gravy. Me and my Mom, and then Me and Sammie, used to eat here all the time.

The next morning I plug my PC in and start looking around San Antonio for old friends to call. I do some searches through an account I'd set up a long time ago with an internet service. Without thinking too much about it, my first attempts are to see if Alice has ever returned to Texas, or if she stayed in Oklahoma. I find her surprisingly fast, at an address back down in Alice, listed under both Kaplan and a new last name, Chase. Many of the girls I'd dated and boys I'd known in high school and college were not showing up in Texas at all, with a few exceptions. The president of my senior class is a lawyer in Corpus Christi. The guy I'd smoked dope with in college is listed as living in El Paso. One of the guys I'd played poker with is dead; a few others are still in San Antonio.

So I try the number listed for Alice; I tell myself it's an innocent call to just say hi to an old girl friend, but I'm very seriously considering hanging up if a man answers. No one at all answers, and the recorded voice that asks me to leave a message sounds a bit like Alice's but young and with an even stronger Texas accent than I remember her having. This could be a daughter without her own phone line.

"Hello, this is Jack Gantt. I'm looking for Alice Chase, if she used to be Alice Kaplan, I was just taking a chance, calling to say hello. I've just arrived in San Antonio for a short visit after many years. I guess I'll try again later today and maybe leave a phone number for the hotel I'm in if I don't reach anyone then. Bye."

Next I check in with the Police Department. The Captain isn't in his office and the woman I speak to takes the message that Jack Gantt is in town and staying at *La Mansion*. She seems to know who I am and tells me Captain Hartmann will be pleased I made it to town. Very gracious.

I'm still tired from the drive, so I lie down on the bed to see if I can nap. This is the first time I've ever stayed in a hotel in San Antonio, and I'd always heard *La Mansion del Rio* was a good one. It has been open since 1970; even earlier it existed as *La Posada*, Spanish for *The Inn*. The bed seems to me both gigantic and my kind of firm, so it doesn't take long for me to drift off....

Weird kind of ringing in my ears, like beepbeep beepbeep, over and over and over. My eyes flutter once, and then open. I squint over to the table where the noise comes from. The red light on the telephone is fluttering in time to the beeping noise. I roll and reach for the cordless phone perched there. "Hullo?" I say. My voice is hoarse, so I clear my throat and say again, "Hello?"

"Jack? Is that you? God, you sound awful!"

It is a woman's voice, but I don't know who she is. "Thank you," I say, "who *is* this?"

"Alice. How many women were you expecting to call?"

"Alice! How in the hell did you find me? Look, I just woke up. Can you give me a minute without heckling me please?"

"Well, I'm in the middle of stuff here, so call me back where you left the message this morning. I should be here till dinner time."

"OK, it'll just be a few minutes, so I can throw some water on my face."

"Fine Jack," she says briskly and hangs up.

I swing my legs off the bed and sit up. I sit for awhile with my eyes closed. When my head drops toward my chest it wakes me up again and I look around the darkened suite. I finally get up and shuffle into the bathroom to wash my face. When I came back out, I'm smiling. *Same old Alice.*

Before I call her back, I take a water out of the little pay-as-you-go fridge and drink. I open the blinds and look down at the river. I can see the heat coming off the concrete bridge that crosses the canal below.

* * * * *

I don't know it is Alice till she starts climbing down from the big blue truck. It is an F450 XLT, and has one of those full width tool chests behind the cab, a big old trailer hitch and standard double wheels in the rear. There are lines of dirt deeply imbedded up and back from each wheel well. A hard working woman's truck, I think.

My first impression of her is how short her hair is now; she is taller than I remember; she has filled out nicely after all these years.

I have recommended a Mexican restaurant named La Fonda in the Sunset Ridge strip mall directly down the hill from my old high school. She is right on time, just like the old days.

She is wearing jeans, boots, and a worn t-shirt that I can barely read. However, being me I make the effort. It looks like *San Diego Tortilla and Catering*, and below that, *San Diego, Texas*. Instead of saying hello, I ask where San Diego Texas is. Alice ignores the question, choosing to reach up to me for a hug. I hold her away for a moment, looking at her face, then into her eyes. Finally, I feel like maybe I see Alice down in there, the one I'd known. So we hug.

Holding each other feels awkward to me, even though we spoke on the phone several times in the past few days, trying to catch up. Of course we'd been intimate a long time ago, but it was so long ago it makes me feel even more awkward. Also, I cannot remember the last time I've held a woman, but I must say that I'm getting more used to it the longer it lasts. Damn, she feels good. She starts once to pull away, but I hold on so she relaxes back into my arms. As I hold her, feeling the strength in her back with my hands, she makes it easier for me to remember what we'd been to each other back then. *Maybe*, I think... *maybe something... again.*

We make a tall couple and we fit together well. She feels softer than she did back then when we were both full of pointy elbows and knees. Finally, I pull away and she lets me. We smile easily at each other.

She says, "It's a few miles west of Alice."

I put my hands on her shoulders and say, knowing I'm going to piss her off but saying it anyway, "But where is Alice?"

She looks as impatient with me as expected. "I'm right here, Jack. Are you going to feed me or not?"

With eyebrows raised I say "I suppose so. I guess we'd better get to it before you start chewing on my arm."

We start walking. "I didn't mean to act like I'm starving, old man. I just have heard the Alice from Alice stuff all my life. It's the only reason I would ever move, is to stop the stupid jokes."

"Old man? I should be offended." *Why can't I just shut up?* We walk in through the main entrance to the restaurant and get in line at the hostess desk. "But I am an old man, I guess." I eye her up and down as we inch forward. "You look about the same, Alice."

She snorts, but says nothing. She is still really nice looking, better than I remember. Yes, her nose is just a tiny bit big, lips a bit thin. I eye her up and down again. Her legs are still slim, she has those big brown eyes and her hair is a practical, short length that looks really pretty around her face, in spite of her height. She also looks a bit tired, probably from the drive. And she still looks like she works out. I notice lines have formed around her eyes and they are just starting a few places above her lips. Her waist isn't pencil thin anymore and that looks good on her, too. The swell of her breasts is much more noticeable than when we were young.

Now we are walking behind the hostess to our table. As we follow, I breathe in deeply the heavy smells of Tex-Mex and realize I haven't had any since getting back to town. Cheeses and peppers and corn masa and flour tortillas and the simmering of cumin in beef, chicken and pork.... "You are acting like you haven't had any Mexican food since you've been back. You're going to start salivating any second, like an old dog." She is looking up at me as we skirt several full tables before settling in at ours.

"Old dog?" We sit down. "You're right, I haven't had any Tex Mex since I left town many years ago. I just realized it and suddenly I'm starving for it. I've never eaten at this La Fonda, but it's part of the original local chain that I went to all my life. The one I remember was upstairs in a strip mall on Broadway close to the old Broadway Theater, back in the day."

She opens the menu the hostess has given her. When I don't open mine, she asks if I already know what I'm ordering. "I don't," I answer, "I'm just going to tell her what I want."

She nods and continues to look at her menu. Then she says she needs to wash up after the drive, tells me what she wants to drink, and leaves me to the chips and salsa.

When the waitress arrives, I order us both iced tea. She leaves, Alice returns and we start talking.

"I read the marriage announcements for you and your wife in the *Corpus Christi Caller-Times*. I'll always remember my reaction to both the engagement and wedding pictures. I was so jealous I could spit, Jack. I'm embarrassed to tell you, but I was." Actually, it is just as embarrassing to hear, and I don't know what to say back.

So I change the subject. "And you have two girls and an ex?"

Stupid. It sounds wrong as soon as I say it. God, I feel uncomfortable!

But Alice laughs easily. "That's certainly one way of putting it, yes. But my ex lives far enough away that I have the girls most of the time. He left about five years ago, when our youngest was nine. We were all pretty relaxed about it, actually."

Now it is her turn to change the subject. She puts her hand on mine. "The accident was all over the news here too. I was so sorry to hear about it and all the police stuff, Jack. It must have been dreadful."

I nod as I look at our hands. "It was. My brother-in-law wasn't easy to be around either, so it was like facing some kind of purgatory, the thought of living the rest of my life in that situation, without... her... there, too."

"I think it was very brave of you to strike out on your own like you did. You seem to have made a success of it."

"I have. But actually it was an act of pure cowardice; I would never characterize it as bravery." I shake my head sadly. "I ran away. Just couldn't face that life. I can never forget this guy - Fred Klein, my ex brother-in-law - telling me we would be seeing even more of each other than ever. It still makes me shudder." As I speak I'm shocked at how much more I am telling her than I'd intended, I'd never told these things to anyone before. "I think I'd have given him everything I owned if I'd had to, to get away."

"I came close several times to calling you back then," she tells me, "but I never could pick up the phone."

"Gosh, Alice, I appreciate your thinking of me but of course I also understand your hesitation. You know, if I'd handled how you and I broke up even a little better, you might have felt more comfortable calling. I mean, we may have even stayed friends this whole time.... Anyway, I've always regretted the way we broke up and you leaving for Oklahoma. Was it not too bad there?"

"Actually it was! We were really miserable the whole time we stayed there. I hated the school even though I did really well, Dad was never comfortable with his new job, and then they found Mom's cancer. He insisted we move back to Alice after I graduated, and he retired and worked in a little retail store there so he could spend more time with her. When she finally died he just withered and was gone a few years later."

We have interrupted ourselves to order through all this talk; she is getting a chicken enchilada plate, and I've ordered a cup of tortilla soup, a pork tamale, a beef enchilada and a guacamole salad. We get an extra spoon, and take turns eating out of the soup cup - I am amazed at the amount of chicken in the bowl. This is just full of the best spicy tasting chicken. I'd forgotten how good eating Tex-Mex is in San Antonio.

Then the main course comes, along with corn and flour tortillas. Both plates also have spanish rice and refried beans. Neither of us speak as we start eating. I mix my rice and beans and scoop the mixture into a flour tortilla, rolling it like a cigar so I can eat it while working on the tamale and enchilada. I am stuffed halfway through the meal, so I pick at the quacamole salad while I watch her eat. She keeps me busy answering her questions about my life in California.

I ask about the life she'd had in Alice with her husband... I pause, not remembering the guy's name. She fills in the blank with "Robert... Bob. I told you his name the first time we talked. Robert Chase. He was a financial analyst at a bank in Alice when I met him, but he's a big muck-a-muck in Houston now."

"Still banking?" I ask.

"No, he's working for an investment firm now."

I wipe my mouth with the napkin. "So Alice Kaplan is now Alice Chase, huh?" I start picking at my salad again, but don't say anything else. She moves on to her girls, now sixteen and fourteen. "When Bob left, Jenny was eleven and Sophie nine, Jenny just starting Middle School. He more and more often had to drive to Corpus Christi and Houston on business. I guess the beginning of the end came when he suggested moving to one or the other and I said no, and the end came when he was offered a promotion if he would move to one or the other and I said no again."

She is now picking at things on her plate, too. The waitress comes by and cleans up the table, then asks if we want desert and I just order more iced tea, Alice some water. No one is waiting for a table so we settle back and continue the conversation. I tell her about my work, Alice about hers. She had graduated with a degree in animal science and is in the breeding and animal health business in Alice. She says this means she is hired by ranchers and farmers from all over that part of Texas to work with their cattle, pigs and chickens.

"Horses?" he asked.

"Not so much," she said, "I'm involved almost completely with animals bred for slaughter."

"So... I don't see how you could move to a bigger city for Bob, if your work is with farmers and ranchers." I'm also thinking to myself that what I'm saying applies to anyone she might end up dating now, myself included.

"Well no, there *are* farmers and ranchers close enough to the big cities, it's just that I don't want to live in one, and I don't want my girls there, either." She looks around, realizing she is sitting "there" at the moment. She waves her arms around and smiles at me, ruefully. "I don't want to live *here*." I keep the smile on my face, but feel as if a chance is being lost.

I am resigned to stick to the original subject. "So Bob just went away without you and the girls? Just... left?"

"Not exactly. He left and took the admin with him who'd been answering his phone - and screwing him for about a year."

"Oh shit. Sorry, Alice."

She smiles. "It's okay Jack, I wasn't thrilled, but I think he started cheating because we weren't too terribly excited about each other by then, anyway. When he finally told me everything, I actually felt a gigantic relief. It was as if he was telling me I'd made the right decision, after all. I mean, that's never stopped me from calling her 'the slut' and getting myself checked for STD's as soon as I found out, but I haven't really hated them for a long time, if ever."

"Well, you seem pretty comfortable with your life, that's for sure. As soon as everything gets settled here, I guess I'll be heading back to L.A., but it sure has been great seeing you again. You really look beautiful, Alice."

"Why thank you Jack. Of course, you look great too. I'd forgotten how great you look, as a matter fact." She checks her watch. "I guess I should head back now so I can get home before it gets dark."

We stand and walk outside. "I sure appreciate the trouble you've gone to to drive in and see me."

"I kind of had to, Jack - I felt like with all the stuff you've been through I needed to tell you eyeball to eyeball how much I hope you get through all this, and, even how much I still enjoy the memories I have of the old days." We are standing at the driver's side door of her truck.

I nod and smile but feel as if I've eaten too much, or have just gotten some more bad news. I open the door for her. She gracefully climbs up and in the truck, as practiced as if she's been doing it her whole life - which is most likely what she *has* been doing. She starts the truck and it growls the way big diesel trucks are supposed to growl. Bugs mark the front windshield, more than you'd expect from one trip from Alice to San Antonio. Her window slides smoothly down and she smiles at me. I fully never expect to see her again. I take a step up onto the running board, lean in and kiss her firmly on her lips. She may have been thinking about opening her mouth under mine, but my lack of balance with one foot on the running board has me pulling away and dropping down before I can find out. As I pull back, I say "Goodbye, Alice from Alice."

She visibly winces at the words, but she smiles down at me and drawls "Goodbye yourself, John Wayne Gantt. Y'all take care a yoreself now, y'hear?"

I smile back as the window slides smoothly back up. With the heavy tint on the window, I can't see her face at all once it closes. I walk over to the curb and turn, grin and wave once, but I'm already walking toward my car as she begins backing out of her spot.

XIII – CHOLO

Jack and I agree to meet for lunch. I talk him into a burger place that I promise him comes close to the original Sill's Snack Shack for a bean burger, but this one isn't on the Austin Highway. My directions will get him there, just off Hildebrand, but way west of familiar territory, on Blanco Road. This is a flat, uninviting part of north San Antonio, heat shimmering off everything, stunted trees and broken fences. I tell him I'm bringing a couple of patrolmen I'm riding with, and when he pulls into the parking lot at Madrid's he'll see our patrol unit backed into a place out where no other cars are parked yet. I've told him to park next to it.

We are seated when I see him walk into the restaurant. The floor is a concrete slab, the walls have old signs and a large electronic board with numbers displayed on it. The music coming out of the speakers is outlaw country. Jack looks relieved to feel air conditioning. The two other cops and I stand up to greet him.

I take Jack's hand, covering it with both of mine, and shake it as I say "Jack. Let me introduce you to these guys and then we have to get in line down that hall over there to order. First this lard bucket here is Sergeant Charlie Briscoe. I've known Charlie since he was slim. Anyway, over here is Officer Leon Parks, Charlie's field partner. Leon is fresh out of the

Atascosa County Sheriff's Office, so Charlie and I have to keep an eye on him.

I hired both these clowns away from other P.D.'s - we go all the way back to Heights, just like you and me. Boys, this is Jack Gantt, officially Fred K's former brother-in-law and in town to answer questions, unofficially he's a friend of the Department - *my* friend - and here to help us with any background he can provide on Fred, the Barnes' clan, and the investigation."

Jack shakes hands all around. He is the tallest in the group but the slimmest. The Chunk is overweight and looks ill: red nose, pale skin, bloodshot eyes, graying sandy hair. Leon appears younger though his hair is also graying. He is kind of wide eyed behind a pair of wireframes, big grin, blue-black skin, almost as muscled as me, but taller and trim. We must look like part of a football team.

"Introduce me to the stranger, Captain Hartmann," says a friendly voice behind us, as we walk through a doorway. We stop in the long hall we will take to the ordering station. I look over Jack's shoulder, and seeing the man who has spoken I say "come by our table after we all order and we'll talk, Bonello." Jack looks back at the man, who is nodding and heading back the way he came. He's a little Italian looking guy, slicked back gray hair, long narrow face, shiny suit.

I order for Jack and me: two tostada burgers, no tostadas, and a large fry for us to split, and won't take no for an answer when I pay for us both. I don't hear what Leon and Charlie order but I hear them both emphasize the word *jalapeños*. We all take our drinks back to the table and sit.

I start teasing Leon about Poteet, suggesting it is tiny, but the largest town in Atascosa County.

"Damn it Captain, that's absolutely wrong," Leon replies, "Poteet's tiny compared to Pleasanton. And neither one's where the county seat is, which is where the Sheriff's office is."

"Aw shucks, podnuh. Whut be's the county seat?" That from Charlie, with a look at Jack to make sure he is enjoying the fun.

"Well, the county seat's in Jourdanton, Charlie. Now we have talked about this a hundred times. Quit showing off for Mr. Gantt!"

Meanwhile, I unbutton three buttons in the middle of my uniform shirt, and pull a bag of Fritos from inside it. I hand it to Jack while I re-button my shirt, and say "Take a big handful when we get our order. You know what to do with it." The bean burger this place emulates is from the Sill's Snack Shack of many long years ago: patty, plain bun, refried beans, cheese whiz, and onions topped off with crushed Fritos.

Our number comes up on the big board before Leon can finish defending Atascosa County. We all get back up to make the round trip with our orders.

Jack settles back down when we return, takes his helping of Fritos and hands the bag back to me. I get busy lifting the top bun off my burger, but there's so much cheese sticking I have to rip the bun to get it off. It ain't cheese whiz. I crush my handful of corn chips and smash them down on the burger. I pull all the cheese that's hanging over up around the Fritos, and replace the bun. I push down on the whole thing so I can get my mouth around it. It's really the only way to eat one of these things. You might figure you'll get full after a few bites, but eating one of these bean burgers is like taking a trip back in time for us Oh-Niners. Every time I bite into one I'm taken back to remembering sitting around at Sills with my old man, eating and watching cars out on the Austin Highway. By the time I hear the crowd around us again, my burger's gone, so are the fries, and Jack's blinking and looking around just like me.

The slicked down Italian named Bonello appears out of nowhere as Jack takes a last sip of water to wash down his meal. He has his hands behind his back like Parade Rest. "I sincerely hope that I am not disturbing your meal, gentlemen, but I did want to catch you before you leave."

He looks at Jack. "You are Mr. Jack Gantt, I believe. May I say," as Jack nods and shakes his hand, "how very sorry I am to have heard of your brother's sudden and unexpected death?"

I interrupt before Jack can decide how to answer. "Mr. Bonello, Mr Gantt is Mr. K's *former* brother-in-law. *I'm* glad to see you, though. I've been tracking you for about a week now, to talk to *you* about Mr. K's sudden and unexpected death."

"Certainly, Captain. I was merely out of touch for a few days. What did you want to talk to me about, exactly?"

"Ah ah, sir," I smile, wagging a finger side to side at him, "we might need you to have your lawyer and your rights read when we discuss this matter. Can we say tomorrow afternoon? My place?"

Bonello looks at Jack and shakes his head sadly. "I'm sorry you have to witness the Captain behaving so boorishly in this sorrowful time, Mr. Gantt. It's his way of dealing with things, I'm afraid." He turns back to me. "You *can* say anything you want, Captain. I'm not saying you *may*, though. You need to call my office to make an appointment. Unless you're arresting me for something...?"

"An important man such as yourself, Mr. Bonello? Goodness me!" I chuckle drily.

Bonello quickly turns back to Jack and shakes his hand. "If there's anything you want or need during your time here, please let me know. I'll do anything for Fred's brother. Goodbye now." And he is gone, walking out the door. His arms only swing from his sides back, as if something's wrong with his shoulders.

Silence at the table. Jack looks around at us all, but no one is looking back.

He asks the table in general "And Mr. Bonello is...?"

"Near as we can tell," I say, squinting at him, "his company was involved in some of Mr. K's more lucrative businesses - lucrative but shady. Things seemed to go south the last few years; Bonello's partner retired and then Frank pulled the company out of the Chamber."

"The Chamber of Commerce?"

"Yeah."

"So you're not saying they were doing illegal things?"

I look at Charlie and ask "Shady?"

Charlie shrugs and nods. "Bonello and a few others, Harvey Reynolds and Lance Drew, all seem to get richer by the minute. Real estate and what they like to call "investments" are the tip of the iceberg, but I don't know enough to tell you what all they are doin'. The SAPD has a small unit assigned to monitor groups like theirs, a small version of a big city organized crime unit. I've been keeping in touch with them, but Mr. K's death seems to have sent everyone underground. I'm thinking seeing Bonello here may be a first sighting since then."

"Wonder why he was looking to introduce himself to me."

The three of us look at him, but none of us look like we have an answer.

"I don't know," I say. "But there are just a few ways he could have known you were coming to San Antonio and fewer to know he could show up at Madrid's to say hi to you. What room did you say you're staying in at *La Mansion*?"

*   *   *   *   *

"I think you should pass this by your wife, George. You *can't* not get her opinion."

Doreen is lying next to me on the bed. We are both on top of the sheets, relaxing, talking business.

I am staring at her in disbelief. "Peggy?"

"Yes," she says, in a teacher's voice, "Peggy *is* your wife, George. She's a very savvy lady, with a great deal of common sense. If you are right, she'll agree too, and you're better off not bringing it to the Department *or* your family till you have a few people agreeing that this is the best way to handle Mr. Gantt and those obnoxious underground types following him around. I mean, I'm uncomfortable being the only person from whom you're getting an opinion. And," she glances at me as she finishes, "I really am just your *mistress,* George. I *love* being your mistress don't get me wrong, and it's all I want - that and my job of course - really. But... you need to talk to Peggy about this, too. Get her buy-in. It's ridiculous to think you'd offer your house to this guy without talking to her first... I mean, in my opinion."

After a while staring at her, I say "God, Doreen you are without a doubt the strangest woman I've ever met. You know what I mean?"

She chuckles but doesn't say anything.

I am surprised about a lot of things. We'd met at the front door and undressed as quickly as usual, watching each other from opposite sides of the bed. Passion is still there, but we are well beyond the stage of trying to kiss and undress each other while flinging ourselves on the bed. Passion *is* still there, but it begins when we lie down together and feel the initial tingling sensations of that first contact mouth to mouth, hand to hip, breast pressed to chest....

Tonight we haven't even started that progression. I had mentioned the scene at Chris Madrid's with Bonello and Gantt and we'd just taken off our clothes and continued to talk while we settled down on top of the sheets. I can't remember ever doing anything like that with any woman. I am surprised how comfortable I feel, and how little I mind.

My brainstorming about inviting Gantt to move out of the hotel and stay with my family was just that, an idle thought I'd brought up to Doreen, just to see how she'd respond, trusting her instincts. Her reaction, that it might be a good idea, pleased me. But now she is suggesting a next logical step that would have been the natural thing I'd have done anyway, but her suggesting it shocks me and I'm not sure why. I decide to tease, too late to hide my reaction.

"Maybe I should go home *now* and talk to her. You know, see what she thinks. Her being *savvy* and all."

Doreen's nipples have always reminded me of small cherries and they rest on breasts of the same translucence as the rest of her body. I study the veins in them as often, in bed, as the ones showing on her temple and forehead when we are dressed.

"Maybe you should, George." Belying her words, she rolls to her side, facing me. She rests her head in her hand and looks at me without expression. She holds her other arm behind her, not wanting anything to get in my way as I look at her. She knows it won't take long before I'll start making love to her.

I feel myself stir as I slowly look her up and down. I cup her cheek with my fingers and run my thumb gently across her lower lip. At the same time she reaches for me.

XIV – JACK

I thank Cholo but there's no way I'm moving into his house. He explains his thoughts carefully as to why he suspects that I'm being watched, bugged, and followed, but, unless he posts a police guard outside my hotel room and a surveillance team to watch my balcony from the River Walk, he has no other ideas about how to keep me safe.

I scoff. I tell him I have nothing, including a relationship with my former brother-in-law, that could possibly attract any of Fred K's associates. "What about the will?" he asks. I can only think of one answer, suggesting this sounds like crooks watching a poker game or a race track two dollar window. "What," I say sarcastically, "they're going to follow me after the reading, when I'm carrying all the money home? So they can rob me at my door? It's silly, Cholo."

"I guess. I'm just pretty uncomfortable because we can't trace these guys to who they really are. Who they work for. Nothing. I would have thought Fred Ks death would end this little soap opera, but Bonello showing up has me thinking... well... I don't really know *what* I'm thinking. I'm worrying."

I smile at the phone. "I don't know what you're thinking either, Cholo. But, you know, even if you are right that something is going on we aren't figuring out, I *can* actually take care of myself."

There is a long pause before he responds.

"No Jack, I don't really think you can."

After another long pause, Cholo signs off and I hang up the phone. I am lying on the bed in my hotel room. I get up and walk to the balcony door, peering through the fabric down at the River Walk, hoping to see someone staring up at me. Nothing.

There are buildings across from mine, mostly restaurants and bars, but some hotels and offices close enough to house someone with binoculars and cameras but there is no way I can see anyone. It is all imagination anyway. Paranoia.

I try the old Barnes' place again. I've called twice and left messages for Jesse, but neither he nor whatever staff is still tending to the place has responded. I have felt a strong urge to at least touch bases with Paige's son since I've gotten back to town and been told that he is is still living in the old mansion, alone.

"H'llo?" says a young, sleepy voice.

"Jesse?" I ask.

*   *   *   *   *

I pull up to 431 Ivy Lane feeling the inevitable déjà vu after all the years. The iron gate is closed and I push the old button, the one I remember from years earlier. After a few minutes, the speaker squawks, and then I hear a young, calm voice. "Yes?"

"Hello, Jesse. This is Jack Gantt."

"OK, just a sec." And a buzz. The gate slowly rolls open.

I ride the drive up to the front of the house. I consider driving around to the back, but decide against it. When I get out of my car, I look around. The boy doesn't come out to greet me so I walk up on the porch. The swing is still there, but an additional table, some chairs, and a few rocking chairs have joined it. I look at the swing for a while. It is dirty, but looks like it might still work. The swing also reminds me of something Sammie told me a long long time ago. She'd had her own personal swing, hadn't she? I look out at the grounds. I have to shade my eyes against the sun, and there about a football field away I see the gigantic live oak with other trees behind it. Sammie and I had talked about that big oak, what seemed a hundred years ago.

I walk back down the stairs and toward the tree. Several of the branches have come straight out from the first forking of its trunk and two of the huge branches even snake down, nearly touching the ground before arching back up. There are thick supports, log-like chunks of wood, placed strategically under those branches. I hear a bird singing somewhere up in the tree. From the songs, I know it is a mockingbird. It sings an unmistakable progression of notes in eight or nine sets, and then starts back through them again, in order. Other than the singing of the mockingbird, it is absolutely still out here under the tree. The shade gives no relief from the heat. I look up where the song is coming from. The bird is up there; just as I look up, I can see it flapping one of its wings as it grooms itself. The wing has the telltale white streak of the mockingbird.

And then I see the swing, over there about halfway between the low hanging branches. A rope is threaded through two holes at each end of the plank that form the seat, so that two ropes make four going up toward the branch way overhead where they are tied down.

The swing is weatherworn but looks serviceable. I sit down in it, facing the mansion. I hear flapping overhead, and then see the mockingbird take off toward the street as the ropes noisily stretch under my weight. I don't swing at first, just look at the house, at what Sammie would have looked at as she swung back and forth when she was growing up.

I look behind me but that way is thick with trees so I imagine she would have preferred swinging toward the house. I remember she'd broken her arm on this tree, this swing. She recounted the story and laughed about how her Dad had run out when she'd screamed, when normally her parents never seemed to hear *anything* the girls did, even *in* the house.

As I start swinging I remember her. Everything about her. I haven't gotten this deeply into my memories - I haven't wanted to - since I left town. The apartment in Wellesley. The wedding and the cruises. That tiny almost invisible patch of freckles across her perfect nose. Her eyes crinkling when she grinned. The powder blue eyes.

Sammie. Oh, Sammie.

"Nice dollhouse," I'd said, long ago. My eyes are burning a little, I tell myself from the sweat; it is a hot day, and I have to wipe my eyes with the sleeve of my shirt.

After swinging for a while, staring at the mansion, I stop, wipe my eyes again, and walk back and get into my car. *The visit will have to wait,* I think. I'll call Jesse later. I will have to tell him something about disappearing like this, but I'll come back another time.

In the meantime, now that I have reminded myself about it, I am thinking about the dollhouse... wondering about something... the fireplace. Had I looked there, after the accident?

I start the car and circle the drive, leaving the way I'd come.

*　　*　　*　　*　　*

I am returning from the trip to the old Barnes place. I am still wondering about Sammie and the dollhouse as I get off the elevator and walk to the end of the hallway. My door is the only one at this end. I slide the card into the slot and the green light comes on above the handle. I open the door. I need to use the toilet, but the sight of the man sitting in the armchair, facing me, raises the hairs on the back of my neck and makes me forget the bathroom.

My 9mm is in the drawer next to the bed. If California and Texas had a reciprocal agreement for the carrying of concealed handguns, I would have it on my hip. But my California license is no good here.

On the other hand, the Latino sitting in the chair is smiling, is dressed well, and is holding his hands up, open to show they are empty, as if to say "I come in peace."

"*Señor* Gantt, you must forgive this intrusion." His accent is slight. "It is necessary not to draw unwanted attention to myself, and to ensure minimum focus on a meeting between us."

I don't respond. I walk over to the door leading to my bedroom, but pause when the man speaks again.

"I have taken the liberty of removing the bullets from your gun. I assure you they will be returned when I leave, and I also assure you that, for the present, I intend you no harm. Please join me here, so we can chat briefly. I will be gone soon, I promise you."

I look into the bedroom and see the drawer beside my bed is open, so I return to the small living area and sit on the couch opposite the man. I sit on the edge of the seat. Before I ask my first question, the man introduces himself.

"Please call me Sylvan. I am only here to give you some information and deliver a message. There is really little that you need to know, and honestly," his natural smile deepens, "the less you know the better for us all, *si*?"

"*Si*," I reply.

The smile has never left his face. His eyes have never reflected it. "You see, *Señor,* I am sent from a concerned *familia*, south of here, terribly sorry for your loss. We also feel your loss in other, more... how would you say... *práctico... pragmático...* ways."

"I understand what you mean, *Señor* Sylvan, but I have no idea why you are telling me this or why you broke into my room to tell me this. I suffered *no* loss when my former brother-in-law died, I assure you. And anything he was involved in -"

Sylvan raises a hand to stop me, so I stop. "We are fairly comfortable with the notion that you are not involved in any of the... dealings... between *Señor* Klein and my... people. Unfortunately, a play for power is occurring because of his death. You may be viewed as a player no matter how hard you deny it. We are comfortable with the notion that you will not change that perception, that you have not returned to *San Antonio de Bexar* for a hidden reason. If we turn out to be wrong, we will be very disappointed. We will react in... I would say... a *negative* way. *¿Entendido Señor* Gantt? *¿Me entiendes?*"

I shrug. After I pause I say "I suppose so, yes. But does this mean the people on the other side will be visiting me next?"

Sylvan chuckles and shrugs back at me. "If they have not already, who can say for sure? But tell them what I've said, if you have a chance before they shoot you." He laughs at his joke.

When his laughter dies down he says "I will leave you now. I trust the remainder of your stay in *San Antonio de Bexar* will be a pleasant one. *Recuerdas Señor Gantt... en boca cerrada... no entran moscas. Adios.*"

As he pauses at the door he smiles again at me. "Oh. The bullets are still in your *automática, Señor* Gantt, the extra magazines still in the drawer. I was... I think 'bluffing' is the word... *ir de farol.*"

Sylvan closes the door behind him and I immediately go to the drawer by my bed. I pick up the gun and push the magazine release as I hold the weapon over the bed. I clear the chamber and a bullet bounces down onto the bed next to the magazine. I take the other magazines and checked them one by one. Then I get the holster out of my suitcase and thread it onto my belt. I reload the extra bullet into the magazine, chamber a round and flick on the safety. I'll wear it from now on, legal or not.

I realize that in the back of my mind somewhere I must have always thought I'd need protection from Fred some day. Ironic, isn't it?

But I am already thinking about something else. I really can't remember checking the dollhouse for messages after the accident.

XV – CHOLO

Peggy is leaning against the door jamb watching me. I'm on the phone, sitting on her side of the bed and though I am looking at her, she can see I'm concentrating on the call.

"God damn it, Jack. Listen to me!" I say for the third time during the conversation. I pause and listen for awhile because, once more, Jack isn't listening.

I can tell Peggy is getting more and more worried. I've already gotten all my clothes back on, except my shoes. And I've armed myself, not only with my carry gun, but also a little something I've wrapped around my ankle and the knife I wore behind my back, from the old days.

As I listen I put on my loafers, using fingers from my free hand to shoehorn my heels down into each shoe in turn.

"Jack!" I try again. I'm not used to being ignored like this. The voice at the other end of the phone finally trails off.

"OK, Jack." I'm trying to be reasonable. "I hear what you're saying and I respect you wanting to stay normal, but what's happening *isn't* normal, and the people you're dealing with aren't, either. *Please* stay in the hotel. *Please* wait till I can get some people over there. You can't believe anything that guy said to you about you being safe, or whatever. Especially if this is some kind of turf war you've been dropped into. I'm not sure what he meant, but it sounds like...."

I stop to listen again. I stand up and walk by Peggy while I listen. "I'll be home as soon as I can," I whisper as I kiss her cheek and head for the stairs. I growl into the phone as I rush down the stairs. I run into the garage and jump in my old Chevy.

* * * * *

The rumbling and feel of the big 383 cruising down Broadway toward downtown makes me feel a little better. I find that, since my promotion to Captain, I very rarely feel as calm as I had in the old days. Maybe it was like I am uncomfortable wearing the mantle of a big shot. I have to dress up most of the time and deliver "sermons" rather than *do* anything. I might as well be out of the Department or be an instructor, telling cops how to behave on the streets now that I rarely get to be there myself.

I remember a month ago, running into that retired Sergeant Rodriguez who had been at my initial interview for the department, who had come outside after the interview to congratulate me for being accepted. I had just gotten out of my new sedan at the car wash, and Frank had walked up to say hello. We had probably not seen each other in ten years and Frank had that look in his eyes of meeting a hero or something.

I, on the other hand, was embarrassed and all I could remember was that back when we'd first met I was just trying to raise myself above the gas jockey job I had. I'd been touched that Frank had come outside after the interview to welcome me to the force, when he probably needed to get back on the job. I think I remember being in Peggy's Pinto that day, and this car

I'm standing next to now embarrasses me in front of Frank. A Captain and driving this overpriced foreign thing, for God's sake.

If it wasn't for Peggy, well, Peggy and Doreen, I wouldn't feel *alive* very often. Lucy has mostly not been around, about to get her Master's in something to do with kinesiology and having a serious relationship going with that young man, that Carl something or other...sincere enough guy, I suppose. But family had always been the most important thing in the world to me. Even when, in some twisted but satisfying way, it includes Doreen. Family. I remember how I felt the day we settled in to the big new house.

Anyway, I'm thinking, as I pass the southern edge of Brackenridge Park and speed up to beat the light at Mulberry, *if Jack gets himself into trouble, I hope I can help. That poor son of a bitch is really asking for it.* I am enjoying this drive though, that is for sure. It's something about the combination of the throbbing feel, and the muted rumbling noise. I think maybe I should drive this car to work more often rather than that new German thing. *Image!* Peggy says.

I decide to cut over to Jack's hotel via Travis since Houston Street is one way the wrong way. I sit at the light at Navarro and put the car in neutral so I can rev the motor without having to hold down the heavy duty clutch I've put in her. I listen for anything out of the ordinary in the sound of the brmmmm brmmmm brmmmm: a stuttering in the plugs, anything wrong in the timing. Nope it sounds good to me. The light turns green as I decide to go straight up to Jack's room after I park. Maybe the fool has done what he's been told, for once.

*   *   *   *   *

I am on the River Walk, on a bridge over the canal at the base of *La Mansion*. Gantt wasn't in his room or in the hotel's restaurant. I have only a few ideas where to look as I stand here scanning back and forth up and down the waterway. It is twilight and not easy to see details out here, although that doesn't mean it is getting any cooler; the heat is oppressive, the darkening sky, cloudless. I have Charlie and two patrolmen combing both sides of the canal up nearer the large mall and parking areas where most tourists hang out shopping, drinking, and eating. Jack's car is still checked in at the hotel, so he's somewhere around here, probably trying to get himself killed - on my watch.

He had mentioned both *La Villita* and *El Mercado* during his phone rant, two places he'll "be damned if I let these crazy outlaws keep me from going to." And then he'd told me he was "packing", for God's sake! That is all this downtown tourist trap needs, a shootout on the river! I'm sympathetic after hearing the details about Jack's hotel room visitor, but for Jack to strap on an old war trophy and parade himself downtown is just crazy, crazy and fucked up.

Matter of fact, Jack *must* be crazy. Like he has death on his wish list, or something. Ironic.

I take the stairs two at a time in spite of the heat. It is a long climb, getting to the surface streets from this part of the river, but I make it fairly easily. I am a bit winded, but not bad enough to be gasping for breath. I am about 6 or 7 blocks from both places Jack could be heading, but in different directions, so I make a guess and get on the radio to Charlie. I tell him to check out *La Villita* since they're not seeing anything on the River Walk heading back from the mall.

I decide to try the Market Square because it is a bigger area. *La Villita* is the original "village" that was San Antonio; just about a block of buildings, curios, artists and food. Some of the art is good; expensive, anyway. Far as I'm concerned you still have to weed out the tourist crap. I'm hoping Jack is more interested in the market stalls, food, and music over at *El Mercado*.

I walk quickly to Commerce Street and head west toward San Saba. It'll take me a few minutes.

I increase my pace, striding along and hoping to make the light at Soledad. The light goes red before I get there. As I slow and stop at the corner, I see Jack in the distance, less than two blocks ahead. I know it is Jack from his height, build, and the way he walks. He is strolling, ambling, really taking his time. He is looking like a tourist, stopping at windows, looking up at buildings, checking his watch, idly looking around. He is also dressed to stick out like a sore thumb. Everyone on the street is in sneakers and shorts and Hawaiian shirts or t-shirts like the brightly colored *I Saw the Alamo and Was Disappointed* ones that are popular now. Jack is in jeans, boots and a short sleeved dress shirt, not tucked in. *To cover his gun,* I think. As I stand there, I even see Jack look back in my direction. *At least he's being careful, like I asked him,* I think.

But the man I see following Jack is being careful too.

*   *   *   *   *

He is holding a map. Every time Jack stops, the man stops and studies the map or ties his loafers or gazes into a storefront. Every time Jack walks, the man follows. By the time the light turns green for me to walk across without being noticed, Jack and the man are more than two blocks ahead. I am far enough behind that neither of them will see my belt holster with the badge attached, but I guess I'm *too* far behind if there is any trouble. The man is wearing a black cowboy hat, felt. I can see few details about him, but his neck is very dark - could be a *Chicano,* but could also be from anywhere south and I'm already thinking cartel from what I heard about Jack's hotel visitor.

So I decide to go a block south and take Dolorosa west. That way I can run the street parallel to the two men and hopefully intercept them at Market Square. I jaywalk across Commerce and take Military Plaza south. While I jog I call for backup, weaving through the noisy tourist traffic. In spite of the hardware on my hip, slapping in rhythm to my running gait, no one seems to notice. Everyone has someplace to go, talking, laughing, singing.

I turn right on Santa Rosa, the sweat starting to soak through my shirt. I figure I've at least caught up enough with Jack's stalker to look for where they are up on Commerce. Besides, there are several ways to enter the area where the market is and I don't want to lose them if they beat me there. As I approach Commerce I hang back, carefully.

First I dart my eyes to the left but see only tourists. I slide along the wall of the Good Bytes Cafe at the corner and peek back to the right but Jack is nowhere in sight that way either. *Shit, they're already in the Market*, I think. I check west again and suddenly see the felt black cowboy hat that had been following Jack. The hat is bobbing up and down in a crowd of people, as the man walks on the same side of the street as me, halfway down the block.

Jack must have already turned onto San Saba and is ready to go into the market. I hurry after the hat. Me and the man I'm pursuing are walking too fast to be hidden on the crowded street, because we are both having to weave through the tourists too quickly. We are obvious, and I know that sooner or later the hat is going to notice me.

It happens sooner.

XVI – EDUARDO MALLICAN

Hijo de la chingada, *my orders are to keep an eye on this gringo and keep him from harm, so why does he make himself such a target? Sylvan gives the orders, but...* ¡maldita sea!

I have been aware of the man, built like *el toro*, who is following me and the *gringo*, have seen the man dash across the street behind us, have seen him reappear behind me but much closer, after the *gringo* turns the corner ahead of me. His *atajo*, his shortcut gives me no time to think this through. I put my hand in my pants and feel the *pistola* hidden in the holster above my other *paquete*. Keeping my hand there, I walk to the corner. The *gringo* I am following, sent to protect, is standing, facing me in the middle of the sidewalk eight, maybe ten meters away. Staring at me. *¡Madre mia!*

I look back the other way. The *levantador de pesas*, the cold-eyed *gringo mafioso*, is pulling a gun and shouting something. I pull my own weapon quickly and point at the man who is yelling at me, who is still in the motion of pulling his own gun. But I am faster and much more accurate because this is what I am trained to do, *uno certero*. I have been given no choice but to react. It is automatic. I quickly raise my *pistola* to make sure of my accuracy in this crowd. The man's head is in my sights and I can not miss.

But something is wrong. I can't pull the *gatillo*. There is a pain in my side that has started as a bee sting but is now all I can feel and it comes from below my right *sobaco*, in my ribs. I look down, I have lost control and the *pistola* falls from my hand; the pain is overwhelming. Much blood on the cement beneath me. I dimly hear people screaming and then can no longer hear anything. My body is on fire. I can't breathe. I lurch and dimly see the sidewalk coming up to meet me.

XVII – JACK

To use the sights on my semi-automatic 9mm Browning Belgique, you have to really concentrate hard. Most modern sights have the tips brightly painted, making it easy to line up the two tips just beyond the hammer with the single tip at the far end of the barrel. But my old Browning just has a small dark notch in the sight at the hammer and a dark tip on the one down the barrel.

The man in the cowboy hat stares at me briefly, and then turns away from me and looks back down Commerce to the east. He is looking in the direction from which we'd come, from which I'd seen Cholo walking, moments earlier.

I draw my gun as I watch the man smoothly draw his.

I cup the palm of my free hand under the hand holding the gun. I line up the sights best I can and point at the side of the man who has drawn his gun lightning fast, doing a quick draw from the front of his pants like in a movie. I hear someone shouting *Police!* around the corner and when I see the guy raise his gun quickly to eye level I know he is about to shoot, so I instinctively squeeze off a round first. My gun is loaded with the hollow points I bought years ago, when I'd first arrived in Los Angeles. I see a puff under the man's armpit and instinctively I'm back in Nam watching Fescola bleed out in the chopper.

The guy doesn't fire. Instead, he looks down at his gun in slow motion and then he drops it, goes to his knees and then onto his face. The cowboy hat rolls slowly away.

I had hardly been aware that I'd fired my weapon. It just seemed like an automatic reaction to the situation, like when you are provoked to take a swing at a guy. I had no idea if I'd been right doing it, I had just done it. It was like I was back in a fox hole, and yet I knew I wasn't. I knew I was in downtown San Antonio and people were screaming and running or throwing themselves to the ground, all around me. I become aware of the sweat rolling down my face.

I hear shouts from around the corner, too. Cholo is suddenly there and two other cops. I know I'm in trouble. I kneel and put the Browning down on the sidewalk. I stay down and raise my hands, palms toward the policemen. Cholo holsters his gun and begins running toward me. The other two cops, in uniform, have drawn down on the man lying on the sidewalk. One of the cops kicks the black hat further out of the way.

*　*　*　*　*

"You're a fucking maniac, Gantt."

Cholo and I are sitting in Cholo's office downtown. We'd ridden in the souped-up Nova while Charlie and two local patrolmen take care of securing the area, the M.E.'s wagon, the reporters.

"And you saved my life," he adds. He hesitates, then says "That guy was fast. He definitely knew what he was doing, like he was a professional. Not like some local punk."

"Who was he?" I ask. "Could he be who killed Fred?"

Cholo shrugs. "How the hell should I know? We haven't gotten him to the morgue, ID'd him, nothing."

His Admin has just arrived from home after getting Cholo's hurried call from his car as we drove away after the shooting. Cholo had asked her to come back to work to field calls for him, etc. She has made us coffee and called Cholo's wife so she won't worry when she hears about it on the evening news.

She brings us both a fresh cup and heads back to her desk. I can see all the lines on his phone are already blinking.

Cholo's eyes follow her out and return to me. "Yeah, that could be Fred's killer. He could be a lot of things. There's really no telling who he is till we know who the fuck he is."

There is a long pause as we both sip our coffee and think about what happened.

"This guy looks old enough to have been around back before you left town for California," Cholo muses.

I take another sip. "You mean when the accident happened."

Cholo is gazing up at the ceiling. He looks back at me. "I'm just saying."

I shake my head and drain my cup. My mind is a turmoil of conflicting thoughts. How could this guy, who shows up right after Sylvan tells me I'm safe, have had anything to do with my wife's death, with Fred? Couldn't he have just mistaken Cholo for Sylvan's enemies out to kill me?

Finally, I shrug and raise my eyebrows. I look down at the floor and try to change the subject. "So when I get released, am I going to get my gun back? If I promise not to carry it any more; if I just leave it in my room when I'm there or my car when I'm driving?"

Cholo laughs in surprise, staring at me. "You've got to be shittin me, man! Even if we let you go, or book and release you, there's no fucking way I'm letting you walk out with that gun! If for no other reason, it's involved in a shooting, for God's sake! You may get it back eventually, but, shit!"

Doreen sticks her head in. "The D.A. agrees with your recommendation, Captain. James says you can release him, but he's to keep in touch. The signed statement can wait till tomorrow, but we will need it then. He's not to talk to the press, not to leave town."

"He probably knows the drill from watching television," Cholo says to her with a smile. Then he looks over at me as the expression on his face turned stern. "By the way, I'm also thinking we should move you to another hotel. And this time, I'm not *asking*."

*   *   *   *   *

"Can I call you Uncle Jack?"

"Of course you can, Jesse." I look hard at my nephew expecting to see a smirk, but Jesse's look appears destined to stay cool and distant, if not guileless. At least I don't see the sneer that had usually been there years ago, even when Jesse was a toddler. I'm pleased to see he appears to have grown into a thoughtful, nice looking, wide-eyed kid. It's hard to think of him as college age.

I had called him this morning to explain why I'd left the mansion grounds without seeing him the last time I came by. I gave him an "I suddenly remembered something I needed to take care of" excuse, trying to keep the lie as vague as possible.

Then I asked if Jesse knew whether Fred had stored any of the things from the house Sammie had lived in with me. Jesse thought so.

"OK, Uncle Jack, here's the ladder."

We had puffed up two long flights of stairs to the third floor of the mansion. I'd never made it past the second floor in my previous life here. There is an old strip of faded paisley carpet running down the middle of the hallway up here, unlike the wooden floors in the hallways below. Jesse reaches up and pulls hard on the rope hanging from the ceiling at the end of the hall. The door it is attached to swings down and open. He reaches up and grabs the ladder, which is folded in thirds and lies flat against the top of the door. He lifts and pulls down on the top third of the ladder, unfolding it as he lifts. I am impressed at Jesse's ability to unfold it, since it appears to require some strength and dexterity. As soon as he puts the feet of the ladder down on the carpet he steps back, for me to climb.

Ever cautious, I ask "Where's the light up there?"

"There's a switch just to the right when you get to the top."

"OK, thanks."

I climb the ladder. Nearly to the top I feel the wood creaking under my weight and a slight bend. As my head clears the attic floor, I spot the light switch against a beam next to my right arm. The lights turn on above me when I flip the switch. I look around and see four flood lights, one in each corner of the ceiling. They are all pointing straight down so that the corners of the gigantic room are better lit than the center. The lights aren't strong, so even the corners aren't too brightly lit.

The room seems as gigantic as the footprint of the whole structure. There is furniture mostly covered with sheets of varying disrepair, boxes of all shapes and sizes stacked as high as two men, and large and small trash bags, some piled neatly, some thrown about. It is an amazing mix of antiques and junk, with much unknown. I hear, then see Jesse climb up the ladder behind me. When the kid straightens up, he says "I can show you where the stuff from your house is. I've done lots of exploring up here through the years."

I question him with the look on my face.

Jesse smiles. "Dad and I have been known to hide stuff up here from time to time."

I nod, but don't return the smile. Eventually, he'll get used to speaking of his father in past tense. Plus, I realize I'm feeling tense, nervous. I am hoping to be disappointed - I still find it hard to believe I had never thought of the dollhouse all these years. I understand why it hadn't crossed my mind initially, because of the shocks and the intense amount of sadness and regret I'd absorbed during that period. But over the years since, I've relived the moments, the days, and the weeks following the accident. Now I remember quite clearly answering Fred, the last time we'd spoken in person, when I was asked about the house I'd shared with Sammie.

"I don't care," I'd said. "I'm keeping the house, but I've hired a management company to deal with leasing it out. They'll clean it up after I leave, and I'm just packing my clothes. If you want anything you need to get it out of there in the next couple of weeks. They're taking it over after the end of the month. They'll deal with her clothes and stuff, donate... whatever they... can to charities." I'd paused, choking up, but got control and continued, "Anyway, take what you want. I can't imagine what you *would* want but I don't care."

Fred had nodded absentmindedly and I had shaken his hand and walked away. Since then we'd spoken maybe once a year, and written letters, mostly between the lawyers, whenever business decisions needed to be made that affected me. Also at my direction, Simpson had set my liability as remotely as was legally possible. I've never trusted Fred, have never shaken the thought that he *had* to have had something to do with the girls'... dying.

Cholo said the man I'd shot in the street hadn't been identified yet. He may have been from South America, prossibly Columbia. He had no ID in his clothes, but a receipt in his pocket was being analyzed. That left me with the feeling that nothing was resolved, that as far as I am concerned, Fred was still generating more and more ripples, even from the grave.

I still figure Sammie was just unfortunate collateral damage in some horrible scheme of Fred's to kill Paige. The businesses, the mansion, the money, the damned boat. Maybe subconsciously that was why I'd left town as soon as I could back then; maybe I knew at some level that sooner or later I'd be involved in an accident myself if I stayed. That was why, consciously, I've kept my war trophy around, oiled and loaded all these years. Why I would feel better now if it was back on my hip, under the t-shirt. I understand why the police kept it, of course - even in a justified police shooting I figure they hold the officer's weapon during the investigation.

Jesse leads the way to the middle of the big room. There, I see an area of seven or eight black outdoor plastic bags that are separated from the rest of the more messily arranged bags, chairs, couches, end tables and the like. There is less illumination here.

Jesse points to them and says, "I'll leave you with this stuff now - I have a Chem lab to get ready for."

Chem lab! Everything's a memory to me lately, I muse.

I get on my knees in front of the bags. I don't hear Jesse leave but the next time I look up, I'm alone.

Dark enough in this place to be spooky.

The trash bags in this group are all secured by big black ties. The first bag I open is filled with Sammie's shoes. Sharp intake of breath as the past fills my head. Sneakers, flats, pumps, heels of varying heights, every color of the rainbow. I remember all the parties, dinners, the lounging around she'd done in and out of all the shoes in the bag. I should throw them away, but I'll probably just tie the bag back up and leave it there. It's a mountain of shoes. Why had Fred kept them?

I try another of the bags. This one is books. Sammie hadn't taken any of her father's collection when we moved; these were the ones I had brought from the old place I'd shared with Mom. *From Here to Eternity* and *Some Came Running, Marjorie Morningstar, Studs Lonigan,* all old stuff. I've noticed the bag that must hold the dollhouse while I'm looking at the books. It is the largest trash bag I've ever seen and it is upside down over the bulky shape. I carefully get my fingertips under one side of the bulk, and though it is heavy I am able to lift the side up at an angle and look under it. The light is barely enough that I can see the masking tape used to close the bag shut. I lower the bag and fish out my keys. I decide not to screw with the tape, so I jam my longest key into the black plastic. The key penetrates the old bag almost immediately. Then I pull up to rip through the material. Within a few inches the key has pulled the plastic into such a big rippled bunch that I'm not able to pull any further.

Oh well. Let's try the tape.

So after examining the shapes within the bag to figure out where the open back of the dollhouse is, I lean it over on its flattest side. That leaves the tape completely exposed. It appears dry and brittle, so after ripping several pieces off the bag, I'm finally able to pry and scrape all of it off. As I pull the black bag away from the exposed side, I can confirm this is the bottom of the dollhouse. I pull the house back upright and remove the bag completely. I fold it a few times and set it aside.

The dollhouse is as gigantic as I'd remembered. It's empty now, of course. One or more of the smaller bags probably holds the little cars, the furniture, the dolls. I refresh my memory, looking through the open space in the back of the miniature mansion, for the location of the fireplace. The chimney isn't perched on top of the structure, I see. When I look for it I see that the hole it is supposed to be in had little snaps on all four sides, so I figure the chimney itself would be in the bags with all the furniture and cars. I find the upstairs fireplace. It appears as unused as I'd remembered. I reach in, two fingers into the fireplace and up the wall behind it. I pull with my fingers. Nothing. I try again, yanking as carefully as I can, afraid of ripping my fingers open on the sharp edges. It still doesn't move. Doesn't even budge.

I tug harder, and then harder still. Finally the snaps give, the *crack!* of the piece coming loose from the dollhouse wall is loud enough to echo in the room. I feel my fingers scrape as they come toward me, holding the wall piece.

First I look carefully at the piece and at my hand. I half expect to see blood, or that the piece is broken. No, I haven't cut myself, and no the wall is still a solid piece. I supposed it had just been frozen in place from years of not being used.

Then I look in the dollhouse at the space above the fireplace that has been revealed. I'm not feeling nervous or expectant. I really feel it's just another nagging possibility that I can dismiss from my mind before getting out of this place again.

But there *is* paper in the secret place. Even in the near darkness I can see a pink card from Sammie's stash of stationary, and several white sheets behind it, folded. She *had* left me a note that morning before she left the house! I am pretty sure I checked the dollhouse when I got home the night before and it had been empty.

*   *   *   *   *

"I don't know, Cholo, I've looked at the note, but not the papers behind it, and I just want you to be here when I look at them. Maybe I need a witness, maybe there's something in here that will tell us what happened or why, I don't know. I think this is as much a police matter as it is a personal one, you know?"

There is a long enough pause that I'm wondering if he's still on the line. I'm about to ask him if he's still there when he says "If we're lucky, we might get some answers. If not, and prepare yourself if it isn't anything Jack, but if not, maybe you've got some closure with what she wrote.

"Give me about twenty, twenty-five minutes. You mind meeting me out front? Frankly, I'd rather you take me up there than Fred's boy."

"Sure, Cholo. Jesse's gone to a class anyway. I'll buzz you in when you get here. It's pretty spooky in the attic anyway, so I'll enjoy the company up here. See you soon."

I head down to the kitchen so I can open the gate when Cholo rings in.

As I back down the attic stairs, I'm remembering all the detective stuff Cholo told me the first time I met with him after I'd gotten to town. He had ticked off all that they'd checked out.

They'd run into nothing but dead ends. The Chief had even suggested they contact John Walsh and see if we could get any leads by airing this on his show. But it was as if Klein's killer was a ghost. No one had seen or heard the shot, the shooter, a suspicious car, an unusual noise, nothing. They'd repeated the neighborhood visits three times to jog people's memories about suspicious vehicles, workers on phone poles or anything unusual thrown away in their trash or down in man holes - anywhere. They also tried asking neighbors to go back into the past a ways, to see if anyone noticed anything unusual in the days or weeks preceding the shooting. The team also went to everyone who did work in the neighborhood the day of the murder and for weeks before - deliveries, mail, meter readers. They'd looked deeper into Fred K's business relationships. They'd canvassed the gangs in San Antonio, Austin, Houston, and Dallas/Ft. Worth for rumors. They'd done an in-depth study of the bullet used and its markings, the possible weapons used, the bullet trajectory, everything they could think of including forwarding everything they had to the central repository in Washington. Nothing.

They also examined any possible link between this murder and the accident that took the lives of Sammie and Paige ten years before. The only similarity anyone could report so far was that they hadn't had any success solving either crime. "If the same guy is involved, he is either the luckiest bastard in the world or extremely thorough in planning perfect crimes, years apart," Cholo had said. He added, "And just in case this guy hasn't *just* pulled off these three murders, I have detectives going through everything in our records, solved *and* unsolved, that have similar M.O.'s."

I had asked him if he really thought the same man killed all three of them. It was something I'd wondered since I first read of Fred's death.

Cholo had shaken his head and simply said "No, but we have to pursue every angle we can think of. I don't want any surprises."

*   *   *   *   *

Paige is waiting so I have to hurry. I love you!

Fred actually turns out to be the bastard I've always said.

I'll fill you in, finally, tonight. I'll explain these papers, too.

Toodles, Jackie-pants ☺

god make my head stop pounding!!!

*   *   *   *   *

We face each other, cross-legged on the wooden floor of the attic. Our knees are close enough to touch. The dollhouse is directly to my right, near enough to us both that we can touch its walls without bending too far.

It is dim where we sit. The lights from the ceiling help, but it is certainly not bright. Hartmann has just finished reading Sammie's last note to me. Every time I review the note in my mind I tear up. Cholo reads it several times, then slides it into an evidence baggy.

He has made me put on a pair of plastic gloves like the ones he's wearing. Though I'd already messed with Sammie's note, neither of us have touched the folded white sheets. He picks them up, opens and looks through them. Even in this light, I can see that each page has numbers and Sammie's writing all over them.

"Thanks for waiting till I got here to handle these papers, Jack. I'm pretty comfortable thinking that these will just confirm what the white collar guys are getting from the state investigators about Klein's accounting. We found his second set of books, what they're calling his "shadow" books, as soon as Judge Carroll issued the warrant and we went through the house. The bank auditors have shut everything down, and there isn't much about any of his businesses that are missing out on being audited. The bank is checking out and most of his public deals are looking like they're on the up and up. His private deals are not, and some of the things in these papers need to be looked at by someone who understands accounting."

"So Sammie put that accounting stuff in the dollhouse to justify to me why she didn't want us to be connected to him, to tell me he was a crook? I mean she knows I wouldn't *understand* them." I point at the spreadsheets and T accounts printed and written all over the white pages.

"Her note sounds rushed. Maybe she just wanted you to force her to explain them to you later, by letting you see them. Kind of like getting it off her mind by putting it on yours. Of course, she had no reason to expect she wouldn't be seeing you later that day."

I think about it. "He was a crook, Cholo. I always knew that, and Sammie said things all the time that hinted at it. I can't imagine him not *staying* a crook ever since the girls' accident. If he didn't cause their accident...."

"I wouldn't be surprised if there's more than just a little connection between the car crash and Fred being shot, Jack. And I really don't like saying it, at least on a personal level, because Fred K was good to me and mine, back in the day."

We stare at each other. I'm feeling something about this big space, some kind of unease. The air in such a surprisingly large area is cool; air conditioning is obviously being pumped in here from hidden vents or the day's heat would have made it insufferable. Perhaps I'm just feeling the effects of the chill and the dark and light spookiness beyond where we are sitting. Dust motes billow under the spotlights.

Cholo's face is in shadow. All I can really see are his eyes, which are bright compared to the rest of his face. He's always been a hard man for me to read, and with his forehead shadowing his eyes, he's even more enigmatic. I think he's staring at me.

Finally he speaks. "This is all conjecture and I'll deny ever saying it, but while I've always suspected Fred could have been behind those deaths, I was always under the impression he wanted *his* wife dead - to inherit or something, I don't know. Maybe, from this note - maybe he wanted *your* wife dead. 'I'll fill you in, finally, tonight,' she said. Do you have any idea what that meant?"

I think about it for a long time. "We both already knew he was a bastard. It sounds like she had been holding something back from the way she said 'finally' but I'm not sure what, unless she was helping him with the illegal stuff he was doing with all the Barnes' holdings. That's what all the paperwork she put in the dollhouse was about, right?"

Cholo pauses again for awhile and finally says "Please understand I'm asking this next question as a detective, Jack. Is there any possibility they were *more* than just in business together?"

I snort. "Jesus, Cholo, there is absolutely no way. How can you even ask? She truly hated the guy, he was slime. She was acting more and more upset about working for him.

"Her habits changed a lot over the years from the time he promoted her to run his Accounting Department. Her not wanting to put in overtime, drinking more and more... complaining about the job and everything he did as the boss."

I pause and look at Cholo, surprised at a memory. "You know...." I'm remembering. Her hand. "A week or two before the accident she suddenly had a hand that looked like it could have been mine after a fight. And I mean a fist fight. She said she'd gotten angry about... something; I don't remember what... and had hit a wall in her office. The skin was peeled back on at least a couple of knuckles, I remember. Maybe... I don't know...." Could he have said or done something so repulsive that she hadn't wanted me to know for fear I'd kill him? Had she changed her mind about telling me the morning she died?

My instincts tell me something is wrong. I hold up a hand to ask for silence. My feeling of unease is becoming palpable, as if the dust motes are moving on cue, or something is just on the other side of them, in a corner of the room. The room itself is actually becoming oppressive. I'm wishing like hell Cholo had let me keep my gun.

Cholo reacts calmly, waiting, listening; not knowing why my hand is up, a questioning look on his face. I also sit quietly, my head cocked, listening. I look at all four corners, wondering if it had been a sound I'd heard, perhaps subconsciously. I peer into the darkness. Then I stand up and walk back to the attic stairs. Looking down, the stairs are still in place. No shadows unaccounted for.

I turn back toward the dollhouse and instinctively crouch down as I turn, half expecting Cholo to be standing behind me, or someone else to be there ready to pounce on me. Cholo is still sitting cross-legged where he'd been, still with a question in his eyes, calm.

The feeling that had bothered me seemed to be ebbing in my mind as I walk back to Cholo and sit down facing him, crossing my legs Indian-style again. "Sorry," I say, "I thought I heard something or felt something, but that's crazy. Maybe it was just a bad feeling.... Hell, maybe it's just a bad feeling about all these memories we're dredging up."

I think back to what we'd been saying. Cholo and I had just been guessing that maybe Sammie's hand hadn't slammed into a wall at the office. "I'm really feeling creepy about all this, especially Paige losing that baby, and what might have happened between Sammie and Fred to set Sammie off like that. I've always thought it, but I'm more and more convinced that he was behind the... what happened on the Austin Highway."

Cholo seems to be thinking about it. We sit a while longer and he looks at me again, then just above me as he seems to start projecting his thoughts again.

"I'm thinking Fred K got someone to kill them. Maybe just to scare them. Maybe the scaring went too far. Who? It could have been anyone Fred dealt with. It could have been a hired gun he paid a great deal to, or just someone who owed Fred for something, or a thug from one of the organizations he dealt with, like that guy today. It wouldn't be unusual considering the way Fred K operated, at least from what we've been able to discover about his activities in the old days. But I imagine that if the killer was supposed to scare them that day, it's possible he just went too far or got carried away or something. It's not beyond reason that Fred K could have *wanted* things to go too far.

"Also, I'm thinking Fred may *not* have been acting when we told him his wife had been pregnant and he seemed so upset. Perhaps his *wife* may have been the collateral damage, he may not have even considered that she might die too, or, if he did, he may not have even cared till he found out she was pregnant. Maybe over the years since, he and the person who killed the girls slowly got to the point where words were spoken, or they stopped trusting each other with their secrets - who knows?"

He speaks slowly, as if weighing his words to be as gentle with me as he can, glancing at me occasionally. "But a man who could run those women off a road and never get caught or slip up in any way over the years, could probably put a bullet through Fred's head without having to work up to it much.

"A psychologist would call that kind of weirdo a sociopath or psychopath, I don't know much about the difference. I can't imagine a person with a conscience ever being able to justify such a thing. On the other hand, the lack of a conscience could also cause the killer to think he is safe, might cause such a person to make a mistake... eventually.

Such a person would have to spend the rest of his life remaining vigilant." He pauses and blinks. "Extremely vigilant." He pauses again and shakes his head. "I doubt we will ever know who, or all the 'why's' behind it. Of course we'll keep trying, but I'm just not sure anyone will ever find out the whole truth." Cholo's eyes move back from where they are gazing, down to mine.

I nod. I mean, he's the cop. I know one thing for sure: we seem to have gone as far as we can with what we've got. I'm thinking it is over for me, here. I can handle whatever is going to happen with the Barnes' holdings and wealth; I can even help Jesse long distance. I don't need to be here for anything, any longer. I can always come back occasionally to visit Jesse and swing under that live oak, go by the Barnes' Mausoleum, eat at Abel's and read the signs, take the right where Broadway forks onto the Austin Highway.

Maybe Los Angeles isn't the answer, either, I'm not sure. It never *has* felt like home to me, anyway.

Maybe I'll go exploring. I don't need to work for awhile. Maybe an extended vacation.

Suddenly I'm aware of a dark form above me, almost completely in shadow with the lights behind it. A monstrous thing with a weapon of some kind in its hand reaching toward me, a monster, unthinking, unfeeling, saliva glittering off its teeth. I blink in fear and just as I feel a moan low in my throat I realize it is Cholo and he is holding out his hand, not a weapon, to me. I have no idea how long he's been standing there. I take his hand and Cholo surprises me with his strength, pulling me up as easily as he would a child. "We should get out of here, Jack. You were right about this place. It's very... depressing here."

I realize I am eager to leave, I'm that spooked.

I wonder in passing about the dollhouse. What should be done with it? "I guess I'll just throw this bag back over the dollhouse. I'll tell Jesse to call some local woman's shelter or something and get them to pick it up. And the other stuff."

"Whatever you do, my friend," Cholo says, "whatever you do, you really need to put this behind you. We all do."

I shrug. "I know that's good advice, Cholo, but I don't know if it's possible."

Together, we throw the bag over the top of the dollhouse. I know I'll never see it again.

I follow Cholo to the ladder. As I back down I take one last look at the attic. I turn off the lights and stare into the darkness. I can barely see where the windows were; it is fast approaching dusk. I climb down the ladder to the third floor. The ladder sags again as I climb the rest of the way down, but my mind is somewhere else.

I am thinking about the long legged girl I'd first seen in home room, freshman year on the first day of high school. The honey blonde hair over the pale green shirt. Fancy Baldwin had hollered hello from behind us, and Sammie had slowly turned around, smiling.

*　*　*　*　*

Cholo follows my car to the gate at the end of the drive. As I edge up to the gate, the mechanism clicks on and the gate slowly rolls open. When I drive through, I turn left onto Ivy Lane and head toward Wilshire. Cholo turns right, and drives east toward Vandiver. He's headed north towards the Austin Highway.

So am I, but I'm taking roads that will allow me to curl back around onto Broadway heading north, so I can turn onto the Austin Highway at the Pegasus. From there I'm not sure where I'm headed, but as I pass the cemetary on the left I glance over but don't pull in. Soon I'll be concentrating on the signs overhead as I near the transitions to I35, Austin to the north, downtown San Antonio to the south, and Loop 410 to the west. I turn south. I know I'll have to make another choice when I hit I37, between sleep and the hotel, or the interstate that could head me toward Corpus Christi and Alice.

At about the same time I'm driving up the Austin Highway, Cholo is turning into the asphalt parking lot at Sunset Memorial Park.

He told me where he was headed before we shook hands and said goodbye. He will get out of his car and walk toward the Mausoleum.

He'll probably stand in front of the small marble building, the name BARNES etched above the double doors between the columns. It is close to nightfall, but there will still be enough light coming from the sky and the highway for him to see. Although I haven't been there since I've been back, I went so many times before I left that I can go there in my sleep and see everything exactly as it was. I still do, actually.

Cholo will open the door on the right and go in, as he has the few times he's been there over the years. "Paying his respects," as he put it. The air conditioning will click on, but the heat inside will be stifling. He will look at the bronze plates above the two casket plates to the far left, the two spaces below those occupied by Belle and David Barnes. The first plate reads:

SAMANTHA FRANKLIN BARNES GANTT

BELOVED DAUGHTER, WIFE, FRIEND

ASLEEP IN JESUS

And the bottom plate:

PAIGE BARLOW BARNES KLEIN

BABY DAUGHTER KLEIN

RESTING IN PEACE

Interlude: 11:16 a.m.

"You're pregnant again, aren't you Paige?" This in a low voice, as she felt a surprisingly sharp stab of jealousy at her chest. My sister has been knocked up again by that bastard!

"What?" Paige said leaning closer too late to hear what her sister had said, so softly in the engine's noise at this speed.

"I said he's knocked you up again, hasn't he!" Sammie shouted.

Paige glanced over at her quickly and flashed a smile.

"You guessed it Sammie!" The smile disappeared. "But that's why I need to talk to you. I want to ask a serious serious favor."

"A favor?" Sammie looked over at her sister, blankly.

"I don't know how to handle Jesse, much less another one," she began, glancing over quickly again, a guilty look on her face. "Jesse's already eight and a half and I don't have a clue about him, how to deal with him. He's the weirdest kid I've ever known. He never talks, hardly comes out of his room unless we make him. I just don't understand him."

Sammie was shocked. Eight and a half? She didn't know how he could be that old. She actually couldn't remember seeing him for... how long? She would swear Jesse could only be four years old. Hadn't she been going to his birthday parties? What was happening to time?

And Paige asking for her help? Her mind flew in spite of the way her head felt. She knew from dealing with Jack that Jesse was an introvert needing space to recharge. She wondered what he did in his solitude. All she could remember was how sweet he and Jack had been together when Jesse was a toddler. They could probably have a lot of fun together now too, reading or whatever. She could even see herself looking in on them carrying a plate of cookies and lemonade. They could have Jesse stay with them at their house as often as they wanted. Finally Jack moving her from the mansion was going to pay off....

She could feel herself tearing up. Paige needed *her to help with Jesse. She looked over at her sister and again remembered the few times she and Jack had babysat their nephew - they had had fun together, almost like how it would have been if they'd had their own - she reached for her sister's hand.*

Suddenly, the car shook and swayed from what seemed like an explosion on the passenger's side. The car beside them on the highway had just smashed into them.

Sammie turned from her sister and looked out her side of the car as the vibration continued from the impact. Control of the Sunbeam wobbled in Paige's hands as she fought the wheel. Sammie couldn't see who was driving the little washed-out blue car next to them. He looked... like a little Mexican... she thought. He didn't look like he realized he'd hit them, he was kind of leaning forward in his seat looking straight ahead. Paige was screaming as she fought the wheel. This isn't happening, Sammie thought as the little sports car slowly began careening in its lane. Paige wasn't slowing down, she actually seemed to have jammed her foot down on the gas pedal! Sammie screamed at her and tried taking the steering wheel but Paige wouldn't let go.

Suddenly another impact - the grinding of metal on metal, that sound you only hear when two cars smash together - and the horrible vibration of the Sunbeam's tires trying to maintain control. Sammie looked over at the blue car again. It was back in its lane as it had been when she last looked. The entire side of the car was dented in and she could see yellow mixed in with the blue. The driver was staring straight ahead as he had been.

Then he looked up at his rear view mirror for what seemed a long time.

Sammie could hear that her sister's screams were even more hysterical than before and that the Sunbeam was once again careening in its lane as if about to lose control. Paige's hands were beginning to rotate back and forth on the wheel as if she wasn't strong enough to hold it steady. Sammie tried to help her keep it steady, but Paige screamed louder and tried to push Sammie's hands away.

The man looked over at them. He looked directly at Sammie. His expression didn't change, but she saw his hands move toward her on his steering wheel. He was coming at them again. For those seconds, she could see him clearly. She could see that he wasn't small but was just hunched over. He wasn't Mexican at all. She could see his eyes, the two scars. As the cars hit again, she felt rather than saw that Paige couldn't keep control of the little sports car any longer. The Sunbeam seemed to rise off the pavement.

No more noise.

Sammie turned and looked ahead and screamed.

Epilogue

"You can't use a phone?" she says, wiping her hands on the chaps she wears over her jeans. No one had answered when I knocked on the screen door, so I'd returned to my car hoping someone would show up before it got late. The big blue Ford truck was parked in front of the house, so I figured I had a chance. Mid-afternoon, I was just thinking about giving up and getting a motel room when she came riding in on as big a horse, a red one, as I've ever seen. So I had gotten out of the car again, relieved.

I don't have any idea what to say in response to her greeting, so I don't answer.

Alice is still up on the horse. She's brought her right leg up and over, comfortably hooking it over the saddle horn with the inside of her knee. She shakes her head, frowning. "You know, I prefer a man who talks, Jack."

"God, don't I remember that," slips out under my breath.

She smiles. She takes her left foot out of the stirrup and brings her right leg on down and smoothly slides the rest of the way to the ground, bending her knees slightly to absorb the landing. She takes off the worn straw cowboy hat she is wearing and slaps it against the front of her thigh, then the back. The effect is a cloud of dust, which I imagine is the objective. I pretend to cough and she laughs as she pulls off her gloves and stuffs them in a back pocket with her free hand.

"You gonna tell me why you're here, Jack? You lookin for work, just drivin through, what?"

"Where are the kids?" I ask.

"Oh, you're safe for the time being, they're visiting their Daddy and the slut for a couple weeks while I deal with sixteen hundred head of cattle who may have to be put down if I'm right about what is making them sick.... But... I'm through worrying for the day. Want to come in and have a drink after we dry out old *Diablo Rojo* here?"

After I nod, she leads me and the horse over next to the barn. I notice she clucks at us both to keep us moving. "This is a big ol' horse, Alice."

She says "Yep, he is a bigun. About sixteen and a half hands. Roan, if you'd like to know. A red based roan, obviously." She pats his neck hard several times. The horse blows some air out through his nostrils and nods his head. After we stop, he strikes a front hoof down into the dirt a few times as if impatient.

We are by a coiled up hose, and as soon as she takes off the horse's saddle, saddle bags and bridle she slips a halter over his head and then hoses him down. He seems pleased and makes a noise through his mouth that I figure is what they mean when they say *the horse nickered.* I am about to ask her to hose me off too when she hands me his reins and tells me to walk him slowly around the barn a couple times. By the time I'm finished with my assignment she is coming out of the barn and the saddle and bridle are gone. She takes the halter from me and walks *Diablo* into the barn. As she comes back out, I can hear the horse slurping up some water from somewhere inside.

I follow her and the saddle bags into the house, and take the beer can she hands me out of the fridge. She opens hers and takes a big slug, maybe half the can. She wipes her mouth with her forearm and makes some smacking sounds. "Jesus God that tastes good," she sighs. "So what's up, my old friend?" She sits at the kitchen table after flipping the chair around so she can rest her chin on her forearms while we talk.

I sit across from her at the breakfast table. "Nothing much, Alice. Yesterday I finished what I needed to do in San Antonio. I regretted how we last said goodbye, so I thought I'd come by and apologize."

"But, Jack.... I thought we understood that saying goodbye was the only place we *could* go, given our very different and very separate lives. I think we parted in a very mature, thoughtful way. You know, although we haven't mentioned it in these pleasant little chats we've had since you first called, there's also a matter of - frankly - I never thought you really liked me nearly as much as I liked you - back at UT, or even over Mexican food last week."

"Maybe you're not as perceptive as you think. Or maybe you are and I've undergone a transformation since then."

She considers the possibilities, and probably whether I am being straight or sarcastic, and then her eyes narrow at me as if a light has turned on in her head. "Or maybe you've been thinking about it, things aren't as easy for an old man up there in the big city, so you came down here to see if you could swing a piece of ass from poor old Alice."

I laugh and so, thank God, does she.

I am still smiling when I say "Well, I guess that'll never happen now, so can we move on? Has anyone ever mentioned that when you finish your work you smell like sweat and cows?"

"Yes darling, Robert mentioned it constantly. It was like having you around calling me Alice from Alice till I was ready to scream."

I take the subtle hint and vow to myself I'll never again tell her how she smells or remind her where she lives. She makes an obvious sniff in the general direction of one of her arm pits, says "whoooey!" and waves her old hat in the same direction. She smiles at me. "Perhaps we could continue this discussion after I clean up a bit, but -" and she pauses frowning and wagging a finger at me, "don't get any ideas. This is not going to end the way you have it planned!"

I put my hands up and try to protest my innocence but she is gone.

*　　*　　*　　*　　*

Why *have* I driven here? I think I first decided that I wanted to track her down because over the years the little nagging things that had caused me to want to break up with her had seemed more and more... silly... to me - just excuses, basically, for not *trying*. Of course I remembered Alice for the things she'd taught me about sex, but I *always* remembered that part. More than that, while I was in California letting myself be lonely, I would occasionally think of her for the very reasons that I'd convinced myself long ago were why I broke up with her. I think I needed to hear the chewing noises and see the imperfections in her face so I could get her back off my mind - or not - but at least so I could make a more mature judgment. When I saw her again at La Fonda I knew pretty quickly that it had to have been Sammie that was really the only reason - Alice was pretty special in her own right - but I'd been fairly well blinded by what I'd loved of Sammie to see what was in Alice. So after all that talk with Cholo in the attic, hearing what made sense in his piecing together what he knew about the girls' accident and Fred's murder, and believing that I was OK with the way we'd processed the last bit of my feelings about Sammie's death, I was now genuinely wanting to see if Alice was interested in whether *we* might have a life. I could meet her girls. Take some time to find out. Relax after a long time of not really relaxing.

*   *   *   *   *

And here she is, showered, walking toward me. Her hair is wet and brushed back. Her face is beautiful, scrubbed clean, whatever makeup she had on is gone, as if she wants me to really see her. She is wearing the fluffiest, whitest robe I've seen in a very long time. She is undoubtedly nude beneath it, but I don't care. She may have a little smile on her face, but the robe is so amazingly bright in the light from the setting sun coming through the windows that it is difficult to see the details of her face, let alone the expression on it. The robe ends mid-thigh. Her legs are long and lean, her feet bare. The nails are painted, but I can't tell the color. She stops and stands there. She leans her head back and shakes her hair, then looks straight at me. She produces a comb and starts drawing lines in her hair with it, straight back. She looks so natural doing this and I'm so comfortable watching her, it's as if we've played out this scene every day for many, many years. I think if we had, I'd have enjoyed every second. I have to blink; she is so bright in the sun. I stand up and now I can see her face clearly. Alice. She smiles.

ACKNOWLEDGEMENTS

I would like to thank the following for their love and their practical support.

Pastor Rick Randall, Senior Pastor, Austin Cornerstone Church, for extending his belief to me, of all people; Katie Laine, the love of my life who not only discovered the edge I didn't know I have, but who married me because of it; Lt. Craig Cannon, Austin Police Department Retired, who knows all about it; Tammy and Luke Kathol, who expand my horizons; Barbara and John Frazell, who have helped me remain insane; Greg McCabe, SSgt, United States Air Force Retired, who gave me great advice about the <enter> key; Jeff Loomis, computer guru, who demanded a horse and more of everything; Erin Brown my sharp-sworded editor, and Google© my unpaid research assistant.

I have heard all the suggestions these friends have offered me. My hope is that they will forgive me for all the times in this book that I've ignored them and blundered along on my own. I also apologize for changing topography and time frames to fit the story.

and finally, all my love to Steve, Frances and their gang, Tammy, Luke and theirs, Lynn, John and theirs, Margo, Kenny and Marcy, Cathy, David and theirs… and to Sean and Deirdre, who have promised not to read this until the year 2030, the little liars.

Alexander Wolf, 2/2010 – 8/2010

HOLD ON NOW,

JACK'S COMING BACK!!

Yes, John Wayne Gantt will be back soon, along with all of his friends and enemies, in a follow-up to *The Austin Highway*. Jack doesn't know everything we do, does he? Well, he is going to find out, on...

THE CORPUS CHRISTI HIGHWAY

Stay tuned to announcements on the author's website:

www.alexanderwolf.net